THE COTTAGE GARDEN
And the old-fashioned Flowers

THE COTTAGE GARDEN
And the Old-Fashioned Flowers

ROY GENDERS

PELHAM BOOKS

First published in Great Britain by
Pelham Books Ltd,
44 Bedford Square,
London WC1B 3DU
1969
Reprinted 1970
New Edition 1983
Reprinted 1984

British Library Cataloguing in Publication Data

Genders, Roy
    The cottage garden.—2nd ed.
    1. Plants, ornamental
    I. Title
    635   SB406

ISBN 0 7207 1442 7

Printed in Great Britain by
Hollen Street Press, Slough
and bound by Dorstel Press, Harlow

To the memory
of my Grandparents
WILLIAM & ELIZA GENDERS
VINCENT & EMMA PEAT
And to
my Grandchildren
MATTHEW WILLIAM & REBECCA MAY

CONTENTS

ILLUSTRATIONS

COLOUR

BLACK AND WHITE

between pages 32 and 33

between pages 96 and 97

Line drawings

PREFACE

Of all flowers I love those of the cottage garden most; the auriculas and primroses, the violets and pansies, those with fragrance and those plants with scented leaves. They have a charm all their own, likewise those gardens in which they grow. For many years they have been my first love and my living and so the writing of this book has given me as much pleasure as the flowers have done through the years. I hope it may give pleasure to those who also love the flowers of a more tranquil age as I do and that it may create interest amongst those who do not as yet grow them in their garden.

Sadly, since the first edition of the book was published, many of the lovely cottage garden plants I described have disappeared from nurserymen's catalogues and with them have gone many of the specialist growers, death having claimed in recent years, Gladys Emmerson of Limavady in Northern Ireland and Margery Fish of East Lambrook Manor, Somerset; also William Chalmers of Stonehaven and many others including most of the auricula and pansy growers who for many years were my north country colleagues.

Gone are the days when one could send a £1 note to a nurseryman on the outskirts of Manchester and within forty-eight hours receive a sackful of plants of that wonderful blood red primrose, Miss Massey, delivered to one's door by British Rail and carriage paid, too. But most of the old flowers still survive to be found in cottage gardens and in small gardens of terraced houses in our seaside towns; whilst several people have recently begun to specialise in pansies and pinks and have opened small nurseries so that others, too, may enjoy them.

The National Council for the Conservation of Plants and Gardens, sponsored by the Royal Horticultural Society and inaugurated in October 1978, is doing much to encourage gardeners everywhere to find, propagate, protect and distribute the old flowers, many of which are now in danger of extinction and which are as much a part of the heritage of our islands as our cathedrals and abbeys, castles and country houses.

As I revise the book it is the high noon of summer and the garden is filled with long borders of sweet williams. The old shrub roses are in bloom and the laced pinks and sweet peas add their delicious fragrance to the garden. Only the old flowers seem to give this richness of perfume and for this alone, should not be neglected.

I am indebted to Marjorie Blamey for the line drawings and water colours which she did for the earlier edition, to John Gledhill for the black and white and colour photographs of some of the old fashioned flowers grown in my garden and to Michael Warren for the additional photographs for this edition.

ROY GENDERS

July 1982

ACKNOWLEDGEMENTS

COLOUR PLATES: water-colour paintings (Plates 7 to 10 and 13 to 16) by Marjorie Blamey; colour photographs by Michael Warren (Plates 1, 2 *top*, 3, 4, 11 *bottom*, 12) and John Gledhill (Plates 2 *bottom*, 5, 6, 11 *top*).

BLACK AND WHITE PHOTOGRAPHS: 1, 2 and 6 reproduced by courtesy of J. E. Downward; 3 by Bruce A. Bailey; 4 by Messrs Sutton and Sons Ltd; 7 to 58 by John Gledhill.

Plants: a select list of suppliers

Old carnations and pinks
Allwood Brothers,
Clayton Nurseries,
Hassocks,
West Sussex BN6 9LX.
Phone: Hassocks 4229

Old roses
David Austin,
Bowling Green Lane,
Albrighton,
Wolverhampton.
Phone: 090 722 2142

Large selection of bulbs
Avon Bulbs,
Bathford,
Bath BA1 8ED.
Phone: 0225 859495

Primulas
Barnhaven Gardens,
Brigsteer,
Kendal,
Cumbria.
Phone: Crosswaite 386

Old roses
Peter Beales,
Intwood Nurseries,
Swardeston,
Norwich.
Phone: Mulbarton 631

Old hardy perennials and alpines
Bressingham Gardens,
Diss,
Norfolk.
Phone: 037 988 464

Primroses and violas
David Chalmers,
Blackbutts Nursery,
Stonehaven,
Kincardineshire.
Phone: Newtonhill 30430

Unusual hardy garden plants
Beth Chatto Gardens,
White Barn House,
Elmstead Market,
Colchester,
Essex.
Phone: Wivenhoe 2007

Groundcover plants
Margery Fish Nurseries,
East Lambrook Manor,
South Petherton,
Somerset.
Phone: South Petherton 40320

*Old cottage garden pinks and
other plants*
Ramparts Nurseries,
Baker's Lane,
Colchester,
Essex.
Phone: Colchester 72050

Haywards Carnations,
The Chase Gardens,
Purbrook,
Portsmouth.

Large selection of old herbs
The Weald Herbary,
Park Cottage,
Frittenden,
Cranbrook, Kent.
Phone: 058 080 226

Part One

THE COTTAGE GARDEN

Soon will the high Midsummer pomps come on,
Soon will the musk carnations break and swell,
Soon will we have gold-dusted snapdragon,
Sweet-William with his homely cottage smell,
And stocks in fragrant blow;
Roses that down the alleys shine afar,
And open, jasmine-muffled lattices,
And groups under the dreaming garden trees,
And the full moon, and the white, Evening-star.

Mathew Arnold: *Thyrsis*

CHAPTER ONE

The English Cottage Garden Through the Ages

I have learned much from the little cottage gardens that help to make our English waysides the prettiest in the temperate world. One can hardly go into the smallest cottage garden without learning or observing something new.

Gertrude Jekyll

Until the beginning of the fifteenth century, the cottage garden as we know it today had not yet come into existence for until then, men were occupied with the ceaseless struggle to secure their liberties and with the waging of wars at home and abroad.

From the time of the Norman occupation until the end of the fourteenth century, the land was under the control of the feudal lords and tended by labourers (serfs) who withdrew to the protection of the castle or fortified manor whenever there was trouble. Gardens as we know them were non-existent or were extremely rare. There was little room for a garden within the walls of a fortified house and only orchards came to be planted without, to be frequently destroyed by marauding bands who would "bark" or cut down the trees. This we are told, happened to the extensive orchards outside the walls of Carlisle Castle during the wars between Henry II and William the Lion of Scotland and described in a twelfth-century poem by Jordan Fantosme.

It was this same Henry II who, at his palace at Woodstock in Oxfordshire, made there a garden and a secret bower, reached only by an intricate labyrinth and where he would meet his mistress, Fair Rosamond Clifford, until she met her tragic fate at the hands of the queen.

But mostly, gardens existed only at the monasteries where the herbarium, under the care of the sacristan, provided the monks with valuable potions to administer to themselves and to those who would seek their help in times of illness.

3

That there were gardens attached to small houses in the city of London we know from a passage in FitzStephen's Life of Thomas à Becket. "On all sides outside the houses," he wrote, "there are adjoining gardens planted with trees both spacious and pleasing to the sight." The trees would most likely be those of apple and pear, thus the first orchards came to be formed. But apart from the monastic gardens, only Henry de Lacy, Earl of Lincoln owned a garden of any note, situated in Holborn where now stands Lincoln's Inn. Accounts of produce of medicinal value sold from this garden during the reign of Edward I show that the sum of 3s. 2d. was obtained for a quantity of red roses; 8s. 9¾d. for herbs; 4s. 1d. for onions and garlic; and £9 for apples, pears and nuts, in each case "tithe being deducted". The accounts also show that 3s. 2½d. was paid for 2 grafts of de Rule "bought for planting". This was a pear named after St. Rule or St. Reggolo, Bishop of Arles, and was the most widely sought variety at the time. An extract from the Exchequer receipts for 1292 shows that 700 'Regulo' pears were supplied to Edward I whilst occupying the castle at Berwick during his wars against the Scots. Gardens came to be made at the earliest scholastic foundations at Oxford and Cambridge as at Trinity Hall and Peterhouse and as more settled times prevailed, the earls and barons and the more important citizens of London and elsewhere, came to make gardens about their homes and to sell the produce in the open market.

In the country, the land was being cultivated by the open field system whereby the people of each village had allotted to them strips of ground, each being divided from his neighbour by a drain. No land was enclosed by wall or hedge, whilst those who cultivated it usually lived some distance away, in what may be described as little more than shacks of wood or of "wattle and daub".

The people did not own their land but rented it from the lord of the manor in return for work done on his lordship's land on certain days of the week, whilst they paid tithe by way of a proportion of the crops they grew. But during the latter half of the fourteenth century, many of the manorial lords saw fit to change the system, a money rent being charged for the use of the strips as against tithes and even in lieu of the fixed working days on his own land, though these impositions could be revived if the lord of the manor thought fit at any time or if rent money was not forthcoming.

It was the Black Death of 1349 which began the break-up of the system of servile labour, for during that year about one-third of the total population of England perished, leaving inadequate numbers of workers available to cultivate the manorial lands. The result was that for the first time, labourers put a premium on their services and were able to demand high wages for the work they performed, whilst it was necessary to accept their terms if the land was not to fall into greater decay. Also, only a small proportion of those who cultivated the open field strips survived with the result that those left took over the vacated land and became in effect small tenant farmers who paid yearly tribute to their overlords.

Around these small areas of farmland, primitive homesteads arose as the labourers became more and more independent of the lord of the manor and they began to build cottages often with a piece of land attached, left untended by those dying of the plague and where they grew herbs and vegetables and kept bees. The growing of flowers for beauty and pleasure did not yet enter into the scheme of things.

The garden was used almost entirely to supply the needs of the household with health-giving herbs and with plants for culinary purposes and for flavouring. All the strongly flavoured herbs were grown, such as enjoyed by Chaucer's Sompnour in the *Canterbury Tales*:

"Well loved he garlic, onions and the leek."

Parsley and fennel were also in daily use, the latter being in demand to stay the pangs of hunger on fast days or whenever food was scarce. In William Langland's *Piers Plowman*, written in 1394, the priest asks the poor old lady:

"Hast thou ought in thy purse?
Any hot spices?"

To which she replies:

"I have peper and piones and a pound of garlic,
a farthingworth of fennel seed for fasting days."

Langland has told of how the poor lived almost entirely on fruit and vegetables with possibly an occasional rabbit poached from the manorial lands:

Benes and baken apples they brought in her lappe
Chibolles and cheruelles and ripe cherries many.

These would be augmented by herbs from the wayside as Chaucer makes mention in the *Clerk's Tale* when describing the destitution of Griseldis:

> When she homeward came she would bring
> Worts or other herbs thyme ofte
> To which she shredde and seeth for her livinge.

In a medieval MS. by one John (the) Gardener, written in 1440 and now in the library of Trinity College, Cambridge, is given detailed instructions for the sowing of onions and leeks on St. Valentine's Day and also for sowing parsley, "in the month of March". The same author also gives instructions for the planting of saffron which was introduced into East Anglia (Saffron Walden) by Sir Thomas Smith, Secretary of State under Edward III. With the herbs were planted cabbages and kale which were used in all manner of ways. An early fifteenth-century cookery book suggests serving cabbage dressed with saffron.

Gradually fruits came to be grown in the cottager's garden including wild strawberries removed from their woodland home, also cherries and gooseberries both of which grew about the hedgerows, and the costard apple (costermonger) which in 1296 sold for a shilling a hundred in Oxford market.

THE EARLY COTTAGE GARDEN

The earliest cottage gardens were small with a few fruit trees planted here and there, giving a little shade from the summer sunshine but not too much for beneath the trees it was necessary to make use of every inch of ground, to provide the household with food and medicinal herbs augmented by those which grew by the wayside.

Gradually a few flowering plants came to be grown not entirely for their beauty but more for their value in flavouring. All were plants growing naturally in hedgerow or woodland or there were those which may have been introduced at an early date in our history, possibly with the Romans or with the Norman invasion, like the clove-scented pink, *Dianthus caryophyllus*, which had become naturalized on old buildings and whose flowers were used to impart their fragrance to drinks. During Chaucer's lifetime the pink was grown in every ale-house garden. From the cowslip and primrose, a wine was made whilst the seeds of the paeony were used as a condiment. "I have peper and piones," quoth the old lady of *Piers*

Plowman. The flowers of the violet were used in salads and were also cooked with other foods as were those of the primrose with milk and honey. They were the flowers mentioned by John (the) Gardener in his poem of 1440 and each had culinary value:

> Periwinkle, violet, cowslip and lily
> Rose red, rose white, foxglove and pimpernel
> Hollyhock, coriander, paeony.

That they became the most common of all cottage garden flowers was only to be expected for in addition they possessed great beauty, though this was of secondary consideration. The Madonna Lily was one of outstanding beauty, and *Lychnis chalcedonica*, both of which were introduced by the returning Crusaders; also the Red Gallica rose. Other native flowers found a place in the earliest cottage gardens such as Herb Robert and the wild scabious, mullein and mallow, columbine and St. John's Wort, each of which were believed to have medicinal value in addition to the beauty of their flowers. All are hardy and persisting, enjoying the shade of each other's company and nowhere do they grow better than in the cottage garden where they have often remained undisturbed through the years, given no more attention than an annual top dressing of manure and decayed leaves.

These same flowers had another important function, that of releasing their sweet fragrance when dried or distilled. During the early years of the cottage garden, toilet facilities were almost non-existent, whilst the houses with their low roofs and the lack of any damp-course were dark and of musty smell. The wearing of crowns or garlands of the Madonna Lily and the sweetly scented red rose (*R. gallica*), held together by the trailing fronds of the evergreen periwinkle was the custom at weddings and on other important occasions, for perfumes were unknown amongst the poorer classes and sweetly scented flowers and leaves were always in demand. Even Chaucer's Sompnour had "a garland set upon his head" and in the *Romance of the Rose* we are told that

> ". . . on his head was sette
> Of roses red, a chapelette."

Emily in her garden, in *The Knight's Tale* seen by the imprisoned knights, gathered flowers "party white and red, to make a sotil [little] garland for her head". So highly esteemed was the red rose that an early fifteenth-century Ave Maria begins:

"Heil be thou Marie, that art flower of all,
As Rose in erbe so red."

To strew over the floors, aromatic herbs were used, many of which like the Meadowsweet which has oil of wintergreen in its leaves, were obtained from the countryside, whilst others were grown in the garden. Chief amongst these were southernwood and wormwood which kept away fleas; hyssop, and rue with its resinous scent flavoured with orange; sage and lavender, the dried stems of which were burnt like incense.

Every plant grown was in some way fragrant, like fennel and coriander with their scented seeds, or the flowers or leaves were scented. Others like *Sedum rhodiola* and the Florentine Iris had scented roots which released their fragrance as the roots became dry. Many plants were grown for distilling, the sweet waters of which were used in the kitchen as well as for medicinal purposes and for the toilet. The household book of the Earl of Northumberland (1502) contain a list of a number of herbs "to stylle": borage, columbine, bugloss, sorrel, cowslip, scabious, tansy, wormwood, sage, dandelion, hart's tongue. Sweet waters were given as presents on saints days and birthdays as are perfumes of commercial manufacture today. The plants were mostly introduced to the cottage garden from the wayside, brought home by those who left at each daybreak to work on the manorial estates and returned with the setting sun, so beautifully described by the Northamptonshire peasant poet John Clare who composed his lovely lines whilst himself toiling in the fields:

The cottager when coming home from plough
Brings home a cowslip root in flower to set.
Thus ere the Christmas goes the spring is met . . .

The observant countryman would not be slow to introduce all manner of rare plants to his garden and which he found growing about the countryside. Perhaps a double yellow primrose or a double white, found nestling amidst their curdled leaves of emerald green. Maybe a violet with flowers of white or palest blue would be found and lifting the plant with a piece of wood, it was set and propagated and perhaps remained in the same cottage garden for generations, fortified by the loving care of those who tended the garden and by a soil continually enriched with humus and decayed manure. For the plants of the first cottage gardens were almost the only possessions of the countryman and he cared for them as those of a later age cared for possessions in the home.

It is because of the cottager's love of his plants that the favourites of long ago have persisted to this day for they were provided with the same conditions that were to be enjoyed under their natural surroundings and this was a constant supply of humus, and the partial shade of other vegetation which prevents the soil from drying out about the roots during summer. It will also prevent the ground from "panning" during periods of heavy rain followed by a drying wind, thus depriving the soil of oxygen and so preventing bacterial activity. The cottage garden needs neither hoe nor hose to maintain the plants in healthy condition, only an occasional mulch of decayed manure and leaf mould such as the plants received during the time when they grew in their native habitat and when the ground was covered with leaves which decayed and provided them with humus.

Besides the value of plants for strewing and for culinary purposes, many came to be planted entirely for their curative powers. During the time when England's archers ruled the western world, the prunella was to be found in every garden for its leaves were said to heal wounds caused by arrows or by the careless handling of carpenters tools, hence its country name of "all-heal".

Winter savory was also prominent in gardens for its leaves rubbed on wasp stings brought immediate relief. It later came to be planted with hyssop, with the cotton lavender and the upright thymes, to surround small beds of flowering plants for as Thomas Hyll wrote in *The Art of Gardening* (1563) "these endure all the winter through green". Horehound and verbascum were used in cough medicines whilst the juice of the poppy was rubbed over the nipples of women's breasts to encourage sucking babes to fall asleep after feeding. The thick leaves of the Mullein were placed in children's shoes and, steeped in tallow, were burned like wick to give light in the home.

From the petals of the red rose and the root of *Sedum rhodiola* a toilet water was distilled, likewise from the leaves of the woodruff (known to countrymen as sweet grass) and with which the ladies bathed their faces. Woodruff leaves were also placed between the pages of books to prevent their taking on the unpleasant musty smell and were also placed, with those of southernwood and lavender, between linen and clothes whilst every cottage room had its bowl of pot-pourris. The Great Yellow Loosestrife was to be found in every garden and in every home for its dried leaves hung from a ceiling would keep away flies.

Every part of the garden was expected to contribute in some way, to the gradually improving conditions enjoyed by the countryman. Every plant had its uses and no part of the garden was left untended and as often plants came to be introduced, they were set wherever space could be found for them. Thus the cottage garden became a place of delightful disorder, green cabbages grew with "cabbage" roses, daffodils with onions and with them grew marigolds, for the leaves were greatly in demand for use in stews with onions. With them too, grew the Madonna Lily and *Lychnis chalcedonica*, both of which are believed to have been introduced by those returning from the crusades.

After the Black Death, when the gardens of the manor lay deserted, some cottager interested in his newly acquired garden would most likely lift a root or two unnoticed when working at the manor and plant them with other favourites of the time, to bloom where none but the cottagers could see them. No two gardens were ever alike and this added to their charm for each personified the individual character of its owner. Mostly the cottage garden continued to be stocked with those plants which were a familiar part of the English landscape, until towards the end of the fifteenth century when the Wars of the Roses brought discontent and disorder and not until the first of the Tudors came to the throne was there a revival of orderly gardening.

Early in the sixteenth century, the cottage garden began to take on a more orderly appearance with the introduction of the new arrangement known as the "knotted" bed by which dwarf box, thrift or marjoram was planted, often in the most intricate designs, to contain the plants which were mostly of dwarf compact habit. Often, a low hedge was planted alongside a path which divided the garden into two more or less equal parts each of which was subdivided into rectangular beds surrounded by rosemary or lavender, both of which withstood hard clipping.

With the Tudors came a new culture and with it a greater skill in husbandry. In his *Book of Husbandry* of 1544, FitzHerbert informs the countryman that "it is necessary, profitable and also a pleasure to have peares, wardens and apples of diverse sorts. Also cherries, filberts, bullaces, dampsons, plums, walnuts and such others. Therefore it is convenient to learn how thou shalt 'graffe'." Increased trading activities overseas brought about the introduction of many new plants including the oriental Hyacinth; *Ranunculus asiaticus*; *Colchicum byzantinum*; and the Star of Bethlehem each of which reached England from the Near East about the middle of the sixteenth century. At the same time, a number of exotic plants were brought over by the Huguenot weavers fleeing from the massacres of St. Bartholomew, the auricula and erythronium being amongst them, plants which were ideally suited to the small enclosed beds as were pinks and primroses, violets and double daisies, cottage garden favourites of earlier days.

For the first time, plants came to be grown entirely for the beauty of their flowers, and fruits and vegetables were usually confined to a part of the garden where they were hidden from view of the sitting-room window, shielded by rows of cornflowers and larkspurs which were in demand for home decoration whilst against the cottage, sun-flowers and hollyhocks grew, often reaching as high as the roof. The garden was gradually taking on a more orderly appearance and with each year, new plants were being grown. Towards the end of the century, came the Crown Imperial and *Ranunculus aconitifolius*, known as Fair Maids of Kent; also the "chequered daffodil", *Fritillaria meleagris*, sent by one, Noel Caperon, an apothecary of Orleans who, we are told "was shortly after taken away in the Massacre". The tulip arrived from Turkey at about the same time and by the early seventeenth century was to be found in every cottage garden where it was known as the Turks' Cap.

But until the Tradescants made their journeys to the New World during the seventeenth century and brought back many new plants, almost all the flowers of the cottage garden with but one or two exceptions, were of blue or purple or of yellow colouring, colours beloved by bees for the seeking of nectar and which rarely visit flowers of any other colouring.

Amongst those blue-flowered plants were:

Aconitum napellus	Wolf's bane
Anchusa italica	Bugloss
Campanula persicifolia	Bellflower
Galega officinalis	Goat's beard
Geranium pratense	Crane's-bill
Iris germanica	Flag Iris
Linum perenne	Flax

Lunaria biennis	Honesty
Lupinus polyphyllus	Lupin
Myosotis palustris	Forget-me-not
Nepeta cataria	Catmint
Nigella damascena	Love-in-a-Mist
Scilla nutans	Bluebell
Vinca minor	Periwinkle
Viola odorata	Sweet Violet

The journey of John Tradescant the younger to Virginia and of others journeying to America saw the introduction of a number of new plants. There were three generations of John Tradescant. The grandfather, a Dutchman, came to England during the reign of James I. His son, known as "the father" was appointed gardener to the first Lord Salisbury, then to the Duke of Buckingham and in 1629, the year of the publication of Parkinson's *Paradisus*, he was made gardener to Charles I. From Virginia, John Tradescant junior introduced the Spiderwort and a perennial aster which bears his name, whilst from Canada came several species of Golden Rod, the Helenium and Rudbeckia, plants of extreme hardiness, able to tolerate the most adverse soil conditions and bearing flowers in shades of golden-yellow, bronze and rust which provided a welcome change to the blue-flowering plants. Moreover, the plants came into bloom during autumn, with the Michaelmas daisies, another valuable North American introduction, thus extending the flowering season of the cottage garden. Later, from Mexico came the dahlia and from China and Japan, the chrysanthemum both of which provided brilliant autumnal colour which was sadly lacking until that time.

It is fortunate that the poor man's garden, the cottage garden of the Restoration period, remained much as it had done since early Tudor times for the gardens of the nobility were being converted to the French style as laid down at Versailles and Malmaison. The vogue began when the Earl of Essex sent his gardener, William Rose, to study the Royal gardens of Louis XIV, and upon his return, Rose was appointed Royal Gardener to Charles II. From then on, newly made gardens carried a strong French influence whilst many old gardens were converted to the designs of Le Nôtre as at Hampton Court where the semi-circular garden was laid out to the directions of the Frenchman.

Under William and Mary, even more prominence was given to

the French and Dutch styles when the parterre superseded the "knot" garden. This was usually made to the front of the house, the beds being cut from turf to designs of embroidery as at Harewood House and Canon's Ashby and filled with hyacinths and tulips and with geraniums and calceolarias for summer display. The day of bedding plants had arrived and the cult was to gather momentum during Victorian times and until the middle of the twentieth century when even the smallest of city gardens followed the vogue.

The enthusiasm for the bedding plant coincided with the new interest being taken in the culture of all manner of tropical plants which had already reached Britain from the Dutch East Indies and from the American continent, plants such as the date palm, the mimosa, the gardenia and banana and which required winter warmth in Britain or N. Europe. Humphrey Repton was the first to suggest the erection of a greenhouse to house the more exotic plants, at the very beginning of the nineteenth century when the use of cast iron was first being given prominence as a material for building. J. C. Loudon was also recommending methods of housing these plants but it was Joseph Paxton, gardener to the 6th Duke of Devonshire who, desirous of growing orchids for his master and wishing to house the great Amazon water-lily, brought about the erection of the first important glasshouse which at Chatsworth covered an acre of ground. This later gave rise to the erection of the great domed glasshouse at the Crystal Palace for which Paxton was knighted in 1851. From that time, the old-fashioned flowers of the cottage garden rapidly lost popularity with the townsmen who, enjoying the prosperity of the industrial revolution, wished to show the world the result of his endeavours to achieve quick riches by a display of the most blatant flowering plants, represented chiefly by the geranium and calceolaria.

The old favourites survived only in the garden of the countryman, still poor in relation to the townsman and in some old vicarage gardens whose owners had not shared the material advantages of the time.

THE OLD FLORISTS

One other section of the populace had preserved the old florists' flowers and this was the weavers of Lancashire and Yorkshire and the lace workers of Paisley who brought to the ranunculus, the auricula, the pink and the gold laced polyanthus, a perfection of beauty which hitherto was unknown in these or in any other flowers. They were cottage craftsmen who worked at home on contract and who wished, in an age of rapidly growing industrial ugliness, to cherish the most exquisite examples of nature's works. It has been said that these florists' flowers, as they were called, found no place in the cottage garden but a garden may be so called whether it is situated in town or country, its functions are the same whilst the plants growing therein were given the same loving care as were those plants of less importance which occupied the country cottage garden of the time. The florists' flowers differed only in that they were suitable for exhibition and were usually displayed in pots, though occupying the cottage garden for most of the year. It was only when the spread of industry compelled the more congested building of houses with the resulting reduction in the size of gardens that the florists' flowers came to be grown almost entirely in pots. The result was that the plants lost vigour and by the First World War had almost disappeared. But not entirely so for some were still to be found growing in country gardens which had escaped town building and, with other favourites of bygone days, had been maintained in vigour and this had ensured their continuity. Here in the humus laden soils, kept moist and cool at the roots by neighbouring plants and knowing nothing of the harsh chlorinated water with which the townsman now waters his plants, they continue to flourish but to quickly perish when transplanted to the smoke-laden atmosphere of a town garden and to a soil impoverished by lack of humus.

One recalls the bed of Rose du Barri primrose discovered in a Wiltshire garden within sight of Salisbury Cathedral. There the plants were as large as cabbages and each spring produced multitudes of double flowers of the size of a 10p piece and of a deep pink colour, flushed with orange, exactly the colour of Picture rose. Or of the Double Cream polyanthus Ralph Spooner, growing in a Sussex cottage garden beneath the Downs with Chanctonbury Ring towering high above. Or again, of the cottage garden in Ireland with its hedge of scented box kept closely cut where grows the rare double scarlet Sweet William known as Bloody William. The old pink Queen of Sheba, known to early Tudor gardeners, may still be found in a Cotswold cottage garden, brought there from an old vicarage garden and Fenbow's Nutmeg Clove carnation, in cultivation during Chaucer's time, was rediscovered as recently as 1960 growing in a garden near Leeds, still owned by the same family which first gave its name to the plant and where records show it to have been planted in 1652. It was planted by one Julian Fenbow to impart its powerful nutmeg flavour to his home-made wines. The late Mr. Montagu Allwood has told of how he found the old Fringed pink in a Lincolnshire garden and crossed it with a perpetual flowering carnation, the result being a new race of perpetual flowering pinks which he named Allwoodii. Those flowers beloved of our forefathers centuries ago have survived in the protection of the cottage garden to enrich modern gardens with their beauty.

The cottage garden has also been the breeding ground of a host of wonderful flowering plants. The story of George Russell and his new lupins which he raised in his tiny garden near York is familiar to all but not so well known is the story of the Histon grocer, W. J. Unwin, who discovered a sweet pea growing in his cottage garden which had attractively waved petals and was of an exquisite shade of shell pink. It resembled the frilly petalled form of Eckford's Prima Donna, found by Silas Cole in the garden of the Countess Spencer at Althorp Park and which was the beginning of the Spencer sweet peas. But Unwin's find was of greater importance for it would breed true, whereas the Countess Spencer variety would not. Unwin named it after his daughter Gladys Unwin and so great was the demand that upon this one variety, discovered in a Histon (Cambridge) cottage garden, the famous seed house bearing the name of W. J. Unwin was founded.

Some years before Unwin's find, the Scottish-born gardener Henry Eckford, in his cottage garden at Wem in Shropshire was working on the sweet pea, introduced into England in 1700. Eckford was able to increase the length of stem and the number of blooms from two to four. His variety Countess of Radnor was the first blue-flowered sweet pea, whilst his other famous introduction, Lady Eve Balfour, was chosen for the presentation bouquet for the 1900 Exhibition held at the Crystal Palace.

In a cottage garden in East Lothian in 1868 was discovered a stock of such outstanding form and pronounced perfume that it began a new interest in these lovely flowers. It was found by David Thomson, then head gardener to the Duke of Buccleuch and it was told to him that the stocks had been growing in this same garden and of others in the district for at least three centuries, since the time of Henry VIII. They grew only 12–15 ins. tall and sown in late July, bloom freely during the following spring and early summer, being ideal for window boxes and restricted bedding. They also bloom well under glass in gentle heat. Shortly after Thomson's discovery appeared Mary Howitt's poem, the *Poor Man's Garden*, in which she referred to the crimson stock and to other cottage garden flowers of her time:

> He knows his red sweet williams,
> And the stocks that cost him dear,
> That well set row of crimson stocks,
> For he bought the seed last year.

That the East Lothian stock would have been lost to modern gardens except for the care it received from Scotland's cottage gardeners is a certainty, likewise so many other plants of our early gardens. They have also been perpetuated by the various florists' societies which came into being about the middle of the eighteenth century and have continued until the present time though they are today kept alive only through the enthusiasm of a few specialist growers who do not wish to see the old favourites disappear.

It was in 1769 that the first recorded exhibition of the gold laced polyanthus was held at the home of one John Barnes at Lichfield, and ten years later Abercrombie wrote that the gold laced polyanthus had become "one of the most noted prize [show] flowers amongst florists". Mostly the shows took place at the local public house. They were "open to all-comers"—"Free to all-England" was how the invitation was worded and the first prize was usually a copper kettle, awarded by the landlord.

As it is reported on more than one occasion that a hundred exhibitors wined and dined at the inn after the event, the landlord could well have afforded his act of generosity.

The first of the shows took place early in April and continued until mid-May when the primrose and polyanthus was exhibited, more than fifty shows being held each year in the counties of Lancashire, Yorkshire, Staffordshire and Cheshire, culminating in the Great Show held in the Cutler's Hall, Sheffield, on the first Saturday of May, on which day the Northern section of the National Primula and Auricula Society still hold their annual show in Manchester.

Then would follow the tulip meetings which would last until the end of May to be followed by the early June ranunculus shows. Then came the exhibitions of pinks and carnations. The Paisley florists, famed for their laced pinks, met every Thursday from "the flowering of the Polyanthus to the disappearance of the Carnation!" The plants were flowered indoors in pots to preserve the quality of bloom from adverse weather. After flowering, they would be replanted in the cottager's garden. The Rev. Francis Horner, writing the introduction to James Douglas's *Hardy Florists' Flowers* (1879) when the old north country florists were fast disappearing, said: "Here is the very window, curiously long and lightsome at which the hand-loom weaver worked behind his loom, able to watch his flowers (in their pots) as closely as his work, his labour and his pleasure intermingled, interwoven as intimately as his silken threads." But the writer goes on to deplore the already passing of many of the old craftsman growers and the following year (1880) a letter from Sam Barlow to a friend mentioned that the most famous of all gold laced polyanthuses, Pearson's Alexander, had already become extinct and the decline of the florists' clubs was almost complete by that same year. By the end of the century, the gold laced polyanthus had almost disappeared, but not quite.

Written from a cottage at Camber, near Rye in Sussex, the author received a letter telling of polyanthuses that had been growing in the garden since the year 1800 at least, and that there were to be found more than 160 years later, a deep yellow polyanthus with a mauve picotee edge and one with a black-maroon ground and silver lacing. This latter variety turned out to be the old Irish Silver Annie, bearing fully double blooms and which may occasionally be found to this day in Irish cottage gardens. But with each year, the lovely old flowers become more scarce. There are few specialist growers who are able to devote their time to the old florists' flowers, the primrose and auricula; the pink and carnation; the pansy and viola, though the smallest of gardens could grow a profitable collection of these antique plant collector's favourites. They may still be found in cottage gardens of the British Isles, hiding beneath the foliage of nearby plants, often hidden from the view of those strangers who would seek them out, their presence known only to their owner. It is to him (or her) that we owe their survival since earliest times for the townsman usually destroys his plants after they have flowered for conditions are against their survival even for a second year. In an age of mass production, the garden plant is no exception.

Nor must we forget the debt the nature-lover owes to those who grew in their gardens a large number of those plants which through the years have become naturalized about the British Isles. Escapes from the cottager's garden they are and they have brought additional beauty and interest to the countryside. The antirrhinum is one, borage another, both early introductions from southern Europe but now an integral part of our flora. The musk-scented Storks-bill and the arabis are others which have made their home in our islands and are warmly welcomed here.

CHAPTER TWO

Making the Garden

In every garden there must be, wherever there may be seclusion,
quiet retreats for rest and retirement, for contemplation.

Reynolds Hole,
Dean of Rochester

The cottage garden has through the centuries presented a panorama
of plants of all types which have reached these islands from all parts
of the world. They provide colour the whole year through and many
will give of their fragrance too and unlike those of the modern
garden, in which the plants of spring and summer form two distinct
groups, those of the cottage garden will intermingle through the
seasons, there being no break or colourless period as is usual with
modern bedding plants.

First comes the Christmas rose, *Helleborus niger*, which in a sheltered
sunny corner will give of its flowers during Christmastide and will
continue until the Lenten rose, *Helleborus orientalis*, comes into bloom
early in March. With it appears the first of the primroses, Gerard's
Double White (*alba plena*) being one of the earliest to bloom, and
Hepatica triloba. From almost the beginning of the year the lovely
polyanthus Barrowby Gem will have thrown up its scented heads of
greenish-yellow, unmindful of the frosts and cold winds. It is seen at
its finest when planted in small groups of four or five near the Christmas roses for they will protect each other. This is the secret of
success with the old-fashioned flowers and by giving some thought to
their planting, they will not only be colourful all the year round but
will remain healthy and vigorous for many years with the minimum
of attention. Both the Christmas rose and the polyanthus appreciate
some shade from the mid-summer sunshine, so plant near them
Tradescant's Starwort, *Aster amellus*, which will be only just pushing
up from the soil when its companions are in bloom and will provide
shade when it is most required, during July and August. In this way
too, the utmost advantage may be taken of every inch of space for

some plants will be dying back after flowering, whilst others will be coming into bloom, the one hiding the other and leaving no untidy or colourless patches about the garden. Every inch of the garden may be made to yield its quota of colour, including the hedge which will protect the plants from drying winds as well as giving privacy to the garden.

Few plants will be happy in a sun-baked soil, except perhaps the geranium, the red hot poker and the sweet pea, plants of warmer climes which do not enjoy shade as do most of the cottage garden favourites. To provide shade at their roots during summer and protection from cold and drying winds as the plants begin to make growth in spring should be the aim of every gardener who grows the old flowers for they are lovers of each other's company, happy with their roots in shade and their heads in the sunlight when they will survive for many decades, providing pleasure for succeeding generations, each year increasing the display of bloom. John Clare caught the mood of the cottage garden in his lines written during the year of Waterloo:

> A little garden not too fine,
> Enclosed with painted pales.
> And woodbines round the cot to twine,
> Pin to the wall with nails.
>
> Let hazels grow, and spindling sedge,
> Bent bowering overhead;
> Dig 'old man's beard' from woodland hedge
> To twine a summer shade.
>
> Beside the threshold sods provide,
> And build a summer seat;
> Plant sweet brier bushes by its side,
> And flowers that blossom sweet.

For making a hedge, the sweet briar or eglantine is perhaps the most satisfying of all plants. Four centuries ago, Thomas Hyll in *The Gardener's Labyrinth* suggested planting "either privet alone or sweet bryar and whitethorn interlaced together, and roses one, two or three sorts, placed here and there amongst them". A delightful suggestion for the interlocking of the whitethorn will give the hedge strength and with it plant the sweet briar with the charming name of Janet's Pride. It quickly makes an inpenetrable hedge and bears its dainty blooms of softest pink, enhanced by the fragrant bottle-green foliage. Here and there at regular intervals, plant the Bourbon rose, Zephyrine Drouhin, its double blooms of satin-pink filling the garden with their exquisite perfume from early July until the end of autumn. And let honeysuckle twine about the hedge, scenting the air when warmed by the sun, its perfume lasting far into the night.

"The garden is best square," wrote Sir Francis Bacon, "encompassed on all the four sides with a stately hedge," and it is thought that he wrote these words after a visit to Hatfield House, now the home of the Marquis of Salisbury where Bacon may have walked in the tiny square Privy Garden so often used by Princess Elizabeth I before becoming Queen. Hatfield was then a Royal House and here it was, sitting beneath a tree, that Elizabeth heard of her accession to the throne. Here, the future Queen of England was to be found, in the garden of what was once the old Palace of the Bishops of Ely from whom it was taken by Henry VIII at the time of the "suppression" and here she held her first Privy Council in the Great Hall. Hatfield later became the home of the Cecil family by the famous "exchange" of houses, James I wishing to possess the Cecils' home, "Theobalds" in Essex, no longer standing.

Sir Robert Cecil wrote: "His Majesty is now come on his journey [from Edinburgh to London] as far as Burghley House [Stamford] and which belonged to Sir Robert's eldest son, later Marquis of Exeter and on Tuesday is expected at Theobalds." The same year (1603) the King persuaded Sir Robert to exchange houses and in 1605 he created him Earl of Salisbury. The gardens at Theobalds were planned and maintained for Elizabeth's celebrated Chancellor, Lord Burghley, father of the newly created Earl, by the famous Gerard to whom he dedicated his "Herbal" (1597).

North of the little garden at Hatfield, and entered by steps, is the Perfumed Garden where eglantine provides protection in the form of a hedge.

Those who live in the more favourable parts may consider a fuchsia hedge as planted by the cottagers in southern Ireland. Mostly native of the higher regions of central and western South America, fuchsias were first grown in England in 1788 and those species and varieties which are considered hardy are delightful plants for a cottage garden with their drooping bells of crimson and purple rocking to and fro in the summer breezes. In the salt-laden winds of the west of Ireland or of Scotland, the finest of all the hardy fuchsias is seen growing. This is *F. riccartonii*, raised in 1853 and it survives in all its glory. It will quickly make a dense bush 5 ft. in height and planted with Ballet Girl which is equally hardy, will prove a source of delight for years to come. But it should be grown only in the west or close to the sea for it is not tolerant of hard frost.

THE ARBOUR

One of the delights of many an old cottage garden was the arbour, usually constructed in a sheltered corner and facing west where the cottager would sit awhile at the end of the day, enjoying his pipe in the cool of the evening, yet warmed by the rays of the setting sun. It was usual for a fragrant hedge to form one side and between the plants and to the front stout stakes were driven into the ground, to make a square retreat, roofed with slatted boarding over which fragrant plants could twine.

Thomas Hyll in *The Art of Gardening* (1564) said, "you may make the arbour straight or else vaulted and enclosed over the head, like to the vine arbours . . . and if they be made of Juniper wood you need to repair nothing thereof for 10 years after; but if they be made with willow poles, then must you repair them every 3 years." About the arbour would be seen growing the· vigorous Musk rose of the hedgerows, *Rosa arvensis*, its white flowers releasing their musk-like perfume especially at eventide and drenching the garden with a heavy scent when the air is calm. Entwined about its thick thorny stems, John Clare's "old man's beard", *Clematis vitalba*, would lift itself to the stars, its greenish-white flowers heavy with perfume as the evening dew begins to form. And the honeysuckles, *Lonicera caprifolium*, in bloom during midsummer and *L. periclymenum* until the autumn.

"If you set roses to run about the arbour," wrote Hyll, "set them in February . . . and in like manner if you would sow [plant] that sweet tree named Jacemine [*J. officinalis*] . . ." Parkinson also advised planting "the jacimine, white and yellow, the double honeysuckle and Ladies' Bower . . . the fittest of outlandish plants to set by arbours . . . to give both sight, smell and delight". In *As You Like It*, Shakespeare makes Hero request "Good Margaret" to go find Beatrice and

> . . . bid her steal into the pleached bower,
> Where honeysuckles, ripened by the sun,
> Forbid the sun to enter.

Shakespeare's friend Ben Jonson, so well describes the bower in his *Visions of Delight* where

> . . . the blue bindweed doth itself enfold
> With honeysuckle and both these entwine
> Themselves with briony and jassamine,
> To cast a kind of odoriferous shade.

It was the white summer-flowering jasmine, *Jasmine officiale*, that was so much desired by Tudor gardeners with its delicious perfume to which Jonson referred, but the evergreen *J. nudiflorum*, which bears its clear primrose-yellow blossoms during winter and spring may also be used. Though scentless, it provides shade and colour when no other plants are in bloom. Likewise the perennial pea, *Lathyrus latifolius*, which bears its magenta-red blooms throughout summer, providing a canopy with its dense twiggy growth, forbidding the heat of the summer sun to penetrate. Each of the climbing plants may also be used to beautify the walls of cottage and outhouse.

Edmund Spenser in *The Faerie Queene* described an arbour of the times which was possibly known to him:

> And over him Art, striving to compare
> With Nature, did an arbour green dispread,
> Fram'd of wanton ivy, flow'ring fair,
> Through which the fragrant Eglantine did spread
> His prickling arms, entrail'd with roses red
> Which dainty odours round about them threw.

Here, in the arbour one may rest awhile and leave refreshed by the fragrance of the flowers, contented and at peace with the world, the solitude broken only by the late song of the birds and the appearance of the Night Hawk Moths searching the honeysuckles for nectar.

THE FLOWER BORDER

Almost all the plants of the cottage garden are of perennial habit so that they will require the minimum of attention and this may be given whenever one's leisure permits. Provided the plants are given an annual dressing of humus which may take the form of clearings from ditches or of decayed farmyard manure, hops or shoddy, the plants will remain vigorous and healthy and may be lifted and divided only when the quality of their flowers begins to deteriorate, whilst certain plants may be left untouched for a decade or more.

As they require more sunlight than most plants, the so-called herbs are at their best when growing together, in an open situation and in a well drained soil. The herb garden could be surrounded by panels of interwoven fencing and should be placed within easy reach of the house. It may be made close to the rose garden, planted with the old-fashioned shrub roses which will require the minimum of attention with their pruning. Once planted, it may be said that they can take care of themselves, requiring no more attention than giving an annual mulching and cutting out dead wood. The remainder of the garden may be planted with herbaceous perennials, using those annuals and biennials which are able to seed themselves, e.g. calendula, oenothera, digitalis, which will be as trouble-free as the perennials.

Perhaps a flagstone path may be laid to divide one part of the garden from another and which will enable the garden to be visited immediately after rain. Chamomile and the carpeting thymes and the most compact of the pinks could be planted between the stones. Or make the path of mellowed brick and on each side set primroses and auriculas; double daisies and thrift; pansies and violettas, interplanted with the miniature bulbs such as the winter aconite and snowdrops, the dog's-tooth violet, and the tiny narcissus species. They would require almost no attention year after year whilst their foliage as it dies back will be hidden by the summer flowering plants. Behind and allowing about 18 ins. from the edge of the stone, there may be planted a low hedge, maybe of lavender using one of the more compact forms and not allowing it to grow more than 15 ins. tall. Behind the hedge would be planted the most compact of the old shrub roses and the border plants. The "hedge" would keep them from coming too close to the tiny plants edging the path which would obtain protection from the sun and wind provided by those plants of taller habit growing behind the hedge and without their being crowded out. These miniature borders could be kept neat and tidy whilst those plants growing behind the dwarf hedge could be left to themselves until late in autumn when the old flowering stems are cut back and ground given a mulch.

On one side of the garden, near the hedge, plant hollyhocks and foxgloves and there let them seed themselves. With them plant the orange-flowered *Lilium croceum* which will grow 4 to 5 ft. tall and the

Madonna lily, *L. candidum*. Several of the Kniphofias, the Red Hot Pokers, and the crimson-purple *Rudbeckia purpurea* will grow to a similar height. The taller Michaelmas daisies would go well with them. With the exception of the foxgloves, all bloom during the latter weeks of summer and through autumn. With them could be planted for the beauty of their foliage, the angelica and the fennel and nearby, *Anchusa italica* with its flowers of clearest sky-blue and which will provide a delightful contrast to the grey-green foliage of the fennel.

In front would come the taller *Phlox paniculata*, growing to a height of 3 to 4 ft. and the Marvel of Peru with its striped flowers and exotic perfume. Both will make dense bushy plants when established and so should be allowed space to develop. The best of the modern phlox with their flamboyant colours of orange and scarlet will provide splashes of brilliance during July and August and plant near them *Chrysanthemum maximum* E. T. Killin and Horace Read, though the latter variety is tall growing and may be more suited to the back of the border. The rather unattractive foliage of the phlox may be offset by that of the Goat's Rue, *Galega officinalis*, with its clusters of purple pea-like flowers and dainty leaves of pea-green. The yellow tree lupins and the purple flowering sages are delightful growing together and here and there plant *Lychnis chalcedonica*, the ancient Cross of Jerusalem which first came to England with the returning crusaders for no flower is longer lasting nor is there one of more brilliant scarlet. All these are flowers of late summer and autumn with *Chrysanthemum rubellum* continuing the display until almost the year end.

It is those plants of more dwarf habit which come first into bloom, the miniatures being earliest of all, endowed by nature with a compact habit to protect them from the cold winds of early spring. We love them all the more for the struggle they make against adverse conditions.

For the middle of the border, no plant is more enduring than the herbaceous paeony, which in some cottage gardens have remained untouched for fifty years or more, and bearing each year their bowls of delicate perfume in ever-increasing numbers. Sarah Bernhardt and Duchess of Nemours and the crimson-black Philippe Rivoire with its "tea" rose fragrance and Kelway's Rosemary with its spicy scent and so well named, should be in every garden for they are the most trouble-free of all plants and none are more eagerly awaited as they come into bloom in the first days of summer. At this time, *Achillea ptarmica* will be in bloom, its snowy-white buttons being most charming when cut and placed indoors with sprays of the yellow-flowering *Ranunculus acris plenus*.

Near them may be planted *Dicentra spectabilis*, the Bleeding Heart which comes into bloom during May and which is always at its loveliest in the coolness of the cottage garden. Also find space for the Japanese anemones. Not of Japan but native of China, they were introduced to our gardens in 1845 when Robert Fortune sent plants from Shanghai, since when they have occupied a special place for they bloom with the Michaelmas daisies when few other plants are in colour. One of the best is September Charm which bears its clear pink flowers on 20-in. stems and is one of the few dwarf plants which is at its loveliest in autumn.

The Peach-leaf campanula, *C. persicifolia*, should find a place in the middle of the border for no plant remains longer in bloom and near it, plant the sweet scented Bergamot, *Monarda didyma*, Cambridge Scarlet which is the brightest of all though Croftway Pink is the most attractive growing near the blue campanula.

Eryngium maritimum, the Sea Holly, with its spiky leaves of purple-green and flowers of steely-blue has since earliest times been a favourite of the cottage garden. It is quite lovely growing near the pink Martagon lily which grows to a similar height and both will be at their finest during August.

To the front of the border come those of more compact habit still, the double-flowered Lady's Smock, *Cardamine pratense flore plena*, with its flowers of silvery-mauve and the hardy geraniums, *G. pratense*, which bears its purple-blue flowers from June until October and *G. sanguineum* which has crimson flowers. The perennial flax, *Linum perenne* with its dainty flowers of clearest blue and *Hypericum perforatum* and *H. calycinum*, the lovely Roses of Sharon which will enhance each other's beauty. And sow annuals, especially those which, like the Calendula and the Californian Poppy, will seed themselves. In such a garden filled with the old-fashioned flowers there will be colour and interest all the year round, scarcely a day when there will not be at least a few plants in bloom, and the original outlay of a few pounds should be the last for almost all will endure for a lifetime.

In a part of the garden may be planted several trees and shrubs to provide colour and perfume the whole year round and beneath which bulbs may be set. Perhaps a tiny spinney could be made to take the place of the orchard which was attached to every cottage of old but with the scarcity of land is now rarely to be seen. In winter, *Viburnum fragrans* will be in bloom and has been found in cottage gardens since its introduction early in the nineteenth century. Its clusters of pink and white flowers are borne from November if the weather is kind. It is a deciduous tree but *V. burkwoodii* is semi-evergreen and makes a more vigorous bush which during early spring is studded with clusters of fragrant white flowers, whilst the blush-pink flowers of *V. juddi* are deliciously clove-scented.

During the bleakest days of winter, *Chimonanthus fragrans*, the Wintersweet, will bear at least some flowers on its leafless stems. The pale yellow and purple blossom is able to tolerate any amount of rain and snow but is not so tolerant of cold winds and should have evergreens for protection. Indoors, the blossom will scent a large room, being amongst the most potent of all flower perfumes.

The Witch Hazels will also bloom during a mild winter. First, *Hamemelis virginiana*, which by late October, before the bracken has fallen, will be covering its bare stems with its twisted blooms of palest yellow and this is a time when there is but little colour and perfume in the garden. Then comes *H. mollis*, its golden-yellow spiderlike blossoms providing delicious scent at Christmastide. And as the spring is patiently awaited, *H. vernalis* will be in colour, its small crimson flowers being tinted with gold and it will still be colourful when the fragrant Daphne comes into bloom, its mahogany stems studded with cerise-pink flowers. Named for the nymph beloved of Apollo, its sweet flowers throw out their beauty in spring's early days.

D. mezereum is of such slow growth that it may be better to plant instead the variety Somerset, raised at the nurseries of John Scott at Merriott. It does well in most soils, though is later flowering, bearing its sweetly-scented flowers of cerise-pink early in May.

To flower in May and early June there are many early shrubs, not least of all being

> "The lilac, various in array, now white
> Now sanguine, and her beauteous head now set,
> Like purple spikes pyramidal, as if
> Studious of ornament, yet unresolved
> Which hue she most approved, she chose them all."

Thus wrote the poet Cowper of one of the loveliest of all flowering shrubs for early summer display.

In his *Sylva Florifera*, Henry Phillips also makes mention of the colourings of the lilac, which by the beginning of the nineteenth century had greatly increased from the original colour which, like the pink, has given its name to the English language to describe the now familiar shade of mauve-blue. Phillips also mentions the white lilac and the Scottish lilac: "The flowers of this lilac are of a much richer colour . . . being of a hue between purple and carmine," he writes and tells us that the first mention of the lilac in England is from a detailed survey of Henry VIII's gardens at Nonsuch Palace in Surrey, made during the latter years of Charles II's reign when he gave the Palace to one of his mistresses who immediately pulled it down. Queen Elizabeth would have known the lilac on her visits to Nonsuch for it was introduced to this country towards the end of the sixteenth century. At Nonsuch, the fountains of the privy-gardens were "set around with six lilac trees, which bear no fruit, but only a very pleasant smell".

It was originally known as the Pipe tree, the wood forming a pipe like that played by Pan, into which the nymph Syrinx was transformed. Hence its name, Syringa. Gerard wrote, "the physitians do name the blew pipe-tree Lilac and some Syringa". Those which bear white flowers always seem to give more fragrance than those of any other colour and especially pronounced is the double, Madame Lemoine, and the single white, J. van Thol. But the lilac is one of the few strongly scented plants to bear flowers other than of white and yellow, one of the most fragrant being the variety Sensation, the dark purple blooms being edged with white and which have a touch of cinnamon in their perfume.

To plant with the daphnes towards the front of the border are the deutzias, such as *D. kalmiaefolia* which blooms in May, whilst those of more vigorous habit, such as *D. pulchra* and Pride of Rochester, bloom at the end of June.

The buddleias, so beloved by bees and butterflies, bear deliciously honey-scented flower spikes during July and August, the variety Black Knight bearing spikes of deepest purple and being quite outstanding both in colour and in perfume. *B. alternifolia* will make a large bush of almost weeping form, its rather unattractive flowers being more strongly honey-scented than any of the genus.

With the buddleias also blooms the Mock Orange, the Philadelphus, in cottage gardens since earliest times. Both plants make canelike growth and should be grown near to each other. Their wood does more greatly resemble the pipe of Pan rather than that of the lilac and there would appear to be some confusion amongst the early writers in this respect. Probably the best of all the Mock Oranges is Belle Etoile, its chalice-shaped flowers of purest white having a refreshing pineapple scent.

To the back of the shrubs may be planted a number of interesting trees including *Laburnum vossii*, its racemes of gold having the scent of freesias, yet Pliny rightly told us that bees never visit its flowers. The laburnum grew in Gerard's garden and was known as the Peascod Tree, for its seed pods are shaped like those of the pea which is of the same family. Its wood, like green ebony, was used for making musical instruments and Matthiolus mentions that (with yew) it made the best bows. Henry Phillips rightly said that "children should be cautioned not to eat the seeds in the green state as they are violently emetic and dangerous".

At the back of the laburnums, the Norway spruce grows with its dark foliage a pleasing contrast to the laburnums when in bloom. From the spruce, turpentine is obtained and from the aromatic fragrance of the trees one may obtain a feeling of great exhilaration on warm days. The story is told of a Mr. C. T. Kingzett who in 1875 after observing the excess of ozone and the exhilarating feeling from a plantation of fir and spruce trees due to the camphoric acid produced by their essential oil on the decomposition of turpentine, conceived of creating the same process by artificial means for use in the home and the now famous Sanitas Company came into being and which happily still exists. In olden times, the tips of spruce shoots were placed in ale to impart their flavour.

In all gardens, the Balsam poplars should be grown. The best is *Populus tacomahaca*. Its buds are covered with resin which is difficult to move from the fingers and if held above a candle flame, the resin will melt to release a powerful incense fragrance. The buds will release their scent even when they have been removed from the tree ten or more years.

In his *Sylva Florifera* (1823) Phillips makes mention that "the buds of both the white and black Poplar have an agreeable perfume early in spring, and when pressed between the fingers yield a balsamic resinous substance which, extracted by spirits of wine, smells like storax". A new hybrid, the result of a cross with *P. trichocorpa* has balsam-scented foliage and is one of the best of the Balsam poplars. Beneath the trees and shrubs, bulbs are planted in generous drifts when

> "Fair-handed spring unbosoms every grace,
> Throws out the snowdrop and the crocus first."

CHAPTER THREE

The Old Shrub Roses

Sweet as scarlet strawberry under wet leaves hidden,
Honeyed as the Damask rose, lavish as the moon,
Shedding lovely light on things forgotten, hope forbidden—
That's the way of June.

Nora Chesson

A rose border or shrubbery will be both labour-saving and colourful
over a long period, and should be considered where space permits.
Once such a border has been planted, it would require no more care
than to be provided with a thick mulch each year, while the plants
would require little more attention with their pruning than the
shortening of long shoots and the cutting out of dead wood.

The old shrub roses, which with the introduction of so many
brilliantly coloured hybrid tea and floribunda roses are now rarely
planted, should be used to make a border, either by themselves or
with other shrubs, for while the bedding roses represent the orderli-
ness of the Edwardian garden, the shrub roses are plants of earlier
days, many of those varieties still happily with us, being widely
planted in cottage gardens during Tudor times. They are of more
robust habit, while their flowers are of those colours, crimson,
purple and pink, usually associated with more leisurely days. Many of
the shrub roses are worthy of planting if only for their fragrance, for
their blooms possess the rich Damask perfume, or have the fragrance
of raspberries, of cinnamon, or of cloves. They also bear flowers of
exquisite form, some having small, rosette-like flowers such as *R.
alba* with its attractive grey foliage, while others bear large double,
globular blooms like those of the paeony and some are attractively
quartered.

A BORDER OF HISTORIC ROSES

A large number of the best of the double-flowering roses were
evolved at the beginning of the nineteenth century, mostly in France,

where they were used to adorn the gardens of the aristocracy who left Paris during the summer months for the coolness of the country. But many of the old shrub roses are very much older than that, and a border could well be planted entirely with those roses famed for their historic interest. The Jacobite rose, *R. alba maxima*, and *R. alba semi-plena*, the White Rose of York would be included. The old cabbage or Provence rose, the enormous "rose of a hundred leaves" (petals), portrayed in so many famous paintings should find a place, and near it plant the Great Maiden's Blush, grown in English gardens since earliest times. The ancient Apothecary's rose, the Red Rose of Lancaster, which is the Gallica rose, and the equally ancient *Rosa Mundi*, also a Gallica, its white blooms striped with crimson, could be found a place; together with the lovely York and Lancaster, a Damask which Shakespeare knew well. The old Painted Damask, known as Leda, and the equally old Celsiana of the same group, could be included, and to remind one of the lovely Empress Josephine, who did so much to perpetuate the beauty of the old roses, a plant of Souvenir de la Malmaison should be included in every shrub border. Several of the lovely hybrid perpetuals, the connecting link between the old shrub roses and the moderns may be planted, for they possess the same vigorous habit and bear the same large, sweetly scented flowers as the old roses. Paul Neyron, Mrs John Laing, with its globes of mauve-pink, and Reine des Violettes, which bears attractively quartered blooms, should find a place in every rose border.

Roses from all groups and heights should be included in the border of historic interest. At the back would be planted *R. alba maxima* and *R. alba semi-plena*, for both grow 6 to 7 ft. high, and near them plant the old blush Damask which comes early into bloom and so will prolong the display. Some 6 ft. away, plant the York and Lancaster rose, another Damask, and which also grows 6 ft. tall. The lovely *R. alba* Celeste should be included at the back of the border for its cool, grey leaves and pale-pink flowers present a most refreshingly cool appearance during the warmest weeks of the year. Besides their beauty and interest, each of these roses has a deliciously sweet perfume. Another rose with grey foliage is *R. alba*, Belle d'Amour. Its flowers are of soft pink and have bright golden stamens. Somewhere nearby, plant *R. rubrifolia*, a thornless rose with red bark and purple-tinted leaves which will also grow nearly 5 ft. tall.

For the middle row use the lovely Apothecary's rose and near it

1 Shrub roses and herbaceous plants in a Cambridgeshire cottage garden

2 An Essex cottage garden with shrub roses and a
hedge of dwarf lavender along the brick path

3 Detail of John Clare's cottage at Helpston

4 A fine example of an English cottage garden

5 Herbaceous plants in the cottage garden

6 A cottage garden framed in an archway of honeysuckle and rambler roses

7   Knotted beds filled with primroses

plant *R. alba maxima* and *R. fedtschenkoana*, both of which bear white flowers. The crimson blooms of *R. gallica officinalis*, used as a symbol by the House of Lancaster, will provide a striking contrast. Near by plant the Great Maiden's Blush with its grey foliage, and the autumn Damask, which blooms from June until the beginning of winter and which was grown by the Romans at Pompeii. The white form Quatre Saisons Blanc Mousseux, could accompany it. This is a moss rose, the buds, stems, and leaves being covered in tiny glandular hairs which are scented.

To remind one of the Empress Josephine's garden, the lovely Souvenir de la Malmaison should be included. It is a perpetual-flowering Bourbon rose, and will bloom even better in autumn than in summer. Near it, plant the Damask, Château Gaillard, from Richard the Lion Heart's castle in Normandy. Then to complete the middle of the border, include the old Centifolia, Rose of Rheims, with its pompon blooms of claret-red, and the lovely striped *R. gallica versicolor* Rosa Mundi, named after Fair Rosamond Clifford. On her tombstone at Godstow Priory in Oxfordshire were inscribed the words:

Hic jacet in tomba rosa mundi, non rosa munda.

To the front of the border, plant Omar Khayyám, a Damask rose which originally came from Omar Khayyám's grave at Nishapur. It grows 3 ft. tall, with grey foliage, and bears flat, pink flowers. Near by plant the double Cinnamon rose, which begins to bloom in May. Gerard, writing in Elizabethan times, tells us that the dark leaves exhaled the fragrance of cinnamon.

The very old *R. centifolia* Robert le Diable, which bears purple-violet flowers splashed with crimson, also grows 3 ft. tall, and near, plant the dainty Damask Petite Lisette, which has grey foliage and bears pretty rosettes of clear pink. Then, the old Gallica Pompon Panachée, its dainty cream-coloured blooms being striped with pink. And Leda, the ancient Painted Damask, which has dark-green foliage and white flowers, tipped with red. Finally, the lovely Gallica Sissinghurst Castle, where it was discovered growing in the gardens by its owner, the late Miss V. Sackville-West (Lady Nicolson). Its dainty blooms are of deep maroon-black with striking golden stamens, a suitable memorial to so wonderful a gardener.

When planting a border of the old shrub roses, all the various characteristics of the numerous species and varieties should be introduced. Besides those roses of historic interest, attention should be given to those roses which have grey and bronzy-green foliage, for this will provide greater interest when the plants are not in bloom, and it must be remembered that the old roses, with but few exceptions, bloom only during the midsummer months. With the introduction of the Bourbons and the hybrid perpetuals, the flowering season will be extended until the autumn, while the inclusion of a few of the more vigorous of the hybrid teas, such as President Hoover and Tahiti, will extend the season until winter.

ROSES WITH COLOURFUL FOLIAGE

A number of those roses which have attractive grey-green foliage have been suggested for inclusion in the border of historic interest, and there are others. Of these, one of the most interesting of all the species is the apple-scented rose, *R. pomifera*, the best of which is the double form, known as Rev. Woolley-Dod's rose. It grows 6 to 7 ft. tall, and bears flowers of clearest pink, followed by crimson hips. Another is *R. spinosissima*, Stanwell Perpetual, thought to be the result of a crossing with a Damask rose, and which makes an excellent hedge. It has an additional value in that its blush-pink flowers are borne through summer and autumn. The lovely dwarf *R. gallica*, Duchess de Montebello, and *R. centifolia*, Rose d'Hivers, both have grey-green foliage, while *R. alba* Jeanne d'Arc has unusual blue-green leaves.

Unlike the modern hybrid tea and floribunda roses, few of the old shrub and wild roses have bronze- or red-tinted foliage. Apart from *R. rubrifolia* and *R. pendulina*, only the Bourbon Mme Ernst Calvat, and the unique *R. centifolia bullata*, which has large lettuce-like leaves, have foliage tinted with bronze. Of modern shrub roses, the hybrid musk Daybreak has coppery tinted foliage.

The *R. rugosa* hybrid, *R. wadei* has golden-yellow foliage, while the Centifolia roses, La Noblesse (which blooms over a very long period), Rose de Meaux, and Gros Choux d'Hollande, the ancient Cabbage rose of Holland, have very pale-green foliage. The foliage of these roses will provide a pleasing change from the usual dark- and medium-green foliage of so many roses.

These roses have grey leaves:

R. alba, Great Maiden's Blush
R. alba maxima

    R. alba semi-plena
    R. centifolia, Juno
    R. centifolia, Rose d'Hivers
    R. damascena, Celeste
    R. damascena, Omar Khayyám
    R. damascena, Petite Lisette
    R. fedtschenkoana
    R. gallica, Duchess de Montebello
    R. spinosissima, Falkland
    R. spinosissima, Stanwell Perpetual
    R. webbiana

Roses with purple-bronze foliage:

    R. bourboniana, Mme E. Calvat
    R. centifolia bullata
    R. pendulina (*flore-plena*)
    R. rubiginosa, Sparrieshoof
    R. rubrifolia

Roses with pale-green foliage:

    R. blanda
    R. bourboniana, Commandant Beaurepeire
    R. bourboniana, Honorine Brabant
    R. centifolia, De Meaux
    R. centifolia, Gros Choux d'Hollande
    R. centifolia, La Noblesse
    R. wadei (Golden-green)

A BORDER OF THORNLESS ROSES

The author has been asked by a lover of roses who had recently lost her sight to name as many species and varieties as possible which carried no thorns, as this would enable the bloom to be cut without fear of damage to the hands. There may be others who would prefer their roses to be without thorns, so here are suggestions for planting a border of roses which are almost devoid of thorns.

To plant a border 10 to 11 ft. in width, three rows should be planted, with those of more robust habit to the back. Of these, *R. webbiana* from central Asia is outstanding, for not only is it thornless but its wood is crimson-red, and its fern-like foliage is grey-green. The single, pink flowers with their aromatic perfume are followed by scarlet hips. It grows 6 ft. tall. Similar is *R. pendulina*, which also has red thornless wood and leaves tinted with bronze, and is one of the very earliest roses to bloom. *R. rubrifolia*, with its bright-crimson wood, is thornless, and grows nearly the same height, while the vigorous Damask Rose of Ispahan, which has practically no thorns and remains in bloom longer than any Damask, attains a similar height. The vigorous, almost thornless moss rose Eugenie Guinoisseau would also be planted at the back of the border. It bears large, cerise flowers, flushed with purple, and near by plant the equally vigorous *R. alba* Madame le Gras de St. Germain, which bears large camellia-shaped flowers of ivory-white.

To the front plant the delightful Bourbon, Zephyrine Drouhin and its pink and crimson "sport" Kathleen Harrop. Both are thornless, and unlike the back row plants will be perpetually in bloom. With them plant the thornless Gallica Belle de Crécy, which bears rose-pink flowers of perfect form, and Belle Isis, which is almost thornless and bears flesh-pink flowers. The very old scarlet Gallica Assemblage des Beautés, with its ball-shaped blooms, is also practically free of thorns, and the floribunda Iceberg, so colourful in autumn.

At the front plant those charming old hybrid perpetuals Mrs. John Laing, Paul Neyron, and Roger Lambelin, all of which are almost thornless, and with them the two lovely old Gallicas Sissinghurst Castle and Henri Foucquier, which grow less than a yard high and bear large, circular blooms of mauve-pink. The dainty Nanette with its pink-and-purple-striped flowers could also be planted. Even more dwarf is the floribunda Rumba, which has very few thorns.

A border of thornless roses would be valuable for a children's garden, while for those who cannot see, almost all those roses mentioned bear sweetly perfumed flowers, an additional quality to their thornless wood.

These roses are thornless or are nearly so:

> Adam Messerich (Bourbon)
> Autumn Delight (Musk)
> Assemblage des Beautés (Gallica)
> Belle de Crécy (Gallica)
> Charles de Mills (Gallica)
> Duchess d'Angouleme (Gallica)
> Eugenie Guinoisseau (Moss)

Henri Foucquier (Gallica)
Kathleen Harrop (Bourbon)
Mme Le Gras de St. Germain (Alba)
Mrs. John Laing (hybrid perp.)
Paul Neyron (hybrid perp.)
Pompon Blanc Parfait (Alba)
Prince Charles (Bourbon)
Rosa Mundi (Gallica)
Sissinghurst Castle (Gallica)
Zephyrine Drouhin (Bourbon)

An open, sunny situation should be selected for the shrub border, for then the plants will receive the sunlight so necessary for ripening the new shoots and to prolong the flowering display. Also, when given a sunny position, the plants will receive their share of the autumn sunshine so necessary for those roses which are to continue to bloom until the arrival of the first frosts of winter. If the garden is unduly exposed, the Gallica and Damask roses will appreciate some protection from the prevailing winds. This may be in the form of wattle hurdles or of those hardy roses of climbing habit which may be trained against rustic poles placed at the back of the border where the winds are most troublesome.

The shrub border should be made where the plants may be best enjoyed, either from the home or when walking in the garden. It may be planted to divide the garden of a semi-detached house from another when, by planting at the back those species of more vigorous habit such as the thornless alba rose Mme Le Gras de St. Germain and the grey-leaved *R. webbiana*, privacy may be obtained without bringing excessive shade to the garden or to that of one's neighbour. The border will be made more attractive if it can be approached by a grass walk or by a path made of crazy-paving stones or of concrete flagstones.

The shrub roses will require more space in which to grow than the hybrid tea and floribunda roses, though the more compact of the Gallicas and Damasks are of similar habit. Mostly they make bushy plants growing from 4 to 6 ft. in height and the same in width, and so should not be planted so closely together that they grow into one another, thus depriving each other not only of food and moisture but of air and sunlight. The result will be that the plants will form an excess of dead wood which gradually result in the plants dying back, while the display will deteriorate each year instead of increasing in brilliance. The plants should be allowed ample space to develop, and it must be remembered that they will be expected to occupy the ground for many years. A well-drained soil, but one retentive of summer moisture, is essential for the shrub roses. The ground should be well prepared by digging at least two spades (spits) deep and incorporating as much of whatever humus materials may be obtained. Clearings from ditches, composed straw, old mushroom-bed compost, decayed farmyard manure, and material from the garden compost heap may be used, not omitting to give the soil of a town garden a liberal dressing with lime before the preparation commences.

As the work proceeds, all perennial weeds must be removed and after the ground has been prepared, it should be allowed at least a fortnight to settle down before planting. If the ground is made ready in October, planting may take place during November, which is the most suitable time and will enable the plants to become established before the hard frosts. Never plant when there is frost in the soil or when it is so wet as to set like concrete after treading in the roses.

When planting, make a hole sufficiently large to take all the roots without crowding. Any unduly long roots should be shortened, and when planting each root should be carefully arranged around the plant so that each will receive its share of food and moisture. The soil should be packed firmly around the roots, and after planting, if the soil is dry, water well. Planting may take place at any time between early November and the end of March, depending upon the condition of the soil. When planting, allow the roses room to develop, and so that there will be room to walk around the plants to cut the bloom and to attend to their needs. Thus, those plants growing 5 ft. across should be planted about 6 ft. apart.

Graduate the planting so that the taller-growing varieties are placed to the back of the border with the less robust to the centre and with those of more compact habit to the front. The border may be completed by planting the dwarf China roses to the front, especially Little White Pet and Cramoisie Superieure, whose blooms resemble those of the old shrub roses.

The shrub border should be given the same careful planning as for the herbaceous border, planting those roses with green- and purple-tinted foliage among those with dark- and medium-green foliage and making use of those species renowned for their colourful hips.

Thought should also be given to continuity of colour in the border, planting those roses which bloom early and those which bloom in autumn on either side of the summer-flowering roses. Colour and perfume should also be considered, so that there will be as wide a variety as possible to give the border the maximum of interest. The shape of bloom and any other interesting characteristics should also be considered.

After planting, the shrub roses require the minimum of attention. They will appreciate a thick mulch to be given each year when any pruning is done early in March. If the mulch be of decayed straw manure or used hops from a brewery, it will provide food and will act as an absorbent for summer moisture. It will also suppress weeds.

CHAPTER FOUR

Evening Fragrance

'Twas midnight—through the lattice, wreath'd
With Woodbine, many a perfume breath'd
From plants that wake when others sleep,
From timid jasmine buds, that keep
Their odour to themselves all day,
But, when the sunlight dies away,
Let the delicious secret out
To every breeze that roams about.

Thomas Moore

Relying upon their scent for pollination by the night moths, those plants which open their bloom as the temperature declines with the going down of the sun, are amongst the most fragrant of all flowering plants, making up in scent for what they lack in colour. In almost every instance, those plants which open their flowers at night-time, bear flowers of tubular or trumpet form in which the honey is accessible to the long tongues of the humming bird hawk moth. The flowers are of delicate colouring, ranging from purest white to blush-pink and palest yellow for colour is not a requirement in the attraction of insects for their reproduction and indeed, those flowers of palest colouring will all the better reveal themselves in the half light of evening.

As the warm daytime temperature begins to fall in the evening, a garden in which the night-scented plants are freely used will become alive again when the rest of the garden is sleeping. For those who must labour during the daytime, returning home only in the evening, the liberal use of the night-scented plants will bring new interest and enjoyment to the garden at the end of a tiring day when a leisurely stroll in the dewy twilight, when all is cool and quiet, will act as a most efficient tranquillizer to a tired mind before the night's rest begins.

A group of the night-scented plants could be set out at the very end of the garden, reached by a path of crazy paving, about which the aromatic carpeting plants will sit in clumps like sleeping tortoises, waiting to release their fragrance when trodden upon. If the air is calm and heavy, a delicious perfume will reach up from the night-scented plants to more than halfway down the garden, drawing to them all who are near, exactly as they do the hawk moth. Night-scented plants have a fascination one is unable to resist, an excitement perhaps with the ghost-like appearance of their pale colour in the half light. And sometimes when too tired to sleep, a walk down the winding path in the moonlight and there, waiting to greet one with their rich, sweet scent are those flowers which are known to all too few garden lovers. All is quiet except perhaps for the sighing of a gentle breeze blowing through the pine trees, diffusing their aromatic scent to add a subtle undertone to the exotic perfumes of the plants: "Perfuming evening with a luscious sweet."

The Evening primroses, of which there are several, come with the going down of the sun into that full beauty of flower which they deny us during the hours of daylight, their pale yellow (ethereal) colouring being almost moon-like, their rich scent almost overpowering, especially so before a storm. The cupped flowers shine bright until the night once more gives way to the daytime when they wither and die for fertilization has taken place. The Evening primroses are biennial plants growing 5 ft. tall. They readily seed themselves if undisturbed and will come up year after year from an original sowing costing very little. They were the favourite flowers of my grandfather, who planted them alongside a fence separating his garden from that of his neighbours with whom he was on most cordial terms, with the sole reason that they too, could enjoy the evening fragrance of the flowers. They would reciprocate the kindly thought by planting on their side, *Hesperis matronalis*, the Damask Violet or Double White Rocket, a familiar plant of old cottage gardens which has given everlasting pleasure to those who would never be without it in their garden. A hardy perennial, though it may also be grown as an annual, it is known as Dame's Violet but I prefer its Irish name of the Damask Violet for its perfume at night more nearly resembles that of the Damask rose. It is one of the most deliciously scented of all flowers and of such easy culture, as one would imagine for it is a member of the wallflower family of plants and like that plant grows well when seed is sown between the stones of an old wall. The flowers are white but sometimes of lilac colouring. The double form, *flore pleno*, is even more strongly fragrant.

William Robinson thought it "amongst the most desirable of garden flowers" as indeed it is for it grows well in full sun and also in partial shade and so may be planted freely in the border where it will grow to a height of 4 to 5 ft. There, the flowers open and give of their fragrance on any cool, dull day of summer. It is to be found in few gardens today yet it is one of those old-fashioned plants which perpetuate the charm of the age in which they were most appreciated.

Several members of the Caryophyllaceae family of plants, which includes the carnation and pink, are fragrant at night and amongst the clove-scented plants is *Lychnis vespertina*, the Night-scented Campion. It is one of those plants whose flowers fill the air with their intense fragrance at nightfall, yet during the daytime, although their blooms remain open, they seem to emit little or no scent at all. The plant is a lover of a chalky soil, like all members of the family and growing to a height of 2 to 3 ft. it is excellent to plant in a sunny border for it bears its fine white flowers uninterrupted from May until September. It is one of the few wild flowers which are even lovelier in the garden though are rarely to be found there.

Closely related to the campions are the catchflies, the Silenes, several of which emit a delicate clove scent at night. *Silene nutans*, which is occasionally to be found growing on cliffs and dry walls, grows 2 ft. tall and during early summer bears its tubular blooms of blush-white which are dimorphic on the first two nights. The blooms are strongly fragrant when the stamens ripen, the styles protruding on the third night when, after pollination, the bloom loses its scent. The plant is perennial but *S. noctiflora* which also opens its flowers at night is an annual, to be found growing in sandy places along the coast. If taken indoors at night, the blooms will fill the largest room with their scent.

The Bladder Campion, *Silene inflata*, so called because its five sepals are swollen to resemble a bladder, also bears flowers which are white and sweetly scented at night and which are pollinated by moths. It is usually to be found growing by the roadside and in waste ground where the soil is of a chalky nature. It is not a plant for the garden though where it can be obtained, the form *puberula*, with downy grey-green leaves, may be planted.

A plant to give delight with its evening perfume is the Tobacco plant, *Nicotina affinis*. Really a perennial and a form of *N. alata*, it is a native of the warmer parts of North and South America and unless given half-hardy treatment, would perish during winter in our islands. Named in honour of Jean Nicot, a diplomat who introduced tobacco to the French Court towards the end of the sixteenth century, its flowers diffuse the most exquisite of all evening perfumes. Growing to a height of 3 to 4 ft., it bears attractive star-shaped flowers of purest white which open only at night. "Heavy nicotinas hidden through the day," wrote Pamela Tennant and they diffuse their delicate sweet odour about the garden as the dew begins to fall. They should be planted, like the Evening primroses, in groups of six or more, spacing them 12 ins. apart and planting out towards the end of May when there will be little fear of night frost. During daytime, when the flowers are tightly closed, the handsome tobacco-leaf foliage provides an attractive background to those plants which bloom by day and so are useful in the garden both by day and night. There is also a dwarf counterpart, Dwarf White Bedder, whose fragrant icy white flowers, green on the outside, remain open both by day and by night and bring to the border an appearance of winter coolness on the warmest day. It is also obtainable in the tall growing form called Daylight, the blooms being larger than those of *N. affinis* and though not fragrant by day, do remain open. What is more, it blooms from July until the frosts of late autumn.

The Tobacco plants grow quite happily in partial shade and will make a pleasing display grouped to the front of mature trees with violas, especially the scented violettas, planted amongst them. Unlike most fragrant plants, the Tobacco plants are most strongly scented where growing in a rich, moist soil which is especially necessary for *N. sylvestris*, a handsome species growing 6 ft. tall and whose large creamy white flowers, which remain open by day, emit so strong a scent in the evening as to almost hypnotize the senses. It is valuable in that it blooms as summer is ending and during autumn.

A wild flower, common in Norway and which was first discovered by Professor Beattie growing in a fir wood at Mearns, near Aberdeen in 1795, is *Linnaea borealis*, the Twin Flower so called because each stem bears two tiny drooping flowers, creamy-white in colour, flushed with pink and which in the evening smell strongly of meadowsweet. A shrubby evergreen of trailing habit, it is a delightful plant to grow about crazy-paving stones or on a rockery and on a warm evening during June and July when in bloom, emits a heavy, exotic perfume, so strong that it would not be thought possible from two such tiny flowers. Remember to provide it with an acid, peaty soil similar to that of its native fir and pine woods.

PLANTING NEAR A WINDOW

Where the garden is small, a delightful idea is to make a small border of the night scented plants immediately beneath the window of a living-room or bedroom where on a warm calm evening in summer, one may lay awake at any time during the hours of twilight and darkness and inhale the perfume of the flowers. For those confined indoors by illness, it gives one a feeling of great contentment to be able to enjoy the delicious scents when the rest of the world are sound asleep.

On one occasion during illness, a bed was placed immediately beneath an old mullioned window, about which a fragrant climbing rose draped itself, almost depriving one of any view. But the rich Damask scent from its flowers, intermingling with the exotic perfumes of the evening-scented plants as the sun gave way to a star-lit sky compensated for any loss of daytime view and for any inability to leave one's bed. Where possible, it is desirable to make up the bed of night-scented plants on the western side of the house so that the plants may be warmed by the late evening sun when they will release their fragrance in more concentrated form, like dried rose petals in a warm room.

To smell the fragrance of the plants from indoors, whether in bed or sitting by an open window, is to convey the same feeling experienced when walking in the perfumed gardens of the East for the fragrance of the flowers on a warm evening is reminiscent of the walled gardens of Syria and the Lebanon.

Though generally grown in pans under glass, in a warm, sheltered border, corms of *Gladiolus tristis* may be planted. A native of Natal, growing 12 ins. tall, it bears in July cream-coloured flowers spotted and pencilled with red which at night have a distinct spicy fragrance. Crossed with *G. cardinalis*, it produced the popular *G. colvillei* which is generally grown under glass for early summer flowering.

The sand verbenas, the Abronias, are not common plants, though at one time were to be found in many a cottage garden. They have a trailing habit and are natives of California and are delightful when used for draping over a dry wall. Especially so is *Abronia latifolia*, which bears heads of pale yellow flowers which in the evening smell powerfully of honey. It remains in bloom from mid-

July until well into autumn. Another species, *A. fragrans*, is not of trailing habit as are most of the abronias but grows to a height of almost 2 ft. bearing white flowers which open only at sundown, breathing out a pleasant vanilla perfume. These two abronias like a humus-laden loam, and in a warm area may be treated as perennials, which they are really, though in northern gardens they should be given half-hardy annual treatment. They grow readily from seed and will be in bloom by August 1st from a March sowing made under glass.

The true verbena, *V. teucrioides*, a native of Brazil, also releases its perfume at night. It is a tender plant and suitable only for sheltered gardens, though a century ago it was to be found in almost every cottage garden. It grows nearly 2 ft. tall and bears large blush-white flowers in hairy heads and which release their lemon scent only in the evening. But what a refreshing scent it is as it comes drifting through the open window when outside the air is warm and calm. It is like the smell of rosemary warmed by the September sun, an aromatic refreshing smell, better than smelling salts to ease a tired mind. "The Verbena strains the point of passionate fragrance," wrote Browning.

To edge the beds of night-scented plants or to sow in little groups to the front of a border or indeed anywhere in the garden, the dainty night-scented stock, *Matthiola bicornis*, will hold its own with the most vigorous plants. Its toughness belies its delicate appearance for it is a plant slender and frail in habit, yet completely hardy. And though its tiny pale lilac flowers are quite insignificant, their fragrance pervades the atmosphere far and wide as the sun begins to set. The scent increases as twilight overtakes the garden and when all is dark and calm, the perfume is more powerful still stealing through the open window for all inside to enjoy. Or fill a tiny jar with the flowers and place it indoors when the fragrance they will diffuse about the home will be greater than the most exotic perfumes. But better, sow the seed where the plants may bloom throughout the summer and where their scent may reach inside the home so that their perfume may be inhaled throughout the night and in the morning awake refreshed in body and in spirit whilst those who are able to spend their summer evenings in the garden will be equally refreshed by the delicious scent. A small packet of seed sprinkled about the garden will provide a most heavenly perfume from June until the summer ends.

All the stocks are night-scented and none more so than the dwarf East Lothian strain, discovered in a cottage garden in that part of Scotland bearing its name. It is the first of the summer stocks to bloom and both by day and by night will diffuse its clove-like perfume over a wide area.

In all her history Greece has given us nothing more exquisite than the Night-scented stock unless it be the Moonflower, *Calonyction aculeatum*, the *Ipomoea bona-nox* of the old garden books. Those who have had the pleasure of inhaling the exquisite fragrance of its flowers, like large convolvulus blooms, when sitting relaxed on a verandah at sundown, with the dark blue water of the Mediterranean far below, will know what Paradise has in store. It is a tender perennial, too tender to grow outside permanently in Britain but it may be grown in a cool greenhouse or garden room where it may be allowed to trail over the roof. Or grow it where it can receive the protection of a covered verandah facing south and there let it twine wherever it desires for it is one of the most exciting plants I know, its pure white trumpets having an ethereal appearance in the half light of evening when the flowers are fully open and when they exhale a delicious spicy fragrance. From a sowing made under glass in February, the plants will be in bloom before the end of July and will continue until too cold for them to bloom more. They should then be removed, treating them as a tender annual. Long neglected for it has been grown in our gardens for more than a century, it should come into its own now that the conservatory has been replaced by the garden room and we can enjoy the more tender plants again.

Yet another deliciously fragrant plant which will prove as attractive in Britain as it does in a warmer climate if treated as a half-hardy annual is the Marvel of Peru. In America it is known as the Four o'Clock Flower, for that is the time when its white or yellow trumpet-shaped flowers begin to open and remain so throughout the night. Grow a few plants against a sunny wall or in a small bed just to themselves for they diffuse a deliciously sweet perfume at night which increases in strength as the evening twilight gives way to complete darkness. Even more exotic is *Mirabilis longiflora*, which grows to a similar height of 2 ft. and whose long tubular flowers emit the unmistakable scent of orange blossom at night. If treated as half-hardy annuals, there is nothing difficult about their culture and when in bloom during August and September, they will never allow one to go indoors while ever the night is warm.

Though nothing like so exotic, a less well-known plant to delight us with its fragrance at eventide is *Hebenstreitia comosa*, named after John Hevenstreit, Professor of Medicine at Leipzig University two centuries ago. It is a plant native of South Africa where it is perennial, though in Britain it should be given half-hardy annual treatment. Its tiny yellow or white flowers, spotted with orange, are borne in spikes and at night diffuse a scent similar to that of mignonette. The plants attain a height of 15 ins. and flowering from June until September, are valuable for planting in small beds.

Some years ago, I made up a bed of these plants outside my garden, along the side of the pavement and in the evening so delicious was their perfume that all who passed by would stop to inquire from where the scent was coming. Especially heavy and sweet was the perfume after a gentle shower and with the plants warmed by the afternoon sun.

Also from South Africa comes a dainty little plant called *Zaluzianskya capensis*. Do not be put off by its name for it is a charming plant which bears masses of white starry flowers, like those of the annual *Phlox drummondii*. Though remaining open by day, it is only at night that the flowers diffuse the fullness of their fragrance which is delightfully aromatic. In its native land it is known as the Night Phlox and growing but 12 ins. high, it is a most pleasing plant to use for small beds where the fragrance of its flowers may be enjoyed from indoors. *Z. villosa* is even more fragrant whilst its white flowers with their orange centre also remain open by day thus giving of its charms both by day and by night.

There are many other plants whose flowers are fragrant at night but as they are also scented by day, they are described elsewhere. Foremost are the honeysuckles which are pollinated by the humming bird hawk moth and open their blooms fully, only during the hours of darkness, raising themselves from a drooping to a horizontal position, when the moths remain suspended above the flowers and with the aid of their long tongue, sip the sweet nectar. The next evening, a change has taken place in the flower. The stamens have become withered but the stigma is ready to be touched by the moth after which, with the setting of seed, the flower takes on a dingy hue and loses its perfume. Its task is complete.

No plant covers a stone gateway quite like the honeysuckle, its creamy-yellow blooms blending with the stone as no other flowers can do and at night diffusing their honey-like fragrance far and wide.

Beneath, so that there will be a similar fragrance in spring, plant a small bed of the old purple double primrose, Marie Crousse, for its honey-sweet perfume at night is especially delicious. It is such a good doer too, hardy and long lasting. In one garden I know, the plants are thought to be fifty years old and with constant division remain as vigorous as ever. It is the most fragrant of all the primroses, equally delightful when taken indoors in pots or in small vases.

NIGHT-SCENTED PLANTS

Abronia latifolia
Calonyction aculeatum
Dianthus caryophyllus
Hesperis matronalis
Jasminum officinale
Lonicera caprifolium
Lychnis vespertina
Matthiola bicornis
Mirabilis jalapa
Nicotiana affinis
Oenothera biennis
Silene nutans
Zaluzianskya capensis

For descriptions see Part II.

Plate 1
Above Rosa centifolia, Fantin-Latour
Left Rosa gallica, Versicolor

Plate 2
Above   Lilium candidum –
Madonna Lily
Right   Borago officinalis –
Borage

CHAPTER FIVE

The Herb Garden

And thou hast fragrant herbs and seed,
Which only garden's culture need:
Thy horehound tufts I love them well,
And ploughman's spikenard's spicy smell;
Thy thyme, strong-scented 'neath one's feet,
Thy marjoram beds, so doubly sweet,
And pennyroyal's creeping twine,
These, each succeeding each, are thine,
Spreading o'er thee wild and gay,
Blessing spring or summer's day.

John Clare

John Clare often wrote of the fragrant herbs of the countryside and of all plants, none provide greater interest nor have more uses about the home. Forty-two were suggested for the kitchen and twenty-two for "sallads and sauces" by Thomas Tusser writing in Elizabethan times. Shakespeare knew of their value too:

"O mickle is the powerful grace, that lies
In herbs, plants, stones and their true qualities."

Thus spoke Friar Laurence in *Romeo and Juliet*. There are few herbs which do not have an aromatic scent in some form, whether it be in the flowers, leaves, root or seed. Several provide pungency from all parts of the plant and may be used in numerous ways about the home, for purposes of medicine, for making pot-pourris and in the kitchen, to give flavour to so many dishes. A leaf of the sweet bay (*Laurus nobilis*) placed in a rice pudding or in a glass of milk will take away the often insipid taste; whilst several of the thymes, rubbed over meat will give flavour to the most tasteless joint. Especially is this so where only small cuts of meat are to be cooked. To improve the flavour try rubbing the meat with *Thymus herba barona*, or use *T. micans* which has a distinct pine-like flavour or perfume. Those who enjoy fish will

49

find it even more palatable if sprinkled or rubbed with the orange-scented *T. fragrantissimus* or the lemon-scented *T. citriodorus*. To give flavour to a stew, add a leaf of Mace or Lovage which imparts the distinctive flavour of celery. And where there is no refrigerator available in which to store meat, if rubbed with Tansy leaves it will keep away flies and maintain its freshness for longer than usual. To preserve fish, fennel was used and as a sauce to serve with it as mentioned in a late thirteenth-century manuscript, whilst it was in great demand for fasting days. It is recorded that both Edward I and Henry VIII were lovers of fennel. In Europe, the plant is still widely used for making sauces as are so many others which have fragrant leaves and are considered indispensable to gastronomic enjoyment.

In France and Italy, dishes of pungent herbs are almost always available on the dining table, to be used with cheeses, to add to soups and stews, to be enjoyed in a salad or to be sprinkled on almost any dish except the sweet course. The dishes consist of chopped chives and sage, of mint and costmary, of thyme and winter savory which in Parkinson's time was held in great esteem to "expelleth the wind". These herbs will help the digestion as well as bringing a new interest to a meal.

There are also the health-giving "teas" to be made from an infusion of the leaves of mint and balm, catmint or bergamot, so valuable for those who suffer from rheumatic and nervous complaints. For pot-pourris, too, the pungent leaves of many plants will be of use and placed beneath the pillow will encourage peaceful sleep. Placed amongst clothes, they will keep away moths and provide bed linen with a pleasant perfume. All have their daily uses and no house or garden should be without them as, indeed, no cottage garden ever was.

MAKING THE HERB GARDEN

A small part of every garden should be provided for those plants with aromatic leaves which in many instances are worthy of planting if only for the handsome form and colouring of their foliage. There are the lovely sages, the silver and gold leaf thymes; fennel; and sweet cecily with its handsome filigree leaves; catmint with its foliage of cool sea-green; cotton lavender with its silvery encrusted leaves of which Parkinson said, "the rarity and novelty of this herb being for the most part but in the gardens of great persons . . ." A number of the herbs have brilliantly coloured flowers, none more so than *Thymus serpyllus coccineus* which, planted between paving stones, will make a mat of darkest green and for three months of summer will cover itself with a multitude of tiny blossoms of brilliant crimson, pink or white. For the border, fennel, hyssop, the angelicas, and the artemesias may be grown for the decorative value of their foliage which will provide contrast to those plants bearing colourful flowers but whose foliage, like that of the phlox, is anything but pleasing. "What greater pleasure can there be than to smell the sweet odour of herbes, trees and fruits, and to behold the goodly colour of the same," wrote Leonard Mascall in 1572.

The most popular way of enjoying herbs in the cottage garden was to enclose the beds with box or cotton lavender, or the most dwarf of the lavenders, each of which will withstand clipping. The shrubby artemesias which retain their aromatic foliage through winter may also be used. With their evergreen silvery foliage, these plants make a delightful surround for small beds of herbs or of other plants, pinks and violettas being at their best when grown in this fashion.

The herb garden may be divided into four beds each surrounded by paths of paving stone, so necessary to reach the plants in winter-time and about which may be planted the creeping thymes; the heath-like *Micromeria corsica* which has the delicious scent of rosemary; the most compact of the pinks; maybe a root of catmint; pennyroyal; and chamomile. Then make the dwarf hedge near the paths and inside, fill up the beds according to size with all manner of fragrant plants. Beds of mixed herbs, as to be found at Sissinghurst Castle in Kent, set by the late Miss Victoria Sackville-West, look perfectly right whereas beds of mixed flowering plants would look anything but happy. Plant those herbs of taller habit at the centre with the dwarf thymes of shrubby habit, the sages and chives about the sides. So that the variety will be as great as possible, different herbs may be planted in each bed and if the beds are made about 6 ft. square, it is surprising how many each will accommodate. If the beds are slightly raised at the centre, the plants will obtain the maximum sunshine, so necessary if they are to store up in their leaves the full complement of essential oil.

For this reason, it is important to make the herb garden in an open, sunny position, for only the mints enjoy shade and moist soil conditions. Wind will not harm the plants for the sunshine will help them to ripen their wood to enable them to withstand the coldest conditions likely to be experienced anywhere in Britain. But if a hedge or interwoven fencing be placed around the small herb garden, with a seat in the sun, it will enable the plants to be enjoyed on all suitable occasions, for the enclosed herb garden will be a place where one may retire, tired after a busy day, to contemplate, like the monks of old who praised God for the beauties around them whilst tending the monastery garden. Here it will be possible to plant the taller growing herbs, not included in the border or shrubbery, but against the fencing, as in the walled gardens of old, rosemary may be tied and will love the protection afforded it.

Here may be kept a hive, for so many of the fragrant herbs bear flowers beloved by the bees. Amongst these are the thymes, especially the wild thyme, *T. serpyllum*, which has purple flowers and of which there are a number of garden varieties with flowers varying in degrees of intensity from white to crimson. So many of the purple flowering plants are favourites with the bees, amongst which is the buddleia and the lilac, catmint and clary (*Salvia sclarea*), clover and melittis which has purple-lipped flowers and whose leaves carry the perfume of musk.

It may be desirable to place a small sundial or bird-bath in the centre of the garden and to surround it with low-growing roses, bearing fragrant blooms. And which should be crimson in colour to blend with the various greens of the herb foliage and their purple flowers. Though Ena Harkness and Chrysler Imperial are in my garden, still the two best crimson roses, to plant around a sundial the low-growing Josephine Bruce would be more suitable. It has Crimson Glory (a suitable alternative) for one of its parents and its crimson-black flowers have the same rich damask perfume. Madonna lilies, too, may be planted above the herbs and look quite lovely growing up through bushes of rosemary and lavender.

A MINIATURE HERB GARDEN

It is sometimes said by those who are busy with household chores that the herb garden is usually made as far away from the house as possible and that this entails much time in reaching it for what may be but a sprig or two of mint and that in winter-time, one may receive a thorough soaking and mud-caked shoes in their getting. All of which may be overcome by making a tiny herb garden near the house or even bringing the herbs indoors.

At the rear of a tiny mews cottage in Knightsbridge may be seen a herb garden, no larger than the size of a cart-wheel. In a sunny corner, a circle 4 ft. in diameter was made and this was divided into eight segments of equal size and separated from each other by sowing parsley seed between. Chives may be planted around the outer rim and both will remain bright green throughout winter. Each section was planted with the most useful of the dwarf herbs which included thymes, sage and the various mints. No manure was given and all that was done was to clear the soil of weeds and stones. At the centre may be planted a dwarf lavender or rosemary, but the tall-growing herbs were omitted. Around the tiny "garden", a path of crazy paving had been made which could also be used to divide the segments and between the stones the prostrate thymes and pinks are planted and a number of the scented miniature bulbs to provide winter colour. Indeed, the tiny garden is colourful throughout the year and provides a continuous supply of herbs for so many purposes

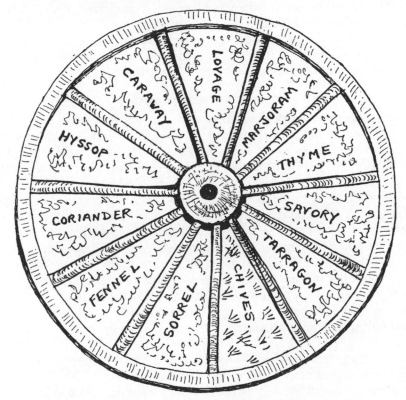

Fig. 1   Herb garden in a wheel

in the home, there being few days when a visit to the little "garden" is not to be made. "The Garden," wrote Thomas Hyll in *The Profitable Art of Gardening* (1568), "which both giveth health to man's body and recovery of strength after long sickness, by commoditie of taking the fresh ayre and sweete smel of the flowers in the same."

A pleasing way of enjoying herbs in the garden is to plant them by the side of a path leading to the entrance of the home. It will then be possible to reach the plants without soiling the shoes and even at night, an outside light will enable the leaves to be collected for use in the kitchen, or in drinks, as required. Or plant the herbs in a small bed beneath the kitchen window. It may be possible to make two beds, one containing herbs to use in the kitchen, the sages and thymes, the other to be planted with those fragrant herbs whose leaves are useful to flavour drinks. Growing near to the house, they may then be removed whenever required and are always more pungent when used fresh.

Where planted by a path, the herbs will release their fragrance when passers-by brush their coats, or dresses, against the plants when the clothes will take on a most refreshing aroma.

PLANTING HERBS IN TUBS

A miniature herb garden may be made in a tub, such as an oak cider barrel cut into two. It will then be possible to grow those plants with fragrant leaves even where there is no garden, such as on a verandah, or terrace, or in the corner of a courtyard, in fact, almost anywhere if the sun may shine down upon them. Several tubs may be used, some planted with herbs, others with sweetly scented flowering plants such as miniature roses, pinks and fragrant annuals, the tubs being placed on bricks to keep the rain water from collecting about the base and being arranged around a courtyard or along a verandah. In this way, as much fun may be obtained from several tubs as from the largest of gardens. Additional colour will be provided if the walls of the courtyard are whitewashed and the tubs painted blue or pink as a contrast. Or oak casks may be treated with wood preservative and left in their natural state.

As the plants will need drainage, holes should be drilled at the base of the tubs over which "crocks" or broken bricks are placed and a layer of turves placed green side downwards. Then fill up the tubs to within 1 in. of the top with fresh turf loam to which some lime rubble has been added to maintain sweet conditions. Manure is not required, all that is necessary is a friable soil, well drained and in no way sour. And the same may be said where plantings are being made in open-ground beds. With the exception of the mints, the plants will require no manure. They like a sweet, well-drained soil and for this reason almost all those plants with fragrant foliage flourish in a shallow, chalk-laden soil.

If the tub is filled to within an inch of the top, there will be room to water when necessary without splashing the soil over the side and

Fig. 2   Tub of herbs

to top dress with fresh soil, probably enriched with some hop manure, perhaps every two years.

Herbs are most appropriate for planting in earthenware pots, especially those of terracotta which provides such a contrast to the various green colours of the plants. Two or three pots may be placed about the herb garden or may be arranged on a terrace and, for satisfying results, they should be treated in exactly the same way as tubs. To plant with the herbs, sweetly scented Madonna lilies make admirable companions especially growing in the terracotta pots or vases.

Another excellent way of keeping herbs in a confined space is by means of a box, a window box placed inside a kitchen window, or in

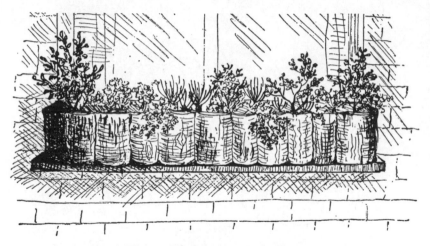

Fig. 3   Herbs in a window box

the sunny window of an outhouse. There is nothing new in the idea. As long ago as 1594, Sir Hugh Platt wrote: "In every window you may make square frames either of lead or of boards well pitched within; fill them with some rich earth and plant such flowers or herbs therein as you like best." The box may be planted with a number of the dwarf-growing herbs such as the thymes, chives, parsley and perhaps a root of sage, which may be kept short by the regular removal of the shoots. Plants of the fragrant leaf geraniums may also be used, their leaves being so delightful in pot-pourris besides being of such attractive appearance. And let trailing nepeta (Ale-hoof) cover the box. With the very minimum of attention, they will remain healthy for many years in an indoor window as will each of the herbs mentioned. Boxes may also be used on the sunny wall of a courtyard. Four or five boxes may be used and should be made about 2 ft. in length, 8 ins. wide and 8 ins. deep. Built of strong timber, they may be fixed to the wall by means of strong iron brackets and should be placed at a height where readily accessible.

If two rows of boxes are to be fixed, one above another, at least 2 ft. between each row should be allowed so that the lower boxes are not deprived of sunlight. The lower boxes should also be fixed between those above to enable them to obtain moisture and so reduce artificial watering to a minimum.

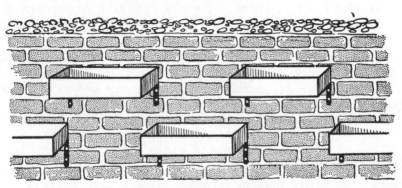

Fig. 4   Boxes on a wall

Do not make the boxes too large, otherwise when filled with soil they may be too heavy for the brackets to support them. In any case, it will be advisable to plug the wall to a depth of not less than 2 ins. into which the screws are fixed. It will also be advisable to fasten a length of strong wire from the two outer edges of the boxes to the wall above and which will provide additional protection should the boxes become heavier than usual owing to excessive rain or snow falling on them during winter-time.

The boxes should have holes drilled in the base before planting and over the holes crocks are placed to prevent soil falling through or filling up the holes and so preventing adequate drainage.

It may be possible to plant each box with a different herb. In one should be planted the thymes in variety, in another the sages. Another may be planted with chives, whilst in one parsley may be sown. There would then be a continuous supply of herbs throughout the year and they would be so easily reached from the kitchen which will usually be on the courtyard side of the house. But any wall will be suitable and there may be one dividing the verandahs of a row of semi-detached houses from each other, suitable for a few boxes of herbs.

The low growing herbs may also be planted on a wall which has been made with a core of soil. Near the edge, plant the trailing thymes and they will brighten up the stone (or brick) with their vivid flowers. Then plant the sages, the most dwarf of the lavenders and balm, with its scent of lemon verbena. Calamintha or the Basil thyme may be grown, chamomile and the Mountain Veitch, whose flowers emit a sweet perfume, especially after rain. In summer, the tiny French marigolds may be planted, with their aromatic foliage and brilliant golden flowers like pompones. Pinks may be grown, especially the Alpine allwoodii which will trail over the sides and which love the dry conditions as do the herbs.

The wall should be prepared in the same way as a tub, placing drainage materials at the base, then turves before filling with good quality loam, preferably removed from pastureland.

BASKETS OF HERBS

Where there is insufficient space for even a tub or box, herbs may be enjoyed by using a hanging basket suspended from the wall of a cottage or in a porch. Or a basket may be hung suspended from the wall of a courtyard or the wall of an outhouse where it will not be dangerous to those who pass by. Where suspended from overhanging eaves, the baskets may be held by strong hooks, whilst if it is to be hung from a wall a stout iron stake should be used, driven well into the wall between the stones or bricks and cemented in. A basket with a diameter of 18 ins. will be suitable, made of strong galvanized wire. To prevent soil falling through and to improve its appearance, the basket should be lined with moisture-absorbing sphagnum moss or with turves which have the green side placed to the outside of the basket. Then fill with fibrous turf loam, mixing in a small quantity of lime rubble or charcoal to maintain its sweetness. Allow the basket several days to settle down before planting, using the taller growing sages to the centre with the most compact herbs around the circumference. In spring, seeds of the trailing nasturium may be pressed into the soil around the edge and with their trailing habit and brilliantly coloured flowers, which are sweetly scented, will brighten the baskets during summer and autumn besides providing a welcome addition to the salad bowl or to sandwiches with their pleasingly bitter pungent leaves. The nasturtiums should be removed in October, but the herbs should remain healthy and require no attention for several years.

Fig. 5   Herbs in a hanging basket

A pleasing custom during Elizabethan times was to grow herbs in pots suspended from a wall both outdoors and in the home, especially in sleeping quarters. Rosemary, so greatly valued for its ability to keep fresh a room with its aromatic perfume, was the most popular plant grown in this way but the thymes were also grown in small pots in a window. "In summertime," wrote Sir Hugh Platt, "your chimney may be trimmed with a fine bank of moss . . . and at either end one of your flower or Rosemary pots," and in his *Florists Vade Mecum*, Samuel Gilbert wrote a century later, "Next comes Martagans, a rambling flower onely fit for flower pots or chimneys . . ." so that by the end of the seventeenth century, flowers (and herbs) were still being used in this way. Rosemary will grow well indoors in pots, whilst it is most attractive hung by the side of an entrance to a house where one may press upon its leaves before entering and when leaving, the fingers retaining its considerable aroma for an hour or more. The shrubby thymes and sages may also be similarly grown. Leminius, a Dutch physician on a visit to this country in 1560 wrote, ". . . their bed chambers and privi rooms with comfortable smell cheered me up and entirely delighted all my senses." Perhaps it may be possible to bring back the custom of having pots of sweet smelling herbs in the bedroom?

HARVESTING AND DRYING THE HERBS

The drying and harvesting of herbs calls for attention to detail. First, it is necessary for the herbs to have reached as perfect a condition as possible before they are cut, for only then will they reveal their full fragrance or flavour and retain it for any length of time. Much will depend upon the season, for most herbs are harvested, whether for their leaves, flowers or seeds, towards the end of summer or in early autumn. To bring the plants to maturity, rich in natural oils, it is necessary for August and September to be dry and sunny months. But whatever the weather, there will be a period in the life of each plant when it will have reached full maturity; afterwards it will begin to die back. The plant must, therefore, be harvested before this happens and the correct time cannot be measured by rule-of-thumb. Those herbs which will be used during the summer in the fresh condition, to enjoy with salads or for flavouring food and drinks will, in most instances, require no harvesting. It is only those grown for their dried foliage or petals and for their seed, which will demand care with their harvesting and drying.

Where the plants are growing under the conditions they enjoy, it will generally be possible to make two cuttings, one in midsummer, the other in autumn, but here again, much depends upon the weather. May and June, however, are often dry, sunny months and it may be advisable to cut about July 1st to make sure of at least one good crop.

Select a dry day for cutting when the time arrives, which is before the flowers or leaves begin to die back, when the valuable oils return to the roots or base of the plant.

Herbs may be dried in the home either by fastening into bunches and suspending from the roof of a dry shed or room (an attic is an ideal place), or they may be spread out on shelves or on trays away from the direct rays of the sun. Wherever they are drying, they should be turned daily so that fresh air reaches all parts of the leaves. The drying should be completed as quickly as possible for only in this way will the herbs retain their full colour and the maximum of fragrance. Especially is rapid drying necessary with those thick-leaved herbs whose leaves contain a large amount of moisture, mildew setting in if drying proceeds slowly. An attic or shed should be selected if possible, for the heat of the sun on the roof will enable quite high temperatures to be maintained, a temperature of 100° F. not being considered excessive where drying mint and parsley.

An efficient rack for drying herbs may be made by using a number of trays about 4 ft. square, using 1-in. timber. To each tray is tacked a square of hessian canvas and the finished trays are held in position one above another by means of four lengths of 2 in. by 2 in. timber fixed to the corners of the frames. About 12 ins. should be allowed between each tray to enable the herbs to be turned and a free circulation of fresh air to reach them. A rack just over 6 ft. high may be inexpensively made and will contain six trays, thus enabling a large number of herbs to be dried.

Where there is sufficient heat, most herbs will have dried within a week, whilst those having thick leaves will take several days longer. Where the herbs have to depend upon the natural warmth of the atmosphere, they may take up to three weeks to become thoroughly dry, at which point they should "crackle" and snap to the touch. The leaves (or flowers) may then be rubbed from the stems between the palms of the hands, after which all unwanted material is removed. The dried leaves are then placed in a fine-meshed riddle so that soil, dust and chaff may be removed, the remaining leaves then being placed in containers for storing. Screw-topped glass jars may be used where small quantities of herbs are grown for home use, each jar being carefully labelled and placed on a shelf away from the sun. When storing larger quantities, possibly for sale, a large container will be necessary. Wooden drums are ideal for the purpose, for wood will not absorb moisture from the atmosphere. For this reason tins of any description should never be used, for they may cause the herbs to become damp. The herbs should be kept in a dry room away from the direct rays of the sun and they may be mixed as required for use in many ways in the home.

It is in the blending of herbs for use about the home that their culture will be most rewarding. To make a fragrant pillow which is sure to bring about sound sleep, the leaves of rosemary, lavender, chamomile and featherfew should be used. The end of the pillow should be opened and the dry herbs placed amongst the down or feathers, or if so wished these may be dispensed with entirely and fragrant hops used to take their place, when the pillow will be soft and fragrant too.

Sachets or small muslin bags may be made to place between bedding and clothes, containing cotton lavender, woodruff, southernwood and featherfew. The mixture will not only provide a pleasant fragrance but will keep away moths. To make a sachet for the handbag to provide an aromatic or refreshing perfume, the leaves of rosemary, woodruff, lemon thyme, geranium, lavender and one or two leaves of southernwood should be used so that the mixture is not too "sweet".

TO HARVEST SEEDS AND ROOTS

Care must be exercised with the harvesting of those plants which are grown for their seeds, such as dill and coriander. While the seed should be fully ripe before harvesting, to allow the seed pods to open will result in the seed being scattered and lost. As they reach maturity, the pods or seed heads should be inspected daily and removed at the first signs of any seed shedding. The seed of annual plants to be used for propagating should receive similar attention, remembering that unripened seed will be devoid of keeping qualities and will not give satisfactory germination.

The seed heads should be removed only when quite dry, or here again mildew may occur. The heads should be cut and dropped into a cardboard box and removed at once to a dry room. There they should be placed in fine muslin bags and hung up to become thoroughly dry, after which the seed is separated by opening the pods over a fine riddle placed above a clean box.

Roots will have reached maturity and their maximum flavour as soon as the leaves begin to die back. Where required for drying, to be grated down when needed, then this is the time to lift. Select a day when the soil is reasonably dry, probably following a dry week which may often be experienced in autumn and lift the roots carefully with a garden fork. They should be allowed to remain on the ground for several hours to become partially dry when as much soil as possible should be shaken off. The roots should then be placed in rows on strips of canvas where they are removed to a dry room, a cellar being suitable. All foliage is cut off and after a few days the roots should be rubbed with the canvas to clean off as much soil as possible before being placed in a warm, open oven to bake. They may then be stored in jars until required for grating.

Where it is required to use the roots either for vegetables or for grating in the raw state into salads, the roots will be washed before use. This, however, should not be done when the roots are lifted. Then any surplus should be removed while the roots will be stored in boxes of moist sand until ready for use. In the more favourable parts, the roots may be left in the ground to be lifted and used when required, though they retain their flavour better if lifted and stored at the correct time.

PLANTS FOR THE HERB GARDEN

Angelica	Angelica archangelica
Bergamot	Monarda didyma
Borage	Borago officinalis
Catmint	Nepeta cataria
Chamomile	Anthemis nobilis
Chives	Allium schoenoprasum
Common Thyme	Thymus vulgaris
Cotton lavender	Santolina incana
Cowslip	Primula veris
Dill	Anethum graveolens
Fennel	Foeniculum vulgare
Golden Rod	Solidago virgaurea
Herb Bennet	Geum urbanum
Hyssop	Hyssopus aristatus
Lad's Love	Artemisia abrotanum
Lady's Smock	Cardamine pratensis
Lavender	Lavendula vera
Lemon Thyme	Thymus citriodorus
Marigold	Calendula officinalis

Marjoram	*Origanum marjorana*
Mugwort	*Artemisia vulgaris*
Mullein	*Verbascum thapsus*
Rosemary	*Rosmarinus officinalis*
Rue	*Ruta graveolens*
Saffron	*Crocus sativus*
Sage	*Salvia officinalis*
Spear Mint	*Mentha spicata*
Sweet Basil	*Ocymum basilium*
Sweet Cicely	*Myrrhis odorata*
Tutsan	*Hypericum androsaemum*
Valerian	*Centranthus ruber*
Wall germander	*Teucrium chamaedrys*
White Pellitory	*Achillea ptarmica*
Winter Savory	*Satureia montana*
Woodruff	*Asperula odorata*
Yarrow	*Achillea millefolium*

For descriptions see Part II.

CHAPTER SIX

Carpeting Plants

... those which perfume the air most delightfully, not passed by as
the rest, but being trodden upon and crushed, are three; that is,
burnet, wild thyme and water-mints; therefore you are to set whole
alleys of them, to have the pleasure when you walk or tread.

Francis Bacon:
Essay On Gardens

Amongst the most valuable of all scented-leaf plants are those of
prostrate or semi-prostrate habit which may be used to make a
fragrant "lawn" or they may be planted between crazy-paving
stone to make a scented path. They possess the same characteristic
in that they enjoy being trodden upon, when they will emit a rich,
refreshing pungent aroma, which lingers long on a calm, sunny
day.

To make a fragrant "lawn", which has the great advantage over a
grass lawn in that it will require cutting only once or twice each year,
the ground must be well drained. Those plants which will be most
used will appreciate a dry soil, well drained in winter whilst the
plants will be able to tolerate dry conditions during summer.
Indeed, like most scented leaf plants, with the exception of several of
the mints, those plants used for a "lawn" will be most fragrant when
growing under as dry conditions as possible. For this reason they
grow best in a light, sandy soil and where this is to be found, the
"lawn" may be made with the greatest of ease. Often the soil will
tend to be on the heavy side which will necessitate the addition of
drainage materials. This may take the form of shingle or grit, though
coarse sand may be used as a less efficient alternative. If the soil is
unduly heavy, it will be advisable to remove the soil to a depth of
6 ins. to allow a layer of broken brick or other drainage material to
be used as a base over which the soil is replaced. Where the ground
is of a poor nature, often to be found about old town properties, a
herb "lawn" will be well able to tolerate such conditions and one

may be planted as an alternative to making up beds of flowering plants. A bank of poor soil in a dry, exposed position may also be made fragrant and attractive by planting it with herbs of prostrate habit. Particularly are the thymes and the chamomile happy under such conditions. Indeed, the wild thyme is generally to be found growing under such conditions. "I know a bank where the wild thyme blows," wrote Shakespeare, and we know from the writings of Ovid that wild thyme covered the lower slopes of Mount Hymettus. In such a position, the plants may be clipped each year with shears to encourage their spreading habit. To rest on a bank of fragrant herbs on a hot summer day and to inhale its aromatic perfume is one of the pleasures of life which should be enjoyed wherever a bank is available.

With their liking for dry conditions, as sunny a position as possible should be selected for the "lawn". Where the ground is shaded by houses or tall trees, a herb "lawn" should not be planted for besides needing a well drained soil, the plants require the sunshine to bring out to the full the fragrance of the leaves.

CARE OF THE PLANTS

The plants should be set 8 ins. apart and though the "lawn" or bank may have a rather sparse appearance the first year, with their spreading habit the plants will quickly form a thick carpet. This should not be cut the first year, apart from the removal of any dead blooms or unduly long shoots, which should be clipped off towards the end of summer. The following year the "lawn" may be cut and rolled like a grass lawn.

It was Falstaff who said of such an aromatic "lawn", "the more it is trodden upon, the faster it grows". Where the ground is well drained, it will be possible to walk over the plants during all weathers and especially will they benefit from treading during the dry summer months. They may be cut with a lawn mower with the blades raised high during midsummer and again at the end of summer or they may be clipped with shears, but where the plants have been trodden frequently, they will require only the minimum of attention, merely to remove any long shoots. By the second summer, the plants will have grown into dense mats which will cover the ground. Several of the thymes will be in a blaze of colour and the flowers much visited by bees.

CHAMOMILE

Probably the most important plant for making a fragrant "lawn" will be the chamomile, *Anthemis nobilis*, and it will be necessary to obtain the true dwarf form. Parkinson likened the pungency of its serrated grey-green leaves to that of the Featherfew and during Elizabethan times, before the introduction of tobacco, its leaves were dried and smoked, its rich aroma being considered a cure for sleeplessness. Its flowers are still used for making a drink, one ounce of the blooms infused in a pint of boiling water, a wine-glassful to be taken twice a day to soothe tired nerves and to relieve indigestion. The same preparation may also be used as a hair tonic, whilst the celebrated Dr. Schimmelbusch recommended its use for a mouth wash. Indeed, the entire herb is used in medicine.

Whereas the flowers of *A. tinctoria*, an excellent border plant which grows 2½-ft. high are bright yellow, those of *A. nobilis* are white, the plant being of woody almost prostrate habit. Plants may be obtained for a reasonable price, or they may easily be raised from seed sown in early summer, a cheap packet producing almost a thousand plants. Sow in drills and keep the soil moist and if sown thinly transplanting will not be necessary until the "lawn" is made in autumn. Where the creeping thymes and possibly the creeping mints are also planted, then plant the chamomile 12 ins. apart and owing to their inexpensiveness and durability use a greater number than of other plants, planting closer together in those parts where other plants are not being used.

After planting and where the soil is light and well drained, the plants may be rolled. John Evelyn wrote that "it will now [October] be good to beat, roll and mow carpet walks of chamomile". The ground must be kept weeded during the first year until the plants spread out and prevent annual weeds from forming. As the chamomile is evergreen, the "lawn" will not lose its green colour during winter, but expect the "lawn" to have rather a miserable appearance until the plants become established and until then, one should refrain from walking over them except to weed. Once established, the plants will remain green during the hottest weather.

For infusing, the daisy-like flowers are removed when just fully open and it is the centre of the flowers which contain the medicinal qualities. When well established, the plants may be clipped hard back towards the end of summer, though not so late as to prevent them becoming green again before winter. A light clipping possibly twice a year may suit them best and they will appreciate being rolled at any time when condition of the ground permits. In the early seventeenth-century play *The More the Merrier* it is written:

"The chamomile shall teach thee patience
Which riseth best when trodden most upon."

MINT

Forming thick mats of green peppermint-scented leaves, studded with tiny mauve flowers, *Mentha requienii*, sometimes known as the Corsican thyme or Spanish mint, is a charming plant. *M. gattefossi* is of similar habit, whilst *M. pulegium* (Pennyroyal), so named by Pliny for it was used to rid houses of fleas, literally hugs the ground. It is to be found naturally growing close to water or about damp ground and was sold in the streets of London, especially to sailors to sweeten drinking water whilst at sea and to make a refreshing bath, "to comfort the nerves and sinews". It was also worn around the head to prevent giddiness and was used in posies given by lovers to denote true love. In Aelfric's *Vocabulary* there is a reference to Pollegia, which may be taken to mean Pliny's *M. pulegium*. Gerard tells us that it was to be found at Mile End, near London.

The creeping mints will grow rampant between stones and may also be used on a dry bank or may be planted with chamomile and thyme to make a fragrant "lawn". Like those plants, the more it is trodden upon the faster it grows and will suppress all weeds growing between a paved path. Their fragrance, when trodden upon, is highly refreshing and unlike the other mints, they will flourish under dry conditions; they will, in fact, grow in any soil and even in partial shade. Though the plants will withstand clipping, this will not be necessary where growing between crazy paving.

Since earliest times, pennyroyal has been used for all manner of ills. Culpeper tells us that when boiled with honey and salt and rubbed on to the gums, it helps toothache and Pliny, who spoke of it more highly than of any plant, said it was a great help for a headache. This was confirmed by Matthiolus, who also recommended it for jaundice and to clear the eyesight.

THYME

Tennyson wrote of "the thymy plots of Paradise" and indeed the creeping thymes are amongst the loveliest of all plants with their tiny flower spikes and small leaves forming a carpet of colour when in full bloom. The thymes may be divided into two main groups, (a) the prostrate or creeping thymes and (b) those of upright bushy habit like miniature shrubs. The former are members of the *T. serpyllus* (serpent-like in habit) group, whilst the latter are representatives of the *T. citriodorus* and *T. nitidus* groups and are valued for their culinary qualities. It was Francis Bacon who wrote of "those flowers which perfume the air most delightfully . . . being trodden upon and crushed, Burnet, Wild Thyme and Water Mint". But not only are they plants for the fragrant "lawn"; they may be used about a rockery or trough garden and planted between crazy-paving stones where they are to be seen at their best creeping over the stones. The foliage of all the thymes is fragrant, each possessing a different aroma.

The thymes are amongst the most charming and cherished of all plants and are extremely hardy and lasting where the soil is light and well drained. Seed of a number of species may be sown in boxes of compost in early summer or in early winter, where they are allowed to remain exposed to the weather until early spring when the boxes are placed under glass. Germination will then be rapid and the young plants may be transplanted to small pots where they remain until set out in autumn or early spring. The thymes, with their woody rootstock resent transplanting after the seedling stage and should be grown on in 3-in. pots. They like a compost containing one-third sand and a small quantity of well-decayed manure.

The thymes may be readily raised from cuttings taken with a heel from the woody stems and when about 2 ins. in length. They will quickly root in boxes, or around the sides of a pot, or planted in frames in a sandy compost. When rooted they may be transferred to individual pots from which they may be planted out at almost any time, though they do seem to enjoy spring planting best. Named varieties from pots will prove the most satisfactory.

A thyme alley, as mentioned by Bacon, may be made alongside a pathway, possibly between a path and a lawn when the alley may be approached from both sides. The plants may be set out in groups of three or four to provide a carpet of rich colour, using those of contrasting colours near together. Set out the plants 10 to 12 ins. apart, preferably from pots and during the first summer hand-weed the bed which if made 5 ft. wide may be reached from both sides without treading. By the end of summer, the plants will have completely covered the ground with their mat-like foliage and if the bed was cleared of all perennial weeds before planting, no further weeding should be necessary.

The upright shrubby thymes are usually confined to the front of the shrubbery or to the kitchen garden where their aromatic qualities will be most appreciated.

OTHER SCENTED CARPETING PLANTS

Anthyllis montana. This mat-forming plant is known as the Mountain vetch and is a member of the pea family. It will grow well in poor soil and like chamomile, may be used to cover an unsightly bank. The leaves are attractively covered with down, whilst the red clover-like flowers emit a sweet vanilla-like fragrance which is most pronounced after rain.

Calamintha acinos. It is known as the Basil thyme and is a plant of prostrate habit bearing its blue and purple flowers in whorls. It is happiest under dry conditions such as provided by a sunny bank or between paving stones where, if walked upon, both leaves and flowers emit a refreshing menthol perfume. A sprig placed in the handbag will remain pleasantly refreshing all day.

Micromeria corsica. It is an uncommon little plant, like a tiny heather and grows only 3 ins. tall with minute grey foliage and bearing pretty purple flowers like those of heather. The foliage is excellent to use in sachets and pot-pourris when dry for it has a strong smell of incense. The plants may be trodden upon and will also withstand clipping and so may be planted about a "lawn" of fragrant plants.

Poterium sanguisorba. It is Burnet and is numbered amongst Bacon's plants "which do perfume the air most delightfully". It is a plant of perennial habit, readily raised from seed which should be sown in spring and is in every way a delightful plant with small serrated leaves borne about twelve to a stem, directly opposite each other. When trodden upon they emit a pleasant sweet perfume, likened to that of balm. It was a favourite with Elizabethan gardeners, to be planted in "walks" with chamomile and thyme.

Whilst the chamomile and dwarf thymes may be planted to form a path of matted foliage which will remain green in winter, there are other plants which will present a most attractive appearance if planted between stones. Several of the pinks like *Dianthus deltoides* and *D. caesius*, the Cheddar pink, both of which form a mat of grey-green foliage and bear fragrant flowers are at their loveliest against stonework. Delightful too, is the dwarf Hyssop, *H. aristatus*, which forms a neat hummock covering itself in dainty spikes of brilliant blue all through summer. Another plant with scented foliage is *Geranium pylzowianum* which spreads out rapidly, covering its stems in multitudes of shrimp-pink flowers from May until September.

The path leading to the cottage entrance should be in keeping with its surroundings. If newly made, it should have an appearance of antiquity and should appear as unobtrusive as possible. Either crazy-paving stone may be used, or old bricks which may be obtained when any ancient outbuilding is being demolished. The bricks may be placed on their sides either straight and allowing a space here and there to take a carpeting plant, or they may be set in herring-bone fashion.

When laying a path of paving stone it is important to have the stones at the same level or it may cause difficulty when walking upon. It should be remembered that the size and thickness of every stone will differ although possibly only slightly. and it will need care in taking out sufficient soil so that the surface is level throughout after each stone has been set in position.

When laying a stone path first begin by marking out the necessary length and width, then remove several inches of soil depending on (a) the depth of stone, and (b) whether it is desired to lay the stone on to a thin bed of concrete or of sand.

The question of the concrete bed is all-important, for not only will it provide a firmer foundation which will prevent various stones from falling below the original level, which in time they so frequently do, but it will prevent the appearance of grass and weeds which are the curse of crazy paving. No matter how carefully the stone is set, placing each piece tightly together with only the minimum of soil, exposed, weeds will eventually push their way up from between the stones and will be almost impossible to clear. And there is no more irksome task in the garden than trying to clear a well-set paving path of grass and weeds. The concreting will be slightly more expensive in the first instance and will take more time to lay, but will be more than worth while. Pockets between the stones may be left free of concrete at irregular intervals to take the plants but do not overdo this, a few look much better than too many. The still wet concrete can be removed from the pockets after sections of the path are set.

First select the stones before the work is to begin and if possible place them into something like order by the side of the path. Small stones may be placed into convenient heaps to be used to fill in any large gaps. A better job can be made of a terrace where either flags or crazy-paving stone is being used if first a solid foundation of clinker, sand or crushed brick is made. This means taking out an extra 2 ins. of soil, but a clinker foundation will make a much better base over which to place the concrete. Even where no concrete is being used on which to lay the stones, a clinker base will prove of untold value in providing additional drainage, especially if the path is at all low lying. The soil may be used to fill up the pocket, or better still, a prepared compost.

Apart from a good spade, the only tool needed will be a spirit level which will not only ensure a neater and more professional job, but will ensure that the stones are laid level and so make for easier walking. Obtain a builder's "level", large enough to span across the path so that the top of the stone may be kept level with the sides of the ground. From the beginning of operations, make use of the level, right from the time the clinker base is put down, for this will ensure that the concrete will also be level and will make the final laying of the stone a much easier matter. Be sure to have the flattest surface of the stone to the top, and of course the sides should be kept as near straight as possible. A neat job can be done by laying a row of bricks down each side of the path, placing them on their sides. The contrast in colour of brick and stone adds to the finished effect and will help to prevent the soil from falling on to the concrete as this is being placed into position, whilst it also makes the laying of the level stone much easier. Remember to set the stones as close to each other as possible, for if concrete is used to point the path on completion, it will spoil the effect. If the stone can be laid close, no pointing needs to be done except to fill up those pockets into which it is not required to set a plant. It is advisable to do the planting as the work proceeds. First make a satisfactory base which is quite level, then lay the stone in possibly 6 ft. lengths, completely finishing the stretch in every way before continuing with the next 6 ft. or so. Pockets for the plants should have the concrete removed whilst still wet and this should be filled up with compost.

Where bricks are to be used to make the path, they should be weathered as much as possible and if setting an edge of brick as previously described, it will first be necessary to take an accurate measurement of the size of the bricks to be used so that they may be laid between the two side rows with accuracy. As each brick will be roughly the same size, the making of a brick path may be done more easily than when using stone but here again, a builder's "level" should be used to keep the bricks to the same level throughout.

On either side of the path a low hedge of lavender may be planted or a most pleasing idea is to make a low dry wall of stone or of cement blocks with a stone finish.

CARPETING PLANTS

Anthemis nobilis
Anthyllis montana
Calamintha acinos
Dianthus caesius
Glechoma hederacea
Mentha requienii
Micromesia corsica
Poterium sanguisorba
Sedum dasyphyllum
Sedum lydium
Sedum oreganum
Thymus micans
Thymus serpyllus

For descriptions see Part II.

CHAPTER SEVEN
The Trough Garden

God Almighty esteemed the life of a man in a garden the happiest
He could give him; or else he would not have placed Adam in that
of Eden.

Sir William Temple (1685)

The stone trough has for centuries been a permanent feature of the
cottage garden and with its miniature trees and shrubs and fairy
roses, a garden in miniature may be enjoyed in a trough. In ideal
surroundings, placed in the garden of the cottage with its roof of
thatch or stone tiles, where the old stone troughs blend so well, a
trough will look equally attractive in the courtyard of a town house
and though there is nothing quite comparable to weathered stone,
the plants will grow equally well in an old sink, provided the surface
is made rough, or in a trough made of concrete. A concrete trough
will have one advantage in that it will be porous. This will ensure
efficient drainage, thus keeping the soil sweet and the roots healthy
with the minimum of attention.

Of whatever material the trough is to be constructed, it should
be provided with drainage holes and will be more efficient and more
easily managed if raised on a suitable base 2 to 3 ft. from the ground.
If the trough is to be of concrete then the base should be built of
breeze blocks. These blocks may also have crushed-stone incorporated which will give them the appearance of stone and will thus
also be suitable for a base for an old stone trough. A sink may be
supported on rustic bricks to good effect, especially where it is
to be used against the walls of a newly-built house of the same
material.

The trough may be placed on a balcony or may be arranged
around the sides of a courtyard. Or where there is no soil to make a
border, troughs may be placed against the wall of a house, especially
beneath a window where they may be observed from inside. It is
important to ensure that the trough is not placed where rain water

may drip on to the plants and so wash the roots out of the soil. Unless the eaves of the house are wide, then the trough is best placed about 2 ft. from the wall. Also, the trough should not be placed beneath overhanging trees, from which melting snow and rain will drip almost continuously through the winter months.

CONSTRUCTING THE TROUGH

The most satisfactory way of constructing a concrete trough is to make two boxes of matured timber, making one about 1½ in. smaller in all dimensions. The smaller box will fit inside the other. For the base and walls of the trough mix up two parts of sand to one part of cement, adding sufficient water to make it into a paste so that it will "pour", yet at the same time it must not be too "sloppy". The cement should be poured inside the first box to a depth of 1½ in., two large corks being held in position to provide the drainage holes. To reinforce the base and sides, a length of wire netting should be pressed into the cement mixture just before it begins to set and this should extend almost to the top of the sides. A second piece of netting should be pressed into the mixture so that it extends up the other two sides in a similar way. Use 2 in. mesh netting, cutting the pieces to the exact measurements of the mould. Thus for a box 30 ins. long by 18 ins. wide by 6 ins. deep, the two pieces of netting will measure 42 ins. and 30 ins. The smaller box does not require a base, just make the four sides and hold them together by small pieces of wood nailed across each corner and long enough to stretch across the corners of the first box to prevent it pressing into the concrete base. The cement is then poured between the two boxes. Insert a piece of stick to hold the netting away from the mould and this will prevent it showing when the concrete has finally set hard, which it will do in about twenty-four hours if not made too thin. Just before the cement has set completely, the sides of the boxes are carefully removed, the inner mould being left in position until thoroughly hardened. The wooden base and the corks are then pressed off.

A glazed sink which is to be used for a trough garden should be chipped as much as possible so that the sink will be more porous, and the roots of the plants will be able to hug the sides in the same way as do plants in earthenware pots. For the same reason plants growing in old stone and concrete troughs have a vigorous root action and as a result, top growth is equally vigorous and healthy.

MAKING UP THE TROUGH

Troughs are extremely heavy, so of whatever material they are constructed, should be given a position of permanency before they are prepared for the plants. Make certain that they are quite firm on a single or double pedestal, using wedges where necessary. Over the drainage holes place several large crocks, or pieces of brick or stone, then over the base place a layer of small stones or crocks to a depth of 6 ins. Over this lay old turves upside down and then fill to the top with the prepared compost, pressing it well down round the sides. This should be composed of:

2 parts fresh loam, sterilized if possible.

1 part top grade peat, which is superior to leaf mould because it contains no weed spores.

1 part coarse sand and grit.

Add a sprinkling of superphosphate of lime to encourage root action, and some lime to keep it sweet; also a little bone meal, a slow-acting fertilizer, and mix the whole together. If one has no garden, sterilized loam, peat and sand may be obtained from a local nurseryman and as a general guide, a barrowful of compost will be required to fill a sink of approximately 36 ins. by 18 ins. by 6 ins. Most stone troughs are several inches deeper, but rarely more than 24 to 26 ins. in length, so that compost requirements will be similar. Some troughs have no drainage holes and so should be given a greater depth of drainage material, whilst some pieces of broken charcoal should be mixed with the compost to maintain its sweetness.

So many ways of making up a trough or sink are available that there is something for every taste. The troughs may be used in much the same way as window boxes or tubs, planting them with spring flowering plants such as primroses and winter flowering pansies to be followed by multiflora begonias, ivy-leaf geraniums or suitable annuals such as verbena and *Phlox drummondii*. However, it is as a more permanent garden that the sink or trough is most suitable. The dwarf roses may be used by themselves to make a miniature rose garden, using possibly four different varieties and dividing them by tiny paths of stone. Or the trough or sink may be made into a miniature rockery, complete with weathered stone, dwarf conifers or shrubs and tiny perennial plants to provide colour all the year round. The smallest of the miniature bulbs may also be used, the whole so laid out as to give a completely natural appearance.

When planting, care must be taken in selecting the most suitable plants for certain soil conditions and situations. Plants requiring a soil containing plenty of lime, such as the fragrant little *Iris reticulata* and the Alpine pinks, should be given some lime rubble in the compost, and the lime lovers should be planted together. Those which are lime haters must also be kept together. There are plants which prefer shade, others a position of full sun. Only the really hardy plants should be used, for the range is large enough to satisfy all tastes, and the less hardy plants may fail to come up to expectations if the winter is unduly wet or cold.

Where possible use plants from small pots so that root disturbance is at a minimum. Planting may be done at almost any time of the year, though autumn and spring would seem to be the most suitable periods. However, before planting allow the soil time to settle down so that there are no air pockets and when making a miniature rockery, place in several stones, grouping them as naturally as possible. Tufa stone from the hills of Derbyshire and Cumbria is the most suitable, but weathered red sandstone or Cotswold stone is almost as good. Set the stone well into the soil so that the plants may send down their roots to reach the moisture which is retained around those portions of the stone which are beneath soil level. Placing the stones well into the soil will also prevent them from being moved when the trough is receiving attention, for established plants will occasionally be replaced with those which may be considered more attractive, whilst others will need trimming to keep them in bounds. The soil will also require stirring to prevent it "panning", whilst all weeds must be removed immediately they are noticed. The soil should never be allowed to dry out during the summer months.

The best effect will be obtained from the trough and sink garden by grouping the plants as naturally as possible. Plant one or two conifers together, with two or three primulas around a stone, with possibly a miniature shrub to give partial shade to the primulas, so building up the garden in such a way that the plants will fit into the scheme just as if nature herself had done the planting.

MINIATURE TREES AND SHRUBS FOR THE TROUGH GARDEN

Abies balsamea. This is the Balsam fir which grows as broad as it does tall and rarely exceeds a height of 8 ins. The foliage is dark green, underlined with silver.

Acer palmatum atropurpureum. This lovely miniature maple has beautifully cut foliage of rich purple-bronze, and is charming used as a specimen tree planted at one corner of the trough or sink.

Alyssum spinosum. A tiny shrublet growing to a height of 5 to 6 ins. with pale silver-white foliage.

Chamaecyparis obtusa ericoides. Of branching habit and extremely compact, it has foliage like that of heather, hence its name.

Chamaecyparis obtusa juniperoides. At eighteen years of age this tree will have reached a height of 6 ins. and with its branched form will be like a tiny oak tree. It is a member of the retinospoar group, *C. nana aurea*, being of similar habit but with golden foliage.

Chamaecyparis obtusa nana. A member of the cupressus family and one of the smallest of them all, its short, rich green branches being most attractive.

GENISTA. For a sun-baked position, the miniature brooms are delightful plants bearing their tiny sweet pea-like flowers during the first weeks of summer. *G. januensis* grows only 6 ins. tall and bears tiny yellow flowers, whilst *G. dalmatica* is like a dense miniature gorse only 4 ins. tall and in May is covered in golden flowers.

Hedera minima. This little shrubby ivy will lift itself up a stone, twisting to a height of 7 to 8 ins., and remaining evergreen all the year round. Plant *H. conglomerata* to trail along the sides of the trough.

HELICHRYSUM. The shrubby Everlasting Flowers are most attractive plants for a dry, sunny position and for a trough which may not receive much attention. *H. bellidioides* grows to a height of 4 ins. and bears its white flowers early in summer; whilst *H. marginatum* bears dusky-pink flowers on tiny silver hummocks.

Hypericum trichocaulon. Throughout late summer this new plant bears masses of bronze buds and exquisite golden flowers on 2-in. stems.

Hyssopus aristatus. This neat shrubby hyssop, growing to a height of 5 to 6 ins. and bearing a profusion of bright blue flowers throughout summer is an excellent trough plant, especially for a dry, sunbaked position.

Jasminum parkeri. This is a delightful summer flowering jasmine growing to a height of only 6 ins. and covering itself in tiny yellow bells.

Juniper communis compressa. Of almost pencil-like form, its dense foliage being of a feathery glaucous green. It will grow about 6 ins. high in six years.

Juniper coxii. It will not grow more than 6 ins. tall and is of weeping willow form, though quite evergreen.

Juniper sabina tamariscifolia. The Carpet juniper with feathery tamarisk-like foliage and of low, spreading habit.

Picea alba albertina. A delightful form of the white spruce found in Alberta and which grows only 1 in. each year.

Picea excelsa gregoryana. A tiny spruce, giving the appearance of little balls of needles.

Picea excelsa nana compacta. This is a dwarf form of the Norway spruce, the horizontal spreading branches giving it an almost globular form.

Picea excelsa pumila. A tiny pine of branching habit, attaining a height of only 6 ins. in six to eight years.

Picea excelsa ramontii. Of pyramidal habit, the lower branches sitting on the ground making a tree of almost compact form and of a rich bottle green.

Ribes alpinus. This is the miniature form of the flowering currant, bearing pale pink flowers, but it is for its rich golden foliage that it should be included in a trough garden. It will grow no taller than 10 ins. and remain compact without attention.

Salix boydii. This tiny willow is truly a remarkable tree reaching a height of 10 ins. only after fifty years' growth. This little gem makes an ideal trough or miniature garden tree, its pale green dancing foliage being most attractive. Almost as dwarf is *S. wehrhahni,* a tiny pussy willow, covering itself with silver catkins throughout early spring.

FLOWERING PLANTS FOR THE TROUGH GARDEN

Miniature forms of cottage garden favourites.

ANDROSACE. The Rock jasmines are amongst the best plants for a trough garden, *A. sarmentosa watkinsii* being umbels of rich crimson blooms held on 4-in. stems above woolly rosettes. *A. lanuginosa* bears clusters of crimson flowers with a striking golden eye. They enjoy full sun.

Antennaria dioica rosea. Above the interesting silver-edged foliage the dainty fluffy pink flowers are borne on 3-in. stems.

Aquilegia bertoloni. A delightful plant for a sink bearing dainty blue and white spur-shaped blooms on 3-in. stems during early summer.

A. flabellata nana alba is equally lovely, bearing its waxy-white flowers on 6-in. stems. They prefer partial shade.

Armeria caespitosa. Six Hills variety. The tiny green cushions are studded with large deep pink ball-like flowers.

Artemesia glacialis. A lovely plant for growing near the dark evergreens, for it is of most compact habit and has attractive silvery foliage.

Aster nepalensis. Its beautiful blue daisy-like flowers are borne on 4-in. stems through summer, the plant making a compact little bush.

AUBRIETIA. Indispensable plants for trailing over the sides of a trough. Of almost prostrate habit, their blooms, about the size of a one pence piece, are borne in profusion during spring and early summer. Outstanding is Kelmscott Beauty, double dusky pink; Studland, light blue; Godstone, deep purple; and the rich crimson, Barker's Double.

Bellis perennis. Quite the most attractive double daisy for a sink is Dresden China, with its tiny double blooms of a lovely shade of shell-pink borne on 3-in. stems.

CAMPANULA. There are dozens of members of this huge family which will prove suitable for sinks. For trailing over the sides none is lovelier than the hybrid E. H. Frost, with its pure white wax-like flowers. Another hybrid, bearing deep violet bells on short, erect stems, is *C. covadonga*; whilst for a semi-shaded position *C. pusilla alba*, like a tiny white harebell and its blue companion, Oakington Blue, remain in bloom from June until October.

Cyananthus integer. A glorious plant, growing no taller than 2 ins., and which bears its powder-blue bells on slender trailing stems through summer and autumn.

DIANTHUS. The neat Rock pinks with their tufts of blue-grey foliage are ideal plants for a trough garden, but they do like some lime in the soil. A lovely variety is Anne, which bears tiny double blooms of cerise-pink; whilst equally charming is Elizabeth, its double pink flowers having an attractive brown centre. But for a real splash of colour Fusilier and Bombadier, both bearing bright scarlet bloom right through summer, are outstanding.

Draba pyrenaica. This is a charming plant for a sink garden, forming a tiny grass-like hummock and mauve flowers.

ERINUS. For a sunny position this is a delightful plant and possibly the most attractive variety is Mrs. Charles Boyle, which bears pretty spikes of clear pink.

Plate 3
Above Knot garden: New
Place, Stratford-on-Avon
Right Violas

Plate 4   Anne Hathaway's cottage garden

GENTIANA. Quite the easiest and best variety for a trough garden is *G. macaulayi*, Well's variety, which is of compact habit and bears its large trumpets, striped with green during early autumn. It likes a lime-free soil containing plenty of peat.

LINARIA. Several species of the miniature Toadflax are ideal for a sink. The blooms are like those of the antirrhinum and are produced from early summer until October. *L. alpina* has grey-green leaves, its tiny violet flowers having a pretty orange lip. *L. pallida*, of similar form, bears lavender flowers with a yellow lip. Both grow only 2 ins. tall.

Lithospermum intermedium. It could almost be classed as a shrublet. It is of upright habit and during May and June covers itself in masses of brilliant blue flowers.

Lychnis alpina. Valuable in that it bears its pretty spikes of rosy-pink from mid-April until June, when few plants are in bloom.

Morisia hypogaea. From March until June it bears its stemless golden flowers above rosettes of bright green ferny leaves and is quite happy in partial shade.

Myosotis explanata. Around its tuffets of bristly leaves it bears its stemless white star-like flowers in midsummer.

PENTSTEMON. Happy in full sun or partial shade, the rock pentstemons are delightful plants and to bloom in April and May one of the best is *P. newberryi*, almost a shrub and which bears deep pink tubular flowers. *P. confertus* bears short spikes of creamy-yellow during May and June.

Phlox subulata. With their dwarf habit and bearing sheets of richly coloured blooms, this phlox is ideal for troughs, but should be planted near the sides. Very compact is the new Aunt May, which bears lavender-blue flowers; and plant near it Temiscaming, which covers itself in sheets of rich crimson.

PRIMULA. Several of the more dwarf and compact *P. juliae* hybrids are suitable for troughs and sinks, especially the salmon-pink E. R. Janes; the pale yellow Keith, like a tiny polyanthus; and Snow Cushion, pure white. A lovely and most distinct plant for a sink is *P. clarkei*, which forms a little tuffet and covers itself with clear rose-pink flowers during March and April.

Early too are the *pubescens* primulas, like miniature auriculas, the flower heads being borne on 4-in. stems from early April until early June. They like a soil containing plenty of peat or leaf mould. One of the best is The Gnome, a delightful plant which bears flowers of rich terracotta red. Equally good is The Cardinal with its blooms of rich crimson and Mrs. J. Wilson, deep purple with an attractive white centre.

SAXIFRAGE. The range of suitable plants for a sink is enormous. In the Mossy Section, in bloom during the earliest weeks of summer, an interesting plant to use close to the dark evergreens is Cloth of Gold, which bears tight tufts of golden foliage and white flowers. Another beauty is Peter Pan, which bears rich crimson flowers and like Cloth of Gold grow only 3 ins. tall.

In the Kabschia Section, *S. apiculata* has attractive bottle-green foliage and bears pale yellow flowers, whilst also growing only 2 ins. tall is the hybrid, Cranbourne, which forms grey rosettes and bears rose-pink flowers. Similar is Grace Farwell, which forms a tiny grey cushion and bears salmon-red flowers. Excellent also is *S. burseriana* Gloria, of compact habit and which bears pure white bell-like flowers. An interesting plant to bloom during August is *S. primulaize* Salmon, which bears attractive sprays of salmon-pink on 4-in. stems.

SEDUM. Happiest in full sun, the stonecrops are excellent for sinks for late summer flowering. One of the best is *S. cauticolum* from Japan, with glaucous foliage and rosy flowers. Delightful, too, is Coral Carpet, the pale-green carpets turning a lovely coral-red; and *S. douglassi*, whose foliage turns vivid scarlet and which bears yellow flowers on 6-in. stems.

SEMPERVIVUM. So easily propagated by offsets, the houseleeks will thrive in the shallowest of soils and in a sun-baked position. There are more than a hundred species in cultivation and a large proportion are suitable for sink and trough gardens. Interesting is *S. borisii,* like a tiny woolly ball; and *S. powelli*, the rosettes being green, pink and red.

SOLDANELLA ALPINA. Happiest in a cool soil and shaded position where it will bear its dainty nodding bells of deep purple during early spring.

THYMUS. The aromatic thymes are quite delightful plants for trough and sink. *T. herba-barona* bears lilac flowers and has caraway-scented leaves, whilst Lemon Curd has lemon-scented foliage. A delightful little white flowered shrublet is *T. nitidus albus*, which grows to a height of 4 to 5 ins. The most colourful thymes are those of cushion habit and which grow to a height of only 1 in. *T. coccineus* covers itself in masses of crimson flowers, whilst *T. serpyllus*, Snowdrift, bears pure white flowers. The variety Pink Chintz bears a mass of lovely salmon-pink flowers.

BULBS FOR TROUGH AND SINK

CHIONODOXA. All members of this family will prove suitable, especially *C. sardensis*, its tiny gentian-blue flowers with their striking white centre being borne on 4-in. stems.

CROCUS. Of the autumn-flowering crocus, *C. pulchellus*, lavender-blue with attractive white anthers to bloom in early autumn, and *C. ochroleucus*, white with orange base in bloom early December will prove suitable. Replace with *C. fleischeri*, with its small white flowers and scarlet stigma, in bloom in February; and with *C. minimus*, bearing its lavender and buff flowers in March. For April plant *C. olivieri*, Jamie, which bears tiny flowers of brilliant gold.

Cyclamen Coum. This is the most suitable of the hardy cyclamen on account of its compact habit. It has dark green leaves and bears its rosy-red flowers on 4-in. stems in March.

ERANTHIS. All members of the winter aconite family are suitable for trough culture.

GALANTHUS. Of the snowdrops, *G. elwesii*, its white globular flowers marked with emerald-green, is ideal for a trough.

IRIS. *I. reticulata* in variety, and especially *I. danfordiae*, bearing its lovely golden flowers on 4-in. stems in February are ideal for a sink garden.

MUSCARI. The best of the grape hyacinths for a trough. is *M. azureum*, bearing its spikes of Cambridge-blue on 5- to 6-in. stems in March. Plant with it the white form, *album*.

NARCISSUS. *N. minimus*, bearing its yellow trumpets on 4-in. stems in March, and *N. canaliculatus*, bearing three to four richly scented blooms of white and gold on a 6-in. stem, are delightful trough-garden plants. Quite charming, too, is *N. watieri* from Morocco, which bears a pure white flower on a 3-in. stem. It is closely related to *N. juncifolius* which bears flat golden flowers in April.

SCILLA. It is the early spring flowering *S. sibirica* which is suitable for a sink, bearing its bright blue flowers on 3-in. stems. The variety *alba*, pure white, is equally lovely. *S. biflora*, bearing dark blue flowers on 3-in. stems, is also a charming little plant.

TULIP. Whilst the colourful dwarf Kaufmanniana tulips may be too large-flowered for a sink garden, several other species are most suitable, and none is lovelier than *T. chrysantha*, the bloom having cherry-red petals on the outside, whilst inside they are bright yellow. Another beauty is *T. dasystemon*, bearing several creamy-white blooms, shaded green on a single stem.

CHAPTER EIGHT

Plants for Walls and Paths

Flower of the solitary place!
Grey ruin's golden crown!
That lendest melancholy grace
To haunts of old renown.
David Macbeth Moir:
To the Wallflower

Many an old wall or tiled roof is a suitable place to grow plants. They bring colour where it is usually lacking and will help to beautify cottage, outhouse or barn. Growing in the narrowest cracks in many a boulder of mountainside, alpine plants are to be seen flourishing in what appears to be a situation almost devoid of sustenance. Yet this is far from being so, for the cracks and chinks contain weathered limestone and perhaps a little soil, sufficient to hold the moisture which penetrated deep down into the fissures, guarded from evaporation by sunlight and wind by the thickness of the stones and here the roots of many a plant find moisture and sustenance. Much the same conditions can be provided by the spaces between the bricks and stones of old walls and roofing tiles where there is usually sufficient space to instert a few seeds of wallflower, stock or antirrhinum and which are helped in their germination by covering them with sand or soil.

Almost all those plants that grow well in a limestone soil will flourish in the weathered mortar of an old wall numbered amongst which are the sedums and sempervivums, the cotyledon, the dianthus species, and wall-gillyflowers. Each enjoys an open, sun-baked situation and is capable of withstanding the most arid conditions. They are fascinating and delightful plants which, once planted will prove almost indestructible, increasing by offsets or seeding themselves. Indeed, they are usually happier under such conditions than where growing in garden soil for they resent an excess of winter moisture about their roots and from this they are

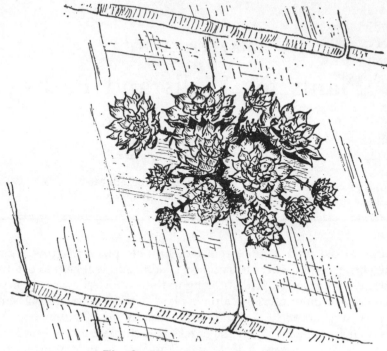

Fig. 6   Houseleek on tiled roof

protected when growing on wall or roof and where they will be little troubled by pest and disease which flourish in rich loamy soils. Again, these plants love the lime content of the mortar.

Where seed is to be sown, first loosen the mortar to as great a depth as possible with a steel meat skewer, then in April, drop into the aperture several seeds, afterwards sprinkling in some finely sifted compost, preferably John Innes Sowing Compost which has been sterilized or use sterilized soil or sand.

There are often quite large apertures in old walls which may be filled with compost and into which alpine plants grown in small pots may be set with the soil-ball intact. Where the opening is limited in size, much of the compost may be washed from the roots and the plant pressed in. Small mounds of compost may be placed on roof tiles, rough Colley Weston stone tiles being ideal, into which the roots of sedums and sempervivums may be planted. Or if there is a space, they may be set between the tiles.

Where making a low dry wall on either side of a path or maybe to divide one part of the garden from another, stone or cement blocks with a stone finish may be used. The blocks may be made by using the Dry Pack Concrete Brick Maker (Higgs Foulkes Ltd. of East Ham) which enables the blocks to be made at a rate of thirty an hour and at a cost of a penny each. The mixture is three parts sand to one part cement, adding the minimum amount of water so that the mixture will bind when squeezed but no surplus moisture will exude.

The wall need be made on 11 to 12 ins. high which will be achieved by using three courses of the stone "bricks". A double wall some 6 ins. apart will enable the space between to be filled with compost and set at the top with suitable plants which will trail over the sides.

If using uncut stones, build each course with as large a stone as possible beneath each joint to give durability but first remove the

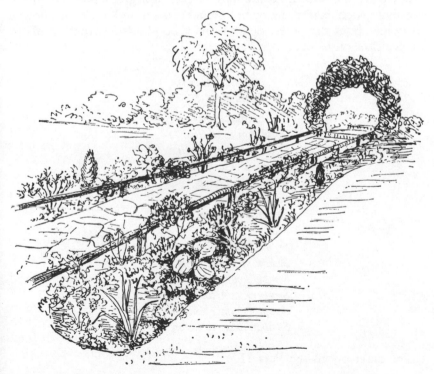

Fig. 7 Rustic poles on each side of crazy-paving path

soil to a depth of 4 ins. before laying the first stones and about them pack with soil for greater stability. Into the cavities between the stones, compost is pressed as the wall is built and into the spaces the plants are set.

Another pleasing way of edging the path is to use pieces of tufa stone and to build up a low "wall" like a miniature rockery, packing the compost round the stones as the wall takes shape. It need be made only 12 ins. wide and a similar height. Lime rubble may be used at the base to assist drainage and to mix with the compost and into it may be planted dianthus, sedums, auriculas and other old-fashioned plants which will provide a most charming effect whilst keeping the path clean and tidy.

Another attractive method of "softening" a path is to drive 16- to 18-in. lengths of pointed rustic poles into the soil to a depth of about 4 ins. and at intervals of 5 to 6 ft. alongside the path. Across the top rustic poles are nailed. At the base of each upright, a scented climbing plant such as jasmine or honeysuckle is set and which is allowed to twine about the poles. Beneath may be planted carpeting plants to overflow on to the path.

WALL PLANTS

Antirrhinum majus
Centranthus ruber
Cotyledon umbilicus
Dianthus caryophyllus
Dianthus plumarius
Matthiola annua
Sedum lydium
Sedum oreganum
Sedum revii
Sedum rubrotinctum
Sedum spathulifolium
Sempervivum arachnoideum
Sempervivum fimbriatum
Sempervivum glaucum
Sempervivum tectorum

For descriptions see Part II.

CHAPTER NINE

Pot-pourris

Laurentinus commands water-lilies . . . to evaporate in the room,
which will make a more delightful perfume if there be added orange-
flowers, pills of citron, rosemary, cloves, bays, labdanum, styrax and
such-like gums . . .

Robert Burton:
Anatomy of Melancholy

Many of the herbs and many more plants besides, may be used for
making pot-pourris to have in bowls about the home.

At one time, pot-pourri bowls were to be found in almost every
home. Now, however, they are confined to country cottages and manor
houses for in their gardens continue to be grown those fragrant herbs
and scented flowers for the sole purpose of making pot-pourris.

The bowls are of wood or decorated china, the latter usually
having a lid in which are pierced a number of holes. This allows the
perfume to escape whilst at the same time keeping the "mixture"
free from dust and from being carelessly deposited about the room.

The bowls or jars are usually square and of a suitable size to hold
about 1 lb. of dried leaves and petals for the greater the quantity
that can be saved, the more powerful will be the scent and the longer
will the perfume be retained.

The petals of flowers and the leaves of such border plants as the
bergamot and lemon verbena may also be used to make a pot-
pourri, it being a matter of taste as to how the mixture is made up,
some finding an unduly "sweet" pot-pourri more pleasing that one
possessing a more refreshing aromatic fragrance. A pot-pourri
which has given many people pleasure may be made by adding to a
three-parts basinful of rose petals slowly dried indoors away from the
sun, a cupful of the dried leaves of thyme, rosemary and marjoram
and the dried and crushed skin of an orange. Add a few powdered
bay leaves if they can be obtained, half an ounce of crushed cloves
and a small teaspoonful of allspice. The whole should be well mixed

and placed in a pot-pourri jar or bowl. The dried petals of the honeysuckle and the scented leaves of the geranium may also be used but, as with all perfumes, one which may be acceptable to a person who may enjoy a sweet, cloying perfume may be unacceptable to one who enjoys a more refreshing fragrance. An alternative to the pot-pourri suggested would be to use the petals of the less powerfully scented roses and to these, in the quantity described, the dried petals of lemon thyme and the lemon-scented geranium leaves may be added. The dried skin of a lemon would replace that of an orange. Southernwood and verbena could also be added and a pinch of powdered nutmeg which would contribute to the refreshingly potent perfume.

Those who favour more of a sweet scent could add the petals of the clove-scented pink and of orange blossom and violets. It is all a matter of taste.

To make a moist pot-pourri which will be even more powerfully fragrant, begin by placing a 6-in. layer of rose petals, undried, into an earthenware jar. Cover with a thin layer of salt and allow it to settle. Then as the season advances add the petals of orange blossom, pinks, lavender flowers (it is the bracts that are scented not the flowers), more rose petals and each time covering with a layer of salt and keeping the jar quite closed. Finally some dried orange skin mixed with a quarter ounce of dried cloves and dried marjoram. Keep closed until whenever the perfume is to be enjoyed.

The scented geraniums are especially suited to the making of pot-pourris. The plants reached this country during the reign of Charles I and were much in demand for sweetening the damp, musty rooms of cottage and manor alike. It is the leaves which are fragrant, not the flowers which are mostly quite insignificant anyway.

The scented geraniums are ideal plants for the town flat or the home with a restricted garden and in this era of small gardens or their complete absence from many of our towns, indoor gardening is the only outlet we have to show our gardening instincts. The plants can remain indoors permanently, or they may be permitted to enjoy the summer sunshine and rains by being placed on a verandah or in a small courtyard. They may be grown in the open in exactly the same way as are the Paul Crampel and Gustav Emich geraniums, used so much for summer bedding but being taller growing they should be given a sheltered situation. The Victorians, who used the scented geraniums whenever possible, would plant them in the protection of a wall or near the house and also close to a patch where the brushing of the leaves with the long Victorian clothes would create the most delicious fragrance.

The plants should be repotted early in spring, using a little decayed manure to mix with the loam. See that the compost is well drained by crocking the pots and incorporating some sharp sand or grit into the compost. At the same time any unduly long shoots should be removed to maintain the compact shape of the plants.

For making up pot-pourris and scent bags, one of the finest of all the scented-leaf geraniums is *Pelargonium capitatum*, the essence of which is now used to replace the more expensive attar of roses in perfume. Another possessing the scent of roses is *P. graveolens*, the variety Lady Plymouth having an additional charm in that its leaves are richly variegated.

One of the loveliest of all is the pyramid-shaped *P. crispum variegatum*, which covers itself in a dense mass of small crimped cream-edged leaves which retain their colour and freshness for years. This variety is deliciously lemon-scented. Besides the enormous range of scents emitted by their leaves the fact that these scents are pungent rather than sweet is a great point in their favour, for indoors a too-sweet perfume tends to become sickly and monotonous but one never tires of the pungent fragrance of nutmeg, sage, lemon and peppermint.

Preferably it is better not to mix perfumes indoors unless they be similar. For instance, the lemon-scented *P. crispum variegatum* is an excellent companion to the *P. crispum minor* which covers itself in small curled leaves carrying the pungent scent of verbena. But to place either of these plants side by side with the peppermint-scented *P. tomentosum* is to kill the fragrance of both.

P. tomentosum is unique in that its leaves are thick and velvety and are joined to the main plant by thin, long stems giving it a most exotic appearance. This is the same plant used by Gertrude Jekyll to make peppermint jelly. She describes the leaves as being "thick as a fairy's blanket . . . and to be found in most old-fashioned gardens". Today we use essence of peppermint and the flavour is not the same. This variety makes a good companion to the eucalyptus-scented *P. clorinda*, a variety which will bear during midsummer a bloom of deep orange-pink shade, quite the equal in size and quality to the best of the Show pelargoniums. The only other of the scented-leaves varieties to equal this in quality of bloom is Moore's Victory which bears a rich scarlet flower and whose foliage carries the not too pleasant aroma of pepper.

For pot-pourri the small leaves of the crispum varieties—there is also *P. crispum major* which is also richly lemon-scented—are the most suitable and retain their perfume for some considerable time. Just remove one or two of the lower leaves so as not to disturb the balance of the plant.

The oak-leaved geraniums carry a rich, pungent scent difficult to describe. To some the scent is of incense, to others it is reminiscent of southernwood. It matters little, for the perfume is rich and pleasant, just right for a warm room on a dark winter evening, while the leaves are richly coloured and edged with gold. The original oak-leaved varieties are *P. quercifolium major* and *minor*.

In the same category of geraniums with perfume difficult to define is the variety *P. fragrans* which to some is pine-scented, to others the leaves smell of nutmeg. An old variety having a definite nutmeg aroma is Lady Mary, listed in the comprehensive catalogue of Messrs. Cannells in 1910. They also suggest that the pungent *P. filicifolium*, with its interesting fern-like foliage is "well adapted for bouquets and button-holes", for which it would be imagined more for its fern-like foliage than for its pungent smell which would not seem quite suitable for a wedding. But for old churches, which so often smell musty, how valuable would be so many of these fragrant geraniums placed where their foliage could be brushed by the coats and dresses of those who come to worship. Perhaps the lemon-scented crispum varieties would be most suitable, or the sweetly orange-scented Prince of Orange which with the minimum of attention will keep fresh and retain its fragrance all the year round. This is an excellent variety for a window box, for it does not grow too tall, likewise the lime-scented *P. nervosum* which today seems difficult to find in Britain.

Frequently used for flavouring apple jelly in countries bordering the far shores of the Mediterranean is the apple-scented *P. odoratissimum*, it being so aromatic that but a single leaf is used in the preserving pan.

A variety slightly sage-scented is *P. asperum* which has attractive sharply serrated leaves. For mixing with bowls of summer flowers, sprigs and leaves of many varieties may be used, especially those of the more delicately perfumed varieties such as the almond-scented Pretty Polly or Little Gem, and the rose-scented *P. capitatum* and *P.*

radula rosea which makes a dwarf, bushy plant, ideal for the window box and hanging basket, and bears rich pink flowers. Like *capitatum*, the foliage is also used in the perfumery trade, for it is said to possess the scent of the old cabbage rose.

Two others with unusual perfume are Purple Unique whose leaves possess the scent of absinthe, and *P. stenopelatum*, the only ivy-leaved geranium with fragrance. It bears bright crimson flowers in summer, whilst its leaves have the aroma of wormwood.

Since earliest times the rose has been held in esteem for use about the home in numerous ways and quite apart from its value as a garden plant. More than four centuries ago, Anthony Ascham wrote in his *Herbal*: "Dry roses put to the nose to smell, do comfort the brain and the heart." He must have been familiar with *The Virtuous Book of Distillation*, published in 1527, but here it was rose water and not the dried petals which was suggested as being a comfort to the brain and heart. It was, of course, the richly perfumed petals of the old shrub roses that were used by those of medieval days, and all herb gardeners had a rosery adjoining where large quantities of blooms were used each year, for not only were the petals in great demand for scenting clothes and making sweet the musty atmosphere of church and dwelling, but for making perfume and for medicinal use.

A manuscript in the Ashmolean Museum describes the method of making perfume for Henry VIII. "Take six spoonfuls of rose oil," it says, "the same of rose water and a quarter of an ounce of sugar. Mix together and add 2 grains of musk and an ounce of ambergris. Boil together slowly for six hours and strain." The result would be a perfume of great richness.

TO SCENT A ROOM

The modern housewife, although having push-button sprays of pleasing fragrance at her command, may never have known the delights of rose-water heated over hot embers to perfume a room. To scent a room in Edward VI's time, having first burnt cypress wood to remove foul air, "take 12 spoonfuls of bright red rose water, the weight of a sixpence in fine powder sugar, and boil it over hot embers slowly. The room will smell as though it were full of roses." In the time of Queen Henrietta Maria, powdered cloves mixed with rose-water and placed on a hot pan "will make a perfume of excellent good odour". Indeed it will, scenting the whole house as if roses were growing indoors. A similar perfume may be enjoyed where that wonderful old climbing rose Guinée is growing near an open window. On a calm summer evening after a shower of rain its rich, fruity fragrance will scent a large room.

Sir Hugh Platt in his *Delights for Ladies* (1594) suggests placing rose petals in a sieve in the oven and there "let them remain until the uppermost of them be fully dried. Then stirr them up and leave them for another half hour until they become dry at the top again and so continue until they be thoroughly dried; then put them hot into an earthen pot having a narrow mouth, stop it with a cork and wet parchment or with wax and hang on a chimney or near a continual fire where they will keep fair in colour and most delicate in scent." Sir Hugh suggests reheating the petals as the scent begins to leave them and if so treated they will give of their fragrance all winter. He also suggests that roses may be dried in much the same way on a hot, sunny day "when they may be put into glasses well stopt and kept in a warm place . . . thus you may keep all flowers but herbs, after they are dried in this manner are best kept in paper bags in closed cupboards".

TO MAKE ROSE-WATER

Rose-water has been used since time immemorial for the beautifying of the hands and face. The women of China have used it along with paeony-water for the complexion, and Shakespeare, in his fifty-fourth sonnet, wrote of the "perfumed tincture of the rose". Pink rose-water is made by filling a saucepan with red rose petals, adding water, and bringing to the boil, allowing it to simmer for a few minutes. Allow to cool and with the lid still on the pan to retain the perfume, then strain, and place into glass jars to be used when required. Select the most fragrant red roses such as Ena Harkness, Charles Mallerin, and Fragrant Cloud with their rich Damask perfume. Not only do red roses possess the most powerful fragrance but make rose-water of a pleasing pink colour, whereas that made from petals of other colourings has an unpleasantly dirty appearance. Henry Phillips has said that "from the petals of the wild rose (*R. canina*), a perfumed water may be distilled which is more fragrant than that from any garden rose".

For those who appreciate something stronger, to be taken as a most refreshing drink, rose wine will provide the answer. A pound of fresh red rose leaves should be obtained and should be covered with a quart of warm water. Then pulp them through a muslin bag, adding more rose petals to the liquid and repeating the procedure until the liquid is a deep crimson colour. To every pint of liquid, 1 lb. of sugar is added together with ⅔ pint of alcohol, brandy being the most suitable. Add 1 oz. of cinnamon, place in a jar, and allow to stand for two to three weeks. Then filter and bottle and use whenever a feeling of tiredness comes over one.

ROSE-HIP SYRUP

It is a pity that since the war rose-hip syrup is no longer in demand, for it is many more times richer in vitamin C than the orange, and is less expensive. Only ripe hips should be gathered, and they are more easily removed from the plants with a pair of scissors. They should be removed during October, after the first frosts and before the birds can get at them. Four pounds of hips should be washed and placed in a pan. Cover with water, bring to the boil, and simmer until the hips are quite soft, so that they may be pulped. Place in a muslin bag and squeeze the juice through. Return the pulp to the pan, simmer again, and repeat the squeezing. The juice should then be placed into a clean, muslin bag, hung up over a basin, and allowed to drip into the basin, when all seeds will be eliminated. Add 2 lb. of sugar and stir, boiling for about five minutes. Bottle and seal while hot, and when cool, give a teaspoonful daily to all children from six months to ten years of age. No better tonic will be found for them.

Anthony Ascham, writing in his *Herbal* (1550), suggests that "some put roses in a vessel and put to the roses hot water and let it stand for a day and a night and of ye water putting to it sugar, they make syrup", and he adds, "In winter and in summer it may be given competently to cure melancholy and choloric people."

In *A Book of Fruit and Flowers* published a century later, there is a recipe for making syrup of Damask roses, "six ounces of them to a pint of water, first well boiled . . . let them stand twelve hours, wringing out the roses and putting in new eight times. Then wringing out the last, put in only the juice of four ounces of roses."

A most delicious jam may be made from rose hips and should be made by all who have access to a supply of fruit. Five pounds of hips, which should have been "tailed" first, should be placed in a jam pan to which 3 pints of water are added. Bring to the boil and simmer for fifteen minutes. Strain the boiled hips and to every pound of the pulped hips add ½ lb. of sugar. Cook and stir for twenty minutes then transfer to jam jars, sealing and placing in a dark cupboard.

Sir Hugh Platt, whose gardens at Kirby Hall were famous in his day, describes among numerous recipes for the rose, in his *Delights for Ladies* (1594), how to candy the petals. Dissolve some sugar by boiling in a little rose-water, then when the liquid is cold, place in the petals. "Let them rest herein until the syrup has pierced them sufficiently," he writes, "then remove and let them candy." He also describes how to preserve a whole rose bloom. "Dip a rose which is neither in bud nor overblown in rose syrup which is simmering, then open out the leaves one by one with a bodkin. Remove the flowers, lay on paper in pewter dishes in a warm room to dry, then put them into glasses [glass jars?] and keep in a closed cupboard near the fire." The writer advises the removal of the seeds if it is intended to eat them.

POT-POURRIS

But it is in pot-pourris that the petals of roses are most in demand, and Sir Hugh Platt repeatedly advises that the roses should be gathered in perfect condition, neither when in the bud form nor when fully opened. At the right stage they will retain their perfume far longer than if gathered at any other time. All too often the roses are allowed to pass their best before being used, so that their beauty may first be enjoyed in the garden. As the blooms die, however, they lose their fragrance.

To make up a pot-pourri, to three parts of a basinful of rose petals, which possess a rich perfume and which have been dried in an airy room away from strong sunlight, add a cupful of dry thyme, rosemary, and the dried and powdered skin of a lightly peeled orange. If they can be obtained, add a few bay leaves, ½ oz. of crushed cloves, and a teaspoonful of allspice. The whole concoction should be well mixed and placed in a pot-pourri bowl. For those who prefer a less "sweet" perfume, the dried orange skin could be replaced by a lemon skin and to which are added the leaves of the lemon thyme or the dried leaves of the lemon-scented geraniums. The leaves of southernwood and a pinch of powdered nutmeg would add potency. It all depends on the individual taste.

To make up a moist pot-pourri, which will possess an even stronger perfume, begin by placing a 6-in. deep layer of highly perfumed rose petals into an earthenware jar. Cover with a thin layer of salt and

8　Old English Pink,
Chaucer's Sops-in-Wine

9　Old English Pink, Unique

10   Murray's Laced Pink   *11*   *Dianthus allwoodii*, Helen

12   Show Pink, Vega   *13*   Garden Pink, Mrs Sinkins

14   Slips or cuttings of pinks

15   Slips or cuttings rooting in a pot

16 Double Primrose, Marie Crousse

17 Double Primrose, Gerard's Double White

allow several days to settle. Then add more rose petals, also the petals of orange-blossom, the more fragrant pinks such as Dusky and Mrs. Sinkins, together with the flowers of the lavender. A layer of salt should be added as the layer of petals becomes thick, always keeping the jar closed as tightly as possible. Finally, add some dried and powdered orange skin and a ¼ oz. of crushed cloves, a little dried marjoram, and keep the jar closed until whenever the perfume is to be enjoyed. When the weather is warm and oppressive release the perfume for a short time upon going to bed. For use beside the bed of a sick person, a moist pot-pourri will provide many months of pleasure and refreshment.

ROSE-PETAL BAGS

During early Tudor times delightful little bags were made of rose buds gathered when just about to open. They should be dried in an airy room away from the sun so that they do not become mouldy. Then take some powdered cinnamon or cloves and let it fall into the petals, while if the buds are made slightly moist on the outsides and the powdered cloves (or cinnamon) is rubbed on, it will adhere if allowed to dry on. The rose buds are then placed in small, muslin bags and tied up, when they may be used among sheets and clothes.

A more simple method of making up a rose bag will be to obtain some petals of roses when at their best, dry them, add the dried leaves of marjoram, together with the petals of pinks and orange-blossom, and to mix with them powdered cloves. Tied into small muslin bags, they may be placed about clothes or hung up over a bed. If the dried leaves of rosemary and bergamot are also used, the muslin bags may be placed beneath a pillow-case, when they will bring about rapid and peaceful sleep.

TO DRY ROSE PETALS

There is quite an art in the drying of rose petals. As previously mentioned, it is most important to remove them from blooms which are just on the point of reaching perfection, at which time they will be most fragrant and will retain this fragrance for a considerable time. Collect the petals when quite dry and after the early morning dew has dried off, otherwise they will become mildewed, for the petals are thick and fleshy and are not easily dried. Do not remove all the good blooms, take just one or two at a time and dry the petals, making up the pot-pourri by degrees during the summer months.

The petals are placed on trays lined with clean paper and should be dried away from the direct rays of the sun which will deprive the petals of their perfume. Select a dry, airy room and turn the petals regularly, to hasten drying and to prevent mildew. As Sir Hugh Platt describes in his *Delights for Ladies*, if placed when fully dry in glass jars and the stopper is covered in with wax, they will retain their perfume for a considerable time and may be used "at your leisure". They must, of course, be kept away from the sun's rays. During the sixteenth century, rose petals were sold by the bushel in the markets, costing from 6d. to 8d. a bushel, and Sir Hugh suggests that if dried and stored in this way, they could be obtained when least expensive, "when you find a glut of them in the market", which showed that those of the first Elizabethan age also thought it necessary to count their pennies.

Mary Doggett, writing in *A Book of Receipts* (1692), suggests the following for "A Sweet Powder for Linen": "Take some ambergris and musk, beat it small and mingle with lemon and orange flower water; then dip some cloves in the liquor, take some damask rose buds and put into every bud a clove. Tie it close and dry, then beat to a powder and mingle with orris root also beaten to a powder." If a small quantity of the powder is placed in a linen chest, it will prove to be so potent that the linen will retain its aromatic perfume for a considerable time when on the beds.

TO MAKE ROSE-SCENTED SOAP AND COLD CREAM

To make your own rose perfume soap, place a few drops of rose-oil in water kept almost on the boil, then add pieces of pure-white soap, which will quickly dissolve. Pour into a container similar to that used to poach eggs and allow to cool, when the small circular "cakes" will be ready to use and will possess a pleasing rose perfume.

For cold cream, use a small, enamel pan in which is melted 1 oz. of white wax and 2 oz. of almond oil. When thoroughly melted, add 2 fluid oz. of rose-water, stirring in with a spoon and when thoroughly mixed in, pour into small, screw-top jars. The cream will become thick as it cools and sets, when it will be ready to use.

ROSE-WATER

To make rose-water at home, gather 1 lb. of the fresh petals of fragrant red roses (those of Ena Harkness being most suitable), and after half filling a large kettle with water, add the petals and put on low heat. A length of rubber tube is attached to the spout with the other end leading to a bottle or jar. Then if the middle portion of the tube is placed in iced water this will cool the steam, and pure rose-water will drip into the jar until almost all the water in the kettle has been evaporated. The rose-water is then sealed down to be used when required. In some countries of the world, containers of rose-water are placed on the table for use with meat dishes, whereas in America tomato sauce (catsup) is used, and either Worcester sauce or vinegar in Britain.

An aromatic bath essence may be made by boiling together the leaves of as wide a selection of sweetly fragrant herbs as possible. With the leaves of the rosemary, bergamot, lavender and southern-wood, add those of hyssop and the flowers of the chamomile, clove pink and rose. Allow to simmer for five minutes, strain and add to the liquid a little alcohol in the form of brandy or whisky and use in the bath as required. It will give both the body and spirits a most refreshing feeling. The use of marigold soap in the bath will improve the skin texture and give a feeling of well-being.

Part Two

COTTAGE GARDEN FLOWERS

Their History and Culture

Cottage Flowers

The timid maid,
Pleased to be praised and yet of praise afraid,
Seeks the best flowers; not those of woods and fields,
But such as every cottage garden yields—
Fine cabbage roses, painted like her face,
The shining pansy, trimm'd with golden lace,
And tall-topped lark's-heels, feather'd thick with flowers,
The woodbine climbing o'er the door in bowers,
The London tufts, of many a mottled hue,
The pale pink pea, and monkshood darkly blue,
The white and purple gilliflowers, that stay
Ling'ring, in blossom, summer half away,
The single blood-walls, of a luscious smell,
Old fashion'd flowers which housewives love so well,
The columbines, stone-blue, or deep night-brown,
Their honeycomb-like blossoms hanging down,
Each cottage garden's fond adopted child,
Though heaths still claim them where they yet grow wild
'Mong their old wild companion summer blooms—
Furze brake and mozzling ling, and golden broom;
Snapdragons gaping like to sleepy clowns
And "clipping pinks" (which maiden's Sunday gowns
Full often wear, catched at by teasing chaps),
Pink as the ribbons round their snowy caps;
'Bess in her bravery too, of glowing dyes
As deep as sunsets crimson pillowed skies,
With marjoram knots, sweetbrier and ribbon-grass,
And lavender, the choice of every lass,
And sprigs of lad's-love, all familiar names,
Which every garden through the village claims.

John Clare, *The Shepherd's Calendar for June*
Helpstone, 1821–24

ACHILLEA MILLEFOLIUM   Yarrow

It is a plant native to the British Isles and like the prunella was at one time used to heal wounds made by carpenter's tools. According to Dodoens it was the Sideritis of Dioscorides. In France, it is the *herbe aux charpentiers* and it takes its name from Achilles, who it is said was told of the qualities of the plant by the centaur, Chiron.

It is a common plant of pastures and hedgerows where it grows to a height of 2 ft. and bears its tiny bluish-white flowers in large corymbs from mid-June until September. The flowers have a peculiar musky scent about them whilst the handsome fern-like leaves which are one of the characteristics of all the achilleas, have the refreshing pungent smell of featherfew. For this reason it was used for bridal wreaths and was known as Venus'-tree to countrymen. It has for long been a popular border plant, the varieties Cerise Queen and the crimson-flowered Fire King being most colourful in the garden during summer and autumn and are long lasting when cut.

An infusion of the leaves in hot water and taken before a meal, acts as a valuable tonic for depression.

ACHILLEA PTARMICA   White Pellitory

Parkinson knew it as *Ptarmica flore plena*, the double wild white pellitory, whilst it is known to the countryman as Sneezewort because as Turner said, "the flowers make one sneeze exceedingly". The small double white flowers also gave the plant the name of "shirt-buttons" for they do greatly resemble the old white calico covered buttons of the countryman's shirt.

A. ptarmica is a native plant, found in meadows and heathlands and is perennial, in bloom during June and July when country brides would make use of the unblemished snow-white flowers in their bouquets. From the leaves, a tea was brewed which had almost the flavour of catmint "tea" and the leaves, dried and powdered were taken as snuff, mixed with chamomile leaves.

The plant grows some 2 ft. tall but the finest form, The Pearl, will attain a height of 3 ft. and is a valuable market grower's flower. The plant may be distinguished from the common yarrow by its undivided but serrated leaves. Its flowers are of purest virginal white, the petals and the disc appearing as if painted with Chinese white: they are the whitest of all flowers.

An open situation and a soil enriched with some humus will ensure the long life of the plants and if cut back after flowering in June, they will come again in autumn. The flowers are long lasting when cut and placed in water and do not drop their petals.

ACONITUM NAPELLUS   Monk's Hood; Wolf's Bane
Though poisonous, it is a plant that has found a place in cottage gardens since earliest time. It is of the northern hemisphere, to be found in the Himalayas, and in the mountainous regions of southern Europe. Shakespeare knew of its poisonous qualities and mentions it in the second part of *King Henry IV* (act iv, scene iv) written during the last year of the sixteenth century and printed in 1600. In this play Shakespeare introduces the rascally character Pistol, though Falstaff is the main attraction with his sharp, coarse wit.

In a room in the Palace of Westminster (the royal residence of Edward the Confessor), Henry IV; his sons Thomas, the Duke of Clarence, and Prince Humphrey, later Duke of Gloucester; together with the Earls of Warwick and Westmorland have gathered together. Henry addresses the Duke of Clarence, beseeching him to think more favourably of his brother, Prince Humphrey:

> "that the united vessel of their blood,
> Mingled with venom of suggestion,
> (As force perforce, the age will pour it in)
> Shall never leak, though it do work as strong
> As aconitum, or rash gunpowder."

In these lines, Shakespeare compares the venomous effects of the aconitum, all parts of which are poisonous, from the root to the pollen of the flowers, to the awful damage to be wrought by using gunpowder. Ovid also wrote of the deadly qualities of the plant in his line:

> *"Lurida terribles miscent Aconitæ Novercæ"*

and Theophrastus observed that the plant yields a poison so potent that it may cause instant death. It was with the pollen of this flower that the ancients poisoned their arrows whilst it was used throughout northern Greece, Italy and France as a bait to poison wolves, hence its name of Wolf's bane. Gerard, in his *Herbal*, tells us that the plant known as Monk's Hood, the shape of its flowers being similar to a monk's cowl, "is universally known in our London gardens" and he mentions *A. napellus* which is still a popular border plant. Of this plant Turner wrote: "let our Londoners which of late have received this blew wolfs' bayne, otherwyse called Monkes-coule, take hede . . ."

The medicinal qualities of the aconitum were first discovered by Dr. Stoerck, a German physician who prescribed it for rheumatism, whilst it is still used as a heart sedative.

"I have heard that Aconite being timely taken hath a healing might . . ." wrote Ben Jonson.

In Aelfric's *Vocabulary of the 10th Century*, it is written "Aconita, thung", this being the Anglo-Saxon word for "deadly poison". By Shakespeare's time, it had received the name Monk's Hood for it is written in Cutwode's *Caltha Poetarum* of 1599: "And with the flower Monk's-hood makes a coule." Granny's Nightcap and Helmet-flower were other names. Phillips (1824) writes of "the common Monk's-hood, *A. napellus*, which elevates its dingy blue helmet flowers on such exalted spikes from the month of May until the end of July, is a native of Germany and of other parts of Europe".

Shakespeare, who must have been acquainted with Gerard's garden in Holborn may have been familiar with the four species listed by Gerard in his *Herbal*. These were *A. napellus*, *A. pyrenaicum*, *A. variegatum* and *A. lycoctonum*, the latter a beautiful yellow flowering species which may still be obtained, whilst *A. variegatum* may be the form we now call *A. napellus bicolor*, the flowers being blue and white, and which were frequently to be found in cottage gardens.

The aconitum is one of the most stately of border plants, growing to a height of 2 to 5 ft. and bearing spikes of various shades of brilliant blue. "We make it the symbol of knight-errantry," wrote Phillips, "because it rears its threatening and gloomy helmet as if to protect the gay favourites of Flora."

The aconitum is a member of the buttercup family and has the same cut or fern-like leaves of bright green as all members of the family and which greatly enhances the beauty of the flowers. Like the buttercup, the plant prefers a moisture-holding soil and is best set out in March. After planting or dividing the carrot-like roots, it is advisable to wash the hands.

SPECIES AND VARIETIES

Aconitum fischeri. Valuable in that it blooms during September and October and so extends the season. It grows 4 ft. tall and bears racemes of amethyst-blue.

A. fortunei. The *A. chinensis* of cottage garden, growing 5 to 6 ft. tall and bearing from July until September, large racemes of brilliant mid-blue.

A. henryi. Spark's variety. It makes a compact plant 3 ft. tall and during July and August, bears branching spikes of Oxford blue.

A. lycoctonum. Native of the Alps, it reached England during early Tudor times and is an outstanding border plant being of bushy habit and bearing, during June, July and August, large flowers of creamy-yellow on 4- to 5-ft. stems.

A. napellus. The common Monk's Hood, occasionally to be found growing wild in Britain in hedgerows and by the side of streams where the soil is continually moist. It bears hooded flowers of darkest blue from July until September and has leaves which are divided into six to seven narrow segments. The poisonous roots are black.

BLUE SCEPTRE. A lovely plant for the front of the border or for a small garden, making a compact mound less than 2 ft. tall and bearing graceful tapering stems of blue and white flowers.

BRESSINGHAM SPIRE. An excellent border plant which grows only 3 ft. tall and bears violet-blue flowers on sturdy, shapely spikes.

A. pyrenaicum. The leaves are hairy on the undersides and held on long footstalks like those of the delphinium, of the same family. It blooms early, during May and June, and bears large golden-yellow flowers on 2-ft. stems.

A. variegatum. It may grow to a height of anything between 2 to 6 ft. with large glossy leaves, whilst it bears, during July and August, large blue flowers, streaked with white.

A. wilsonii, Barker's Variety. Suitable only for the back of the border for it grows 5 to 6 ft. tall and bears flowers of amythyst-blue on graceful racemes.

KELMSCOTT. Similar in all respects to Barker's Variety but its flowers are of brighter and richer blue.

AGROSTEMMA CORONARIA Rose Campion

This, the perennial form of the Corn-cockle *A. githago*, is one of the most delightful of all cottage garden plants and is one of the oldest. It is mentioned in a garden book of the fourteenth century and by Elizabethan times was to be found in almost every garden. At that time it was known as the Gardener's Delight and one form was known as the "Painted Lady" for the flowers were splashed and streaked like the carnation of the same name.

The countryman's name for the plant is possibly a corruption of the word "champion" for the flowers were much in demand for making garlands to decorate the heads of sporting champions during the time of the Stuarts and every cottage garden made its contribution. John Rea who published his *Flora, Ceres and Pomona* in 1665, the year before the Great Fire, spoke of the plant as Rose Champion, so too did the Rev. Samuel Gilbert who married Rea's daughter, Minerva. He published his *Florist's Vade Mecum* in 1683.

The plant has broad leathery leaves covered in woolly down which accentuates the brilliance of the flowers in the same way that the use of Chinese white accentuates the water-colours of R. P. Bonington and of other water-colourists of his time. It was from the thick woolly leaves that the genus also takes the name Lychnis, a lamp for in ancient times the leaves were used to make candle wicks.

The plant requires a well-drained sandy soil to be long lived and planting is best done in April for then they may grow away, stimulated by the summer sunshine. Growing about 20 ins. tall, they are admirable subjects for near the front of a border and will remain in bloom from June until September. At one time the plant was so popular that roots were sold in the streets of London.

The best form is *astrosanguinea* which bears flowers of crimson-red whilst Abbotswood Rose is the best pink, the flowers being of vivid carmine-pink. During the eighteenth century a double form was known but now seems to have vanished from gardens.

ALTHAEA ROSEA Hollyhock

No cottage garden is complete without the stately hollyhock which towers above its neighbours, lending an air of antiquity to the garden. Planted in groups against a garden wall or near a house, they give the impression of having been there since time immemorial, seeming to push up a little more each year until the tops of their noble stems are out of reach to all but the tallest of men.

Exactly when the plant reached England is not known but it is mentioned in the fifteenth-century poem of John (the) Gardener, and Turner spoke of it as a "common" flower. As it is native of the Near East (where it is found in every garden), it may have come with the returning Crusaders who gave it the name Holy-hock, which name was still in use early in the eighteenth century when Mortimer published his works on husbandry (1707). Dr. Prior Laveire, in his *Popular Names of British Plants*, believes the name to be from Colly, a cabbage, from the doubling of the flower.

Sir Thomas Hanmer writing in 1650 listed numerous varieties, including a double yellow raised, he tells us by the Duke of Orleans. By the beginning of the nineteenth century, Thomas Hogg, a nurseryman of Paddington Green, in his *Treatise* lists eighty named varieties and by that time the hollyhock had become a florists' flower along with the ranunculus and auricula. It remained so until the end of the century, the last to raise the hollyhock to the status of a florists' flower being William Chater of Saffron Walden whose double-flowering strain is still the best obtainable for it breeds remarkably true from seed.

The hollyhock is a perennial and is readily raised from seed which should be sown in drills in the open, during April. By early autumn, the plants will be large enough to transplant to the flowering position and they will bloom the following summer. To prolong the life of the plant, the stems should be removed as soon as they have flowered.

In early times, an infusion of the flowers was considered a valuable help towards relieving diseases of the lungs, bringing relief to those suffering from tuberculosis and to those who suffered from inflamation of the bladder. If only for its curative qualities, it may have been given the name "holy".

ALLIUM   Molly; Golden Garlic
A large genus which includes the onion, garlic and shallot. The ornamental species and varieties are known as the "ornamental onions" or "flowering garlics". They were widely grown in Elizabethan gardens and were known as "mollies", a name derived from *Allium moly*, the Golden Garlic, said by Pliny to be amongst the most

precious of all plants. Gerard called it "a stately plant", though Rea, described it as being "too common for a good florist's collection", whilst Parkinson, writing shortly before Rea, considered it the least satisfactory of the fourteen species he grew. He did, however, say that alliums "do abide a great while blown before they fade".

Parkinson mentions that John Tradescant, who achieved fame early in the seventeenth century as a collector of plants from the New World, obtaining them for his patron, the Duke of Buckingham, grew *A. moly* in his own garden at Canterbury and adds that "it was he who sent me a root to plant in my garden". The two must surely have been firm friends for in the year (1629) of the publication of the *Paradisus*, Parkinson was appointed botanist to Charles 1 whilst Tradescant was made head gardener to the king.

The ornamental onions are perhaps interesting rather than beautiful but are most valuable plants to naturalize in a dry soil. They will seed themselves or they may be increased by the small offsets. Plant the bulbs 2 to 3 ins. deep and 6 ins. apart.

SPECIES

Allium moly. The golden yellow star-like flowers are borne in dense globes, resembling *Primula denticulata* and on 10- to 12-in. stems. A native of southern Europe, it blooms during midsummer.

A. neapolitanum. The first to bloom, in a sheltered corner in full sun, opening its loose umbels of purest white during the first days of springtime. A native of southern Italy, it blooms on 12-in. stems above dark green strap-like leaves, but in the British Isles is not completely hardy away from the South West. The sun brings out the scent of the flowers, the plant being free of any onion smell.

A. schoenoprasum. Chives are hardy plants in the herb garden or front of a border and when in bloom in May and June, bearing their brilliant purple globes on 10 in. stems, no plant is more colourful. The hollow grass-like leaves are used in summer to flavour soups and stews and are chopped into omelettes or sprinkled into salads to give a delicate onion-like flavour. The plants are set 12 in. apart. They die down in winter when they are lifted and divided.

AMARANTHUS   Love-lies-Bleeding; Prince's Feather
This hardy annual, Milton's "Immortal Amaranth", now rarely to be seen in cottage gardens, was at one time the most popular of all

plants and was named the Purple Flower-gentle. Growing 2 to 3 ft. in height, Gerard said that the plume-shaped flowers were "of a shining light purple, with a gloss like velvet, but far passing it . . . and being gathered, do keep their beauty a long time, in-so-much that being set in water, it will revive again as at the time of gathering", hence it was regarded by the ancients as the symbol of immortality. It is Spenser's "Sad amaranthus in whose purple gore meseems I see Aminta's wretched fate" and it takes its name from a Greek word meaning "incorruptible". This plant is now named Celosia. *A. caudatus* was known to Gerard who called it the Great Purple Flower-gentle. It was also known as Love-lies-bleeding or Princes' Feather on account of its drooping crimson plumes.

Yet another form, *A. tricolor* was grown in Tudor gardens. It is the three-coloured amaranthe, native of the East Indies and named Floramor in Tudor times. Gerard said that "evry leaf resembleth in colour the most fair and beautiful feather of a parot . . . a stripe of red, a line of yellow, a dash of white, a rib of green . . ." The plants are raised under glass, sowing in gentle heat in February and planting out, after hardening, in June when they reach their full beauty during the early weeks of autumn.

A. tricolor, Molton Fire, has most striking foliage, being blotched with shades of crimson-red, bronze and amaranthe purple. It makes a compact plant 2 ft. tall.

The true Princes' Feather is *A. hypochandriacus* which reached this country from Virginia in 1684. Like all the species, the plants require ample supplies of moisture during dry weather.

ANAGALLIS ARVENSIS   Scarlet Pimpernel
This pretty little native wild flower has since earliest times been a prominent member of the cottage garden chiefly for its ability to forecast the weather. Indeed, it was known as the Poor-man's Weather-glass because when there is moisture in the atmosphere, the flowers fail to open and it is a forecast of rain. The flowers also close up in the evening to protect the anthers and the discharge of farina. John Clare knew well of the flower's qualities. In *The Shepherd's Calender for May* he wrote:

> . . . with its eye of gold
> And scarlet starry points of flowers,
> Pimpernel, dreading nights and showers,

Oft called 'the shepherd's weather-glass',
That sleeps till sun has dried the grass
Then wakes and spreads its creeping bloom
Till showers with threatening shadows come.
Then close it shuts to sleep again.

The common or scarlet pimpernel is an elusive, almost prostrate
plant and it is an annual, in bloom throughout summer, its tiny
scarlet flowers having a circle of purple at the centre. It takes its
name from a Greek word meaning "to extract" for the freshly
gathered plant pressed against the flesh was able to extract splinters
for which purpose it was also highly revered by countrymen. A
decoction of the plant was also used to combat convulsive disorders,
and even the bite of a mad dog.

The blue form, *A. coerulea*, is also a native plant which is to be
found on hilly pastures above Malvern and on the South Downs;
also in Devonshire, near Honiton. Each petal has a spot of carmine
at the base, possibly to attract and guide insects for its pollination.
Pliny said that sheep avoided this species but ate the scarlet
pimpernel.

ANCHUSA   Alkanet; Bugloss

It is *A. officinalis* and was also known as Alkanet and with borage
and comfrey is a member of the forget-me-not family. The flowers,
borne in dense inflorescences are all similar and with the gentian
are the truest blue coloured of all flowers:

> The spiny stem of bugloss flowers,
> Deep blue upon the outer towers.

Evelyn described it as being "in nature much like Borage" and
recommended the flowers to be used as a conserve for they were
thought to be "greatly restorative". The leaves are hairy, like
an ox's tongue from which its name bugloss is derived and they have a
musky fragrance when dry.

The anchusas are perennial only where the soil is light and well
drained. In a heavy, badly drained soil, the roots will decay if the
winter be unduly wet. Like most blue flowering plants, they are best
planted in spring when they may be propagated by lifting and
dividing.

SPECIES AND VARIETIES

A. italica. This is the Italian bugloss, with shining lance-shaped leaves of which there are a number of beautiful varieties growing from 2 to 5 ft. tall. The tallest is Morning Glory, which grows nearly 5 ft. tall and bears flowers of deepest blue, whilst Loddon Royalist bears flowers of brilliant sky-blue throughout summer and grows 3 ft. tall.

ANETHUM GRAVEOLENS   Dill

It is the only species of the genus, distinguished from other umbelliferæ by the absence of any involucre to the umbel. It is very similar to fennel in that it grows 3 ft. high with attractive feathery foliage which has a spicy taste and smell when handled and it bears yellow flowers. It is a very old herb, receiving its name from the Norse word *dilla*, to lull, for its seeds were used to lull young children to sleep in the same way that today it is used in sedative mixtures. The word is to be found in the vocabulary of Aelfric, Archbishop of Canterbury. The leaves were at one time used to flavour salads and sauces to serve with fish in the same way as those of fennel. In ancient times the plant was to be found in every cottage garden, for it was believed to have powers to safeguard the home against witchcraft. The leaves, with their spicy smell and taste, may be included with new potatoes and with peas, but as the flavour is strong, they should be used sparingly. Joseph Cooper, cook to Charles I, gave a recipe for pickling dill and cucumbers.

Seed is sown in March, in a well drained soil and in a sunny situation. If the seed is required, the plants are cut towards the end of summer and stores in a dry room for several days before the seed is removed. Remember, dill is an annual.

ANEMONE CORONARIA   Garland Anemone

Though now so widely grown in the West of England to provide cut flowers during the spring of the year, the anemone has a history comparable to that of the lily and the rose. *A. coronaria*, the Garland or Crown anemone, is to be found growing wild in all the lands of the eastern Mediterranean and may well have been "the lily of the field" of biblical days. It was well known to the ancient Greeks who named it wind-flower because it was usually found growing in exposed situations. Both the ancient Greeks and the Romans used the flowers to make coronets, hence its name, whilst in the Middle Ages the brilliant crimson-red flowers were believed to have sprung from the blood of the early Christian martyrs.

The Garland anemone, which we now call the St. Brigid or double anemone, was well known to the Tudors and was to be found in every cottage garden. Turner, Dean of Wells, called it the Rose Parsley "because there groweth a flower like a single rose in the middle of this herb which is like parsley in the leaves". Gerard, writing thirty years later said, "I have in my garden 12 different sorts," and later, Parkinson said that it was "sufficient to furnish a garden with its flowers for almost half the year" which is indeed so. Parkinson included it with those flowers "that are strangers to us and which give the beauty and bravery of their colours so early and which are to be found almost in all places, with all persons".

By the end of the seventeenth century the Garland anemone was to be obtained, as Rea said, in some 300 varieties and for the next 100 years it remained one of the foremost of florists' flowers, with the auricula, tulip and polyanthus. M'Intosh, a Scotsman who was gardener to H.M. King of the Belgians, describes in detail the flower in his book *The Flower Garden* (1838). He mentions that "one hundred fine named sorts may be purchased from 3 to 5 gns. a hundred" and prices the Single Red at one shilling and the Single Violet at sixpence. The flower was equally popular in France. A letter from a Paris nurseryman dated September 8th, 1881, said that "the anemone in France as a florist's flower is of ancient date, the finest strains coming from Caen more than a century ago". The single-flowered type, descended from *A. tenuifolia,* was that form most grown in the Caen and Bayeux districts of Normandy so that it came to be known as the Caen anemone, by which name it is known to this day. Parkinson's illustration of *A. tenuifolia* shows a bloom differing but little from the modern Caen anemone.

The St. Brigid (St. Bridget?) form with its double row of rayed petals is descended from *A. latifolium* and possesses more of the oriental make-up one would expect to find in this native of Turkey, Syria and the islands of Greece. Sir Thomas Hanmer, in *The Garden Book* (1659), said that "the doubles kinds we call Star Anemones, lying spread open like a star or marigold, showing no seed in the middle ... the flowers Gridelines, Reddes and Ash colours. And some are beautifully striped."

So great is the quantity of bloom grown in Cornwall each year and supplied to the wholesale markets that it is surprising that not until 1924 did the commercial cultivation of the anemone begin. In that year, seed was obtained from the garden of Canon Boscawen at Ludgvan Rectory and was germinated at the Gulval Experimental Station where the technique of corm and flower production was evolved and which was the commencement of the present prosperity amongst commercial growers in the county.

The anemone is one of the easiest of all plants to grow and from a planting of the corms made in March, there will be bloom for cutting and for garden decoration by early June. Those gardens enjoying a favourable climate will produce bloom the whole year through if a planting is made in spring and another in early autumn.

It is a mistake to use large corms which have become acclimatized to their original soil conditions and which may have lost their vigour. Plant "pea"-size corms, 2-cm. size, and set them 1 in. deep and ¾ in. apart, as M'Intosh says, placing the "eye" uppermost. They resent being planted too closely. They like a friable soil which is not deficient in lime.

Plantings of mixed colours may be made, or of separate colours from the many named varieties which are obtainable.

SINGLE OR CAEN OR POPPY ANEMONES

HIS EXCELLENCY. The blooms are large, of rich velvet red with a white central ring.

HOLLANDIA. It is somewhat shy in blooming during cool weather but its fiery scarlet bloom has no equal in the garden.

MR. FOKKER. Most prolific of all, its large refined blooms are purple-blue, paling towards the centre.

THE BRIDE. A most striking flower, being of purest white with a contrasting black centre.

STAR OR ST. BRIGID ANEMONES

LORD LIEUTENANT. The large double blooms are navy-blue with a velvety sheen.

MOUNT EVEREST. Like the old-fashioned Garland anemones, the white blooms have a red ring midway between the black centre and petal tips.

THE ADMIRAL. The large semi-double blooms are of deep magenta-purple.

THE GOVERNOR. The fully double blooms are of pillar-box red.

ANEMONE JAPONICA   Japanese Anemone
It has been grown in cottage gardens since its arrival in 1845, having been found by Robert Fortune, growing in a graveyard near Shanghai though it had first been seen by Dr. Cleyer in Nagasaki in 1685. It is, however, a native of China and which must have reached Japan at an early date. It bore purple flowers and is now almost extinct in Europe for those now known as Japanese anemones are hybrids, the result of crossing the original species with *A. vitifolia*, the pink-flowered anemone of the Himalayas. The first named variety was raised by M. Jobert of Verdun and it bore a flower of purest white. He named it Honorine after his daughter and more than a century later it is still in commerce. It was that which came to be most widely planted in cottage gardens during the latter part of the nineteenth century. It is now being superseded by Louise Uhink, a white of great beauty, whilst Whirlwind is equally fine and bears semi-double flowers. Of the pinks, September Charm is most attractive whilst Lady Gilmour bears flowers which are fully double. Another of great merit is Bressingham Glow which bears semi-double blooms of rich ruby-red.

The modern varieties grow from 18 to 24 ins. tall and make bushy plants which are a mass of bloom during September and October. They like a well-drained loamy soil and are quite happy in partial shade.

ANGELICA ARCHANGELICA   Angelica
This handsome herb is to be found growing in all parts of northern Europe, from Greenland, to Sweden and Norway; in the British Isles and in northern Germany; as far west as eastern Russia.

> Angelica, that happy counterbane,
> Sent down from heav'n by some celestial scout,
> As well the name and nature both avow't.

It is perennial and may live for several years but is usually treated as a biennial, the seed being sown in August as soon as collected, in the position where the plant is to mature though the seedlings will transplant if necessary. It may be kept growing almost indefinitely if one or two plants are cut down in June each year, when they will send out strong side growths which may be allowed to grow to maturity the following year. It will grow up to 6 ft. tall and should be grown at the back of the border where it will appreciate the shade given to its roots by other plants. There it will seed itself and may even become a nuisance, but it does enjoy a moist soil.

It is a handsome plant with stems, tinted with purple and which appear as if polished, whilst they are covered with a plum-like "bloom".

The stems are cut in June, when young, to candy and are used in confectionery, also to flavour apple tarts and tomato chutney. The stems have a musky smell and may be used for stewing, together with those of rhubarb to which it will impart its unusual flavour, also to rhubarb jam. It should be said that the wild form *A. sylvestris* is almost flavourless.

To candy the stems, after cutting drop them into boiling water for a few minutes. After removing, peel off the outer skin. The stalks are then boiled again until they have become a bright green colour and are almost transparent. Then make up a syrup of sugar which is poured over the angelica stems and they are then boiled again until the liquid is quite clear when they are removed and placed on wire trays to drain and dry.

Turner wrote that in his day, candying was done abroad and he tells us that "the roots are now condited in Danske, for a friend in London called Master Alleyne, a marchant man, who hath ventured over to Danske, sent me a little vessel of these, well condited with honey; very excellent good!"

From its aromatic seeds an aromatic oil is obtained, also from the scented roots. The seeds yield 1·15 per cent of essential oil, which has a musk-like smell and is used to flavour liqueurs, especially Chartreuse. In his *Callender for Gardening* for July, written in 1661, Stevenson suggests that one should "be sure every morning to perfume your house with angelica seeds, burnt in a fire-pan or chafing dish of coales, then which nothing is better". It does indeed send a delicious aromatic scent to all parts of the house.

Bees visit its white flowers whilst its leaves and roots are used in the making of Vermouth. Parkinson tells us that the dried roots powdered and taken in water "will abate the rage of lust in young persons", whilst it will also help "tremblings and passions of the heart". "The whole plant, leafe, roote and seede is an excellent, a comfortable scent, savour and taste," he wrote. The plant was mentioned by Phillippe de Comines in his account of the Battle of Morat in 1476, when its leaves were used to cure wounds which were made by an arquebus. Taken hot, the leaves infused in boiling water to which lemon juice and honey are added it is an excellent drink for a cold. The stems may also be blanched to use like celery and are delicious when boiled.

ANTHERICUM LILIASTRUM St. Bruno's Lily
Closely related to the asphodelus, it is St. Bruno's lily of the European Alps. It has white fleshy roots, like those of alstroemeria from which arises a 2-ft. stem, carrying at the top funnel-shaped flowers of sophisticated beauty. The pure white flowers are more than 2 ins. across, each segment being tipped with green and they appear in May, diffusing their sweet lily-like perfume over the Alpine meadows.

It has been growing in cottage gardens since early Tudor times and is to this day usually found only in the same surroundings, revelling in the cool, humus laden soil and the shade provided by nearby plants. It was dedicated by the French to the founder of the Carthusian Order and is a most delightful plant but will flourish only where conditions suit it.

The tuberous roots should be planted in March, some 4 ins. below the surface of the soil and spreading them out before packing soil around them. Gerard likened the roots to the legs of a spider with the central crown like its body.

ANTHEMIS NOBILIS Chamomile
No plant is more suitable for making a fragrant "lawn", for as Falstaff remarked in the Boar's Head Tavern in Eastcheap to Henry, Prince of Wales, so soon to become King Henry V: "Harry, I do not only marvel where thou spendest thy time, but also how thou art accompanied; for though the camomile, the more it is trodden the faster it grows, yet youth, the more it is wasted the sooner it wears." Prince Hal it was who lived in idleness in his youth and who was to become victor of Agincourt a few years later.

When once established, only occasional weeds will need removing

from the "lawn" whilst it should be extremely long lasting, for it is
only when newly planted that there is any tendency for the young
plants to die. For this reason a few plants of chamomile should be
held in reserve for filling in any gaps, or pieces may be removed from
established plants.

Besides the value of its medicinal properties, the chamomile
figures greatly in folk-lore. In Germany it is thought that if a wreath
of chamomile is hung up in the home on St. John's Day it will guard
the home against thunder and lightning. William Browne, writing
in the *Britannias Pastorals* advocated that chamomile be good for fish.

> "Another from her banks in sheer good will,
> Brings nutriment for fish, the camomile."

The chamomile is dedicated to St. Anne, Mother of the Virgin,
though Culpeper maintains that it was originally dedicated to the
sun by the Egyptians because of its properties of curing agues,
though agues, being watery diseases, would come under the influence
of the moon.

Its name is derived from the Greek meaning earth-apple, for the
plant when trodden upon emits the smell of ripe apples. In Spain it
is called Manzinella, little apple. Lawson, in his *New Orchard*,
described the value of having banks of chamomile planted about the
garden which "delights the mind, and brings health to the body",
for which reason it was widely used to make chaplets and garlands.

> Diana!
> Have I (to make thee crowns) been gathering still,
> Fair-cheek'd eteria's yellow camomile?

To the early writers the plant with its prostrate form was the
symbol of humility. Parkinson likened the pungency of its serrated
grey-green leaves to that of the featherfew. During Elizabethan times,
before the introduction of tobacco, its leaves were dried and smoked,
its rich aroma being a cure for sleeplessness. Its flowers are still used for
making a drink, one ounce of the blooms infused in a pint of boiling
water, a wine-glassful to be taken twice a day to soothe tired nerves.

ANTIRRHINUM MAJUS   Snapdragon; Calve's Snout
"The flowers grow on the top of the stalks and are of a purple
colour," wrote Gerard, "fashioned like a dragon's mouth from
whence the women have taken the name Snapdragon." The writer

also says that the seed is black, contained in husks fashioned like a calve's snout, hence it was also known by the name of Calve's Snout. Dioscorides, alive when Christ walked the earth, said that "the herb being hanged about one, preserveth a man from being bewitched". The plant was held in high esteem during ancient times and indeed in Russia and the Balkans until quite recently for its seeds yielded an oil which was said to be little inferior to that obtained from olives, the plants being grown solely for this purpose.

It is native of southern Europe and was believed to have reached Britain with the Romans for at an early date it had become naturalized on the cliffs of Dover and later, on castles and abbeys built by the Normans who may possibly have brought it with them. It is a plant that, like the wallflower, will beautify an old wall, where with its roots in mortar, wrote Hyll in 1564, "it will propagate itself from year to year without his [the gardener's] care". It was a familiar plant in Elizabethan gardens and was described by the writers of the time. Lyte (of Lytes Cary in Somerset) said the flowers were "like those of the Toadflax . . . of a faint yellowish colour" and it is of the same family. By Parkinson's time, it had become an "English" flower.

Though often growing high up and exposed to the elements, the parts of fructification are guarded against adverse weather by the unusually shaped corolla which defies any insect to gain entry until pollination has taken place. The "mask" then falls away to allow air to reach the seed vessel. The plant is self-pollinating and so does not need scent to call to it the pollinating insects. It was only in 1963 that the first scented variety appeared, with the introduction of a trio of F1 hybrids named Super Jet, Vanguard and Venus. Growing to a height of nearly 3 ft., the blooms are fully double with attractively frilled petals and have a soft clove-like fragrance.

During early Victorian times, antirrhinums bearing striped flowers were to be seen in cottage gardens and some bore double flowers like the Double Glamour Parade strain of today. Plants too, grew several feet tall and formed dense bushes, alight with their spikes of flame and gold, like the modern F1 Rocket hybrids. There is now a dwarf strain, Tom Thumb Floral Carpet, growing only 6 ins. high and making rounded ball-shaped plants covered in tiny spikes from July until November.

Though really a plant of perennial habit, the antirrhinum is best treated as a biennial, sowing the seed under glass (a box covered with a sheet of glass will be suitable) in July and transplanting the seedling into boxes when large enough to handle. The plants should be given the protection of a cold frame for the winter months when they will be ready to plant into their flowering quarters (after hardening) as soon as the spring flowering display has ended in May. Or they may be planted to the front of the border. They will come into bloom in June, six weeks earlier than if treated as annuals.

ARMERIA MARITIMA   Thrift; Ladies' Cushion
It is a British maritime plant which came to be used during Tudor days for edging small beds of "knot" gardens "for the which it serveth very fitly", said Gerard who classed it with the gillyflowers for it was then known as the Sea-pink. Pliny mentions it under the name of Statice, to stop or retain for the plant was able to stop the movement of shifting sands. It was given its English name of Thrift, the passive participle of threave, meaning to keep together, or retain one's earnings, to spend wisely.

It is a delightful plant, found on mountain sides as well as by the sea shore, making a neat tuft of evergreen grass-like leaves and it bears its tiny rounded heads of brightest pink on 6-in. leafless stems from May until September. In Elizabethan times it was named Ladies' Cushion.

It does, indeed, make a delightful edging for a border or bed and it will withstand clipping which should be done in autumn after it has flowered and which will keep the plants neat and bushy. As it does not drop its petals readily, it is advisable to remove the dead flower heads periodically for they turn brown and detract from the display. Propagation is by lifting and dividing the roots after flowering or early in spring. Every piece, however small, may be replanted and will quickly grow into a large clump.

The best forms of *A. maritima* are Vindictive, bearing flowers of deepest pink on 4- to 5-in. stems, and *alba*, pure white. For the border, the best is the hybrid, Bee's Ruby, which grows 12 ins. tall and bears large heads of glowing ruby-pink. Ruby Glow is equally fine and is intermediate in its vigour.

ARTEMISIA ABROTANUM   Southernwood
The Lad's Love or Southernwood, so called to distinguish it from other artemisias because it is a native of southern and not northern

Europe, though it will survive a severe winter in the British Isles. The pinnate leaves are grey-green in colour with a refreshing lemon-like perfume so were much used in pot-pourris and to place amongst clothes for it is said that the clothes-moth will keep away from it. Hence its French name of "Garde-Robe".

Believed to have been introduced into Britain by the Romans, the plant, which is deciduous and grows about 3 ft. tall, was grown in the ninth century by the monk Walfred Strabo in his "Little Garden" by Lake Constance. He tells us that its "hair-like leaves" are good for wounds and that the plant has as many virtues as leaves.

It was and still may be used as a help against sleeplessness, placing the dried leaves in muslin bags beneath the pillow-case whilst one writer of old suggests pounding the fresh leaves with sugar in a mortar until it is like a paste and "three times a day take the bigness of a nutmeg of this . . . It is a composer and always disposes persons to sleep".

It is a plant which grew in every cottage garden for apart from its charm it had so many uses, not least in lover's posies.

> With marjoram knots, sweet brier and ribbon-grass,
> And lavender, the choice of ev'ry lass,
> And sprigs of lad's-love, all familiar names
> Which every garden through the village claims.

These delightful lines were written by John Clare in *The Shepherd's Calender for June*, in which he so well describes the daily happenings of the Northamptonshire countryside in the early years of the nineteenth century.

Gervase Markham, living at the time of Bacon, suggested using an application of yarrow, southernwood, cummin seed, fenugreek and ditany, bruised with black soap to draw out deep-seated splinters and thorns, and Turner in his *Herbal*, said that when sprigs of southernwood were burned, the fumes would drive away serpents. Here, he must have intended those unsavoury creatures which enjoy cool, damp conditions and which frequently entered those buildings with a stone or earthen floor. It is amongst the plants described in John Gent's *New England's Rarities Discovered* (1672), it being one of the earliest plants to be introduced into America from England.

To propagate, the long woody shoots are removed in spring when forming new leaves. They will quickly root in sandy soil in the open. The plants should be allowed 3 ft. in which to grow but to maintain them thick and bushy, they should be cut down to 18 ins. of the base in March each year.

ARTEMISIA VULGARIS   Mugwort

The common artemisia or Mugwort is to be found amongst hedgerows throughout the British Isles. The dark-green leaves are smooth above but are covered with down on the underside. In ancient times, the leaves were used to feed to poultry, being healthful, whilst if placed in shoes, it would keep a man from weariness.

In *The Art of Simpling* (1656), William Coles said that if a footman put mugwort leaves into his shoes in the morning, "he may go forty miles before noon and not be weary"!

But the real use of the plant was for flavouring drinks and for brewing and it obtained its name from its use in flavouring beer, a leaf being placed in a mug for several minutes before consuming. Inn-keepers usually grew the plants for this purpose and also to brew mugwort beer. The herb is gathered when in bloom and dried. When quite dry, a quarter pound is placed in a preserving pan to which is added two gallons of water. Simmer for an hour and add a pound of brown sugar. Strain into an earthenware pan and add a teaspoonful of brewer's yeast, allowing it to ferment for a week. Then when fermentation has finished, strain into jars and after several weeks it will be ready to use.

ASPERULA ODORATA   Woodruff

With its sweet scent of hay, it is one of the most alluring and daintiest of plants with tiny leaves, borne in whorls like ruffs (Anglo-Saxon: Rofe) and which increase in fragrance as they dry. Tusser advised using the leaves to make "sweet water" for bathing the face, whilst to the Tudors it was known as Sweet Grass. The leaves were hung up in houses to keep the rooms cool and fragrant during summer. Gerard tells us that made up into garlands, "they do make fresh the place to the delight and comfort of such as are there-in", whilst it was the custom to place the leaves between the pages of books for their sweet smell and also amongst clothes. The leaves were also placed in cases of pocket watches during Georgian days, to be inhaled whenever learning of the time.

The plants are best raised from seed sown as soon as it is ripe and if sown where the plants are to grow the seedlings should be thinned to 12 ins. apart. The plants grow only 6 ins. tall and so may be grown alongside a path. In May they bear multitudes of tiny white flowers.

The plant contains coumarin, also present in the Sweet Vernal grass of meadows, hence the likeness of its fragrance to that of newly mown hay.

SPECIES AND VARIETIES

The tiny woodruffs are amongst the loveliest plants for a crazy-paving path where they may be planted with the thymes to give fragrance all the year. They are also suitable for the rock garden.

Asperula gussoni. It forms a wee tuft only 2 to 3 ins. high and is studded throughout summer with tiny pink bugles. The foliage is fragrant.

A. lilaciflora caespitosa. Of carpeting habit, it forms a mat of emerald green, covered throughout summer in deep-pink flowers.

A. odorata. The Sweet Woodruff and a native plant which grows 5 ins. tall with square stems at the end of which are borne eight leaves in a star-like whorl. The whole plant has the smell of new-mown hay including the small white flowers which appear in May and June.

A. suberosa. Its fragrant grey-green tufts are in direct contrast to the emerald green of *A. lilaciflora* and are enhanced by the flowers of soft shell-pink.

ASPHODELUS LUTEUS
Asphodel

It is a plant which has a similar rootstock to the anthericum, the roots being thick and fleshy. It is a native of southern Europe where it was held in great esteem by the early Greeks and Romans for its roots were used as "potatoes":

> Asphodel forsakes her bed,
> On whose sweet root our rustic fathers fed.

Ruskin wrote of

> The Asphodelus, the flowers of the Elysian fields . . .

and Milton described it as forming part of the nuptial couch of Adam and Eve.

The plants have narrow strap-like leaves from which arise flower spikes which carry a most satisfying perfume. The flowers vary in height from 1 to 5 ft. and rival the sweet-scented eremurus in their stately border habit. They require a well-drained soil and an open position.

Daffodil is a corruption of its name and the plant was introduced at an early date in our history together with the white narcissus from southern Europe.

It was possibly introduced by the Romans and was known to Gerard who grew four species, one of which was *A. luteus*, now named *Asphodeline luteus*, which is the most powerfully scented of all the species. The flowers are characterized by having a central line down each petal.

ASTER AMELLUS   Star-wort

For so long associated with the cottage garden, the star-worts are not native plants but have become so much an integral part of the garden scene that we cherish them as such.

The first species to reach Britain was *Aster amellus*, native of southern Italy and which should be planted in springtime. It is Parkinson's Purple Italian star-wort and may be the plant referred to by Virgil when describing how the "altars of the gods" were decorated with the flowers, hence its name during Parkinson's time of *Amellus virgilii*. It is a stiff woody plant growing 18 ins. to 2 ft. tall and bears multitudes of starry purple-blue flowers during July and August, before the Michaelmas daisies appear. It has hairy lance-shaped leaves which have a greyish appearance and the flowers are enhanced by their golden centre. It is a plant which resents disturbance.

Of the several lovely varieties, still outstanding is King George V, introduced in 1914 and which bears large flowers of deepest blue. Lovely too, is Vanity which bears flowers of violet-blue whilst Lady Hindlip is deep rose-pink. Nocturne bears flowers of a unique shade of lavender-pink which are most pleasing under artificial light.

ASTER NOVÆ-BELGIÆ   Michaelmas Daisy

This well-known plant which bears its flowers during Michaelmas (autumn) was first identified by the Belgian botanist Hermann in 1687 and named in honour of the Dutch settlement of New Amsterdam, near where the seed was first collected. In 1664, however, the settlement had been taken by Britain and the town renamed New York, in honour of the Duke of York, later King James II. With its almost indestructible habit, it quickly became established in European gardens but with its tiny flowers of lavender-blue never achieved popularity until the late Mr. Ernest Ballard took up its culture in his garden at Colwall, in Worcestershire. Ernest Ballard did for the Michaelmas daisy what George Russell did for the lupin and within a few years, the sickly looking garden weed had been transformed into a graceful lady of sumptuous colouring and clothed in healthy green foliage from tip to toe. His first, Beauty of Colwall, appeared in 1907 and henceforth the plants took on a compact habit, rarely growing more than 3 ft. tall and so requiring the minimum of staking. Flourishing in almost any soil, including one of a heavy clay nature, the hybrids of Ernest Ballard will beautify the garden from late August until late November when it is beginning to lose some of the brilliant colour of its autumn loveliness.

Of many lovely varieties, Flamingo bears large fully double blooms of clear flamingo-pink and Apple Blossom, flowers of softest pink. Moderator bears large double flowers of deepest violet-purple; Royal Velvet of glowing violet and Winston Churchill, masses of small flowers of a unique shade of beetroot-red.

BELLIS PERENNIS   Double Daisy
A daisy, symbol of humility, figures in the badge of Lady Margaret Beaufort, mother of Henry VII by her marriage to Edmund Tudor. She was founder of St. John's College and Christ's College, Cambridge, and from the time of Chaucer, the flower has been held in greater esteem by our poets and nobility than have any of our wild flowers with the possible exception of the primrose and the violet. For its hardiness, its daintiness of habit and for its earliness to bloom it has few rivals. In *The Legend of Good Women*, Chaucer has written these delightful lines:

> Of all the flowers in the meade
> Then love I most those floures white and redde,
> Such that men call daisies in our town;
> To them have I so great affection,

> As I said erst, when comen is the May,
> That in my bed there dawneth me no day
> That I n'am up and walking in the mede
> To see this flow'r against the sunne spread,
> When it upriseth early by the morrow;
> That blissful sight softeneth all my sorrow.

Again, he alludes to its Anglo-Saxon name of daeges-eage, "the eye of the day", for it is the first flower to open each day and there are few days of the year when the countryman will be unable to find at least one of the familiar white flowers, splashed with red or pink.

The French know it as Paquerette because it comes into full bloom at the approach of Paques (Easter), but its name bellis is from the Latin, bellus, meaning pretty.

A most pleasing and inexpensive scheme for spring and summer bedding may be obtained by planting together Violetta, Heather Bell or Le Grandeur (purple-blue) with double pink daisies of the Pomponette strain. The plants will come into bloom in March and continue right through spring and summer and the plants always remain neat and tidy. They will bloom for several years without attention. They are plants which grow well in almost every type of soil, though they do appreciate the addition of a small amount of humus which may be of used hops or leaf mould or decayed manure. Plant in autumn or in spring and propagate by root division. Or the plants may be grown from a sowing of seed made outdoors early in spring in a frame or in a box covered with a sheet of glass. They are amongst the easiest of all plants to grow well for they possess extreme hardiness and are able to give as good a display in a town garden as in the country. They are of perennial habit.

SPECIES AND VARIETIES

Bellis perennis.

DRESDEN CHINA. A named variety and one of the finest garden plants ever raised in spite of its humble origins. It grows only 3 ins. tall and is almost perpetually in bloom, sending up its tiny button-like flowers in endless succession. The colour is of a lovely shade of dusky pink.

THE PEARL. The pure white counterpart of Dresden China, except for colour being in every respect the same.

ROB ROY. In size, the flowers are similar to those of Dresden China

18 Double Polyanthus,
Ralph Spooner

19 Polyanthus, Barrowby Gem

20 Gold Laced Hose-in-
Hose Polyanthus

21 Alpine Auricula, Argus

22   Hose-in-Hose Primrose, Brimstone

23   Jack-in-the-Green Primrose

24 English Tulip, Sir
Joseph Paxton (flamed
bizarre)

25 Old English Tulip,
Sam Barlow (flamed
bizarre)

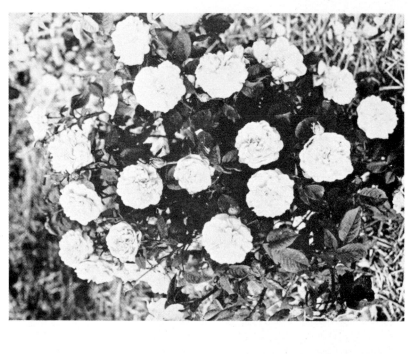

27   *Rosa alba*, Belle Amour

26   *Rosa muscosa*, Common Moss

and The Pearl but are produced on stems 4 to 5 ins. long. The colour is a lovely shade of richest crimson.

SUTTON'S MINIATURES. The tiny double buttons are similar in size and shape to the named varieties and are borne on 4-in. stems. The colour range includes dusky pink, salmon and shell-pink, many of the blooms having deeper coloured centres.

POMPONETTE. Of compact habit and growing only 6 ins. tall, the tightly quilled pompon-like flowers are obtainable in shades of pink or red, the latter bearing flowers of the most brilliant crimson-scarlet.

Bellis prolifera.

The Hen and Chickens daisy, a very old plant in which tiny flowerets develop from the central bloom and dangle down like chickens about the mother hen. It is a charming plant for pot culture, but is now rarely seen though plants are obtainable from several growers in Northern Ireland who specialize in old-fashioned flowers.

BETONICA GRANDIFLORA Betony

Syn: *Betonica macrantha*: *Stachys grandiflora*. It is a delightful plant with its grey woolly foliage and bearing erect spikes of purple-red. Pliny believed it to be named Vettonica, after the Vettones, a people of Spain in whose territory the plant was discovered. It reached England at an early date in her history, possibly with the Romans who used the leaves as a blood purifier.

It is an excellent plant to edge a border for it grows only 12 to 14 ins. tall and remains in bloom from June until September, its flowers being much loved by bees. It is propagated by root division in March.

BORAGO OFFICINALIS Borage

It is a native biennial plant, growing 12 to 15 ins. tall and though usually found by the side of ditches, has since earliest times been grown in cottage gardens for the beauty of its flowers and for its leaves. The plant takes its name from a Celtic word "borrach", meaning to have courage for it was believed that an infusion of the leaves gave a person courage. They have a pleasant cucumber-like taste and are delicious in a salad or may be cooked as spinach. A sprig, placed in claret cup or in lemonade not only greatly improves its flavour but gives the drink an icy coolness. An infusion of the leaves will also bring relief to one suffering from a sore throat or tight chest.

It will readily seed itself after flowering and makes an upright, branched plant with oblong leaves and a stem covered in stiff hairs. It blooms throughout summer, the flowers being of an exquisite shade of sky-blue with a spot of jet-black at the centre and at the mouth of the tube are two rows of projecting stamens.

Gerard said, "those of our time do use the flowers in salads to exhilarate and make the mind glad"; whilst Francis Bacon has written "that the leaf hath an excellent spirit to repress the vapour of dusky melancholy".

CALENDULA OFFICINALIS   Marigold
"The marygolde," says Lyte in his *Herbal*, "hath pleasant, bright and shining yellow flowers, which close at the setting down of the sunne and do spread open again at the sunne rising." And from the Castle of Carisbrooke, during his imprisonment, Charles I wrote rather pathetically:

> The marigold obeys the sun,
> More than my subjects me have done.

There was a popular belief that the flowers followed the sun, an idea to which Shakespeare has alluded in *Cymbeline* when the musicians enter Imogen's apartments singing:

> Hark! hark! the lark at heaven's gate sings:
> And Phoebus 'gins arise,
> His steeds to water at those springs
> On chalic'd flowers that lies;
> And winking Mary-buds begin to ope their golden eyes;
> With everything that pretty is—My lady sweet, arise.

Of all our common flowers, the marigold is most sensitive to the sun's rays. The ancients knew it as ymbglidegold, "that which moves round the sun". "All yellow flowers," wrote St. Francis de Sales, "not only rejoice in the sight of the sun but follow with loving fidelity, the attraction of its rays, gazing at it and turning towards it from its rising to its setting."

Marguerite de Valois, grandmother of Henry IV, took for her armorial device a marigold flower turned towards the sun with the motto

Je ne veux suivre que lui seul.

In *A Winter's Tale*, the scene is set in the shepherd's cottage, and here Shakespeare reveals his abounding love for flowers and an intimate knowledge of garden craft when Perdita says:

Here's flowers for you;
Hot lavender, mints, savory, marjoram;
The marigold, that goes to bed with the sun,
And with him rises weeping.

The plant received its name Calendula because it is usually in bloom on the calends (first day) of every month, whilst it is dedicated to Our Lady for a similar reason, being in bloom at the time of all the festivals of the Blessed Virgin. The word "gold" is a reference to the golden rays seen around the head of the Virgin and this name was that most often used by the writers of old. "Ye golde floure is good to be seene," it is written in an ancient medicinal manuscript in Stockholm and in Fuller's *Antheologia* of 1655 it says, "we all know the many and sovereign virtues . . . in your leaves the Herb general in all pottage", hence its name of Pot Marigold. At that time, the plant was to be found in every garden for with its extreme hardiness, there was scarcely a day in the year when there was not at least a few flowers to use to flavour broths, together with the almost ever-green leaves. Tusser includes it amongst those "herbs for the kitchen"; and he also included it in his list of flowers suitable "to grow in windows".

The calendula is one of the most accommodating of plants, preferring a place in the sun but growing in partial shade where it may receive the early morning sunshine. It also demands no special treatment in its culture. Being an annual, it is grown from seed, sown broadcast or in shallow drills early in spring where the plants are to bloom, or they may be transplanted when large enough to handle.

Or the seed may be sown in a cold frame, or beneath cloches in the autumn, treating the plant as a biennial and moving the plants to their flowering quarters some time in March. From an original sowing, they will seed themselves with the greatest of ease and new plants will appear year after year to provide a never ending succession of colour.

VARIETIES

Calendula officinalis.

CAMPFIRE. The flowers are produced on very long stems and are of a lovely shade of burnt orange, the deepest coloured of all the marigolds.

GEISHA GIRL. It is an entirely new "break" in this lovely old plant, the blooms being likened to an incurved Japanese chrysanthemum, hence its name. The blooms are large, tightly packed with petals and are of glowing orange with an overtone of glistening red.

INDIAN MAID. It grows taller than most calendulas, reaching a height of nearly 3 ft. by the end of the summer. The pale orange flowers have a dark maroon centre.

KELMSCOTT GIANT. The flowers are possibly the largest of all the calendulas and are of clear deep orange.

PACIFIC APRICOT BEAUTY. The colour is quite unusual in the calendula, being of a true shade of soft apricot enhanced by the dark centre.

PACIFIC CREAM BEAUTY. The first of its colour and a distinct "break" from the usual orange and gold for the large flowers are of rich Jersey cream colouring.

PACIFIC LEMON BEAUTY. One of the newer "Pacific" varieties, bearing large refined flowers of a lovely shade of soft lemon-yellow.

RADIO. One of the finest cut flower plants ever raised. The habit is ideal, never becoming tall and "raggedy" whilst the flowers with their attractive quilled petals are of clearest orange.

CALONYCTION ACULEATUM   Moonflower

A native of Greece, it has long been grown in cottage gardens but to modern gardeners is almost unknown. It was called *Ipomoea bona-nox* (Beauty of the Night) for its large trumpet-shaped flowers resemble those of the convolvulus, having a waxy-white appearance at eventide, hence the name of Moonflower.

It is a plant of climbing habit and in a warm summer will attain a height of nearly 20 ft. in a single season, bearing from July until October in one long succession, its large trumpets. The blooms of ten measure nearly 6 ins. across and diffuse a powerful scent at night.

As it is not fully hardy in the British Isles it should be planted against a bower or porch with other plants against which it can twine and receive protection. The roots should be covered with ashes during winter whilst Christmas roses planted close-to will provide additional protection.

CALYSTEGIA ALTHEOIDES   Bindweed
Of the Great Bindweed, *Calystegia sepium*, which twines about our hedgerows, handsome with its lance-shaped leaves and bearing, in July and August, its trumpets of dazzling white, Pliny in the *Historia Naturalis* wrote:

"There is an herb named in Latin *Convolvulus*, growing among shrubs and bushes, which carrieth a flower not unlike to the lily, save that it yieldeth no smell . . . [it was] as if Nature in making this flower, were alearning and trying her skill how to frame the lily indeed."

A most delightful description of the plant and its flower and Pliny was absolutely right in saying it is without perfume though Gerard has described it as "sweet of smell". That species which is scented is *Calystegia* or *Convolvulus arvensis*, the Lesser or Small bindweed, an obnoxious but attractive weed of countryside and gardens with its underground roots, difficult to eradicate wherever it takes hold. It is Wordsworth's "Cumbrous bind-weed, with its wreaths and bells". Its flowers are white, suffused with pink and often striped green.

Calystegia altheoides is a plant of vigorous growth and will quickly cover an unsightly bank or a trellis. It has attractive silvery foliage and from early June until October bears masses of small pink trumpets. It is the best of all the bindweeds for use in the garden.

CAMPANULA   Bell-flower
A large genus of mostly perennial plants, confined to the northern hemisphere of which several are native of the British Isles. A number of species have been growing in cottage gardens since earliest times for they are of easy culture and appeal to the countryman with their dainty dangling bells whilst they had various uses, to ease a sore throat or to clear the skin of obtrusions.

Best known is *C. rotundifolia*, the Harebell, which is the rightful bluebell of Scotland, a name the English give to *Endymion non-scripta* (Scilla). It is a plant of northern Europe which Linnaeus is said to have seen growing by the steps leading to the University of Uppsala. It is a delightful plant, to be found mostly about the sheep-cropped hillsides of Northumberland and Lanarkshire, and is in bloom from June until September for most of the bell-flowers remain long in bloom. When the first cottage gardens were made, plants were dug from the fields and replanted, in the same way that John Clare's ploughman would lift a root of cowslips from the meadow and replant it in his own garden upon returning home at eventide.

The flower is delightfully shown in the background to Millais's painting, "The Blind Girl", in the Birmingham City Museum and Art Gallery. The painter has faithfully reproduced the colouring and habit of the demure bells which contribute greatly to the charm of the picture.

The Canterbury Bell is known to every cottage gardener but is now less widely grown, possibly because it is a biennial and requires yearly attention. Yet it is too valuable a plant to be neglected for it blooms during those few weeks of June when the spring display has ended and just before the flowers of summer begin to unfold their petals.

Canterbury Bell is the name we give to *C. medium*, the biennial but until recent times the species known by that lovely name is *C. trachelium*, a native plant which Gerard said "do growe very plentifully in the low woods and hedgerows of Kent, about Canterburie, Sittingbourne and Southfleete" and which acquired its name because its dainty bells resembled those which Chaucer's pilgrims used to decorate their horses. The modern Canterbury Bell was named the Coventry Bell. There is some doubt as to whether this plant is a native, though it grows naturally about the hedgerows of northern France and may have been introduced by the Normans. Gerard tells of it being found in hedgerows near the city of Coventry and they "are called Coventry-bells".

C. pyramidalis, the Steeple bell-flower has a similar ancestry and is also biennial but is now rarely seen. It was at one time grown almost entirely in pots to decorate the home and Henry Phillips has told of it being used to garland a window indoors "or rustic grate of a country parlour" for its stems were sufficiently pliable to train into any shape. Phillips has said that it "could be bent around a hoop, to form a complete circle".

The Peach-leaf bell-flower, known to gardeners of Tudor days, is a perennial of outstanding garden value, in bloom during June, July and August and bearing its cups of blue or white in elegant spikes some 3 ft. tall. It is a native of southern Europe though it is perfectly hardy and has foliage of the shape of a peach leaf. The Italians call it *Campanella*, whilst the cottager knew it as the Paper-flower from the almost transparent texture of the corollas.

All parts of the plant, including the blue bell-shaped flowers, yielded a distilled water which was beneficial to cure sores of the mouth and a sore throat as well as to cleanse the skin whilst the roots were sliced and boiled to serve with meat in the same way that the close-related Rampion, *Campanula rapunculus*, was eaten.

Milton knew of its healing powers and in his poem "Ode on the Death of Demon" he writes:

> There thou shalt cull me simples, and shalt teach
> Thy friend the name of healing powers of each,
> From the tall Blue-Bell to the dwarfish weed,
> What the dry land and what the marshes breed.

What delightful names the country folk gave to our native flowers and especially to those of the campanula species. Is there any one more lovely than Venus's Looking Glass, a name given to *C. specularium*? The brilliant corollas seem to reflect the sun's rays, hence its name. Gerard found it growing wild in a cornfield at Greenhythe in Kent, home of so many campanulas, and which take their botanical name from the Latin meaning a "tower of bells".

C. specularium was named the Corn violet by Parkinson from the violet colour of its blooms which Sir Thomas Hanmer said "stand open all day . . . and make a handsome show". An annual, it is now rarely seen in cottage gardens.

The campanulas enjoy a light, friable soil and like most blue flowering plants, do well in one of a chalky nature. For this reason, several of the trailing species grow well when planted in the mortar of an old wall. The perennial forms, again like most blue flowering plants are best planted in March but the biennials are raised by sowing the seed in boxes (or pans) or in shallow drills in the open, in May. The seedlings should be moved when large enough to handle, planting them 4 ins. apart and they should be set out in their flowering position in autumn, moving them with as much soil attached to the roots as possible. Plant 15 ins. apart for they grow into bushy plants.

SPECIES AND VARIETIES

Campanula carpatica. Native of the Balkans, it reached Britain about two centuries ago and making a dainty mound, in bloom from early July until September, came to be planted in every cottage garden as an edging to a border or to small beds. The fresh green foliage is studded with large cups of china blue, held on 8-in. stems. The plants grow as wide as they grow tall.

One of the finest varieties is Wheatley's Violet which grows less than 6 ins. tall and bears large bells of violet-blue. The long flowering and equally compact Hannah, an old country name, is a happy companion.

C. glomerata. The Clustered bell-flower and a perennial plant of the British Isles, growing 12 to 18 ins. high. It is found in hilly pastures and bears funnel-shaped flowers in terminal clusters. They are of deep violet-purple and are in bloom from July until October.

The variety Joan Elliott bears flowers of violet-blue on 20-in. stems and is an excellent long-lasting flower when in water whilst Purple Pixie of compact habit, bears flowers of deepest violet of refined form.

C. medium. This, the Canterbury Bell, or more correctly, the Coventry Bell, grows 3 ft. tall and is a biennial, dying after it has ripened its seed. A plant of shrubby, branching habit it bears large bells of 1 in. or more in diameter in violet, blue, rose or white. The double or cup and saucer form, *calycanthema*, is obtainable in the same colours and for long has been a quaint inhabitant of cottage flower borders.

The dwarf single form of recent introduction is a charming plant for small gardens, growing 18 ins. tall and forming a neat pyramid covered in dainty bells of blue, pink or white.

C. persicifolia. The Peach-leaf bell-flower, introduced during early Tudor times and which requires a more open, sunny situation than most campanulas. It bears its open bells of deep blue on 3-ft. stems and remains long in bloom. The variety Telham Beauty is a most striking plant, in the words of Miss Sinclair Rohde "one of the loveliest flowers of the midsummer garden" with its large cups of powder-blue on wand-like stems. Snowdrift makes a pleasing contrast with its snow-white bells whilst Pride of Exmouth bears double blooms of darkest blue.

C. rotundifolia. The Harebell, common on downland pastures. It grows 8 ins. tall and is a glabrous plant with slender stems and kidney-shaped lower leaves. It bears its drooping flowers of pale blue in a small raceme and though scentless, they dangle prettily in the summer breezes. The best form is Olympica, with its large bells of violet-blue whilst Spetchley White has pure white flowers and is rare.

C. trachelium. This, the true Canterbury Bell, also known as the Nettle-leaf bell-flower, grows 3 ft. tall and has nettle-like leaves with serrated edges and covered with bristles. It bears its purple-blue flowers in axillary clusters of two or three from July until October and is a perennial. The finest form is Bernice which bears double flowers of soft powder blue.

CARDAMINE PRATENSIS   Lady's Smock
The plant flourishes in damp places, by the side of streams and in low-lying meadowland, the pale silvery-mauve flowers appearing early in April. It is one of those delightful plants of childhood days, dedicated to Our Lady, so that it should really be called Our Lady's Smock. It comes into bloom at Lady-tide. It is also known as Meadow Cress, Bittercress, Mayflower and Cuckoo Flower.

Izaak Walton wrote of "the meadow, chequered with water-lilies and Lady's Smocks" and again he writes, "looking down in the meadow, [I] could see there a boy gathering lilies and lady's-smocks . . . to make garlands suitable to this present month of May".

> And some to grace the show,
> Of lady-smocks do rob the neighbouring mead.

Thus wrote Michael Drayton of this flower in the *Polyolbion* and Shakespeare associates it with other familiar plants of the Warwick-shire meadows that he and Michael Drayton knew so well and where, along the Avon's banks, lady's-smocks grow in profusion today in the company of buttercups and cowslips as they did in the time of the dramatists.

> When daisies pied and violets blue
> And lady-smocks all silver white
> And cuckoo-buds of yellow hue
> Do paint the meadows with delight.

So sang Spring at the conclusion of *Love's Labour's Lost* and it is not difficult to imagine Shakespeare's thoughts as, in his lodgings in London, he toiled at his first important play. It may have been that

he was writing it during Maytime when the meadows of Warwickshire's Avon were a patch-work of nature's subtle hues, and where
at a distance, the flowers of the Lady's-Smock have the metallic
appearance of polished silver.

In the next verse, he alludes to the flower again

"And Maidens bleach their summer-smocks"

for the pale flowers resembled the smocks or chemises laid out by the
maidens to bleach in the sun, a custom which must have been a
familiar sight along the banks of the Avon.

The plant takes the name Cardamine from the one-time belief
of its value for strengthening the heart, but it was most in demand
for its leaves which have the pungent bitter taste of watercress and
were used in salads when lettuce was in short supply. It is, indeed, of
the same Cruciferae family as the watercress, the edible leaves
springing from the root in orbicular segments, whilst those which
appear from the stem do so as narrow divisions. Parkinson has
written that "divers have reported them (the leaves) to be as affec-
tual for scurvy as the water cresses" and were in great demand by
those peoples who relied chiefly on fish and meats for their diet.
Phillips in *The World of Words* (1696) described the Lady's-Smock as
"a kind of water-cress, of whose virtue it partakes".

The Cardamine is also known as the Cuckoo Flower for it is in
bloom when the cuckoo is heard most clearly.

The plant is of interest in that it will reproduce itself from the tiny
plantlets which appear upon the leaves and if detached and laid on
top of a box of soil, they will form strong plants to bloom the following year. The plants may also be propagated by root division in
autumn. Several of the species are attractive in the border but
must be given a soil containing ample supplies of humus to retain
summer moisture. They will grow in partial shade.

It is the double form, *C. pratensis flore plena* that has for so long been
grown in cottage gardens. It is a delightful old-fashioned plant
which Phillips in the *Flora Historica*, says deserves a place in the
choicest garden especially where the soil tends to be damp. It occasionally appears amongst meadow plants and grows 12 ins. tall.

CARDUUS   Thistle
It is perhaps the most widely known of all plants and of the legends
and traditions surrounding it, a book could well be written. It takes

its name from Thor-sel, Thor being the god of the thunderbolt for it was believed that plants of the Sow Thistle (*Sonchus oleraceus*) planted near a cottage would protect those who entered from being struck by lightning. William Browne who wrote the *Britannius Pastorals* spoke of it as the "chief cherisher of vital power":

> And for the chiefest cherisher she lent
> The Royal thistle's milky nourishment.

Here, Browne's reference to the "Royal thistle" is surely meant to be the Royal Thistle of Scotland, the Milk or Dappled Thistle, *Carduus marianus*, the tender stems of the lower leaves of which may be boiled to make delicious eating whilst the stalks of the leaves may be chopped into a salad after soaking them for an hour or so to remove their bitterness. The roots too, may also be eaten, braised like those of the celeriac. Culpeper wrote: "In spring if you boil the tender plant, it will change your blood as the season changeth" for which purpose it was to be found in every cottage garden.

The Thistle of Scotland ranks next to the Rose of England in heraldic importance and as a national symbol is said to date back to the Battle of Largs when the Danish invaders are said to have retreated by stepping on thistles. Its first appearance as a national symbol was on the coinage of James III of Scotland in 1474 when it is thought to have been taken by the king as his emblem. In 1540, it was recognized for all time as a national emblem in the foundation or the Order of the Thistle when it is represented as a flowered head upon a short stalk with a leaf on each side.

On the arms of the National Bank of Scotland, two thistles appear, together with St. Andrew and the cross of his martyrdom.

Shakespeare made several references to the thistle as in *Henry V* when they are mentioned as a symbol of ground which has been badly neglected over a period of years, in this instance during the long war between France and England:

> And nothing teems
> But hateful Docks, rough Thistles, Kecksies, Burs.

Thistles, however, did not represent soil that was barren for Tusser tells us that their presence told quite the opposite:

> "If Thistles so growing proove lustie and long,
> It signifieth land to be hartie and strong."

Both the Field Thistle and the Holy Thistle bloom during July and August, their purple flower heads being composed of more than a hundred tiny florets which secrete an abundance of nectar. This rises high in the tube so that it is readily available to the bees, though there are some thistles where the flower tube is so long as to be out of reach of the honey bee.

It is the European thistles (Echinops) which are now mostly grown in the cottage garden. They are natives of the Mediterranean and are plants of extreme beauty with globular flower heads and spiny leaves which, together with the stems, are of a brilliant steely-blue colour. They grow well in any soil and are propagated by division and from pieces of the root.

CENTUREA CYANUS Cornflower
It is a plant native to the British Isles where it has been growing since the beginning of time, enhancing many a cornfield with its flowers of deepest blue. It was named *Centaurea cyanus* from a Greek word meaning centaur and which is thought to represent the centaur Chiron who taught mankind the use of medicinal plants.

It was introduced to gardens in very early times and was mentioned by Dr. Turner in the *New Herbal* (1564). He called it the great Blewbottle and told us that "some herbarists call it Baptisecula, because it hurteth sicles". Gerard knew it by the name of Hurtsickle "because it hindereth the reapers by dulling their sicles in the reaping of corn". The flowers were, however, in demand by artists for the rich true blue colour which could be made from it by removing the centre petals and pounding with a mortar. To the juice a small amount of alum was added and the preparation stored in large shells until ready for use.

In Germany, the flower was used to make a drink by boiling in water and which was considered to be a reliable cure for jaundice.

Growing 3 ft. tall, the annual cornflower has for long been a feature of cottage gardens for it remains long in bloom and few flowers can rival its rich blue and pink colourings.

Seed should be sown in circles of about 15 ins. diameter where the plants are to bloom and if a sowing is made in August, the plants will bloom early in July. Another sowing made in April will prolong the season for the plants will bloom in September and continue until November if the weather is favourable.

The cornflower took on a new popularity in 1935 by the introduction of a dwarf variety, Jubilee Gem, which makes a bushy plant 12 ins. tall and the same across. For weeks, it covers itself in flowers of brilliant blue whilst Rose Gem bears flowers of deep carmine-pink and is lovely to plant with it for bedding. Red Ball, bearing flowers of crimson colouring is still more compact.

The musk or Sweet-scented cornflower, *Centaurea moschata*, was introduced from Turkey about the year 1600 and was named Sweet Sultan after the Sultan of Turkey who is said to have discovered the plant on an expedition into Persia. Parkinson tells us that "it is a kind of cornflower of such beauty, lately obtained from Constantinople . . . the Turks themselves do call it the Sultan's Flower". And he adds, "it is of so exceeding a sweet scent that it surpasseth the finest civet there is . . ."

C. montana is of the mountains of central Europe and is the blue perennial cornflower.

The old "whitewashed" cornflower, once to be found in cottage gardens everywhere, is *C. dealbata*. Its beautifully cut leaves are grey-green, and white beneath, as if "whitewashed".

The flowers of the variety John Coutts are of deep clover pink. A perennial, it blooms May and June.

CENTRANTHUS RUBER Valerian; Setwall
It is a native plant though not a common- one and is usually to be seen growing on the walls of monastic buildings as at Ely and Lincoln and in the garden of the Grey Friars at Canterbury, together with the wallflower and sedum for it loves to have its roots in lime-stone rubble. In ancient times it was called Setewall or Setwall, an Anglo-Saxon name which persisted until Tudor times for Dr. Turner, who compiled his *Herbal* during the reign of Mary Tudor, used the name, and Chaucer wrote of

> ". . . herbes great and small,
> The licquoris and the setewall."

It is a perennial of extreme hardiness and has its admirers, including Gerard who called it Mercury's Blood and who said that "it groweth plentifully in my garden, being a great ornament to the same. . . ."

There is an attractive deep crimson form, *coccineus*, and a white, *alba*. The plants bloom from mid-June until October.

CHEIRANTHUS CHERI   Wallflower

With their richness of colour and thick velvety petals, as well as their sweet clove perfume, no plant better personifies the cottage garden and none is more appreciated when it blooms in spring. Native of southern Europe, it probably reached England with the Norman builders of our castles and abbeys for the plant was, and still is, found on old walls and may have come attached to stone imported from Caen. The writers of old called it "wall-gillyflower" for its flowers have the warm scent of cloves (gilofre is French for clove). In the *Paradisus*, Parkinson describes seven kinds, including the old double yellow, re-discovered early this century by the Rev. Harpur Crewe and which still carries his name. The old double crimson is known as the Bloody Warrior. Both are propagated from cuttings as they do not set seed. In *The Floricultural Cabinet* for December 1848 the writer mentions both and says: "They are so highly esteemed in the North that they rank as prize (show) flowers and some have spikes 24 ins. long".

CHRYSANTHEMUM MAXIMUM   Moon Daisy

One of the loveliest flowers of pastures, the Ox-eye or Dog daisy has been grown in cottage gardens since earliest times. It is *Chrysanthemum leucanthemum* and came to be called the Marguerite when Margaret of Anjou, queen of Henry VI, at the age of 15, took the flower as her emblem in 1445, perhaps as a reminder of the alpine meadows of Anjou where it also flourishes. But it was the Moon Daisy of the Pyrenees, *C. maximum* which came to be so much planted for it flourished in all soils and in the coldest of gardens, bearing its large snow-white single flowers from July until October. It was used by the Read family of Deopham in Norfolk to raise a number of magnificent double-flowered varieties which are amongst the finest of all garden plants.

C. *maximum* reached Britain early in the nineteenth century and quickly superseded the old Marguerite for it was more robust in every way. Autumn is the most suitable time for its planting, dividing the roots into offsets and planting them 15 ins. apart. They will quickly grow into large clumps each capable of bearing, on 3–4 ft. stems, fifty or more flowers in a single summer.

Of many fine varieties, all of which last long in water when cut and in the garden, Horace Read grows 5 ft. tall and bears large double blooms like a greenhouse chrysanthemum and Wirral Supreme grows 4 ft. tall. It has an attractive pin-cushion centre. Cobham Gold, found by Lord Darnley in the gardens of Cobham Hall, has similar flowers but with a flush of gold.

CHRYSANTHEMUM PARTHENIUM   Featherfew
The peculiar pungent scent of its foliage is well known to all country lovers for it is a native plant and no cottage garden was ever without it. It is a perennial, retaining its curled leaves of palest green throughout winter, whilst it bears its tiny white button-like flowers from early July until September.

It was one of the plants recommended by Thomas Tusser for strewing. Tusser was an Essex man, born at Rivenhall in 1525 and as a boy sang in the choir of old St. Paul's. He was educated at Eton and Cambridge from where he came to Court and where he remained for ten years. He then took a farm at Cattiwade, on the borders of Essex and Suffolk and there in 1557 published his poem, "One Hundred Points of Good Husbandry" in which he gives advice on garden cultivation; on housekeeping; about how to keep Christmas; and on how to treat one's wife and servants. He died in 1580 and was buried in St. Mildred's in the Poultry. On his grave appeared this inscription:

> Here Thomas Tusser
> Clad in earth doth lie,
> That sometime made
> The Points of Good Husbandrie.

The plant takes its name of Featherfew from the Latin febrifuge, "to drive away illness" due to its tonic properties and in Europe, its bitter-tasting leaves were friend with bacon and eggs and were often served in like manner in cottage homes in Britain, to counteract the grease and add interest to the meal.

C. parthenium is an erect branched plant growing 15 ins. high and during Victorian times was often used for summer bedding, especially the variety *aureum* with its leaves of golden-yellow and which formed a striking contrast to the Paul Crampel geranium and purple heliotrope. The double flowered form was known to and described by Parkinson as *Parthenium flore pleno*. "We have this kind only in gardens," he wrote and he described the flowers as being "like unto the double chamomile". Parkinson mentions that it was used as a cure "for those who had taken opium too liberally". Little is known of the early life of the author of the *Paradisus*, the loveliest of all the old garden books, except that he was born in Nottinghamshire in 1567 and was appointed Apothecary to James I and Botanist to Charles I. He died in 1650 and was buried in St. Martin-in-the-Fields.

The Featherfew is readily raised from seed sown in gentle warmth early in the year or in a seed bed outdoors in April. Where it is to be used for bedding, the seedlings should be transplanted to 2½-in. pots from which the plants are set out in May. Ordinary soil is suitable but the plants should not be allowed to lack moisture.

CHRYSANTHEMUM RUBELLUM   Chusan Daisy

Though held sacred in the gardens of China and Japan since earliest times, the chrysanthemum, the most popular flower after the rose, is a comparative newcomer to gardens, the Old Purple flowering for the first time in Britain in the nursery of a Mr. Colville in the King's Road, Chelsea, in 1796. This had been brought from China to France several years earlier by a Captain Blanchard of Marseilles but there is on record that plants grew in the Chelsea Physic Gardens about fifty years before though they were soon lost and may not even have flowered.

The purple-flowering chrysanthemum was *C. morifolium*; it had double flowers and an upright habit and it became, with *C. indicum*, a single yellow-flowered variety, the ancestor of all the now so common early and late-flowering varieties. Two other forms of *C. morifolium* were to be found in China, a yellow and a white which were mentioned in *The Book of Odes*, revised by Confucius in the fifth century B.C. During the Sung dynasty, which coincided with the Norman invasion of Britain. The monograph recognised thirty-five forms of the flower and by 1700, an encyclopaedic work on flowers recognized 300 kinds. The Chinese regarded the chrysanthemum as a medicinal plant, one which promoted long life and the dews from the leaves were collected and drunk. From the flowers, a wine was made and which was thought to increase the vitality of man.

The plants had reached Japan by the fifth century A.D. and two centuries later the flower was taken as his emblem by the Emperor and also incorporated into the flag of the country.

Plate 5
Left Old English
tulips
Below Old pompon
chrysanthemums

Plate 6
Left Old laced pinks
Below A selection of the
best modern pinks: *left to
right from the top:* Mizar
Doris Mars Margaret
Fortuna Vega Monty
Hugh Show Pearl Ian
Susan Show Cameo
Prudence Robin Helen

In 1846, Robert Fortune introduced into Britain the Chusan Daisy, *C. rubellum* and in 1866 Mrs. Beeton wrote that "this little favourite has tended in no small degree to resuscitate the cultivation of the chrysanthemum".

Able to withstand severe cold, the plant had a neat habit and bore small circular double flowers resembling the pompons on the caps of French sailors, hence its name of Pompon chrysanthemum and it quickly came to be planted in every small garden in Britain and in France. Careful hybridizing saw the gradual development of this plant until today there are some varieties which grow less than 12 ins. tall and during autumn, cover themselves in a mass of flowers no larger than a ten pence piece.

Readily increased by division of the roots in spring or by detaching the rooted offsets, the plants appreciate a well-nourished soil and though requiring ample supplies of moisture in summer, resent excess moisture about the roots in winter. 12 ins. should be allowed between the plants and they should be divided every four years.

Varieties of C. Rubellum

ALLAN RUFF. It grows only 12 ins. tall and comes into bloom late in August, the flowers of chestnut-bronze being fully double and of the size of a fifty pence piece.

CLARA CURTIS. Growing 2 ft. tall, it bears small buttons of deepest pink.

DENISE. Growing 12 ins. tall, the flowers are of five pence size and borne in neat sprays of deep golden-yellow.

DUCHESS OF EDINBURGH. The blooms are of fiery scarlet and borne with freedom.

JILL. Growing 18 ins. tall, the large circular poms are of a unique shade of creamy apricot.

LITTLE LOUISE. It grows 18 ins. tall and during September and October bears button-like flowers of palest lilac over a white ground.

MARY STOKER. Of compact habit, the dainty flowers are of soft primrose-yellow.

PAUL BOISSIER. An old French pompon growing 4 ft. tall and in bloom October and November, the flowers being of rich coppery-orange.

WISBECH PINK. It grows 18 ins. tall and bears a large pom, packed with petals at the centre and the colour is rosy-red flushed with purple.

CLEMATIS VITALBA   Traveller's Joy; Old Man's Beard
A genus of shrubby plants which climb by means of their leaf stalks.
The calyx consists of four or more petal-like sepals with no corolla
whilst the fruit is a head of sessile or stalked achenes with long awns
or styles which adds to its winter beauty. One species, *C. vitalba*,
Traveller's Joy or Virgin's Bower is native to the British Isles, particularly to the chalky south-eastern part of England. Gerard mentions that it was common in every hedgerow from Gravesend to
Canterbury "making a goodly shadow" beneath which travellers
could rest, "thereupon have I named it Traveller's Joy". In an
Anglo-Saxon vocabulary of the eleventh century it is called "Viti-
cella-woodebinde".

The word clematis is derived from the Greek *klema*, meaning
"vine branch", probably because it resembles the vine in climbing
by means of tendrils. The plants are always happiest in the company
of other plants to which they look for support and possibly for protection from cold winds. They love to have their roots in lime rubble
whilst they will appreciate an annual mulch of decayed manure.

SPECIES AND VARIETIES

Clematis cirrhosa. It is evergreen and is said to have been discovered
in Spain by the botanist Clusius and to have reached England during
Elizabethan times. It will grow to a height of 8–9 ft. and in a mild
part of the British Isles, will come into bloom early in the New Year
and continue until April or May, bearing bell-shaped flowers and
polished leaves.

C. flammula. The Fragrant Virgin's Bower it was called and it
reached Britain from Spain early in the seventeenth century. It is
one of the beauties of autumn when it will bear masses of small
creamy-white flowers which have the pronounced scent of Meadowsweet, almost too powerful to be enjoyable if inhaled near to. It is
a vigorous climber, retaining its leaves almost until the year end
whilst its flowers are followed by fluffy silvery seed heads. The form
rubra-marginata, a hybrid of *C. flammula* and *C. viticella*, also bears
fragrant flowers of a lovely shade of soft port-wine. It should be
pruned hard in February each year.

C. vitalba. It is one of the loveliest of our native climbers and
though not now considered worthy of planting in the garden, was at
one time to be found in most cottage gardens, bearing throughout
summer clusters of greenish-white flowers which are sweetly scented.

These are followed in autumn by clusters of feathery fruits, hence, its country name of "Old Man's Beard". The seed heads persist until almost the year end and appear like a grey mist during autumn when seen from a distance.

COLCHICUM AUTUMNALE   Naked Lady; Meadow Saffron
It was named Colchicum because it grew in abundance around the Armenian City of Colchis, celebrated as the birthplace of Medea and for its poisonous plants. Horace, in the Thirteenth Ode of his second book, wrote of

". . . every baleful juice
which poisonous Colchian globes produce".

This is the plant known as *C. byzantinum* and is described by Gerard in his *Herbal* who tells us that the French called it "Mort au chien" for it caused the rapid death of dogs or of any animals that chewed it. For that reason it was always confined to an orchard near the house or to a corner of the cottage garden where farm animals were not permitted to roam and where it was seen by William Cobbett who described it in his *Rural Rides*.

The Common Colchicum is indigenous to the moist meadows of Essex and Gerard mentions that it was also plentiful around Bath and in Northamptonshire. Its poisonous properties would seem to be known to grazing animals which always ignore its presence, as if by instinct.

From the walnut-sized roots (bulbs) the drug colchichine is obtained and which was used by the ancient Egyptians to cure gout. The modern apothecaries have found a new use for it for it has the amazing property of increasing the number of chromosomes in a plant so that hybrids which are sterile may be made fertile.

The bulb sends up its flower in September and October and is entirely without foliage, hence its name of Naked Lady. When established, the plants increase rapidly, covering the ground with their white or rosy-lilac crocus-like flowers, the six petals being united at the neck of the corolla to form a long tube which reaches down to the bulb. The large leaves appear in spring. The colchicums are especially suitable for a border shrubbery where their large coarse leaves will be hidden in summer. It is distinguished from the autumn-flowering crocus by its six anthers whereas the autumn-flowering crocus has only three.

Colchicum autumnale. The Common Colchicum, which bears its rosy-lilac star-shaped flowers rather later than those of *C. byzantinum*. There is a double form of great beauty, *roseum plenum* and a white, *album*.

C. byzantinum. This is the broad-leaved form, which bears numerous star-like flowers of rosy-lilac from a single bulb whilst of the new large-flowered hybrids, the double pink, Waterlily, and the vivid purple, Lilac Wonder, are outstanding.

CONVALLARIA MAJALIS   Lily of the Valley

A genus of a single species and it is one of the loveliest of native plants, exquisite in its purity. Those who for the first time may have come across a bed of the flowers, deep in the heart of the woodlands, drawn by its exotic spicy fragrance as the night-scented flowers draw the hawk moth, will have enjoyed an experience never to be forgotten. The flower has an ethereal beauty unknown in any other flowers with its dangling bells of greeny-white backed by the bright green lance-shaped leaves which display the bloom as if in a sheath. This was the flower so much loved by the poet Shelley:

> And the naiad-like lily of the vale,
> Whom youth makes so fair and passion so pale,
> That the light of its tremulous bells is seen
> Through their pavilions of tender green.

Hartley Coleridge, contemporary of Shelley, considered it to be the loveliest of all scented flowers, his lines to The Lily of the Valley being amongst the most beautiful in our language:

> Some flowers there are that rear their heads on high,
> The gorgeous products of a burning sky,
> That rush upon the eye with garish bloom,
> And make the senses drunk with high perfume.
> Not such art thou, sweet Lily of the Vale!
> So lovely, small, and delicately pale,—
> We might believe, if such fond faith were ours,
> As sees humanity in trees and flowers,
> That thou wert once a maiden, meek and good,
> That pined away beneath her native wood
> For very fear of her own loveliness,
> And died of love she never would confess.

Its name is derived from Convallis, a valley. It is also known as the Wood Lily and was mentioned by Thomas Hyll in *The Profitable Art of Gardening* (1564). "The Wood lily or Lilly of the Valley is a flour marvellous sweet," he writes, "flourishing especially in the spring time and growing properly in woods but chiefly in vallies and on the sides of hills. But now . . . is brought and planted in gardens." Henry Lyte in his *New Herbal* (1578) calls it the Lilly Convall and describes the flowers as being "as white as snow and of a pleasant strong savour. The water of the flowers comforteth the heart. The same water as they say, doth strengthen the memorie and restoreth it again to its natural vigour, when through sickness it is diminished." In *The Flower Garden* (1726) John Lawrence wrote, "The Conval-lily is esteemed to have, of all others, the sweetest and most agreeable perfume; not offensive or overbearing, even to those who are made uneasy with the perfumes of other sweet scented flowers."

Gerard tells us that it grew plentifully on Hampstead Heath (four miles from London, where in Ken Wood it still grows) and at Lee, in Essex. He says that flowering in May, it was also known as the May Lily whilst the French call it Muguet.

Sweet May Lillies richest odours shed
Down the valley's shady bed.

wrote Sir Walter Scott. The flower was also known as Our Lady's Tears, the tiny dangling bells of Virgin whiteness being like large tear-drops from a distance.

"The flowers . . . distilled with wine, . . . restore speech unto those that have the dumb palsie . . . and are good against the gout and comforteth the heart," wrote Gerard.

In ancient times, the distilled water was held in such esteem as to be kept only in vessels of gold. Hence Matthiolus called the water *Aqua aurea*.

The belief that the plant was able to restore the memory is substantiated by the ability of the dried flowers and roots when inhaled to act like snuff, exciting a discharge of mucous to clear the head and to bring relief to a tired mind.

The manner in which the bells are suspended from the stem gives them a lightness possessed by few other flowers. Keats said of them:

> No flower amid the garden fairer grows
> Than the sweet lily of the lowly vale,
> The Queen of flowers.

And Barton has captured their delicate charm in his lines which tell
us that

> The lily of the vale, whose virgin flower
> Trembles at every breeze beneath its leafy bower.

The plant is indigenous to almost all parts of Europe from Britain
to the Caucasus and it grows freely in the woods of France and of
Germany where it is known as Meyen Blumen. It is a plant with a
creeping rootstock by which it increases rapidly and it requires the
same conditions in the garden as in its native woodlands. That is
either a situation facing north or beneath trees or shrubs. But it must
have moisture about its roots and this is encouraged by working into
the soil humus in the form of peat, leaf mould or used hops which
will retain much of winter's moisture during summer-time.

Specially retarded crowns (roots) are imported from nurserymen
in Germany for forcing in gentle heat in pots to be taken indoors for
winter flowering when their fragrance is more than usually
appreciated.

There is a double form, *flore plena* and also one bearing pink
flowers, *rosea*, but neither are as gorgeous as the single white form
with its flowers of richest perfume. A small shaded bed, with the
fragrant pink polyanthus, Enchantress, planted about it will present
a delightful picture of pink and white in May and the two are right
in every way to accompany each other in small vases. A few roots of
each will give hours of pleasure year after year.

COTYLEDON UMBILICUS   Wall Pennywort; Navelwort
This remarkable succulent, with round leaves serrated at the edges
and depressed in the centre was known to cottagers as the Wall
Pennywort for like the House Leek, it always grew on old walls.
With its saucer-shaped leaves it was also known as the Navelwort. It
takes its botanic name from the Greek, *kotule*, a dish, from the shape
of its leaves which country children used to call "Penny pies".
Gerard had a great affection for it, also for the Great Navelwort, a
larger form which he described in detail, the flowers being of an
"incarnate" colour or flesh, the word Falstaff used to describe the

colour of the carnation, hence the name. Gerard has told that the Great Navelwort was to be seen growing from the walls of Westminster Abbey, "over the door that leadeth from Chaucer's tomb to the old Palace" whilst he tells that the Wall Navelwort was native in the Alpine regions around Piedmont though it was introduced into England at so early a date as to be classed (with *Sempervivum tectorum*) as a native plant.

The leaves are held on stalks of about 2 ins. long whilst from the base arise the succulent flower stems which often attain a height of 12 ins. or more. The greenish-white flowers, like tiny bells are borne in racemes and have the appearance of miniature red (or green) Hot Pokers. It is a perennial, in bloom from June until the end of August when the whole plant begins to take on a pinkish tint, making it even more attractive.

CROCUS SATIVUS   Saffron
"The flower of saffron doth rise out of the ground nakedly in September," wrote Gerard, and he continues; "it groweth plentifully in Cambridgeshire; at Saffron Walden; and other places thereabout, as corn in the fields."

Crocus sativus is one of the oldest of all cultivated plants, being grown throughout the Eastern world since the beginning of civilization for, with the exception of the Flax, it had greater commercial value than any other plant. It takes its name Saffron from the Spanish *Acafron* and the Arabic *Sahafarn*, meaning "thread", from the thread-like stigma from which the product Saffron is obtained. It is estimated that it requires more than four thousand blooms to yield one ounce of saffron which is collected from the dried stigmas.

It is believed to have been first introduced into Britain by the Romans, for it is mentioned in a tenth-century Leechbook, "when he bathes, let him smear himself with oil mingled with saffron" and in an early English vocabulary, the name appears: "Hic crocus, A safarroun". There is, however, some doubt as to whether the plant then grew in England or whether it was the finished product which was imported by those who traded with the Mediterranean peoples for there is no record that it grew in England before 1330. It is said to have been introduced into that part of Essex, now called Saffron Walden, by Sir Thomas Smith, Secretary of State to Edward III, and who was a native of that town. His object was to initiate a new industry for the villagers and his idea was greatly successful for the plants flourished exceedingly, bringing considerable wealth to the district. When Saffron Walden was granted her charter and arms it incorporated three flowers of the purple *Crocus sativus*, "walled in". Saffron flowers are a charge upon the arms of Player of Nottingham, famous in the cigarette industry.

So successful did Sir Thomas Smith's venture prove to be that during the fifteenth century, the culture of saffron had spread to other districts. Hakluyt (1553–1616), writing in Vol. II of his *English Voyages* said that the saffron crocus grew also "in Herefordshire by Wales, where the best of all England is". Bullein in his *Government of Health*, published in Armada year, a few weeks after Shakespeare had arrived in London for the first time wrote, "our English honey and Safron is better than any that cometh from any strange or foreign land". Saffron had many uses. It was used to die clothes yellow and during the fifteenth century, as an alternative to gold thread to make church vestments. It was used to colour the garments worn by the knights at the Field of the Cloth of Gold during the reign of Henry VIII. It was also used instead of gold leaf in the illumination of missals. Hendries' translations of Theophilus, writing in the tenth century gave these instructions. "If you wish to decorate your work in some manner, take tin pure and finely scraped; melt it and wash it and apply it with glue upon letters or other places you wish to ornament with gold; when you have polished it with a tooth, take Saffron with which silk is coloured, moisten with white of egg and when it has stood a night, cover with a pencil the places you wish to gild."

Today, saffron is used in Cornwall and in parts of Ireland to lend colour and flavour to cakes, especially during Lent, to provide one's diet with greater interest.

"Let me see," says the Clown in *A Winter's Tale*, "what am I to buy for our sheep-shearing feast? . . . I must have saffron, to colour the warden pies. . . ." These were pies made with Warden pears, the pastry being given a richer appearance by the use of saffron.

From the large globular corms arise narrow grey-green leaves which appear before the reddish-lilac flowers. The pistils are long and hang down. They are of vivid blood-red colouring which greatly enhances the beauty of the flower.

The plant requires a porous soil enriched with decayed manure and if to bloom with freedom, require lifting and dividing every third year. Of the variety, *Cartwrightianus*, with its smaller flowers, E. A. Bowles has written in *A Handbook of Crocus and Colchicum*, "I found it on the lower slopes of Mt. Lycabettus under the Aleppo pines in loose soil, where clumps of its large corms were easily acquired."

CYCLAMINUS Cyclamen; Sowbread

A genus of corm-bearing plants of dwarf habit, suitable for naturalizing beneath mature trees. By planting several species, a number of which bear fragrant flowers, the blooms may be enjoyed almost throughout the year.

The plant reached England early in her history, the corms being much in demand to assist in child-birth. The first species to be grown in gardens was *C. coum*, a winter-flowering species bearing carmine-pink flowers. It is possible that *C. hederifolium* (*C. europeum*), the Common Sowbread and native to most European countries, was also a native plant for Gerard tells that it "groweth upon the mountains of Wales and on the hills of Lincolnshire; and Somerset" (presumably the Quantocks). It is also to be found naturalized in parts of Kent and Sussex, usually growing on limestone formations.

When planting the corms, they should have the upper surface exposed, merely pressing them into the ground which should first have been enriched with leaf mould and some decayed manure and with mortar or limestone chippings. A well-drained friable soil is necessary, otherwise the corms may decay during periods of root inactivity when excessive rainfall is often experienced. *C. hederifolium* is the exception to the need for shallow planting for it requires to be set 6 ins. deep where the soil is light and friable. This species is also the exception to the rule of planting the hardy cyclamen in July for it will then be in bloom and is best planted early in spring, remembering to place the round or smooth side downwards and to keep the corms moist until established. Most of the species will not bloom during their first season but will more than compensate by their beautifully mottled foliage.

Those species requiring shallow planting should be given a top dressing each year as they tend to push themselves out of the ground. Leaf mould should be pressed around the corms after flowering and they will benefit from an occasional dressing with mortar or lime rubble whenever obtainable.

SPECIES

Cyclaminus cilicicum. It should be planted in July when it will come into bloom early in September, continuing to produce its pretty pink flowers with their attractively twisted petals until November if the weather is mild. Like all the hardy cyclamen, the dainty flowers hover above the foliage like moths and they have a delicious vanilla perfume. *C. cilicicum* is a native of the pine forests of the Lebanon and grows only 3–4 ins. tall. Its rounded leaves have a pretty heart-shaped zone of silver. In exposed gardens, the plant should be confined to the shelter of trees or shrubs whilst it is also suitable to plant in the trough garden.

C. coum. It comes into bloom before the end of January, with the snowdrops and continues until the end of March. It was discovered on the Isle of Cos, Asia Minor and has a corm which is flatter than the other species. Its pretty short-petalled flowers of magenta-red are borne on 3-in. stems above shining dark green leaves. There is an attractive white form *album*, the flowers being blotched with maroon.

C. europeum. It is Gerard's *C. hederifolium*, the Ivy-leaf Cyclamen and may be said to be a native plant for it was grown in the knot gardens of Elizabethan times. It bears the most sweetly scented flowers of all the hardy cyclamen, and it is summer flowering, remaining in bloom from mid-June until the autumn-flowering species take over. It is native of the limestone mountainous regions of all parts of Europe and during Parkinson's time had become naturalized in south-eastern England. From the heavy perfume of its flowers, it was also known as *C. odoratum*. The heart-shaped leaves are marbled with white and are purple on the underside whilst the flowers of purple-red colouring darker at the base.

The plant is a lover of shade and appreciates some moisture about its roots when under the right conditions an established corm will bear upwards of a hundred fragrant blooms.

The corms are flat and will increase in size for fifty years or more until they are more than 12 ins. across. They will appreciate a mulch each year after flowering as they tend to exhaust the soil.

C. repandum. It is to be found in mountainous regions of central and southern Italy, at altitudes of 5,000 to 6,000 ft. and though the corms are small, its is the most free flowering of all the species, an established plant bearing as many as 200 blooms of rosy-white, spotted with purple at the base. They are sweetly scented and appear during April and May, a few weeks later than *G. libanoticum* but before those of *C. europeum*.

DAHLIA Mexican Daisy

The dahlia which takes its name from the Swedish botanist Andreas Dahl was unknown to European gardens until 1790 when seed reached Madrid from Mexico where the plant grows wild. It would have been growing in the gardens of the Aztecs, possibly for food for the tubers are full of nutrition and were a valuable substitute for potatoes. The plant was first recorded by Francisco Hernandez, botanist to Philip of Spain, shortly after the conquest of Mexico. But 250 years were to elapse until Cervantes, keeper of the botanical gardens in Mexico City, sent seed to the keeper of the Royal Gardens in Madrid from which was raised a pink and a red dahlia.

Plants first reached England in 1798, sent by the Marchioness of Bute whose husband was then our ambassador in Madrid but they soon perished and the plant had to be re-introduced by Lady Holland in 1804 (also from Madrid), in the year that Napoleon was made Emperor of France. It is said that the Empress Josephine grew dahlias in her famous gardens at Malmaison near Paris, a number of which eventually reached England.

By 1830, the dahlia had become, as Loudon's *Encyclopaedia of Gardening* tells us, "the most fashionable flower in the country". This is confirmed by M'Intosh, then gardener to H.M. the King of the Belgians, who in *The Flower Garden* (1838) lists 730 named varieties, those held in most esteem being what were known as the Shows. The blooms were large and were tightly filled with quilled petals, like the small modern decoratives. They were included amongst the florists' flowers of the day and were especially prized (like the laced pinks) with the weavers of Paisley. They reached a peak of popularity about a century ago and by the end of the century, like so many florists' flowers, had declined almost to the point of extinction, surviving in a few cottage gardens where the pompon and miniature ball dahlias, with flowers of less than 3 ins. diameter held pride of place for they were ideal plants for the small garden, being of compact habit whilst they flowered from July until cut down by the frosts, often well into November.

Though only half hardy, in the most favourable districts, the tubers may be left in the ground permanently, lifting only when there is need to divide. There, in the cottage garden, growing amongst plants which will provide them with winter cover, they will be as permanent as any plants and as an extra precaution should be covered when cut down near the base, with decayed strawy manure.

Nor is a warm greenhouse necessary to grow dahlias in the more exposed gardens. The tubers, after lifting in November and storing in boxes of damp sand or peat over winter in a frost free room, may be started into growth in deep boxes of soil covered with glass or in a cold frame, giving additional moisture as the sun gathers strength and the days lengthen. The tubers with their new shoots may be planted into the open early in June and will come into bloom before the end of July.

To increase the stock, the shoots from a number of tubers should be detached with a sharp knife, removing a small piece of tuber with each shoot. These are placed in boxes (or pots) containing sand and peat and should be covered with whitened glass until rooted, at all times keeping moist the rooting medium. The rooted cuttings should then be planted into small pots containing the John Innes potting compost and should be placed in deep boxes or in a frame and grown on through summer. Any flower buds should be removed to enable the plant to concentrate its energies in building up a sturdy tuber to provide large numbers of bloom the following summer.

Dahlia tubers should not be planted too deeply; no more than 1 inch of soil should cover them. They are copious drinkers and gross feeders, revelling in a well-manured soil and appreciating regular feeding with diluted manure water. The tubers of the small flowering varieties should be planted about 2 ft. apart. They may be planted in a border to themselves or between plants in the herbaceous border to which they will give fresh colour when the other plants will mostly be finishing flowering.

SMALL POMS AND MINIATURE BALL VARIETIES

ANDREW LOCKWOOD. One of the most free flowering of all poms, the blooms being of a lovely shade of soft pure lavender.

BURWOOD. Outstanding on the show bench and one of the brightest plants of the garden. The blooms are golden-yellow, tipped scarlet.

DR. J. GRAINGER. The blooms are of perfect ball shape and of antique bronze and old gold colouring, borne on long stems.

GOLDEN FIZZ. The dainty globular blooms are of a lovely shade of primrose yellow.

WILLO'S VIOLET. A pom of great merit, the deep violet mauve flowers with a white base being borne with greatest freedom.

ROTHESAY SUPERB. The finest pure scarlet form.

DAPHNE MEZEREUM   Mezereon

Of the two native daphnes, *D. mezereum*, found in woodlands of most parts of Europe was cultivated as a garden plant as early as the sixteenth century. It makes an upright bush and is slow growing, adding less than 12 in. to its stature in about as many years. For this reason it was widely grown in cottage gardens where it also appreciated the company of other plants which provide the cool conditions which its roots so much appreciate. No winter flowering plant is more colourful for from the early New Year and until the end of March, its naked branches are wreathed in tiny flowers of purple-pink. The flowers have thick petals and curl back, to reveal their bright orange stamens whilst they emit a delicious sweet perfume, a characteristic of all the daphnes. William Cowper speaks of its beauty in *The Winter Walk at Noon*:

> . . . mezereon too,
> Though leafless, well attired and thick beset
> With blushing wreaths, investing every spray.

There is a deeper coloured form, *rubrum* and a white form, *alba*, its beauty accentuated when growing with the purple flowering varieties. Its snow-white blooms are followed by amber-yellow berries whilst those of the type bear purple-red berries which appear in June. The form *grandiflora* comes into bloom in October and bears larger flowers than the others.

The secret of success with *D. mezereum* is to provide it with a cool soil, one which is deeply worked and is enriched with leaf mould and a little decayed manure. The best plants are those raised from seed which, however, take more than two years to germinate and it will be another decade before the plants reach 12 ins. in height. It is unwise to cut the flower spikes to enjoy indoors however tempting it may be to do so for *Daphne mezereon* resents cutting in any way, especially when in bloom and the plant may die back. It should be left to beautify the winter garden.

Daphne laureola is the Spurge Laurel of the woodlands and remarkable for its smooth upright stems which are bare of leaves except at the ends, has never been widely planted in cottage gardens though it is evergreen. It flowers from January to April, bearings its green blossoms in drooping sprays and they are delicately scented especially when the weather is mild and calm. It is a plant that enjoys dense shade and a cool, moist soil for which reason it is always happiest in its natural surroundings.

DELPHINIUM CONSOLIDA · Larkspur

When mentioning this flower in the introductory song to *The Two Noble Kinsmen*, Shakespeare used its country name of Lark's-heel:

> Oxlips in their cradle growing,
> Marigolds on death-beds blowing
> Larks-heels trim.

We know it as Larkspur, or *Delphinium consolida* the annual native delphinium, a member of the buttercup family of plants, to be found growing in corn fields around Stratford-on-Avon and in the countryside around Norton Lindsey where it is still known by its ancient names of Lark's-heel and (Lark's-toe) from the unusual spur formation of calyx and petals. During early times, distilled water from the flowers was used to strengthen the eyes and was so potent that the writers of old believed that merely to behold the flowers growing would have the same effect.

The bloom was also thought to resemble a dolphin in form, the Greek word for Larkspur being *Delphinion*, a dolphin. There are two forms of the annual larkspur, *D. consolida*, the Branching Larkspur which grows to a height of 2 ft. and *D. ajacis*, the parent of the single-stemmed forms. From *D. consolida* the modern Imperial-flowered strains have been evolved. The plant was mentioned by Thomas Tusser in 1575, who also noted *D. ajacis*, not a native plant but one which had become established in the cornfields of southern England about that time. Gerard called it the Wild Larkspure, to distinguish it from our native form, by then a garden plant. *D. ajacis* was so called on account of it being supposed to have sprung from the blood of Ajax, a story also associated with the hyacinth. Indeed, this form of Larkspur is today known as the Hyacinth-flowered and may have been named because of its likeness to that flower.

Parkinson, writing in 1629 said of the larkspur, "the most usual name with us is Delphinium but whether it be the true Delphinium or the Poet's Hyacinth or the Flower of Ajax, another place is fitter to discuss than this". He described the leaves as being "finely cut, like those of Fennell" and tells us that, "the root perishes every year . . . raising itself from the seed sown in the springtime", thus confirming its annual habit.

By the mid-seventeenth century, *D. ajacis* was to be found bearing bloom in nine colours and in both the single and double forms. Sir Thomas Hanmer writing at that time said, ". . . (they) have stalks so thick with flowers that the stalks are not to be seen."

Growing to heights varying from 12 ins. to nearly 6 ft., the larkspurs are valuable to use to fill in gaps left in the border by the failure of perennial plants whilst it is one of the most useful of all plants to provide cut flowers for home decoration. For this purpose, sow the seed thinly in drills for the seedlings will not readily transplant. For early bloom, a sowing should be made during September, treating the plant as a biennial, with another sowing to be made early in spring and thinning the seedlings to 6 ins. apart. An open sunny situation should be selected.

VARIETIES

DWARF DOUBLE-HYACINTH-FLOWERED. (12 ins.). Evolved from *D. ajacis*, it comes early into bloom, the spikes being short and sturdy, very like a hyacinth and without the branching habit of the *D. consolida* varieties.

GIANT IMPERIAL (3 to 4 ft.) the florets are larger than those of the other forms whilst it branches from the base, providing long stems for cut flowers. Outstanding varieties are Miss California, salmon-pink and Dazzler, rosy-scarlet.

DIANTHUS BARBATUS Poet's Pink; Sweet William

Oeillet de Poëteit (*Dianthus barbatus*) it is called by the French, in the same way that the bunch-flowered Narcissus is known as the Poet's Narcissus. Its other name is Sweet William, possibly in honour of the Conqueror for as Phillips says, "it grows on the hills of Normandy, west of Dieppe but the flowers are scarcely larger than those of the

London Pride". Miss Alice Coats, however, believes that it may have been originally named Sweet St. William, commemorating St. William of Aquitaine and may have been introduced to our land at an early date possibly by Carthusian monks, along with *Dianthus carthusianorum*, its close relation and which is recorded as being amongst those plants originally used to beautify the gardens of Hampton Court.

The first to mention *D. barbatus*, so named from the hairy scales on the calyx was Dr. Rembertus Dodoens, who in 1554 when physician to the Emperor Charles V of Germany, published his *New Herbal or History of Plants*. This was later translated by Henry Lyte (of Lytes Cary Manor) in 1578, a copy of which made £500 when auctioned at Christie's sales room on November 2nd, 1966. In the book, the plant is called "colmenier", col being an ancient word meaning "embrace", possibly used here as the flowers could be said to be "embraced" by those who wore them close to their bosoms, being decorative and sweetly scented.

As Turner (1568) makes no mention of the plant, we may infer that it was not widely grown at that time and may even have been lost and reintroduced at a later date. Gerard, however, speaks of it as a common flower and for the first time refers to it as the Sweet William (maybe in honour of his friend and neighbour William Shakespeare). He says, "these plants are not used either in mete or medicine but esteemed for their beauty, to deck up gardens and the bosoms of the beautiful."

During the early eighteenth century the plant was taken up by the weavers of Paisley, along with the laced pink and achieved the status of a florists' flower. It is surprising that with the rich clove perfume we are accustomed to enjoy with the modern Pink Beauty strain, Phillips should write in 1829, that "its want of perfume unfits it for the salon".

Though perennial, the plant is usually treated as a biennial for it is so readily raised from seed sown in drills or where it is to bloom, in June. It will come into bloom in just twelve months. It enjoys a friable soil, enriched with some lime rubble and requires an open, sunny situation.

STRAINS

AURICULA-EYED. The blooms are similar to those of the show auricula or Gold Laced Polyanthus with a ground colour of crimson-scarlet or pink, edged with white and with a white eye.

DUNNETT'S CRIMSON. A magnificent Sweet William, the blooms being of deepest fiery crimson with a sheen of black whilst the foliage is also crimson.

DWARF RED MONARCH. It is an annual and should be sown in March where it is to bloom, or in boxes under glass for planting out in April. It grows 6 to 8 ins. tall and throughout summer bears trusses of brilliant scarlet.

PINK BEAUTY. The large trusses are held on 15-in. stems and are of soft pink, flushed with salmon. The market grower's favourite.

SCARLET BEAUTY. The scarlet counterpart of Pink Beauty and one of the brightest flowers of the early summer garden.

DIANTHUS CARYOPHYLLUS   Carnation; Pink
A genus of about 100 species of annual or perennial plants with narrow grass-like glaucous foliage and bearing their flowers either solitary or in terminal clusters. They are mostly of the N. temp. regions, able to survive intense cold and a number of species and varieties bear clove-scented flowers.

The Athenians held the plant in so great esteem that they named it Dianthos, Flower of Jove, awarding it the highest honour. It was the chief flower used to make garlands and coronets, hence its early English name of "coronation" from which the name carnation is a derivative.

It was the opinion of Canon Ellacombe, the Victorian authority on the history of plants, that *Dianthus caryophyllus*, a native of southern Europe, reached England with the Norman invasion, possibly attached to stones imported from northern France (Caen) by the Conqueror for the erection of castles and houses of worship. Canon Ellacombe reported having seen it in bloom in 1874, on the walls of the Conqueror's Castle of Falaise (where he was born) and in England it is to be seen to this day, growing on the walls of the castles of Dover and Rochester in Kent, both built by the Normans and on the walls of Fountains Abbey in Yorkshire where it blooms early in July. Indeed, several of the writers of old believed its country name of "Gillyflower" to be derived from "July-flower". Herrick was of this opinion:

> A lovely July flower
> That one rude wind or ruffling shower
> Will force from hence and in an hour.

Sir Francis Bacon also wrote that "in July come gillyflowers of all varieties . . ." from which it would appear that the reference was to double pinks or carnations (which Gerard called the Great Double Carnation) rather than to single pinks for he suggests growing the pink for earlier flowering. In his essay "Of Gardens" he wrote that in May and June "come pinks of all sorts especially the blush pink", with possibly in mind *D. plumarius*, parent of the hybrid pinks or *D. caesius*, a native plant, both of which bloom early and were known to gardeners of the time.

With the scent of the flowers resembling the perfume of the clove, the plant was called by the French "giroflier" which name accompanied the plant to England with the Norman invasion. Whether it was *D. caryophyllus* or *P. plumarius* to which Chaucer alluded in the Prologue to the *Canterbury Tales* (begun in 1386) is uncertain but all those plants bearing clove-scented flowers were at the time much in demand to flavour wine (and ale) possibly a French custom and pinks, known as sops-in-wine, were to be found until the end of the sixteenth century, growing in tavern gardens of which Chaucer makes mention:

> And many a clove gilofre,
> And notemuge to put in ale,
> Whether it be moiste or stale . . .

Chaucer's spelling of the word differs but little from the early French whilst the poet Shelton, wrote of "The Ielofer amyable". By Shakespeare's time, it had become "gillovor" or "gillyflower", the word being used for all clove-scented flowers, such as the Queen's Gillyflower (*Hesperis matronis*) and the Stock Gillyflower.

D. caryophyllus takes its botanical name meaning "nut-leaved" from the name of the Clove tree, *Caryophyllus aromaticus*, not because its grass-like leaves have any resemblance to those of the clove tree but because the clove scent of the flowers resembled the fragrance of the fruits of that tree.

By Tudor times, there would appear to be two groups of dianthus, those with single flowers, known as the pinks and descended from *D. plumarius* and those bearing double (or semi-double) flowers, offspring of *D. caryophyllus*, both species reaching England at possibly the same time with the Norman invasion or shortly afterwards.

In the New Herbal of 1578, Lyte distinguished between the two forms by his use of the word "coronations" and of "the small feathered Gillofers, known as Pynkes, Soppes-in-Wine and small Honesties". Writing at the same time, the poet Spenser separates the two in his lines from *The Shepherd's Calendar*:

> Bring hither the pincke and purple cullambine,
> With Gilleflowres;
> Bring Coronations and Sops-in-wine,
> Worn of paramours.

Spenser here also differentiates between the pink, the carnation and sops-in-wine which may be a distinctive form of the dianthus (possibly a small semi-double pink) for it is doubtful whether the earlier reference to "the pinke and purple cullambine" really meant Columbines of pink and purple colouring as the word "pink" signifying the particular colour was not introduced into the English language until late in the eighteenth century. Before that, the colour we now call "pink" was always described as "flesh" or "blush" or even "carnation" as in Byron's line:

> Carnation'd like a sleeping infant's cheek.

The earliest carnations (or semi-double pinks) bore flowers of cut flesh colour which may be described as deep "pink" and alluded to in *Henry V* when in Mistress Quickly's house in Eastcheap, the Boy says ". . . and (he) said they were devils incarnate". To which Mistress Quickly replies: " 'A could never abide carnation; 'twas a colour he (the dead Falstaff) never liked."

But to the Elizabethan poet Shenstone, both the colour and the perfume of the carnation was most agreeable:

> Let yon admired carnation own,
> Not all was meant for raiment, or for food
> Not all for needful use alone;
> There, while the seeds of future blossoms dwell,
> 'Tis colour'd for the sight, perfumed to please the smell.

The Roman historian Pliny has told of how the clove-scented pink was discovered in Spain during the reign of the Emperor Augustus when it received considerable attention in Rome to flavour wine. The plant had been found in that part of Spain bordering the Bay of Biscay, then inhabited by the warlike Cantabri after whom the plant was originally named. As late as the mid-sixteenth century, Dr. William Turner, a close friend of Bishops Latimer and Ridley and himself Dean of Wells, called the pink the *Cantabrica gelouer* in his

New Herball, the first part of which was dedicated to Queen Elizabeth.

John Tradescant reported that on several islands in the Mediterranean he found the clove-scented pink "growing naturall, of the best sort we have in Ingland, with the edges of the leaves (petals) deeply cut. . . ." More recently, Mr. Will Ingwersen reported having seen *D. plumarius* growing about the limestone rocks on the western coast of Corsica where its bright pink flowers seen against the dark rocks created a lasting impression with him.

In his *Herbal* (1597), Gerard distinguishes (the name Dianthus was not in use until Linnaeus compiled his binomial system of plant classification) between the "Carnation Gilloflower (the Great Double Carnation) and the "Clove (or Pink) Gilloflower" from which it would appear that by then, the carnations had not the same clove perfume as the pinks, though of the Great Double Carnation, Gerard said its flowers "had an excellent sweet smell" though maybe not of cloves.

That there were many different species and varieties is confirmed by Gerard who said: "A great and large volume would not suffice to write of every one at large . . . and every year every climate and every country bringeth forth new sorts . . ."

Gerard also distinguishes between the "wild (native) Gilloflowers" as they had smaller flowers than the "Carnations and Clove Gilloflowers". Earlier, Tusser had written of "pinks of all sorts" and at a later date, Milton wrote of "the white pink", possibly the Old Fringed and still obtainable, to be included amongst other flowers to strew over the hearse of Lycidas.

That there were at the time, "streaked gillyflowers" is confirmed both by Shakespeare and in the *New Book of Flowers* by Maria Merian, a copy of which is in the British Museum and in which there is a colour illustration which shows the "streaked gillyflowers" much as we know the flaked carnations of today.

In *A Winter's Tale*, which Shakespeare wrote in lighter vein, upon his return to take up residence at his home, New Place in Stratford-on-Avon in the spring of 1611, Perdita speaks of

> "The fairest flowers o' the season
> Are our Carnations and streak'd Gillyflowers."

Later in the play Polixenes exhorts Perdita to "make your garden rich in gillyvors".

At the time of Shakespeare's death, carnations and pinks had become amongst the most popular of all garden plants. Gerard wrote that ". . . they are well known to most, if not to all" and William Lawson in *The Country Housewife's Garden* (1618) said, "I may well call them the king of flowers, except the rose."

Possibly for their hardiness were they so popular and though native of south and eastern Europe, quickly became acclimatized to English gardens for which they were most suitable for the small "knots" of the time. John Fletcher has commented on their hardiness:

> Hide, O hide, those hills of snow
> Which thy frozen bosom bears,
> On whose tops the pinks that grow
> Are of those that April weares.

By the beginning of the seventeenth century, the pink and carnation had become very popular indeed. Parkinson writing shortly after Shakespeare's death said, "What shall I say to the Queene of delight and of flowers, carnations and gillyflowers, whose bravery (hardiness), variety and sweete smell joyned together, tyeth every ones affection with equal earnestness both to like and to have them?" Writing about the same time, Gervase Markham in *The English Husbandman* (1613) said, "Gilliflowers are of all other flowers, most sweet and delicate" and in *The Complete Gardener's Practice* (1664), Stephen Blake wrote, "Carnation gilliflowers for beauty and delicate smell and excellent properties, deserve letters of gold." "I wonder that Solomon did not write of this flower when he compared his spouse to the Lily-of-the-valley".

Exactly when the dianthus received it name "pink" is not known. Mr. Stanley B. Whitehead believes the name to be a derivation of the Celtic "pic" meaning peak, possibly the "peak of perfection" amongst flowers; on the other hand, Mr. L. J. Brimble in his *Flowers of Britain* suggests the name was obtained from the verb "to pink" or "to pierce", indicating the extremely serrated petals of *D. plumarius* and its offspring, the Old Fringed Pink and Mrs. Sinkins. Again, it has been suggested that the name is from Pinksten, German for Pentecost, for it is at this time when the pink comes into bloom, a late Whitsuntide and on the Continent the plant is known as the Whitsun Gillyflower.

The native pinks of the British Isles remained very much neglected, until Parkinson (1629) said that ". . . some grow upright like gilly-flowers or spreading over the ground". It was from the so-called

Matted Pink, *D. caesius* that the modern Alpine Allwoodii were evolved and which bear scented flowers. During the reign of Charles I, a number of pinks were introduced from France by Queen Henrietta Maria, for the pink is said to have been her favourite flower. But by the time of the Restoration, John Rea in his *Flora* remarked that "there were few carnations to be found in any of our gardens". However, in a later edition of his work he lists 360 varieties of carnation and pink and wrote:

> "But yet if 'ask and have' were in my power,
> Next to the Rose, give me the Gillyflower."

The early nineteenth century was perhaps the Golden Age of the pink, and in *The Flower Garden* (1839) M'Intosh, has listed 192 varieties, including several which were introduced by such well-known florists of that time including Barlow, Hogg and Keen. M'Intosh mentions that "it is pre-eminently the cottager's flower as it takes less care and skill to cultivate than the carnation and other florist's flowers".

Thomas Hogg, a nurseryman of Paddington Green, writing in 1822, lists 121 varieties in his *Catalogue of Pinks*, and in addition, a dozen Scottish pinks, one of which had the charming name of Robertson's Gentle Shepherd. Another of the old pinks was called Kilner's Cricketer. It was raised in Yorkshire as one would imagine when recalling those stout-hearted cricketers the late Norman and Roy Kilner. That there must have been many varieties of the pink during Hogg's time is obvious in reading the introduction to his Catalogue of Pinks for he says, ". . . and if I have not published a numerous list, let it be remembered that quality, in respect to flowers, is always preferable to quantity." And he then lists 121 varieties!

In the same way that the miners of Yorkshire and Derbyshire took up the culture of the pansy, and the cotton workers of Lancashire devoted their hours of leisure to the Show auricula, so did the weavers of Paisley, near Glasgow, toil to reproduce the intricate oriental patterns of their shawls on the flowers of the pink.

The object of the Paisley weavers was to impart the characteristic of rounded or smooth edges to the flowers, thereby eliminating the serrated petal edges of *D. plumarius*. At the outer edge of the petals was to be a band of black, with which colouring the blooms were also marked at the centre. The variety was recognized by the degree of black about the bloom.

The plants must be given an open, sunny situation for on no account will they tolerate shade. Here again the plants are valuable in that they are quite happy in a completely exposed situation, where strong winds are experienced and the direct rays of the sun beat down on them, drying out the soil but without causing them the slightest distress even during long periods of drought. Where the garden is exposed, the first choice of flowering plants should be members of the Dianthus family.

The gardeners of former times, without exception, made mention of the pink's liking for an open, sunny situation, though strangely they make no mention of the plant's liking for a soil containing an abundance of lime. Large quantities of manure as for auriculas and polyanthus was the fare for pinks a hundred years ago, and it is surprising that plants flourished under such conditions, for manure encouraged "soft" growth and disease. Perhaps the Laced pinks of Scotland were lost because of this treatment.

In *A Winter's Tale*, Polixenes describing the art of grafting fruit trees to Perdita, also exhorts her "to make (her) garden rich in gillyvors" but Perdita, not liking the streaked gillyflowers replies:

"I'll not put
The dibble in earth to set one slip of them."

In the British Museum copy of the *New Book of Flowers* "diligently produced for the enjoyment, usefulness and service of all connoisseurs of the arts of the year 1680" the coloured illustration of the streaked pinks is almost indistinguishable from the flaked carnations and enable one to appreciate Shakespeare's reference to them in derogatory terms. For all that, they were extremely interesting.

Layering is done during July and August, to allow the shoots to root before the arrival of the frosts and June is not a satisfactory month as it is usually too dry. Unflowered shoots are selected close to the ground around the outside of the plant and where their stems may be brought into contact with the soil without severing them. First, the lower leaves are removed, then a strong joint immediately below is selected. About 1 inch below the joint, a cut is made into the stem in an upwards direction. The shoot will be partly held to the main plant whilst the tongue is opened to the joint to allow a small stone to be inserted to prevent it from closing. The partly severed shoot is then pressed into the soil, just covering the joint and is held in position by a layering pin. The soil, into which some peat should have been added, must be kept comfortably moist when rooting will take place within a month. The shoot is then severed from the main plant and set out in the open ground or in a pot where it remains throughout winter. "For my part," wrote William Cobbett, "as a thing to keep and not to sell . . . I hesitate not a moment to prefer the plant of a fine carnation to a gold watch set with diamonds."

The Carnation too, possibly reached its peak of popularity during the early years of the nineteenth century, when the florists, usually the weavers of Lancashire and Yorkshire and of Paisley, took up their culture as a hobby together with the auricula, the gold-laced polyanthus and the laced pink. Carnations were then divided into three main classes, Flakes, Bizarres and Picotees. The Flakes were of a single colour, with the flaky stripes going right through the petals. The Bizarres were of two colours, variegated in irregular stripes, whilst the Picotees had a white ground, edged with red, rose or purple. It is said that the best collection of Picotees in England was that at Windsor Castle during the time of Queen Adelaide, consort of William IV, who gave her name to the Australian city. According to the rules then formulated for the exhibiting of a carnation, "the stem should be strong and tall, not less than 30 ins. and not more than 45 ins. long, whilst the bloom should be at least 3 ins. in diameter. The petals should be long, broad and substantial, particularly those of the outer circle."

Shakespeare used the term "slips" which is used to this day when speaking of the propagation of carnations and pinks, though carnations are also increased by layering. "Slips" are unflowered shoots carefully pulled away from the main stems so that they come away with a short piece of stem attached and which is known as a "heel". It will enable the shoot to root more quickly, a "tip" which Shakespeare may possibly have learned from Gerard or one of the other famous gardeners when in London.

SPECIES AND VARIETIES

D. caryophyllus. A native of southern Europe it is also found on several islands of the Mediterranean, growing amongst rocky limestone formations and is a much-branched perennial growing up to 2 ft. tall with linear awl-shaped glaucous leaves 4 to 5 ins. long. It comes into bloom towards the end of June, its flesh-pink flowers measuring 1½ in. across with broad petals, slightly toothed. From this plant have been raised over the years many varieties of hardy garden habit which are known as Hardy Border Carnations, a number of which carry the rich clove perfume of the parent. Amongst these may be included the Old Crimson Clove, of which Parkinson said, "none will give so gallant a tincture to syrup". No perfume is present in the orange and yellow flowering varieties. This species is also the parent of the Perpetual Flowering Carnation.

Hardy Border Carnations with Clove Perfume

CORAL CLOVE. The blooms are of an unusual shade of coral-red, of outstanding substance and shape and with the clove perfume developed to a marked degree.

CRYSTAL CLOVE. A delightful companion for Scarlet Fragrance as it is equally free-flowering. The medium-sized blooms being of clearest white with pronounced clove perfume.

DONN'S CLOVE. It bears a profusion of medium-sized bloom of perfect form and with outstanding clove perfume.

EGLANTINE CLOVE. A lovely old variety, still growing strong and healthy and bearing flowers of a unique shade of salmon-rose. Also known as Rose Eglantine.

EDENSIDE CLOVE. It has long been a premier winner on the show bench, the white blooms, edged and striped with maroon, having exquisite form and pronounced scent.

FENBOW'S NUTMEG CLOVE. It is one of the oldest garden plants still in cultivation dating from the fourteenth century, and may well be Chaucer's Sops-in-wine. It was re-discovered in 1960, by Mr. Sanderson of Leeds, growing in the garden of Colonel Fenbow in whose family are preserved records to say that the Nutmeg Clove was growing in the same garden in 1652, planted there by a certain Julian Fenbow to impart its powerful nutmeg scent to flavour wines. It bears a small but fully double flower of crimson-maroon with slightly feathered petals and measures little more than 1 inch across. The leaves are blue-green and upright.

NEYRON CLOVE. A charming variety bearing a profusion of medium-sized blooms which remain fresh when cut longer than any other variety and which are of a lovely shade of rose-neyron.

OAKFIELD CLOVE. An old variety, still the finest crimson border exceptional in the rich glowing colour and the pronounced clove scent of its bloom.

PINK CLOVE. The late Mr. Montagu Allwood who did so much for the dianthus, considered this to be the most fragrant of all his borders, whilst the large blooms are of a lovely shade of soft powder pink.

ROBIN THAIN. A superb variety, the white blooms being striped with crimson and they are deliciously scented.

D. plumarius. It is distributed throughout S. Europe as far east as the Caucasus. It has glaucous linear rough-edged leaves which it forms into compact hummocks and bears rich pink flowers on 9-in. stems. The petals are bearded and jagged whilst the flower diffuses a powerful clove scent. It received its name "plumarius" from Gerard, on account of its feathered petals and in his *Herbal*, he lists and illustrates twelve varieties which he calls "Wild Gilloflowers". They all bear single flowers as did almost all pinks up to the beginning of the eighteenth century. Of these that have survived from the sixteenth or early years of the seventeenth century, all bear single flowers with deeply serrated petals and all are deliciously scented. They bloom in June and early July.

Fourteenth-century Pinks

SOPS-IN-WINE. A plant of this name still survives and may well be the original of Chaucer's time for it is believed to have reached England during the early years of the fourteenth century, from a European monastery garden which is believed to be situated near Orleans. It flourishes in cottage gardens in Berkshire where it is still called by its ancient name. The white flower is extremely fringed and has a black central zone whilst its perfume resembles that of the Old Nutmeg Clove Carnation which may have reached England at about the same time.

Fifteenth-century Pinks

CAESAR'S MANTLE. It is the Bloody Pink of early Tudor and Elizabethan times and may well date from the end of the fifteenth century. It bears a flower larger than a half-crown, of a dark blood-red colour, covered in grape-like "bloom". The crimson-red becomes almost black at the centre whilst the petals are deeply toothed. It has a powerful clove scent.

Sixteenth-century Pinks

FOUNTAINS ABBEY. It resembles the equally old Queen of Sheba in appearance, the flowers being less than 1 inch diameter but they are semi-double. The petals are beautifully fringed whilst the black lacing on a white ground is the equal of the old Scottish pinks. To my knowledge it has no connection with the famous abbey.

NONSUCH. It is of "Painted Lady" type and is believed to have been discovered in the gardens of Henry VIII's palace of Nonsuch though it may have received its name from its great beauty. The petals are more deeply fringed than others of this type whilst the ground colour is pink with ruby-red flashes.

OLD MAN'S HEAD. Dating from the early seventeenth or late sixteenth century and rediscovered in a N. Yorkshire garden. It is a sturdy grower bearing white semi-double flowers, curiously spotted and splashed with purple and with a powerful clove perfume.

PAINTED LADY. It was rediscovered in 1950, growing in a Monmouthshire garden and resembles in all characteristics an illustration of "Ye Gallant's Fayre Ladye" pink which appears in a book of garden flowers of the first year of James I's reign. It bears a bloom only one inch across and is semi-double with fringed petals which are white, flashed with purple. In his book *Old Carnations and Pinks*, Rev. Oscar Moreton tells that it grows in his garden at Chipping Norton and has the "strongest and sweetest clove scent of all".

QUEEN OF SHEBA. A pink of the "Painted Lady" type, bearing single flowers 1 inch across, with neat serrated petals which are laced with magenta-purple on a white ground. Of the late Elizabethan era, either late sixteenth or early seventeenth century.

UNIQUE. Of the same age as those surviving members of the "Painted Lady" type. The flowers are single and of outstanding beauty, the ground colour being red and covered all over with flashes of black and pink.

Seventeenth-century Pinks

BAT'S DOUBLE RED. It is a pink which has been growing in the Botanical Gardens at Oxford since the very end of the seventeenth century and is believed to be that raised by a Thomas Bat in London and until 1950, believed to be lost. It has blue-green foliage and bears flowers with bluntly toothed petals of rich ruby red over a long period.

BRIDAL VEIL. One of the old fringed pinks, possibly of the late seventeenth century, the double blooms of ice white, having a crimson patch at the base of each petal. They are heavily scented.

FIMBRIATA. Its origin is lost in antiquity but it is most likely a late

Elizabethan pink, the creamy-white flowers with their fringed petals having pronounced perfume.

GREEN EYE. Also Charles Musgrave or Musgrave's Pink, named by the late Mr. George Allwood after the owner of the cottage garden where it was rediscovered. It is said to be identical with plants which have been growing in the Palace garden at Wells since the end of the seventeenth century. The blooms are single, of 1½-in. diameter and are of purest white, with slightly fringed petals which overlap and they have a conspicuous green eye or zone. The blooms have outstanding fragrance.

OLD FRINGED. It is one of the oldest pinks in cultivation, most likely grown in gardens of the late Elizabethan period. It is a delightful plant of dwarf, compact habit, and bearing semi-double flowers of purest white with extremely fringed petals and of exquisite clove perfume. The seed-bearing parent of the first *allwoodii* pink.

PHEASANT EYE. One of several Pinks surviving from the early seventeenth century though each of them may be older. It is to be found in both the single and semi-double form with the petals deeply fringed whilst the ground colour is white or blush, with a conspicuous purple-brown "eye" at the centre. Occasionally the flowers have lacing of the same colour.

Eighteenth-century Pinks

BEVERLEY PINK. It was found in a cottage garden of a Mr. Williams at Beverley where it had grown since at least early in the century. The small semi-double blooms of crimson-red are flaked with white and yellow and have the true clove perfume. It was first noted by Miss Gladwin who described it in the Journal of the Royal Horticultural Society.

CHELSEA PINK. Also Little Old Lady. It was to be found in Chelsea gardens early in the century. It is like a Painted Lady, with glorious perfume, the small double flowers of crimson-red being edged and splashed with white.

GLORIOSA. An old Scottish pink, possibly having a carnation for one parent for the flowers are of beautiful shape and fully double, being of pale pink colouring with a crimson eye and having outstanding fragrance.

INCHMERY. It makes a neat compact plant and bears a profusion of double flowers which open flat without splitting their calyces and are of an attractive shade of bright clear pink which are a pleasing foil for the silvery foliage. It has outstanding perfume, "as heady as that of Mrs. Sinkins but not so cloying", wrote Mr. Ingwersen.

MONTROSE PINK. Also the Cockenzie Pink for it was discovered in the Scottish fishing village of that name and was found growing in the garden of Montrose House where it had been since early in the century. It is still listed by Forbes of Hawick and is a beauty, growing 9 in. tall and bearing on stiff stems, fully double blooms of brilliant carmine-pink.

Nineteenth-century Pinks

AVOCA PURPLE. It may be very much older for it is to be found in many Co. Wicklow cottage gardens. It bears a small purple flower, streaked with lines of darker purple and it is sweetly scented.

BLACK PRINCE. An old Irish variety now rarely seen and somewhat resembling Sops-in-Wine, its semi-double flowers being white with a large black centre or eye and with similar nutmeg scent.

EARL OF ESSEX. One of these much loved of garden pinks which always splits its calyx but is always welcomed in the garden. The clear rose-pink blooms with their fringed petals have a small dark zone and sweet perfume.

EMILIE PARÉ. One of the truly outstanding pinks, raised in 1840 in Orleans, France, by André Paré, probably having the Sweet William for one parent for it bears its double salmon-pink flowers in clusters and will survive only a few years so that it should be propagated annually.

LINCOLNSHIRE LASS. It has been known since the beginning of the century and may be much older. The flowers are of an uninteresting flesh colour but the delicious scent makes it worthy of cultivation.

MRS. SINKINS. It was raised by a Mr. Sinkins, Master of Slough Workhouse and named after his wife. The plant, which has the distinction of being incorporated in the Arms of the Borough of Slough, was introduced by the Slough nurseryman, Charles Turner, one of the great florists of the time and who had introduced the Cox's Orange Pippin apple to commerce. It is a pink of great character, its large white cabbage-like blooms, borne on 12-in. stems above a mat of silvery-green foliage, possessing an almost overpowering perfume.

NAPOLEON III. Raised by André Paré in Orleans in 1840 from a Sweet William crossing and like Emilie Paré will flower itself to death in two years. It bears on 10-in. stems, large heads of double clove-scented flowers of a striking scarlet-cerise colour.

PADDINGTON. It was raised about 1820 by Thomas Hogg, a nursery-man of that part of London on which now stands Paddington Station. Of dwarf habit, its double pink blooms have serrated edges and are richly scented.

ROSE DE MAI. It may be traced back to the beginning of the century and it is a beauty, the double blooms being of a lovely shade of creamy-mauve with fringed petals and glorious perfume.

RUTH FISCHER. Dating from the end of the century, it is a most attractive variety of compact habit and bears small fully double flowers of purest white with a rich, sweet perfume.

SAM BARLOW. At one time it was to be found in every cottage garden though is now rarely seen. Like Mrs. Sinkins and so many of the old double pinks it splits its calyx but blooms in profusion, its white flowers having a maroon blotch at the centre and with a penetrating clove perfume.

WHITE LADIES. To the grower of cut flowers, it is with Scabious, Clive Greaves, the most profitable of all plants, bearing its sweetly scented blooms of purest white throughout the summer and they do not split their calyces. Obviously a variety of D. plumarius for it has the same fringed petals, it is a plant of neat habit and is tolerant of all conditions.

Twentieth-century Pinks

DUSKY. The result of back crossing the Old Fringed pink with an Allwoodii seedling and it is free and perpetual flowering. The blooms have fringed petals and are of a lovely shade of dusky-pink.

ENID ANDERSON. A most striking pink, its semi-double clove-scented flowers of glowing crimson being enhanced by the silver-grey leaves.

FRECKLES. An Imperial pink, it bears a double bloom of unusual colouring, being dull salmon-pink flecked with red and with a penetrating spicy scent.

GUSFORD. An outstanding pink, bearing large double blooms of rosy-pink on 12-in. stems and which are deliciously scented.

HASLEMERE. Raised at the Ipswich nurseries of Thompson and Morgan, the large fragrant double flowers have a deep chocolate centre and fringed petals.

ICE QUEEN. A "sport" from Dusky, it bears a highly scented double bloom of icy white which does not burst its calyx and which has fringed petals.

LILAC TIME. Raised by Mr. C. H. Fielder of the Lindabruce Nurseries, Lancing, it is an Imperial pink and bears fully double blooms of a lovely shade of lilac-pink with a powerful scent.

MISS CORRY. Raised in Holland, it bears large double blooms of richest wine-red with the true clove perfume.

Laced Pinks

Several are thought to have survived from the time of their greatest glory in Scotland and from them, possibly re-named, a number of scented laced pinks were raised by the Allwood Brothers between the two world wars. They have the habit of the Allwoodii pinks and from them Mr. F. R. McQuown continued the programme in raising a number of laced pinks to which he gave the London prefix. They had as parents, the laced Allwoodii, the Herbertii pinks and perpetual flowering carnations.

CHARITY. The habit is short and tufted whilst the plant is free flowering. The semi-double blooms have a white ground with clearly defined lacing of bright crimson.

FAITH. The first of the laced Allwoodii (1946). The blooms are small but fully double with the petals broad and fringed. The ground colour is rosy-mauve with lacing of cardinal-red.

JOHN BALL. Raised and introduced by Turners of Slough about 1880. The bloom is large and double with a white ground and lacing and zoning of velvet-purple.

LONDON SUPERB. The large double blooms have a pale pink ground and are laced with purple. The fringed petals and perfume give it the old world charm.

VICTORIAN. A laced pink of early Victorian times bearing huge blooms which often burst their calyx but is a most attractive variety. The white ground is zoned and laced with chocolate.

WILLIAM BROWNHILL. It dates from about 1780 and is one of the best of the laced pinks, the beautifully formed blooms being white, laced and zoned with maroon and they do not burst their calyces.

Allwoodii

The result of crossing the Old Fringed pink, *D. plumarius* with the Perpetual Flowering carnation. Several varieties have a pronounced perfume whilst the plants are perpetual flowering, remaining in bloom from early June until September.

ANNE. The blooms are held above the foliage on 12-in. stems and are double, and of a lovely shade of salmon-pink.

BLANCHE. Very free flowering, the double blooms are of purest white with deeply fringed petals.

DORIS. The double blooms of salmon-pink with a darker eye are sweetly scented and are of ideal exhibition form.

MARY. The first Allwoodii, bearing double blooms of lavender-pink, zoned with maroon and with a delicate sweet perfume.

MONTY. The blooms are as large as a five-shilling piece and are of solferino-purple, zoned with chocolate.

WILLIAM. One of the best of all white pinks with broad petals and outstanding clove perfume.

WINSTON. The large double blooms are of bright crimson, borne in profusion and with outstanding clove perfume.

Show Pinks

The result of a cross between the Allwoodii and Herbertii pinks. The plants have a habit more vigorous than either parent and bear a refined bloom, like a border carnation.

SHOW ARISTOCRAT. The plant has beautiful silver foliage and bears sweetly scented double blooms of flesh-pink with a deeper pink eye.

SHOW CLOVE. The rose-pink bloom is smaller than usual in this group but it carries the true clove perfume.

SHOW EXQUISITE. The bloom is almost as large as a Malmaison carnation and of a lovely shade of soft pink with a sweet perfume, with spicy undertones.

Hybrid Alpine Pinks

They have been evolved through the years by crossing *D. allwoodii* with *D. alpinus* and *D. erinarius* and with *D. caesius* and *D. squarrosus*, all of which bear scented flowers. They range in height from 3 to 6 ins. and are delightful plants for the trough or alpine garden.

ELIZABETH. A real treasure for the alpine garden, with erect silvery-green foliage and bearing, on a 4-in. stem a tiny double bloom of dusky pink with a brown centre. The scent diffused by so tiny a flower is truly remarkable.

ERNEST BALLARD. Raised at the Old Court Nurseries, Malvern, it forms a dense prostrate mat of grey foliage above which are borne on stiff stems, double flowers of crimson-red which have the old clove perfume.

Plate 7   Double Primrose, Madame Pompadour

Plate 8   Murray's Laced Pink

GRACE MATHER. A real gem for the trough garden forming a prostrate mat of neat blue-green foliage and bearing, on 5-in. stems,
large double blooms of deep salmon-pink.

MARS. One of the 'great' plants of the alpine garden, forming a
dense tuft of silvery-grey above which it bears bright crimson-red
flowers with the true clove perfume.

MISS SINKINS. A tiny replica of the more robust Mrs. Sinkins and
found in a garden at Henfield, Sussex. The heavily fringed blooms of
purest white have a delicious perfume.

NYEWOOD'S CREAM. A delightful plant forming a hummock of grey-
green above which it bears scented flowers of Jersey cream.

DICENTRA SPECTABILIS   Ladies' Heart; Ladies' Locket
Though it has been a favourite of the cottage garden for more than a
century, and has more country names than any other plant, it was
not introduced until 1846 when Robert Fortune found it on the Isle
of Chusan. Within a few years it was to be found in almost every
cottage garden bearing its drooping heart-shaped flowers from early
April until the end of June. From the shape of its flower, it was also
known as Ladies' Locket.

The plant enjoys a cool, leafy soil and partial shade. It also likes the
company of other plants and once established should never be disturbed. It is not completely hardy in the British Isles, but ashes
heaped about its crown in autumn should provide it with all the
protection it requires and even in an exposed garden it will rarely
perish.

DICTAMNUS FRAXINELLA   Burning Bush; Dittany
It was named *fraxinella* because its leaves resemble those of the ash
tree and it is a most interesting plant, being completely hardy. A
native of S. Europe, it is probably the bush that "burned with fire"
mentioned in Exodus. Like all members of the order, the flowers
emit an orange-like fragrance and also exhale from rusty-coloured
glands an inflammable vapour which is particularly pronounced at
night. As with the buds of the Balsam Poplar, it is possible to set
alight the vapour if a match is held immediately above the flowers
on a calm evening, without causing any harm to the plant. When
the leaves are pressed, they emit the refreshing aromatic perfume of

balsam. Indeed, the whole plant is extremely resinous. Tournefort wrote, "The flowers and stalks are aromatic, balsamic and sweet," resembling the leaves and stems of rue when bruised.

Dictamnus fraxinella is a plant of great beauty, forming a dense bush 2 ft. tall and bearing, in mid-summer, racemes of pale purple flowers, veined with deeper purple. There is also a pure white form, *alba*.

The plant does not take kindly to root division and is best propagated from seed, sown when ripe towards the end of summer. It requires a light soil to be long living.

DIGITALIS PURPUREA   Foxglove

A plant native to the British Isles, it has been found growing in every cottage garden since earliest times. Abraham Cowley wrote:

> The Foxglove on fair Flora's hand is worn,
> Lest while she gathers flowers, she meets a thorn.

But from where it obtained its name, none would seem to know. Parkinson said that some call it "finger-flower", hence its name Digitalis for the flowers are similar in shape to the fingers (of gloves). The flowers of purple (or white) appear early in July on noble stems up to 5 ft. in length. When the flowers advance from the calyx, they are tightly closed by the four clefts of the corolla so that air cannot enter until the parts of fructification have reached maturity. The lips then open to form a trumpet and this remains for several days until the anthers have discharged their farina when the guard or trumpet falls away to enable the sun to ripen the seeds. Coleridge wrote:

> The Foxglove tall
> Sheds its loose purple bells . . .

The lower flowers open later and it may be early September before the stems have finished flowering.

From the plant the poisonous drug digitalin is obtained and which is used for diseases of the heart, causing diminution of the frequency of the beat of the heart. The ancients used the juice to treat external sores. Turner was the first English writer to mention the plant saying that it was "to be found in divers woodlands".

It is perennial but to be long lived the stems should be removed after bearing flowers for about six weeks and before the plants use up their energies in ripening seed. They are readily raised from seed sown in early summer. The young plants will be ready to move to their flowering position early the following spring when they will bloom in July. Plant 12 ins. apart at the back of the border, preferably in groups of three or four plants. They are happiest in the partial shade of other plants.

SPECIES AND VARIETIES

Digitalis ambigua. The Giant Yellow Foxglove of Central Europe, to be found in the alpine regions of Austria and Switzerland. It was growing in cottage gardens during Elizabethan times and is a most enduring plant, bearing spikes of palest yellow. It grows only to half the height of the native Foxglove and remains long in bloom. Plants may be obtained today at a relatively low cost and why it has almost disappeared from gardens is not understood.

D. lutea. Gerard grew it in his London garden and said, "we have in our gardens another sort thereof, which bringeth forth most pleasant yellow flowers and somewhat lesser than the common kind." It was called the Small Yellow Foxglove and as it grows to about the same height as *D. ambigua*, it could be that species of which Gerard was writing. It was to be found about shady mountainous places in northern Italy and Austria.

D. purpurea. The Common Foxglove of which the finest strain is Excelsior in which the florets or fingers completely encircle the stem whilst the enormous spikes are densely crowded with flowers of shades of purple, pink, crimson and white with the throats heavily spotted. They grow 6 ft. tall.

DODECATHEON   American Cowslip; Shooting Stars
A small genus of N. American plants of perennial habit which bear their flowers late in spring in nodding umbels. Like all members of the family, they require a cool loamy soil which does not dry out during summer and so a position of partial shade, such as an orchard, will be suitable. The soil should be enriched with either peat or leaf mould whilst the plants love a little well decayed manure in their diet.

The plants die back after flowering to re-appear the following March, the most suitable time for planting, lifting and dividing the rosettes.

D. meadia was the first species to reach Britain, arriving during the first years of the eighteenth century where it was to be found growing in the gardens of Fulham Palace, having been obtained by that famous collector of plants, Bishop Compton. The plant carries the name of the celebrated Dr. Richard Mead, in practice during the time of its introduction. In America its country name is Shooting Star, after the unusual and pretty reflexing of the petals which Henry Phillips likened to a half-opened parasol.

> Meadia's soft chains five suppliant beaux confess,
> And hand in hand the laughing belle adress;
> Alike to all she bows with wanton air,
> Rolls her dark eye and waves her golden hair.

In his *Flora Historica*, Phillips says that *D. meadia* is the only known species and it remained so until the introduction of *D. hendersoni* towards the middle of the nineteenth century. All the species carry the unmistakable scent of cloves, unusual in flowers which grow in shade.

SPECIES AND VARIETIES

Dodecatheon dentatum. A precious pet for the alpine garden growing less than 6 ins. tall and from the rosettes of brightest green arise dainty heads of purest white, smelling deliciously of cloves.

D. hendersoni. Its home is the Rocky Mountains and it grows 6 ins. tall with smooth leaves of emerald green and it blooms in April. The flowers are crimson with a yellow ring around the centre and though they emit the clove perfume, it is not so pronounced as with the other species.

D. integrifolium. Readily distinguished from *D. meadia* by its fleshy bracts, it grows only 4 ins. tall and bears cinnamon-scented flowers of outstanding beauty, being crimson, shaded white at the base and having orange shading in the throat.

D. meadia. Known as the Virginia Cowslip, it will attain a height of 15 ins. in a cool, moist soil, bearing tufts or large, erect toothed leaves above which arise tall scapes of rosy-purple or lilac-pink flowers with protruding yellow anthers. It is the most richly scented of all the species.

D. pauciflorum. It blooms later than the others, in June, bearing its flowers of rosy-lilac on 10-in. stems. The variety Redwings is a superb plant, bearing large heads of deepest crimson with a pronounced scent.

DORONICUM PLANTAGINEUM   Leopard's-Bane
This early intruder to our cottage gardens is native to Central
Europe where its poisonous roots were dried and mixed with meat to
rid the countryside of unwanted animals, hence its ancient name of
Leopard's-bane. There is a story that the famous botanist Conrad
Gesner killed himself by taking 2 drams of the root as an experiment
and Matthiolus, after whom the scented stock is named, gave it to a
dog which died immediately. Yet it is a much appreciated plant for it
blooms early in the year, during April and May when few other
border plants are in bloom and enjoying partial shade, will brighten
the darkest corner with its golden flowers for which reason it was to
be found in every cottage garden.

Gerard tells that it grew in his garden in Holborn whilst Lyte
speaks of it as "the aconite that killeth panthers" to distinguish it
from Wolf's-bane. Gerard also mentioned that a friend of his found it
growing wild in the hilly regions of Northumberland but it may have
at some time become naturalized, having possibly been introduced
by the Romans for the poisoning of wild animals.

It is a plant of extreme hardiness which will flourish in all soils. It
has stalked heart-shaped leaves and is covered in glandular hairs. On
the end of 3 ft. stems, solitary flowers are borne and which have
rayed petals of deep golden-yellow. A variety named after Rev.
Harpur Crewe is the best form whilst Spring Beauty is a most outstanding introduction, bearing fully double blooms of deepest yellow
on 20-in. stems.

ENDYMION (SCILLA)   Bluebell
During Elizabethan times the bluebell was known as the Harebell:
Milton's "sanguine flower inscribed with woe", which is also the
plant referred to in *Cymbeline*:

> Thou shalt not lack
> The flower that's like thy face, pale primrose, nor
> The azured harebell, like thy veins

Today the bluebell of Scotland is the flower called in England, the
harebell! It is *Endymion non-scripta* or *Scilla nutans* as it used to be
called botanically and is to be found throughout our Islands but
nowhere in greater numbers than through the counties of the
Midlands.

F. A. Homfray in *A Spring Fancy*, so well describes the feeling one enjoys upon seeing the first bluebells of Maytime:

> Comes not this sunshine at my heart
> In the still azure-sheeted dell
> From music; like the tears that start
> At some far wind-borne bell?
>
> Then let me follow Fancy's bent,
> And dream this little dream of spring
> That in the wafting of the scent
> I hear the bluebells ring

In the *Rape of Lucrece*, Shakespeare refers to "Her azured veins" and possibly as he was writing, the poet's thoughts were a hundred miles away, in those woods of oak and elm which are a feature of the Warwickshire countryside to this day. "The blue Harebells grow wilde in woods, copses and in the borders of fields everywhere through England," wrote Gerard, and adds, "the roots being beaten and applied with white wine, hinder or keep back the growth of hairs." Gerard called the flower the English Jacinth or Hyacinth and at that time, bluebells were known as Sea Onions for the bulbous roots were lifted with their foliage, if possible, and hung up on board ship in exactly the same way as we hang onions today, to use when required.

A writer of early Stuart times, said that the bluebell "is wholly used physically because we can perceive no pleasure from the sight of the flower".

Wood hyacinths or bluebells may be planted about the shrub border or beneath mature trees and will be perfectly content under pine and fir trees, revelling in the acid soil caused by the cones and needles over the years. They are also particularly attractive when seen flowering against a background of silver birch trees, planted in grass which need not be cut short until the leaves of the scillas have had time to die down in July. They also provide a pleasing display beneath ornamental cherries or in an orchard for they will bloom at the same time as the fruit trees whose pink and white blossom will present a delightful cover for the azure scene below.

Plant with them the Spanish hyacinths, like refined bluebells but also obtainable in shades of pink and blue and also white.

The bulbs should be planted 3 in. deep and 3 in. apart in autumn, setting them in circular groups of a dozen or more. They will multiply rapidly and will seed themselves when established.

Endymion campanulata. Syn. *Scilla hispanica.* Growing to a similar height as the English bluebell, the Spanish hyacinths appear on more sturdy stems above the strap-like foliage. The flower spikes are more densely packed with bells and like our native bluebell, they are sweetly scented.

alba. The bells of purest white are borne on 12-in. stems and prove a pleasing contrast to the others.

BLUE QUEEN. It bears large pyramidal spikes of clear porcelain-blue.

EXCELSIOR. It grows 18 ins. tall forming a dense spike, its large blue bells being of delicate lavender, veined with navy-blue.

FRANS HALS. Outstandingly beautiful with its large dangling bells of purest soft pink.

QUEEN OF THE PINKS. It bears its tightly packed spikes of enormous bells on 18 in. stems and the colour is dark rose-pink.

WHITE TRIUMPHATOR. The outstanding white with the huge bells borne on graceful arching stems.

EPILOBIUM HIRSUTUM Willow Herb

This native plant which Gerard described as growing in his garden with flowers "of an orient purple colour . . . very goodly to behold" has now almost vanished from cottage gardens because of its creeping roots which tend to invade the ground occupied by other plants. Growing 4 to 6 ft. in height with leaves like those of the willow, it bears purple-red flowers in long elegant spikes. Parkinson said that it was a useful plant to fill up spaces about the border and he named it *Chamaenerium flore delphinii* for the flower buds much resembled the buds of the larkspur.

In the 1st Edition of *The Gardener's Dictionary*, Miller advised planting in the border with its roots confined to a pot to prevent it from over-running nearby plants.

It is found in the wild state from northern Italy as far north as Lapland and was dedicated to St. Anthony whose favourite flower it was. In Lapland, its dried leaves were used to make a "tea".

ERANTHIS HYEMALIS Winter Aconite

A small genus of five or six species, native of S. Europe, of Siberia and N. Japan, being perennial tuberous plants of extreme hardiness.

They bloom from the early years of the New Year and continue, depending upon species, until May, bearing their golden chalices as the snow melts from them. They are suitable for planting beneath mature trees, where the summer shade prevents the grass from growing and where against the brown earth, the glowing bowls of gold, born on 2-in. stems present a delightful picture in the depth of winter. The flowers are backed by an attractive green ruff.

> . . . and winter aconite
> It's buttercup-like flowers which shut at night,
> With green leaf furling round its cup of gold.

Its name, Eranthis, means "flower of the earth". It is also known as the Winter Aconite, Thomas Noel's "gloom-gilding aconite" of which Gerard wrote, "it groweth upon the mountains in Germany; we have great quantities of it in our London gardens. It bloweth in January . . . yea, the colder the weather is and deeper the snow, the fairer and larger is the flower." Parkinson told us that "it groweth upon bare and naked rocks, which the Greeks call Aconas", hence its name of aconite. *E. hyemalis* was known to Lyte who mentioned it in his *New Herbal* in which he called it the Little Yellow Wolfsbane. "It seemeth well to be that aconitum the which Theophrastus hath spoken of and is now called *A. hyemale* because . . . in the winter it flowreth." Lyte was correct in calling it the Wolfs-bane for it is of the same plant order as the poisonous blue aconite. Plant the corms (tubers) 2 ins. apart and 2 ins. deep.

ERYNGIUM MARITIMUM Sea Holly

A genus of more than 100 species of thistle-like herbs with spiny leaves whilst the flower heads are surrounded by a whorl of spiny bracts. The eryngiums are perennial border plants of great beauty, delighting in a sandy soil for they are plants of the seaside, *E. maritimum*, the Common Sea Holly being native to the British Isles. It is this species which has fragrant roots resembling those of the parsnip, of the same family.

The Common Sea Holly which grows to a height of 2 ft., its glaucous leaves having a whitish hue whilst they are extremely spiny, resembling those of the holly. The ball-shaped flower heads are bluish-white and if cut and placed indoors without water, will retain their beauty for several weeks.

In Elizabethan times, the fleshy roots were much in demand as a vegetable, to be cooked and eaten like parsnips which they resemble in their sweet smell and taste. The candied roots of the Sea Holly were known as Eringoes and were a favourite food of Falstaff. To this Shakespeare refers in *The Merry Wives of Windsor*: The scene is set in the Great Park of Windsor when Falstaff enters wearing a buck's head.

> Falstaff: Let the sky rain potatoes; let it thunder to the
> tune of Green Sleeves; hail kissing-comfits;
> and snow eringoes . . .

The reference to "snow eringoes" may have been to the boiled roots, to accompany the potatoes whilst "kissing comfits" are believed to have been the candied roots which later came to be known as eringoes. Shortly after Shakespeare's death, one Robert Buxton of Colchester in Essex, achieved considerable fame for his eringoes which he made from the long tuberous roots gathered on the nearby coast and sold to all parts of the country.

ERYTHRONIUM DENS-CANIS   Dog's Tooth Violet
The Dog's Tooth Violet was introduced into England towards the end of the sixteenth century by the Dutch botanist de L'obel, after whom the lobelia is named and it quickly became a favourite of the cottage gardener. Gerard tells us that it was believed to be the Satyrion of Dioscorides, an orchid thought to be the food of the Satyrs. He would most likely have obtained bulbs from L'obel for his garden in Holborn for the Dutchman was superintendent of Lord Zouch's botanical garden in nearby Hackney and he was later appointed physician and botanist to James I.

Clusius, botanist to the Emperor Maximilian was the first to name the plant, calling it *Dentali* and this had become *Denscaninus* in the *Paradisus*. It was so named because of the long shiny white bulb resembling the tooth of a dog whilst "violet" was a word often given to purple flowers. It is in no way connected with the sweet-scented violet and is in fact, entirely scentless. But it is a most handsome plant, native of the woody mountainous slopes of Switzerland and northern Italy. It is found as far north as Siberia and will flourish in the coldest of gardens.

It loves a friable soil and partial shade and from between two curiously purple-spotted leaves arises the bloom with its reflexed petals on a purple stem. The flower has six purple anthers and is a symphony in purple, at its loveliest during April beneath dwarf trees or near the front of the border where in the half shade of other plants it will spread by self-sown seed. The bulbs should be planted 3 to 4 in. deep.

ESCHSCHOLTZIA CALIFORNICA   Californian Poppy

It is a "new" plant to cottage gardens for seed did not reach these islands until early in the nineteenth century since when few country gardens have been without the brilliance of its summer flowers. A native of California where the land is carpeted with the golden flowers throughout the summer months, it is known as the Californian Poppy and gave the name of "Golden West" to the most famous of all the United States and which has taken the flower as its emblem.

E. californica is a hardy perennial of the Poppy Family, growing about 12 ins. tall with attractive glaucous leaves which are finely divided and throughout summer it bears bright golden-orange cup-shaped flowers which close up in the evening. The whole plant has the appearance of frailty when really it is most robust, flourishing under the hottest conditions.

The biennial or annual form *E. douglasii* is that most widely grown today, a pinch of seed being sown early in spring towards the front of a border in full sunlight when the plants will come quickly into bloom. Growing about 12 in. high, the flowers appear in the most striking shades of scarlet, cherry and gold as well as in the most delicate art shades and have an ethereal beauty all their own.

FOENICULUM VULGARE   Fennel

Because of its pronounced hay-like smell, the Romans gave it the name of *foeniculum* and it is one of the oldest of cultivated plants, steeped in history. The seed, which has an aromatic smell like that of Aniseed, is used to flavour gin and the leaves to consume with fish, either boiled with the fish or to make sauce to serve with it. It was Falstaff in *Henry IV* in a room in the Boar's Head Tavern in Eastcheap who said in reply to Doll's question as to why Prins was so fond of Prince Henry: "And he plays at quoits well; and eats conger and fennel . . . and swears with a good grace . . . for the prince himself is such another." The herb was appreciated in Shakespeare's day as an accompaniment for fish.

From the accounts of Edward I (1281), eight pounds of fennel seed were bought for the King's household for only one month's supply and in *Piers Plowman*, a priest asks a woman for "a farthingworth of fenel seed, for fastyng days" for it was said that the seed allayed the pangs of hunger. Chaucer mentioned the old custom of growing mint and fennel together:

> "Down by a litel path I found
> Of mintes full and Fennell greene."

During Tudor times, fennel was made up into wreaths or garlands to present to lovers in the same way that it was used as an emblem of flattery with the Romans.

Fennel grows to a height of nearly 6 ft. and bears yellow flowers in June, whilst its feathery leaves take on a bronze tint which makes it a most handsome garden plant. It grows in any soil but prefers one of a chalky nature and likes plenty of sun to ripen its seeds which in commerce are distinguished as "shorts" and "longs". Like Rosemary, it grows well in sight of the sea. The leaves are used throughout summer as required, while the water from which the seed has been steeped is excellent for stomach disorders. The roots may also be eaten, braised, like those of celery. A row of seedlings should be set out for this purpose, planting them 9 ins. apart and earthing up the plants as they grow.

Until the beginning of the nineteenth century, fennel was grown for its attractive foliage which was cut and taken indoors for mixing with other leaves and flowers, a custom which could commend itself today. Oliver Goldsmith, the Irish poet, in *The Deserted Village*, mentions the use of fennel for decorating a fireplace during summertimes in his lines:

> The hearth, except when winter chilled the day,
> With aspen boughs and flowers and fennel gay.

FRITILLARIA IMPERIALIS Crown Imperial

The Crown Imperial, *Fritillaria imperialis* is a native of Persia and Turkey (where it grows wild in the woods) and was introduced into Europe by Charles de l'Ecluse (Clusius) in 1576, reaching England shortly afterwards. Clusius was then employed by the Emperor Maximilian II in Vienna with the sole object of collecting plants from all parts of the world. He was friendly with Sir Francis Drake through whom he obtained plants from America. He may, in exchange, have sent bulbs of the Crown Imperial to Drake or to his friends for shortly after Drake had returned in the *Golden Hind* from the circumnavigation of the globe in 1580, the plant was to be found in several of London's most famous gardens. Gerard said that "this plant hath been brought from Constantinople, amongst other bulbous roots and made denizons in our London gardens, where of I have great plenty."

George Herbert who died in 1633 and probably looking for plants for his own garden, wrote:

> "Then went I to a garden, and did spy
> A gallant flower,
> The Crown Imperial."

And Chapman, writing in 1595 spoke of the

> "Fair Crown Imperial, Emperor of Flowers."

By the time Shakespeare left London to retire to his New Place home in Stratford-on-Avon, he would undoubtedly have taken with him some bulbs of the Persian Lily which, as he rightly observes blooms in spring, usually on March 18th, the day of St. Edward, king and martyr, to whom this flower was dedicated. Parkinson began the Paradisus (1629) with a description of this plant: "For its stately beautifulness (it) deserveth the first place in this our garden of delight, to be here entreated of before all other lilies."

Shakespeare mentions the flower in *A Winter's Tale*, written in 1611 and which was the playwright's last comedy. In it he tells of the joys experienced once again in his wanderings about the countryside of his home town, of the customs of the district and here he reveals his love of flowers more so than in any of his works. Perhaps the play was commenced during the cold bleak days of January when the playwright was thinking of the warmer days of springtime and the advent of those flowers he loved so well. In the Shepherd's cottage Perdita says, "I would I had some flowers o' the spring" and then follows some of the loveliest words written in the English language

> O, Proserpina,
> For the flowers now . . .
> Daffodils,
> That come before the swallow dares and take
> The winds of March with beauty.

And included amongst the flowers of springtime loved by Shakespeare and Perdita is

"The Crown Imperial; (and) lilies of all kinds, the flower-de-luce being one!"

That Shakespeare wrote so lovingly of the spring flowers is only natural for in his time there were few autumn and wintering flowering plants and roses gave but a single flush of bloom, during June and July. From then onwards, until the spring flowers appeared again, the garden was almost devoid of blossom for the autumn flowering plants were only beginning to arrive from America. They were different flowers in all respects, mostly tall growing and scentless and they have never attained the popularity of those flowers of the English springtime with their fragrance and humble charm.

Shakespeare may well have obtained bulbs of the Crown Imperial from Gerard's garden (now Fetter Lane) for Gerard said that he had "plenty".

Though the Crown Imperial has a most unpleasant smell, one writer suggesting that it had the smell of a fox combined with that of garlic, it is one of the most interesting of all garden flowers. Early in spring it sends up a stem 2 ft. in length on top of which is a circle of corollas which turn downwards with the stigmas protruding below the rim, resembling church bells. The flower head is crowned by a tuft of bright green leaves. Nature has bestowed on it the pendulous position of the corollas to protect the organs of reproduction until fertilization has taken place.

The flowers have another peculiarity in that at the base of each bell is a drop of liquid, like a tear which Gerard compared to a "pearl of the Orient". The drop will defy the laws of gravity, remaining in position in spite of the drooping flowers. It is nectar which is produced from a tiny cavity in the base of each petal.

Gervase Markham, writing in *The English Husbandman* which he published in 1613 whilst Shakespeare was still living wrote: "this Pearle, if you taste it upon your tongue, is pleasant and sweet like honey."

Those bells from which the nectar is removed by hand will produce no seed, the anthers and stigmas withering rapidly as if deprived of nutriment. To make this discovery, it is necessary to remove the nectar tears three times a day for they will form continuously. Gerard mentioned this. ". . . which drops," he wrote "if you do take away, there do immediately appear the like; notwithstanding if they may be suffered to stand still in the flower according to their own nature, they will never fall away, no not if you strike the plant until it be broken."

> "The Crown Imperial, ever bent on earth,
> Favouring her secret rites, and pearly sweets."

wrote Fanster whilst Shelley speaks of "Heaven's collected tears".

The Crown Imperial is best planted very early in spring so that the bulbs may begin growing at once and become established without fear of their decaying through excessive moisture which may lodge in the scales. For a most attractive display, plant in groups of three or four, in the border or shrubbery and spacing out the bulbs 9 to 10 ins. apart for they will multiply rapidly when established. Plant the base of the bulb 6 ins. deep, with 3 to 4 ins. of soil over the top. It is advisable to set the bulbs on a bed of sand to encourage drainage, and packing peat about them before filling in with soil.

It is remarkable in this age of rapid change that nothing has changed the Crown Imperial since Shakespeare's time. The same two varieties, the red (rubra) and the yellow (lutea) are still available at a reasonable price. They are not expensive when it is considered that they will last a lifetime if planted with a little care. Parkinson has written that "the root doth grow sometimes to be as great as a childes head" which they will do, if left undisturbed. The Crown Imperial was so named by one, Alphonsus Pontius, on account of it having been grown in Europe for the first time by the Emperor of Austria but perhaps its crown of leaves had something to do with its naming.

FRITILLARIA MELEAGRIS   Chequered Daffodil
Canon Ellacombe, an authority on the plants of Shakespeare, contended that in his poem, "Venus and Adonis", entered for publication on April 18th, 1593, and dedicated to the handsome Earl of Southampton, later to become his patron, Shakespeare's lines:

> And in his blood that on the ground lay spilled
> A purple flower sprung up chequer'd with white

referred to the anemone, yet it would seem more likely that it was *Fritillaria meleagris* that was intended rather than the anemone.

Shakespeare wrote "Venus and Adonis" shortly after his arrival in London and it established him as a poet of renown before he turned to writing plays. It was written whilst the intimate knowledge of the Warwickshire countryside was fresh in his mind for the work is full of those little details observed with his own eyes.

Shakespeare's description of the Chequered Daffodil as Gerard named the Fritillary, seems to fit this flower (which could have been known to the poet) admirably, also his description, in the following verse of the fleshy stem issuing green sap, like the bluebell, when severed.

> She crops the stalk and in the breach appears
> Green dropping sap, which she compares to tears.

F. meleagris bears its drooping bell-shaped flowers on 12-in. stems and blooms during May and June. The flowers are pale purple, marked with squares of white, pale yellow or green. The old form *nigra*, bears flowers of almost black which is most striking when planted with the pure white *alba*, said to have been found on the battlefield of Poitiers in France. The variety Aphrodite is a most robust white whilst Artemis bears flowers of an unusual shade of mauve-grey. Poseidon bears blush-white flowers veined purple and Saturnus, large flowers of a lovely shade of pink, heavily checkered.

The flowers are divided into tiny squares; "like the board at which men play at chesse", wrote Gerard. It was also called the Ginny-hen flower, for at a distance the petals have the appearance of the feathers of the Guinea fowl, surpassing "the curiousest paintings that art can set downe". It was also known as the Snakeshead Fritillary for the blooms do greatly resemble the head of a snake whilst the markings of purple and black resemble those of the adder's skin. It was also the Chequered Lily for Phillips, in his *Flora Historica* says that the flower is "chequered with purple and white". It was at one time thought to be a cross between a lily and a daffodil and was named *Lilia narcissus*.

From Gerard we learn that it was introduced into England about 1575 by "the curious and painful herbalist of Paris, Jean Robin" who sent Gerard many "new" plants for his Holborn garden but the plant was first discovered by Noël Caperon, an apothecary of Orleans and who was shortly after killed in the Massacre of St. Bartholomew.

It is an ideal plant for orchard planting or for planting beneath an old apple tree for it is always at its best in short grass but as it blooms during May, the grass should not be cut until the end of July when the foliage has had time to die down.

The bulbs are planted in autumn, about 4 ins. deep and 6 ins. apart. Some sand or peat should be placed over the bulbs to prevent them decaying.

FUCHSIA   Lady's Ear-drops

Native of Mexico, Chile and Peru the fuchsia did not reach Britain until towards the end of the eighteenth century. Miss Sinclair Rohde tells the story of Mr. James Lee, a nurseryman of Hammersmith who saw what is thought to be the first plant to reach this country, growing in a pot in the window of a lady's cottage in Wapping. It had been brought to her by her husband, a sailor whose name was Hogg and Lee was able to persuade her to part with it for 8 gns. It was a plant of *F. magellanica* and from that one plant was raised many thousands which came to be grown in almost every cottage window and planted in every garden in the western parts of the British Isles; "in those parts", says Sir Sacheverell Sitwell in his *Old Fashioned Flowers*, "where the Celtic language is still spoken." The fuchsia hedges of Wexford, Cork and Kerry, of Devon and Cornwall, of Wales and of the Western Highlands of Scotland are a sight which the peoples of the world travel miles to see in late summer and autumn. In these parts of the British Isles it will attain a height of 20 ft., forming a dense bush with crimson-green leaves and bearing drooping flowers of rich scarlet with crimson sepals.

James Lee who was always quick to size up the merits of a good plant, sold three hundred within two years of his original purchase at 1 gn. each and started the vogue for fuchsia growing which has continued to this day.

The fuchsia was discovered in 1700 by Jean Plumier, the French botanist and he named it after Leonhart Fuchs, the sixteenth-century German botanist.

From *F. magellanica* and *F. corallina* with its plum-coloured flowers was raised at Riccarton near Edinburgh in 1850, *F. riccartonii* possibly the hardiest of all fuchsias and which bears its bright scarlet flowers on compact twiggy branches throughout summer and autumn.

GALANTHUS NIVALIS   Candlemass Bells; Snowdrop

A genus of about a dozen species, one of which *G. nivalis* may be indigenous to the British Isles but may have become naturalized at an early date in our history for it is to be found in the deciduous

28 Pompon Dahlia,
Edinburgh

29 Pompon Dahlia,
Autumnal

30 Paeony, Duchess de Nemours

31 Paeony, Sarah Bernhardt

32 Imperial Paeony, King George VI

33 Clump of single paeonies

34 Rosemary growing by the side of steps

35 *Santolina incana*—Cotton Lavender

36 Viola, Woodsmoor

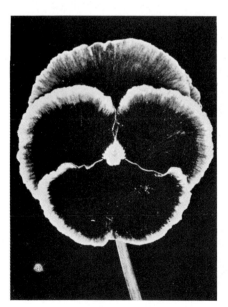

37 Fancy Pansy, Roslin

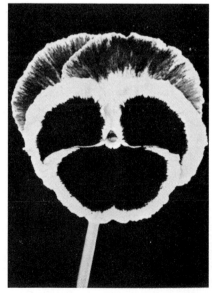

38 Fancy Pansy, Doreen Dow

woodlands of Central Europe extending from northern France to the Caspian Sea. It is a plant of extreme hardiness, pushing up through the melting snow often to come into bloom before the end of January. Because of this, the French named it Pierce Neige, though in Italy it is called the Milkflower from the Greek words *gala* and *anthos*.

That the snowdrop was growing in England during Elizabethan times has been confirmed by Gerard who called it the Early Flowering Bulbous Violet. In the revised edition of the *Herbal* (1633) it is written, "some call them also snow drops", which is the first occasion on which the name we know so well has been used to describe the flower. The name is derived from the German "schneetroppen", a "drop of snow" or "snow-drop", the "drop" denoting the globular shape of the drooping bells.

It is a flower held in great esteem by all for

> The snowdrop is the herald of the flowers
> Sent with its small, white flag of truce to plead
> For its beleaguer'd brethren—suppliantly,
> It prays stern winter to withdraw his troop
> Of winds and blustering storms . . .

To William Wordsworth it was the

> Chaste snowdrop, venturous harbinger of spring,
> And pensive monitor of fleeting years.

John Keble also sang its praises in his lines "To the Snowdrop";

> Thou firstborn of the year's delight,
> Pride of the dewy glade,
> In vernal green and virgin white,
> Thy vestal robes arrayed.

G. nivalis, the hardy European snowdrop, brings with it the soft mossy fragrance of the woodlands as it pushes up through its winter covering of russet-coloured leaves. A solitary flower will carry little scent but in small bunches and in a warm room they will diffuse a spring-like perfume difficult to describe but which may be likened to that particular perfume given off by other early flowers, the primrose and the Winter Aconite and the Lent Lily, a soft refreshing perfume which becomes more pronounced in the later flowering violet. It is similar to the satisfying scent released when treading upon the damp moss and decaying leaves of the woodlands, an earthy smell, refreshing, like the smell of cucumber.

The snowdrop is a plant which enjoys cool conditions and in Britain grows better in the North, along the estuary of the Forth, in the woodlands of Berwickshire and Northumberland, near the exposed East Yorkshire Coast and in the Peak District of Derbyshire. Sir Henry Dorian-Smith in a letter to the author, said that they could not grow *G. nivalis* in the gardens at Tresco in the Scilly Isles. It was too warm in summer.

Snowdrops should be lifted, divided and re-planted as soon after flowering as possible, when the clumps are still green or like the primrose, they may be moved when in bloom. If planting bulbs, the 3 cm. size should be used for anything smaller will not bear bloom the first year.

SPECIES

Galanthus elwesii. It comes into bloom in March and continues until the end of April. The flowers, borne on 9-in. stems have deep green margins on the tips of the petals and at the base.

G. latifolius. Known as the Caucasian Snowdrop, it is found about the mountains of that name throughout the southern states of Russia. The blooms are free of any green segment markings which gives them a milk-white appearance. The form Ikariae, found naturally only on the Island of Nikaria in the eastern Mediterranean, may be distinguished by the long outer segments. It grows only 5 in. tall and bears a bloom which has a more pronounced perfume than any other snowdrop.

G. nivalis. It comes into bloom during January, depending upon the weather and is often to be found in bloom during April. From the bulb springs two glaucous leaves 6 ins. long between which appears a solitary drooping flower on a stem 6 ins. long. The form *viridi-spice* has attractively green-tipped petals whilst there is also a double-flowered form, *flore pleno*. The variety *flavescens* has pale yellow markings whilst Colesbourne, which received an Award of Merit from the R.H.S. in 1951, grows only 4 ins. tall and bears flowers of great substance which carry the pronounced "mossy" perfume.

GALEGA OFFICINALIS   Goat's Rue
G. officinalis, the Common Goat's Rue was at one time to be found in every cottage garden for its valuable qualities in feeding livestock.

Most cottagers kept a few hens and a goat and Gerard has said that the seed fed to poultry "causeth them to yield a greater store of eggs" and the foliage fed to goats was thought to increase the supply of milk. Its planting persisted until the beginning of the present century when it gave way to plants of greater beauty but with its attractive pinnate leaves of brilliant green, resembling those of wistaria, it had its attractions for back of the border planting.

A member of the Pea family, it bears its vetch-like flowers in axillary and terminal racemes and they are purple-blue. The best form is Her Majesty which bears flowers of deepest blue and they continue to appear throughout the summer months.

G. officinalis is believed to have been introduced by the Romans, possibly for its stock-feeding qualities and at an early date had become naturalized in several parts of England whilst Turner and the other early writers mention that it was an established garden plant.

Growing 4 to 5 ft. tall, the spring is the best time for planting, allowing at least 2 ft. between each. They enjoy an open position, like dahlias, with which they make a pleasing contrast to the brilliance of the bloom.

GERANIUM PRATENSE   Crane's-bill
A genus of mostly perennial plants several of which are natives of the British Isles and N. Europe, the best known being *G. pratense*, the Meadow Crane's-bill, a plant which has been growing in cottage gardens since earliest times. With its deeply cut foliage and large cup-shaped flowers of purple-blue, it enjoys an open, sunny situation and is usually to be seen growing over the garden path, most attractive against the rough stone. It is one of the longest flowering of all plants, remaining colourful from early June until October, bearing its flowers in never-ending succession. The plant takes its name from the Greek *geranos*, a crane, from the long-beaked fruit which resembles the bill of a crane. It forms a low bush, growing as wide as it grows tall. Two forms of exceptional loveliness are the double purple, *purpureum plenum* and the double white, *album plenum*, now rarely seen.

Another interesting form which grew in every cottage garden was *G. sanguineum*, the Bloody Cranes-bill, a native plant to be found on dry rocky slopes and near sea-shores. Growing less than 12 ins. tall, it is also long flowering and bears small solitary flowers of crimson, magenta or pink on long stalks.

As Parkinson has said, the Crane's-bills were considered to be valuable wound herbs, the fresh leaves stemming the flow of blood when pressed against the wound. For this reason, G. *sanguineum* may have been so named rather than for the colour of its flowers which are of dull magenta colouring rather than blood-red.

GEUM URBANUM   Herb Bennet; Holy Herb
A native plant of the British Isles, it takes its botanic name from the Greek *geuo*, "I taste", for its roots are pleasantly aromatic. To cottage gardeners of old it was named the Holy Herb or Herb Bennet, the Blessed Herb on account of its medicinal properties whilst the root taken internally was considered an antidote against serpents' bites and as Culpeper says, "by its warm savour was useful to expel crude humours from the belly".

Mary Quelch in her *Herbs and How to Know Them* has told that the roots tied into small bundles and placed in an apple tart are a substitute for cloves, imparting a delicious aromatic flavour. Culpeper also mentions their clove-like scent. In the Middle Ages, the dry roots were used to flavour beer in the same way that the flowers of the pink (sops-in-wine) were used to impart their clove-like perfume. The foliage too, releases the same clove fragrance when handled.

It is a perennial plant of hedgerow and thicket and with its bright yellow flowers is seen to advantage in the border, enjoying the shade created by nearby plants and moisture at its roots. It is an erect, hairy plant bearing its rounded flowers on 18-in. stems. It blooms from June until August and to the countryman, the five petals of the flowers represent the five wounds of Christ so that apart from its numerous valuable qualities, it was considered a sacred plant.

GLECHOMA HEDERACEA   Ground Ivy; Ale-hoof
Syn.: *Nepeta glechoma*. At one time it was a popular plant for hanging baskets when it was known as the trailing Nepeta, for it is of the cat-mint family, its leaves having the same pungent mint-like smell. It is a native plant and is perennial, considered by some to be a weed but if so, it is a charming one, trailing over the ground in the manner of ivy, by roots formed at the joints of the dainty kidney-shaped leaves which are variegated white and green. Like all the "mints", it enjoys a rich moist soil and a cool, semi-shaded position. It bears its

dainty whorls of purple-blue lavender-like flowers during June and July when they are often mistaken for violets. In medieval times, the plant was known as Ale-hoof for its leaves were used to clarify ale, as a substitute for hops whilst in rural districts, the leaves were dried and made into "tea".

HEDYSARUM CORONARIUM   French Honeysuckle
A genus of silky-haired perennial plants and shrubs, one the French Honeysuckle being fragrant and suitable for planting in the border. Like the laburnum, the flowers are borne in racemes and appear throughout summer.

Parkinson tells us that the plant, a native of Italy, was first grown in Britain in the garden of a Master William Coys (who introduced the artichoke into Britain) at North Okenden and he describes it as being "of an excellent shining red or crimson, like unto satin of that colour".

Francis Bacon, who published his delightful essay *Of Gardens*, at the time Parkinson was writing his *Paradisus*, includes the French Honeysuckle amongst those plants to bloom early in summer when "the cherry tree (will be) in blossom . . . the white thorn in leaf (bloom), and the lilac tree", plants which are of "the greatest refreshment to the spirits of man".

Hedysarum coronarium grows 4 ft. tall and as long as it has an open, sunny position will be happy in any well-drained soil. The flowers are borne in crowded racemes throughout summer and are enhanced by the roundish leaflets which are hairy on the underside. It has a scent similar to that of clover and from its flowers the children of Italy, where it is used as a forage crop, suck the sweet nectar.

HELLEBORUS NIGER   Christmas Rose
It is one of the oldest cultivated plants, said to have been used by Melampus about the year 1500 B.C., shortly after Moses, to cure the daughters of Proetus, king of Argos of a mental disease. Pliny has said that the daughters of Proetus were restored to health by drinking the milk of goats that had fed on hellebore. It is the Black Hellebore, *H. niger*, possibly introduced in Roman times and so called from the black colour of its roots. Gerard said that "a purgation of hellebor is good for mad and furious men . . . and those molested with

melancholy". Robert Burton, author of *The Anatomy of Melancholy* (1676), wrote that:

> Borage and Hellebor fill two scenes,
> Sovereign plants to purge the veins
> Of melancholy . . .

At that time the roots were dried and ground to a powder, to be taken like snuff for the relief of headaches and moods of melancholia. Gerard mentioned that in Holland it is called Christ's Herb because it blooms "about the time of the birth of Our Lord". It is also called the Christmas Rose because it blooms during mid-winter, and because its pure white flowers resemble the Dog Rose of the hedgerows whilst it received its botanical name from two Greek words, *hellein*, to destroy and *bora*, pasture, for its presence was thought to cause harm to grassland and grazing animals.

The Christmas Rose is perennial and to have bloom the first year 2-year plants should be planted in well-manured ground in March or April, spacing them 18 ins. apart. At all times they should be kept moist and they will appreciate a top dressing of decayed manure given each year in October. For this reason they always bloomed to advantage in the cottage garden. The plants also love some lime rubble in their diet. If one plant at least, is covered with a cloche in November, not only will the bloom be earlier but it will also be clean whatever the weather. Earlier bloom may be enjoyed by lifting a root and planting in a large pot (or box) which should be placed in a temperature of 50° F. *H. niger* is like the paeony, a plant of extreme longevity, if regularly top-dressed, and requiring no attention for as long as sixty or more years when each winter it will bear more and more bloom.

It should be said that the plants appreciate protection from the cold winds of winter and early spring and as they do not mind partial shade, may be planted at the foot of a wall facing north but where the plants may be sheltered from prevailing winds.

SPECIES AND VARIETIES

Helleborus atrorubens. Possibly Parkinson's red-flowered Hellebore which was known to him but which "perished quickly". A native of deciduous woodlands of S. Europe, it bears crimson-purple flowers on 18 in. stems. The lower leaves are divided into 5 to 9 lobes whilst the upper ones are palmate. A slow grower, it blooms during

January and February and is still obtainable from several plantsmen.

H. corsicus. Native of the island of Corsica, it has bright green foliage and sends up its flowers on stems 3 ft. tall. The leaves have spiny edges like those of the holly whilst the bright green flowers are borne in bunches of a dozen or more and are a most striking feature of the cottage garden in February.

H. niger. The earliest into bloom is *H. niger maximus* which grows 2 ft. tall and bears white flowers, tinted with pink which measure 4 ins. across. The flowers, which resemble those of the hypericum when open, are like small tulips when in bud. The leaves are palmately lobed and are of darkest green. Equally fine is the variety Potter's Wheel, bearing enormous pure white flowers while *angustifolius* with its narrow leaves of apple green and flowers of purest white, does not bloom until early March.

H. odorus. Native of Hungary, it is the only helleborus which bears scented flowers. It was introduced early in the nineteenth century and is now rarely seen. Growing 12 ins. tall, it is hardy, of easy culture and is a long time in bloom with fern-like leaves and bears on nodding stems, small green flowers of delicious perfume. It is in bloom during February and March.

H. orientalis. This is the Lenten Rose, native of Syria and Asia Minor and a familiar member of cottage gardens since Tudor times. It blooms during March and April, during Lent when it bears large rosy-purple flowers on 20-in. stems. The leaves are downy and divided into 7 to 9-toothed segments whilst the flowers are borne 2 to 6 to a stem. Crossing with other species, it has given rise to hybrid varieties of various shades of pink, purple and red.

HELIANTHUS ANNUUS Sunflower

Both the annual and perennial forms have for long been growing in cottage gardens, the one *H. annuus*, growing to a height of 6 to 7 ft. and showing its face above the hedge for all to see. It is a delightful plant, the epitome of warm July days and the brilliance of the sun which seems to be reflected in the golden-rayed blooms. It is a native of Peru and was named Helianthos, Flower of the Sun, for to those who worshipped in the Temple of the Sun, the flowers bore a marked resemblance to the god of day.

The plant was first mentioned by Dr. Monardes (after whom the Monarda is named) in the first American book on botany published in 1569 and it was described by Gerard. In his Holborn garden, he tells us that it grew to a height of 14 ft., bearing flowers which measured 16 ins. across. Gerard also called it the Marigold of Peru for like the calendula, the flower was believed to follow the sun all day, hence Moore's lines in the Irish Melodies:

> As the sunflower turns to her god when he sets
> The same look which she turn'd when he rose.

Parkinson called it a "goodly and stately plant" and illustrates it in the *Paradisus* calling it *Flos Solis*. He mentioned that "the whole plant, every part above ground, hath a strong resinous scent of turpentine, and the middle parts of the flower do sometimes sweat out a fine thin or clear resin or turpentine, as in drops in the heat and dry time of the year, in smell, colour and in taste, like unto Venice turpentine". Nowadays, in many countries a valuable salad oil is extracted from the seeds which is also fed to poultry and large commercial plantations have been set up.

From a sowing of seed made in early April where they are to bloom, the plants will have reached a height of 6 ft. or more by the time they begin to flower at the end of July. They require a sunny situation and must not lack moisture whilst growing. There is also a semi-dwarf Sungold strain which bears flowers 9 ins. across and which grows only 2 ft. tall, a replica in miniature of the Sunflower of Peru, so admirably painted by Nicolas Robert for the collection of Louis XIV, at Versailles, symbol of the Sun King.

The perennial form of the Sunflower is a North American plant, *H. multiflorus*, native of Virginia from where it was possibly introduced into England by Raleigh. It was known to Gerard but seems to have escaped the attention of most writers of the time. It was, however, a popular cottage garden flower of the seventeenth century and was of easy culture, flourishing in all types of soil and as Phillips has written: "this plant is remarkable for not being affected by the smoky atmosphere of London."

VARIETIES

CAPENOCH STAR. It makes a bushy plant 4 ft. tall and blooms from July until September, bearing large flowers of clearest yellow.

MORNING SUN. A variety of outstanding merit bearing fully double blooms of soft lemon yellow.

TRIOMPHE DE GANDE. The flowers are semi-double and of deep golden-yellow, produced with great freedom.

HELIOTROPUM PERUVIANUM Cherry Pie

Native of Peru, it was to be found in every cottage garden during the nineteenth century and in favourable districts was wintered in the open. It is a half-hardy perennial but may be treated as an annual for if sown in gentle heat early in the year, it will come into bloom in July of the same year. The cottager would often lift the plants and winter them in pots in the home when they would bloom through winter. They would be planted out again in May.

Of the borage family, the flowers have the unusual scent of ripe cherries baked in a pie, hence its country name. The plant grows about 18 ins. tall and is of woody branching habit with hairy lance-shaped leaves which have a grey-green appearance, blending attractively with the dark purple of the flowers which act as a pleasing foil when growing near scarlet geraniums.

One of the finest varieties is Marguerite which makes a bushy plant 15 ins. tall and bears umbels of darkest blue. The lilac-flowered Lemoine's Giant, raised in France is also outstanding, likewise the beautiful White Lady.

In its native land as in the most sheltered parts of S. Ireland, the plants are grown as a hedge and will attain a height of 5 ft. or more, diffusing their fragrance about the countryside for miles around.

HEMEROCALLIS FLAVA Day Lily

Though of the Lily family, it has thick fleshy roots and is increased by division in autumn, treating it in the same way as for the Alstroemeria. The plants require a deeply dug soil and will flourish either in full sun or partial shade. They bloom during July and August, lasting only for a day but others take their place in one long succession over a period of eight weeks. The funnel-shaped flowers are borne in clusters on 2 to 3 ft. stems above a clump of grass-like leaves. Those of yellow colour usually carry the sweet perfume of the sweetly scented *H. flava*, a native of Central Europe which is to be found growing in pastureland like the cowslip of the English midlands, scenting the air for a distance when warmed by the summer sunshine. Many strikingly lovely hybrids have been raised during the past decade varying in colour from blackish red to orchid pink, all of them descended from *H. flava* and *H. fulva*, the latter a scentless species bearing orange flowers. They were to be found growing in Gerard's Holborn garden and may have been familiar to Shakespeare. They were then known as Asphodel Lilies for they have roots like those of the Asphodel and bear a flower of lily form. Gerard in his *Herbal* wrote that "these lilies do grow in my garden and also in the gardens of herbarists and lovers of fine and rare plants".

Henry Phillips tells us that the flowers of *H. flava* "give of their agreeable fragrance . . . more particularly when planted in a moist soil and in a shady place".

VARIETIES

GOLDEN SCEPTRE. It grows 3 ft. tall and bears large clusters of bloom of a unique shade of bright Empire yellow.

GOLDEN WEST. Taller growing than most, reaching a height of 3½ ft. and bears large flowers of deep golden-yellow.

HONEYSUCKLE. Like all the yellows it is tall growing, the deep golden-yellow blooms having a rich honeysuckle perfume.

HYPERION. It grows 2 ft. tall and bears large blooms of pale citron-yellow with a delicious sweet perfume.

IRIS, LADY LAWRENCE. It grows only 18 in. tall and bears large flowers of a lovely soft shade of creamy-apricot which are sweetly scented.

JAS. KELSEY. It bears sparkling clusters of medium-sized flowers of soft buttery yellow.

MARY RANDALL. It grows 30 ins. tall and bears flowers of a lovely shade of soft lemon-yellow with a deeper yellow line down each petal.

RADIANT. Received an Award of Merit for its bright golden-apricot flowers which possess exceptional perfume and are borne in profusion.

HEPATICA TRILOBA Liverwort

"Next unto the Winter Wolfesbane, these making their pride appear in winter, are the most welcome early guests," wrote Parkinson of the Hepatica and he grew ten kinds, including the double purple, "sent from Alphonsus Pontius out of Italy, as Clusius reporteth and which was also found in the woods near the Castle of Starnberg in Austria." As Parkinson said and Turner before him, the plants were used for liver complaints and were used in this way until early in the eighteenth century. It is a delightful plant and will be in bloom with the snowdrops if the weather is not too severe when it bears its dainty anemone-shaped flowers on only 3-in. stems so that it is well able to survive strong winds. It enjoys, like most spring flowers, partial shade and may be planted in the alpine garden or at the margin of a border. It is most attractive planted near an entrance to home or garden where the dainty blooms may be observed as soon as they begin to open.

Hepaticas love a well-drained loam and like snowdrops are best planted in March, when in bloom, spacing them 6 ins. apart. They should never be lifted and divided, except when it is necessary to increase stock for the plants resent disturbance, and bloom only after occupying the same place for at least three years. Hence they have never achieved the popularity with the modern gardener as they did with those of old who exercised greater patience with their plants. Care is also needed when planting never to bury the crown below soil level. Hepaticas are readily raised from seed sown in July, in small pots where they remain over winter until planted out in April where they are to bloom eventually.

SPECIES AND VARIETIES

Hepatica angulosa. Native of the Caucasus, it differs from *H. triloba* in that it has 5-lobed leaves and its flowers come rather later, in March and April. The blooms are sky-blue with striking black anthers and are held on 6 to 8 ins. stems. It grows well in a chalk-laden soil and is almost evergreen.

Lodden Blue is the finest form, bearing large flowers of the most brilliant blue on 5 in. stems.

H. triloba. Known to Elizabethan gardeners as Trinity Flower from its 3-lobed leaves. The flowers, which are pink, white or sky-blue are held on 3- to 4-in. stems. Sometimes, like the primrose, the flowers will double when they take on the attractive camellia-shape of the double white primrose.

HYACINTHUS ORIENTALIS   Hyacinth
A genus of some thirty species, only a few of which are in cultivation in the British Isles. Almost all are native of the eastern Mediterranean regions and being closely allied to the scillas, require an

open sunny situation and a well-drained soil. The dwarf species are suitable subjects for the alpine garden where they will bloom at the same time as the scillas and crocus species and at a height of about 6 ins. It was these dainty hyacinths alluded to by Homer as being amongst those flowers which formed the Couch of Juno. In Book 14 of the *Iliad* it is written:

> And clust'ring Lotus swell'd the rising bed,
> And sudden Hyacinths the turf bestrow,
> And flow'ry Crocus made the mountain glow.

Crowns of hyacinths were worn by young Greek girls who assisted at the weddings of their friends. Pliny tells us that the hyacinths had the "smell of the grape flower", a perfume similar to that of the stock.

Percy Bysshe Shelley in *The Sensitive Plant*, more admirably describes the scent of the hyacinth than anyone, making mention of its strength which is most penetrating, like that of the stock and wallflower but which has also a sweet, delicate quality:

> And the hyacinth purple and white and blue
> Which flung from its bells a sweet peal anew
> Of music so delicate, soft and intense,
> It was felt like an odour within the sense.

To the Elizabethans, the hyacinth with its flower spikes of sombre purple-blue was, like the violet and other flowers of similar colour, associated with sadness. "The melancholy hyacinth" it is written and Spenser in *The Faery Queene* alludes to the flower which is supposed to have sprung from the blood of Hyacinthus, a youth loved by both Apollo and Zephyr but who, preferring the sun (Phoebus) to the winds, created jealousy which caused his destruction.

> And all about grew every sort of flower,
> To which sad lovers were transformed of yore;
> Fresh Hyacinthus, Phoebus paramoure
> And dearest love.

The large flowered hyacinth, *H. orientalis*, was introduced into England by Anthony Jenkinson from Persia in 1560 and each year its popularity increased. Parkinson (1629) grew several varieties including the White Roman and a hundred years later, Philip Miller tells us that the Dutch grew some 2,000 varieties. One, bearing a double flower called King of Great Britain, earned for its raiser, Peter Voerhelm, £100 for each bulb.

The Florists' hyacinths as they came to be called, were grown in pots for winter decoration as they are to this day, and owe much of their popularity to Madame de Pompadour who decided that the Court should adopt them as the fashionable flower for indoor decoration in winter and early spring.

Top size bulbs should be used for Christmas flowering, planting three or four to a pot or bowl in September and keeping them in a cool dark place for 8 to 9 weeks when they may be introduced to room temperature. They may also be grown entirely without soil by placing them in the neck of glass jars filled with rain water to the base of the bulb. They should then be placed in a dark room until they have formed shoots about 2 to 3 ins. high when they may then be introduced to the light and warmth.

When planting in beds outdoors, second size bulbs may be used and which should be planted in a rich soil in October 4 to 5 ins. deep and spacing them 6 to 8 ins. apart. They will bloom during May and early June. Towards the month end the glossy strap-like leaves will begin to wither when the bulbs may be taken up and dried off to be replanted in October. They are generally used for bedding to alternate with pelargoniums and other summer bedding plants needing half-hardy culture.

The Roman hyacinths (really a French form of *H. orientalis*) have the same delicious perfume but a more graceful branching habit. The so-called Fairy or Miniature hyacinths are similar. They may be massed outdoors beneath ornamental trees (the blue-flowered Borah is delightful beneath pink-flowering cherries) or in the shrub border where it should be left undisturbed, or "prepared" bulbs may be planted in pots in September and forced into bloom by early December.

SPECIES AND VARIETIES

H. orientalis. Native of those countries of the Middle East, especially of Persia and Turkey, it is a charming plant in its own right, bearing a dozen or more nodding bells of palest mauve on stems 10 ins. long. The bells open like stars and diffuse about them, a perfume equalled only by that of the stock. From this lovely plant, the enormous spikes of the Dutch or Florists' hyacinths have been evolved and from the variety *albus* with its blooms of virginal whiteness, a native of France, has been raised the early flowering Roman hyacinth.

VARIETIES OF H. ORIENTALIS

ANN MARY. The huge thick spikes, arising from upright straplike leaves are of clearest pink with perfect placement of the bells around the stem.

BEN NEVIS. The finest of all the whites with a powerful balsam-like perfume whilst the large balls of ivory-white are fully double.

BISMARCK. Long in commerce, it has never been surpassed in its colour which is light porcelain-blue with a delicious perfume.

CITY OF HAARLEM. Later flowering than most which will prolong the season, it forms a flower spike of great substance and of a lovely shade of soft creamy-yellow with a soft sweet perfume.

JAN BOS. It forms a magnificent spike of ox-blood red which does not fade as the spike ages.

KING OF THE BLUES. A magnificent late flowering variety with a powerful scent and bearing an enormous spike of deep indigo, flushed with purple.

LADY DERBY. It forms a beautiful broad spike of a most attractive shade of bright salmon-pink.

L'INNOCENCE. Probably more widely grown indoors than any variety, it forms the largest spike of all, with enormous bells of purest white with a ravishing perfume.

MYOSOTIS. The finest of all the light blue hyacinths, exactly of forget-me-not colour, the bells having a silver centre and delicious perfume.

ORANGE CHARM. It bears a large compact truss of exquisite colouring being of an unusual shade of buff-yellow with orange shading.

OSTARA. The finest in its colour, bearing a spike of exhibition form, its large fleshy bells being of clear dark blue and free of any purple shading.

PRINCESS IRENE. A variety of uncommon beauty, bearing a handsome spike of soft silvery-pink.

SCARLET PERFECTION. A fully double form of Tubergen's Scarlet, bearing a spike of perfect symmetry and of deepest scarlet.

YELLOW HAMMER. It forms a compact spike of a lovely shade of deep creamy-yellow with a pronounced scent.

H. romanus. This is the true Roman hyacinth which is widely distributed throughout S. Europe. It may be said to resemble the

Musk Grape Hyacinth in its inconspicuous flower and its delicious scent for it bears bells of dingy greenish-yellow with a rich incense-like perfume.

HYPERICUM Tutsan; St. John's Wort
Included amongst the species is the native Common Tutsan or Sweet Amber with its scented flowers and leaves, also the beautiful but scentless Rose of Sharon (*H. calycinum*) which is naturalized in parts of Britain if not a native plant. There are a dozen species native to the British Isles where they are to be found in woodlands and thickets. All bear flowers of brilliant yellow colouring and have evergreen foliage.

Several species are known to give off a most unpleasant musty goat-like smell when handled. This is due to minute oil glands in the leaves. These may be observed by holding a leaf to the light when the tiny glands or cells devoid of protoplasm, no bigger than pin pricks, may be seen in the leaf. It is from these glands which contain caproic acid, that the musty, goat-like smell is released. But of all herbs, the hypericum has most medicinal value. An infusion of the leaves is valuable for a bad cough and was at one time used to prevent children from wetting the bed. Gerard tells us that the oil obtained from the leaves is the best remedy for deep wounds of the flesh "made by a venomed weapon" whilst modern medical practitioners recommend its use to treat bed sores, an ointment being prepared from the flowers and olive oil.

The plant takes its country name from St. John and its association with the mystic rites of Midsummer's Eve, a celebration which goes back to pre-Christian days. The plant was also hung above the entrance to a dwelling to prevent the entry of evil spirits.

SPECIES

Hypericum androsaemum. The Common Tutsan or Sweet Amber frequenting woodlands and shady places usually about the western side of England and Scotland. It is a most handsome plant, growing 3 to 4 ft. in height with a woody stem and leaves 3 ins. long. These are covered in pellucid dots which release a resinous smell when bruised. The golden flowers of five petals are most attractive, with radiating stamens formed in bunches of five. They appear in July and are followed by crimson-black fruits. It takes its old English name from the French, Toute-saine, All-heal, for the leaves contained antiseptic properties and were used to cover open wounds.

H. elegans. A native of Siberia growing 12 ins. high, with stems which are covered with black oil glands. The blunt, lance-shaped leaves are also dotted, the whole plant emitting a powerful goat-like smell, most pronounced when wet. Said to be named in honour of St. John owing to the many uses the plant enjoyed in ancient medicine, the hypericums have red sap in their leaves and stems which was thought to be the blood of the saint.

H. hircinum. It smells so strongly of goats that it has been named the Goat-Smelling St. John's Wort. It is native of S. Europe and forms a multi-branched shrub 4 ft. in height with ovate lance-shaped leaves which have the oil glands concentrated down the edges. When brushed against, the glands release a most unpleasant smell. This species should not be confused with *H. hirsutum*, whose leaves are entirely without the oil glands and which emits no unpleasant smell.

H. perforatum. The Common or Perforated St. John's Wort, native of the copses and shady hedgerows of the British Isles and it is in partial shade that these plants flourish, providing valuable ground cover beneath deciduous trees. It grows 2 ft. tall with brown stems and oblong leaves of dark green covered with transparent dots. To this plant genus the French have given the name millepertuis, "plants of a thousand perforations". The petals and anthers are also covered in glandular dots, black in appearance so that when in bloom, the whole plant gives off a most unpleasant smell when approached.

H. prolificum. A native of North America where it inhabits damp situations in partial shade. Unlike most of the species, the stems are round with lance-shaped leaves covered in transparent dots which give off a smell of wet fur.

H. quadrangulum. The Square-stemmed St. John's Wort frequenting moist woodlands and ditches and whose leaves are a mass of tiny perforations. The star-like flowers have the stamens bunched together, an attractive characteristic of these plants.

HYSSOPUS OFFICINALIS　　　　　　　　　　　Holy Herb; Hyssop

Though Hyssop was mentioned only once in Shakespeare, that being in Iago's famous speech in *Othello*:

. . . "Set hyssop, and weed up thyme . . ." it was, since earliest days, held to be so sacred that it was used in the Consecration of Westminster Abbey. "Hyssop is a herb most prime," wrote Michael Drayton, and Parkinson opens his *Paradisus* with these words: ". . . the golden hyssop was of so pleasant a colour that it provoked every gentlewoman to wear them in their heads with as much delight as many fine flowers can give."

The hyssop is native of the colder regions of Central Europe and had reached this country by Tudor times and possibly long before, being used to surround beds of flowering plants and herbs. It is to be found today growing on the walls of Beaulieu Abbey, possibly introduced by Cistercian monks for it had all manner of uses and retained its green through winter. Hyll, in *The Art of Gardening* (1564) wrote, "It (marjoram) may either be sette with Isope and Time or with winter savoury and Time, for these endure all the winter throwe greene." It was then known as Isope. The poet Spenser writes of the "Sharp Isope" as being good to heal wounds whilst it was also used for strewing floors. The plant was mentioned so often in the Bible that it became known as the Holy Herb and is indeed, named from the Hebrew word *Azob*, "a holy plant". There is an item in the fifteenth-century accounts of Adam Vynour, gardener to the Lord Bishop of Ely at his Manor of Holbourne, for "one quart of ysop seed".

SPECIES

Hyssopus aristatus. It is a dainty aromatic plant making a neat bush only 9 ins. tall and bearing, through summer, a profusion of tiny bright flower spikes. It is charming when used to edge a shrub border or path or it may even be planted on a rockery in a position of full sun.

H. officinalis. It makes a neat evergreen bush about 2 ft. tall and bears bluish-mauve flowers in racemes and which are much frequented by bees. The flowers which are of pink, white or blue possess a rich aromatic fragrance and should be cut when fully open. Though, like the lavender, the santolina and the rosemary, the hyssop is a plant to give beauty to the shrub border, it is now rarely to be seen, though in olden times it was widely grown for flavouring broths and stews. Both its leaves and dried flowers may also be used in pot-pourris.

IBERIS Candytuft

The annual Candytuft, *Iberis umbellata* has been a familiar plant in cottage gardens since its introduction in about 1550 from Candia (Crete). Lyte mentions it, and Gerard tells us that he raised plants from seed brought from Crete by Lord Zouche "for which I think myself much bounde unto his good lordship". Gerard later had charge of Lord Zouche's garden at Hackney and so would often obtain presents of seed and plants for his own garden in Holborn.

Seed of the Candytuft was introduced, not for bearing flowers but for use as a substitute for mustard, for serving with meats for it was "hot" and was thought to aid digestion.

The plant grows about 9 ins. tall and may be sown in April, as an edging to a bed or border, as it was in cottage gardens of old for it comes up uniformly and always retains its compact habit.

The original strain bears flat or slightly cone-shaped flowers in shades of purple, mauve, rose and pink, also white. The flowers have no perfume but retain their colour for a long period.

Two outstanding strains for the border, or for sowing where the plants may be grown to provide cut blooms for the home is the Hyacinth-flowered White and Rose Cardinal, the latter bearing flowers of brilliant cardinal-red. They grow 15 ins. tall and bloom from June until September.

The evergreen perennial form, *Iberis sempervirens*, was first grown in the Chelsea Physic Garden about 1740, having been sent from Persia, its native land. It forms a bushy plant 12 ins. tall and where long established, is often to be found some 20 ins. in diameter. It has small dark green leaves above which it bears multitudes of flowers of glistening white, as pure as driven snow. It is a plant of great endurance and hardiness.

IMPATIENS SULTANII Busy Lizzie; Balsam

The Busy Lizzie of cottage windows was introduced from Zanzibar as recently as 1896 and named *Impatiens sultanii* in honour of the Sultan there.

It makes a compact plant growing less than 6 ins. tall and is readily raised from seed sown in gentle heat in March, or by cuttings removed immediately beneath a leaf joint and inserted in a glass of water. Rooting will take place in 2 to 3 weeks when the plant may be potted and brought into bloom so maintaining a succession.

The variety Scarlet Baby bears flowers of brilliant red whilst Salmon Princess, a plant of low spreading habit bears flowers of a luminous shade of salmon rose.

The Common Balsam, *I. balsamina* was known to gardeners of early Tudor times although a native of tropical Asia. An annual, it is today grown almost entirely indoors yet during Gerard's time was wisely used for summer bedding, planting as he advised "in the most hot and fertile place in the garden". It grows 18 ins. tall with lance-shaped serrated leaves and it bears its rosy-red flowers during July and August when during periods of drought and intense heat, it will retain its freshness and beauty. Phillips reported having seen plants of shrub-like proportions growing in the Tuileries Gardens and with flowers of crimson, scarlet, purple or white "as large as a moderate rose".

It takes its name Touch-me-not from the characteristic of the seed capsule which releases the seed when ripe at the slightest touch. The plants are readily raised from seed sown in pans or boxes in gentle heat in March and transplanted to small pots when large enough to handle. At all times, the Impatiens needs a well-nourished soil and where growing in pots indoors, needs regular watering with dilute liquid manure to prevent is leaves from falling. Nor should the plants be allowed to dry out at the roots.

The finest strain is the Double Camellia-flowered, the large flowers being closely set along the whole length of stem. The Double Scarlet Bush-flowered strain is also excellent for bedding or as a pot plant.

Being tender, the plants should not be set out until early June when fear of frost damage should be negligible.

INULA CONYZA Ploughman's Spikenard

Its leaves form a rosette which covers the ground some 12 ins. across, destroying the grass beneath wherever it is to be found, which is usually on dry banks. It is in bloom during July and August, when both the flowers and leaves emit a refreshingly aromatic scent. Wrote John Clare:

> Thy horehound tufts, I love them well,
> And ploughman's spikenard's spicy smell.

For its fragrance, it was previously named *Inula odora*, for all parts of the plant are aromatic, especially the roots, which in olden times were burnt upon the fire to scent a room. "Have you smelled the bud of the briar or the nard on the fire?" asked Ben Jonson. For this reason it came to be planted in the cottager's garden.

IRIS Fleur-de-Lys

A genus of hardy perennials which for convenience may be divided into two main groups, those having a rhizomatous root stock and those which grow from a bulb. They must be considered amongst the most beautiful of all garden plants, entirely at home in the mixed border but perhaps happier in a border to themselves. The plants require a deeply worked soil and appreciate some lime in their diet which is usually given in the form of lime rubble or mortar whilst they like a soil that is well-drained in winter. They also require a position where the summer sunshine can ripen the rhizomes, so essential if they are to bear a full complement of bloom each year.

The Flag Iris is an excellent town garden plant being tolerant of deposits of soot and a sulphur-laden atmosphere which will in no way harm the sword-like leaves. Usually, however, the plants are confined to a shady corner or to the shrubbery where the sun can rarely reach them and where the soil is devoid of nourishment and so they are never seen in the same glory that they achieve when planted in a specially prepared border to themselves.

The plants should be divided every four years as they so quickly exhaust the soil. The most suitable time is late in July, after flowering which commences mid-May. Or they may be lifted and divided in October or in March though no bloom can be expected that year.

The roots may be divided into sections by cutting with a sharp knife, but each piece must have an "eye" from which the leaves arise and from which the new plant can develop.

Set the pieces 2 ft. apart, laying them just below the surface with the fibrous roots downwards and the top of the rhizome exposed to the sun to encourage ripening.

The rhizomatous irises may be divided into three groups:

(a) The Bearded Iris, descended from *I. germanica.* They have a creeping rootstock from which arise dark green sword-like leaves some 18 ins. long and an erect scape with several flowers attached at the end. The flowers are like large orchids in shape and colour and have "fall" petals which are bearded or crested.

(*b*) The Beardless Iris. Into this group come the difficult *I. stylosa*, the winter-flowering iris and several other species whose large, handsome blooms are free of any beard.

(*c*) The Cushion or Oncocyclus Iris. Here the bud appears at the end of a short stolon whilst the scape bears only a single flower, usually of great size and beauty. The Regalia irises of this section bear more than one flower to a scape. Each of them likes a well-drained gritty soil and shallow planting. The flowers are not scented.

SPECIES AND VARIETIES

Iris albicans. At one time classed as a variety of *I. florentina* but now classed as a distinct species. Native of the Yemen, it is now to be found around the Mediterranean where it is used to bind the sandy soil against erosion. It bears a flower of purest white and may have been introduced into Britain by the Romans.

I. florentina. The Florence Iris whose roots, when dry, possess the fragrance of the violet and in medieval times were used as powder to be placed amongst clothes and linen and to perfume the hair. The dry roots when burnt will perfume a musty smelling room whilst chewed, it will sweeten the breath.

I. germanica. The Common Flag or German iris is a native of Central Europe and is the oldest iris to be given garden culture. It is believed to have been grown in the ninth century, in the monastery garden of Reichenau by its Abbot, Walfred Strabo. The plant is one of the hardiest and toughest in cultivation, well-nigh indestructible but though by its rugged constitution persisting through the years, it received little attention from breeders until the present century. Though the modern flag irises are always classed as being the off-spring of *I. germanica*, this species has played little part in their raising in comparison with the scented *I. pallida*. Under this heading however may be listed a number of varieties of outstanding beauty and which are richly scented.

ALINE. It is an older variety but one of great beauty, being a pure azure blue self and carrying a more powerful perfume than any other variety, perhaps obtaining its scent from *I. pallida* which bears flowers of similar colouring. 3 ft.

BLUE SHIMMER. A most handsome iris, bearing a large crisp white flower, feathered with blue and sweetly scented. 3 ft.

CHRISTABEL. One of the few irises to bear copper-coloured blooms and to be scented. It is an iris of exquisite texture with coppery-purple fall petals and blooms with freedom. 3 ft.

CLEO. Described by its raiser as chartreuse-green in colour, it is a most interesting iris in any company and in addition it has the scent of orange blossom. 3 ft.

EBONY QUEEN. Like a number of the darker coloured irises, this one is also deliciously scented. The blue-black flowers have great substance and come into bloom before all others. 3 ft.

FASCINATION. A gorgeous iris to plant near those of darkest colouring for its flowers are of a lovely shade of dusky lilac-pink with a sweet perfume. 4 ft.

HARIETTE HALLOWAY. A new iris of outstanding form, the ruffled flowers of great substance being of a lovely shade of medium blue with a powerful perfume. 3 ft.

INSPIRATION. Though introduced in 1937 no iris bears a flower of the same rosy-cerise colouring and none has a sweeter fragrance. 3½ ft.

IVORY GLEAM. The huge refined blooms are of solid ivory with touches of gold at the edges of the falls and diffusing a perfume like lily-of-the-valley. 3 ft.

LAGOS. Valuable in that with Coastal Command, it is the latest iris to bloom, its large cream and gold flowers with their soft sweet perfume, opening about mid-June to extend the season by several weeks.

MAGGADAN. One of the most unusual and sweetly scented varieties. The standards are slate-blue, the ivory-white falls being flushed with slate. 3½ ft.

MANYUSA. One of the outstanding pink irises, the flowers with their exquisitely ruffled petals being of soft orchid-pink with a sweet orange perfume. 3 ft.

MATTIE GATES. A most attractive variety and surprisingly, one of the few yellows with pronounced perfume. The standards are of soft, almost primrose-yellow with the falls of brightest gold, blazoned with white. 3 ft.

MOONBEAM. With Mattie Gates, it is the most richly scented of all the yellow irises, the large blooms of clear sulphur-yellow having the scent of lily-of-the-valley. A variety for the front of the border. 2 ft.

RADIANT. This fine iris will be a valuable addition to the front of any border for its bright apricot-orange standards and terracotta falls ensure that it receives the attention it deserves. In addition, it is free flowering and richly scented. 2½ ft.

ROSE VIOLET. A front of the border bi-colour with rose-pink standards and violet falls, the whole being a bloom of great substance. Valuable for its lateness of flowering and its rich gardenia scent. 2½ ft.

I. pallida. A Flag Iris similar to *I. germanica* and which has had a considerable influence on the raising of the modern hybrid varieties. It is native of S. Europe, arriving in the British Isles during Elizabethan times. Gerard mentions that it grew in his garden in Holborn with "leaves much broader than any other (iris) and . . . with fair large flowers of a light blue or (as we term it) a watchet colour". And he adds, "the flowers do smell exceeding sweete, much like the orange flower". To some, the perfume more nearly resembles vanilla; to others, it is likened to civet.

I. pseudacorus. It is the Yellow or Water Iris to be seen growing by the side of rivers and in marshlands throughout the British Isles and in France, whose King Louis VII took the flower as his blazon during the Crusades and gave it his name, "flower of Louis". It is the yellow "Vagabond Flag" of Shakespeare's *Antony and Cleopatra* and it became the national symbol of Medieval France, in Heraldic language: "Azure powdered with fleurs-de-lis or". In 1339 when Edward III made claim to the throne of France and began hostilities against Philip VI (Philip of Valois), he took for his arms the three Plantagenet Lions and the *fleur-de-lis* of France.

It is a delightful plant with a scented flower some 3 ins. across and of a soft shade of golden-yellow. The flowers are produced in succession from May until August amidst sword-like leaves. From the dried rhizomatous roots, a delicately scented essential oil is obtained which at one time was used to adulterate oil of *Acorus calamus*.

I. sibirica. It was grown in Elizabethan gardens and in spite of its name, is native to all parts of Europe. It makes a pleasing waterside plant but will flourish in the border provided lime is not present in the soil. It has elegant grass-like foliage and bears two or three flowers together of brightest lilac-blue.

Two outstanding varieties are Helen Aster, a rose-red and Nottingham Lace, introduced in 1960, the wine-red flowers being laced with white.

I. Susiana. The Mourning iris, "so fit for a mourning habit", wrote Parkinson. "I think in the whole compasse of nature's store, there is not a more pathetical . . . among all the flowers I know, coming neare into the colour of it." It takes its name from the ruined city of Susa in Persia where it was discovered, the enormous flower being white, veined and marked with black. It must be given a dry, sunny situation.

Gerard said "it doth prosper well in my garden" and he likened its bloom to the Ginny Hen. He also called it the Turkey Flower de luce, having reached England from Constantinople early in the sixteenth century.

BULBOUS SPECIES

Iris persica. It is the Persian Iris and was described in the *Paradisus*. It also has the honour of being the first plant to be featured in the *Botanical Magazine* of 1787. The bulbs are about as large as a bantam's egg and from which arise in March almost stemless flowers some 3 ins. across. The waved fall petals are of bluish-green with a golden keel, in front of which are spots of violet-black. *Purpurea* bears flowers of richest purple whilst *isaacsonii* has cream coloured flowers tinted with green and with violet veins. It is characterized by its sickle-like leaves.

JASMINUM Jasmine

The Arabic name for the plant is Ysmyn whilst the Persian is Jasemin, changing but little in English and it is likely that the White Jasmine, *J. officinale* had reached Britain from the Near East early in Tudor times. Gerard and later Parkinson and Ben Jonson mention it as a plant in common use for covering arbours whilst Spenser, who may have been familiar with Gerard's garden in Holborn, includes it amongst those lovely scented flowers which we have come to associate with the cottage garden in these lovely lines:

> Her breast, like lilies, ere their leaves be shed;
> Her nipples, like young blossomed jessamines;
> Such fragrant flowers do give most odorous smell
> But her sweet odour did them all excel.

William Cowper who, it is said, better understood flowers and plants than any of our poets with the possible exception of Shakespeare and Clare, also wrote of

The jasmine, throwing wide her elegant sweets
The deep dark green of whose unvarnish'd leaf
Makes more conspicuous and illumines more
The bright profusion of her scatter'd stars.

In *Lalla Rookh* (The Night of the Harem), Thomas Moore describes the delicious perfume released by the White Jasmine and which is especially pronounced at night-time.

Twas midnight—through the lattice, wreath'd
With woodbine, many a perfume breath'd
From plants that wake when others sleep,
From timid jasmine buds, that keep
Their odour to themselves all day,
But, when the sunlight dies away,
Let the delicious secret out
To every breeze that roams about.

From the flowers of the White Jasmine, the perfume "oil of jasmine" is obtained whilst the ancients captured the evanescent odour of the blossoms by means of enflouage, embedding the fresh flowers in fat from which they made odoriferous ointments.

It is a genus of more than 120 species of evergreen and deciduous shrubs, all indigenous to the East, to be found from Persia to Central China, though one, *J. azoricum* is native of the Azores and *J. odoratissimum* of Madeira. Many are completely hardy in the British Isles and are successful in ordinary soil whilst with their small glossy leaves, like those of the privet and other plants of the family they are tolerant of town garden conditions. They are readily increased from cuttings of the half-ripened wood, removed in August and rooted under glass. Any pruning should be done in April after flowering.

SPECIES AND VARIETIES

Jasminum azoricum. It is a twining species, vigorous and evergreen but in Britain is suitable only for the mildest localities in which it will bloom almost throughout the year. The flowers are white and heavily scented.

J. beesianum. It rarely exceeds a height of 6 ft. but may be planted against a low wall. It makes a slender plant and blooms during July and August, its small deep rosy-red flowers having a powerful spicy scent.

J. humile glabrum. Native of Nepal, it is a plant of vigorous habit growing 8 ft. in height and from May until August bears clusters of deliciously scented yellow flowers.

J. nudiflorum. This native of China did not reach English cottage gardens until quite recent times when it came to be appreciated for its winter blossoms which appear in opposite pairs along the twiggy stems, devoid of leaves at this time of year. Any pruning should be done in April, after flowering so that the new shoots produced during summer will be able to carry the full compliment of blossom. It is not scented but its primrose-yellow flowers are always appreciated when the days begin to lengthen and the cold intensifies.

With its flexible stems and small narrow leaves, it may be trained about trellis or against a wall and always remains neat and tidy, whilst no degree of cold will harm it.

J. odoratissimum. Native of Madeira, it is suitable only for the mildest parts of Britain where it will bear its primrose-yellow flowers in threes from the tips of the branches. The flowers have a heavy sweet perfume.

J. officinale. The Common White Jasmine of Tudor gardens, a strong-growing twining plant which will attain a height of 10 ft. or so and is evergreen in all but the coldest localities of the British Isles. It is a plant now rarely to be found though with its deliciously scented blossoms, borne from June until October, it is a charming companion for the Winter Jasmine which comes into bloom early in November and continues until late in March when *J. revoltum* comes into its scented loveliness.

KNIPHOFIA UVARIA   Red Hot Poker

The Torch Lilies were introduced into Britain from South Africa at the beginning of the eighteenth century and were soon to be seen in every cottage garden. Though requiring a sunny situation, they enjoy the winter protection of nearby plants and so have continued to flourish in the cottage garden for the past two and a half centuries.

The plant was named after Professor Kniphof of Erfurt whose claim to everlasting fame lies in the production of the largest of all herbals, comprising twelve enormous volumes. Perhaps the fact that the plants do not bloom over a long period has reduced their popularity but they add a touch of brilliant colour to the late summer and autumnal border, often remaining in bloom until cut down by frost.

Readily increased by division of the crowns in autumn, the Red

Hot Pokers grow 3 to 5 ft. tall with lily-like strap-like leaves and they bear their flowers in dense spikes at the end of leafless scapes.

Mr. Herbert Samuel of Wrexham succeeded in raising, after the 1939–45 war, a number of magnificent hybrid varieties which have greatly increased the popularity of the plant.

Like all members of the Lily family, the plants require copious amounts of moisture whilst making growth during summer but require a well-drained soil and the minimum of moisture about the roots in wintertime.

The plants will quickly make clumps of dense foliage and should be given a square yard of ground in which to grow.

VARIETIES

ALCAZAR. Growing 2 to 3 ft. tall, it bears in July and August, dainty spikes of fiery red.

BEES LEMON. A variety of great beauty, bearing large spikes of clear lemon-yellow.

K. galpini. A delightful small garden species, introduced in 1930 and named after Ernest Galpin. It makes a neat, compact plant 18 to 20 ins. tall and bears its slender golden wands from July until October. It has passed on its golden colouring to several hybrids.

MAID OF ORLEANS. A magnificent almost white variety, bearing from July until September elegant spikes of creamy-white on 3-ft. stems.

MODESTA. An unusual and charming variety, its graceful ivory spikes being tipped with rose. It grows only 2 ft. tall.

ROYAL STANDARD. An old favourite growing 3 ft. tall and bearing handsome spikes of scarlet and gold.

SAMUEL'S SENSATION. A giant of a variety, sending up its enormous spikes of coral-red to a height of 5 to 6 ft.

LATHYRUS LATIFOLIUS　　　　　　　　　　　　Everlasting Pea

The Perennial or Everlasting Pea, *L. latifolius* is a native of S. Europe and is not a British plant as Henry Phillips says, though it is closely related to the native *L. sylvestris*. Since its introduction early in our history, it was to be found in every cottage garden as it is to be to this day. Gerard called it Tare Everlasting or Chickling, and Parkinson said that "the purplish blossoms borne on a long stem are very beautiful to behold" and surprisingly adds that they have "a pretty scent or smell". As they have since the beginning of the century been quite scentless and as Parkinson could not have known the Sweet Pea to cause confusion, it would seem that the Perennial Pea lost its scent soon after its introduction, if it ever had perfume.

The plant is readily raised from seed sown in small pots in July, the young plants being set out in their flowering quarters the following April. They will quickly pull themselves up a trellis or over nearby trees or shrubs and will smother themselves and their hosts in flowers of purple-red during July and August. Once they take hold they are almost indestructible for as Parkinson said, the root goes down to a considerable depth and is "of the thickness sometimes of a man's arm".

LATHYRUS ODORATUS   Sweet Pea
A genus of more than 100 species of annual or perennial plants, only one, *L. odoratus*, so named by Linnaeus, having perfume. It is an annual, discovered in Sicily early in 1697 by a monk, Father Cupani, and he described the plant in his *Hortus Catholicus* of the same year.

In 1700 he sent seed to a Dr. Uvedale, a schoolmaster at Enfield Grammar School, one of the few people in England at the time to possess a warm greenhouse. The seed produced a weedy looking plant with tiny flowers of maroon with a standard of deep purple but as would be imagined from the colour, the flower possessed a powerful sweet fragrance. Its appearance in the garden, however, was so poor that 100 years later, the number of varieties had increased to no more than six, all with flowers as inconspicuous as those of the original plant. The one exception was the Painted Lady, a reddish-pink and white bi-colour which had a particularly sweet perfume.

The flower was first called the Sweet Pea by the poet Keats though apart from the name, he made no reference to the perfume:

> Here are sweet peas, on tiptoe for a flight
> With wings of gentle flush o'er delicate white,
> And taper fingers catching at all things,
> To bind them all about with tiny rings.

In spite of Thomas Fairchild's exhortation that "the sweet-scented pea makes a beautiful plant" (1722) it was so inconspicuous in the garden that it is surprising that it persisted for it produced but little bloom and only in "ones" and "two's" on short, weakly stems.

It took someone with considerable foresight to consider this flower worthy of development. But in 1870, Henry Eckford, a Midlothian man, whilst gardener to Dr. Sankey at Sandywell in Gloucestershire began cross-fertilizing sweet peas and, realizing the commercial possibilities, he left his employment to devote his entire time to the raising of new varieties, working in his garden at Wem, Shropshire. So successful was he that at the Bi-centenary Sweet Pea Exhibition held at the Crystal Palace in 1900, that of the 264 varieties exhibited, half had been raised by Henry Eckford. His variety Lady Eve Balfour, described in Robert Bolton's catalogue of 1908 as being "pale lavender, shaded grey", was chosen as the most outstanding variety ever raised and was used for the presentation bouquet at the Exhibition. The flowers were deliciously scented.

In the same year, in the garden of the Countess Spencer at Althorp Park, Northamptonshire, appeared the first sweet pea with frilled petals. It was noticed by the head gardener, Silas Cole, who named it after the Countess and almost overnight, Silas Cole and his new sweet pea earned universal fame. From a single seed pod came the world's most beautiful flowers which had a perfume transcending all others. But Countess Spencer had one great fault, it did not always breed true to type. Nature, however, has a way of correcting these things for in the following year, there appeared in the garden of a Cambridge grocer, Mr. W. J. Unwin, a form of Eckford's Prima Donna which also had waved petals and which he named Gladys Unwin, after his eldest daughter. As soon as Unwin realized that it would breed true, he sold his business and set about the raising of the new sweet peas for the commercial cut-flower markets and quickly achieved success with the introduction of many lovely varieties. Mr. Charles Unwin has told that Prima Donna had been grown for at least eight years before producing its changed form, which it did at almost the same time and in three different places, and never did so again, this being one of the greatest enigmas in all horticultural history.

The Sweet Pea is a hardy annual but like so many hardy annuals responds better to half-hardy or biennial culture, being sown in a coldframe either in August or in March or in gentle heat early in the year, the plants being moved to their flowering quarters in April when they will come into bloom in June. The seed should be sown individually in small pots or in boxes spaced 1 inch apart so that the young plants will have space to develop from the moment of germination. When about 4 ins. high, the growing point should be removed to persuade the plants to develop a more bushy habit. It requires an open, sunny situation and will not tolerate shade.

It is a plant of climbing habit and requires to be grown up canes or against a trellis about which it climbs by means of tendrils. It may also be grown up twiggy branches when it will make a delightfully scented "hedge" some 6 ft. tall. If the dead blooms are continually removed before they set seed, the display will continue into autumn. The plants die down in winter and grow again in spring.

VARIETIES

BRIAN CLOUGH. An Unwin introduction which won the Clay Cup for the Best Vase at the 1979 National Sweet Pea Show. The flowers, with their beautifully frilled petals are of a striking shade of deep salmon-orange.

CREAM BEAUTY. A vigorous grower which blooms profusely, bearing 4 and often 5 frilly flowers of ideal placement on 12 in. stems; the colour is rich cream with a powerful scent.

CRIMSON EXCELSIOR. The most richly scented crimson, the enormous blooms being of a striking shade of crimson-red.

ELIZABETH TAYLOR. The best of its colour which is a lovely rich deep mauve with an equally rich perfume. An exhibitor's favourite.

EVENSONG. One of the most beautiful and sweetly scented of all sweet peas, shades of soft blue and lilac merging with delightful results whilst it is unsurpassed by any variety in vigour and perfume.

GIGANTIC. Introduced in 1932 when it received the Gold Medal of the National Sweet Pea Society, it has never been surpassed. It also received the Abol Trophy "for the greatest advancement since the First World War in any one species or strain of plants". The florets are enormous and the petals so heavily frilled as to give rise to a "double" effect, whilst no variety has a richer perfume.

JOHN NESS. Raised by the late Mr. John Ness, it is an outstanding exhibitor's variety, the flowers which are borne in "fours" and "fives" being of an attractive shade of clear mid-lavender with a delicious spicy scent.

LEAMINGTON. Raised by Rev. Kenneth Colledge and introduced in 1958, no variety carries a more pronounced perfume nor is there one which has received more honours including the Award of Merit from the R.H.S. and also from the National Sweet Pea Society. The frilly-petalled flowers are large and of a lovely shade of deep, clear lilac with ideal placement.

MABEL GOWER. A long established favourite being introduced in 1949, the blooms are of a most attractive shade of clear medium blue with a sweet vanilla perfume.

MRS. BERNARD JONES. Raised by Unwins, it is a Clay Cup winner, bearing heavily ruffled flowers of a lovely shade of soft rose-pink.

NOEL SUTTON. One of the finest blues ever raised, it carries 4 or 5 flowers of a unique shade of mid-blue on 12 in. stems.

RED ENSIGN. It was the 1981 Clay Cup winner and carries 4 or 5 large ruffled blooms of brilliant red on stems up to 18 ins. long. It is sweetly scented.

ROSE FONDANT. Raised by Messrs. Unwins of Histon, it has the richest perfume of any sweet pea of its colour, and is one of the most beautiful and richly scented of all sweet peas. The frilly blooms are of a lovely shade of soft rose-pink suffused with salmon.

ROSY FRILLS. A picotee of great charm, the huge frilly blooms, the largest since Gigantic, having a white ground and a wide edge of rose-pink with a most delicious perfume.

WELCOME. An old favourite and still a winner on the show bench for its huge ruffled crimson blooms, borne 4 or 5 to a 16 in. stem.

LAVANDULA Lavender
A genus of twenty species, *L. vera* being that most widely grown. All are native of S. Europe but several reached Britain early in her history, possibly with the Roman invasion.

> Here's flowers for you;
> Hot lavender, mints, savory, marjoram.

said Perdita in *A Winter's Tale*, coupling all those strongly flavoured herbs which Shakespeare loved so well.

Langham in *The Garden of Health* (1579) wrote, "boil it in water, wet thy shirt in it and dry it again and wear it", and because of its clean, fresh smell, the person whom we now know as a laundress was in Elizabethan times, known as a *"lavendre"*.

From the plant an essential oil has for long been produced from it at Mitcham in Surrey whilst no cottage garden was without it, to supply dried flowers to make up into small muslin bags to place between linen and clothes and beneath the pillow to encourage sleep whilst the dried stems were burnt in sick rooms like incense. Turner delightfully suggested placing the dried flowers in the front of a cap "to comfort the brain" during warm weather in the same way that lavender water will bring comfort to a tired mind. Parkinson said that it would "pierce the senses . . . to comfort and dry up the moisture of a cold brain" meaning that it brought comfort to a cold in the head, hence Shakespeare's reference to "hot lavender".

Lawson in *The Country Housewife's Garden* wrote, "This flower (lavender) is good for bees, most comfortable for smelling except roses." Izaak Walton paints a delightful picture of the "honest alehouse where we shall find a cleanly room, (with) lavender in the windows . . ." for like Rosemary, the herb was made up into bunches and grown in pots to be placed in windows to purify the air of house and inn.

No plant has more greatly retained its popularity through the years yet it is remarkable that it is not more freely planted in the garden of today. It is of such easy culture, too. Possessing attractive silvery-grey foliage, the plant will always be colourful and aromatic, even where perhaps not bearing a large amount of bloom, and no plant makes a more decorative low evergreen hedge. Planted to surround a bed of highly scented crimson-red roses such as Ena Harkness or Josephone Bruce, or a bed of fragrant pinks, the dwarf lavenders remain neat and compact and may be clipped into shape when the plants are young. The most compact variety is *L. nana compacta*, the French lavender, its habit being erect and with careful clipping in spring, which is the best time to trim all lavenders, the hedge may be kept at a height of no more than 12 ins. It bears pale lavender-mauve flowers and is one of the latest to bloom. Even more compact is the White flowered counterpart, Queen Henrietta Maria's favourite which will grow little more than 9 ins. tall, likewise Hidcote Blue with its flowers of old-fashioned lavender-blue:

"It's perfume wrapt in the sky's own hue"

wrote Lady Lindsey.

Little more vigorous than *L. nana compacta* is the Munstead variety, famed for its deep purple-blue flowers. It rarely exceeds 12 ins. in height and blooms over a longer period than any other. It was raised by Miss Gertrude Jekyll at her Munstead home in Surrey. Another lovely variety is Jean Davies which grows 15 ins. tall and bears flowers of a lovely shade of strawberry pink.

The most vigorous form is the Old English, *L. spica*, that known as

39 Crown Imperial in
Shakespeare's garden

40 *Echinops ritro*—
Globe Thistle

41   Above left: Scabious, Clive Greaves. *42   Above right: Geranium pratense. 43   Below: Kniphofia uvaria,* Maid of Orleans

44 Helianthus, Triomphe de Gande

45 Double-flowered Balsam

46   *Above: Lilium candidum—* Madonna Lily

47   *Left:* Annual Cornflower

Grappenhall, growing 3 to 4 ft. tall and forming a dense aromatic hedge.

Like all aromatic herbs except the mints, lavender prefers a light, sandy soil and will always be more fragrant growing along the drier eastern side of Britain than elsewhere. Soil of a chalky nature suits it most of all, bringing out its full fragrance. It also likes plenty of sunshine which is essential where it is grown for oil extraction. It requires neither manure nor humus in the soil at planting time, though a little top manure may be forked round the plants in autumn. The more robust varieties should be planted between 3 to 4 ft. apart, slightly closer together where planting a hedge. For a dwarf hedge, plant the compact lavenders about 15 ins apart, for the plants will grow as wide as they grow tall. Always plant in spring.

LILIUM   Lily

A large genus of flowering plants growing from a (usually) scaly bulb. On an erect leafy stem branched at the end, it bears one or more drooping or erect flowers in racemes. The flowers consist of six segments, the three inner petals being larger and broader than the three outer petals. The lily is widely distributed throughout the N. temp. zone from Oregon in the West, across N. Africa and Europe to China and Japan, usually growing where they are exposed to a severe winter with little rain, followed by long periods of sunshine.

Few plants are more steeped in history. As a flower it has no rival except possibly the rose. The ancient world consecrated the White Lily to Juno from whose milk it was thought to have come forth. This was the White Lily of the East, *L. candidum*, the Madonna Lily so named for its purity and rich sweet perfume. It is used to decorate the church on July 2nd, the celebration of the Visitation of the Blessed Virgin. It is the only flower mentioned in name by Jesus though there is some doubt about it being the flower intended. It is depicted more than any other flower in the paintings of the masters. In Phillipino Lippis' "Virgin and Child", St. Dominic is seen holding the Madonna Lily. It is also mentioned more often than any other flower by the poets to whom the White Lily served to typify all that was good and beautiful. Chaucer in the Second Nun's Tale wrote:

"First wol I you the name of St. Cecilie . . .
It is to say in English, Heven's lilie."

In the Gardeners' Rolls of Norwich Priory of that time, the Rose and Lily were the only flowers mentioned, both being used to beautify the chapel on special occasions.

The Order of the Blessed Lady of the Lily was inaugurated by Garcias, 4th King of Navarre following an image of the Holy Virgin which miraculously appeared in a flower of the Madonna Lily and which was thought to have cured the King of a dangerous disease.

The Madonna Lily is believed to have reached England at the time of the Crusades though may have come much earlier for it is shown in a tenth-century miniature of Queen Etheldreda, foundress of the abbey at Ely, now the Kings' School where Edward the Confessor received his early education. It was noticed by Chaucer in armorial bearings of his time:

> Upon his crest he bore a tower,
> And therein stalked a Lily flower.

During Edward III's reign, the flower was incorporated in the armorial bearings of Winchester College as a token of respect for the king who had, in 1340, incorporated the fleur-de-lis in his own crest and in 1440, in the bearings of Henry VI's College of Eton, the arms granted by the king being "three garden lilies argent upon a sable field with the fleur-de-lis of France and lion of England". Thus, it may be taken that the fleur-de-lis was not the flower we call the lily but some other flower, most probably the Flag Iris for both flowers appear in the College Arms being clearly distinguished by the Pursuivants at Arms. The Madonna Lily is clearly shown (on either side of the Madonna and Child) in the arms of the Borough of Marylebone (Mary the Good) and it also appears in the Arms of Aberdeen University; of Corpus Christi College, Cambridge; and in those of the Royal Burgh of Dundee.

The Madonna Lily was a familiar plant in cottage gardens in Elizabethan times; it was so common that Gerard speaks of it as a native plant. "Our English White Lily groweth in most gardens in England," he wrote. Shakespeare also treated it as a common garden plant and in his works, mentions it on twenty-eight occasions, yet, like other writers, always alluding to its ethereal whiteness never to its scent. "A most unspotted lily", as in Henry VIII; "Most lily-white of hue", in *A Midsummer Night's Dream*. On only one occasion does Shakespeare allude to its scent and then in less than pleasing terms as in sonnet xciv:

For sweetest things turn sourest by their deeds;
Lilies that fester smell far worse than weeds.

The smell of lilies as they die is far from pleasant and perhaps the poet found it equally oppressive at all times. In *King John*, the fragrance of the violet is given the highest praise but once again it is the Lily's whiteness that is more wondrous to Shakespeare than its scent.

To gild refined gold, to paint the Lily,
To throw a perfume on the Violet . . .
Is wasteful and ridiculous excess.

Oppressive when indoors, having something of the animal smell, the perfume of the Madonna Lily in the garden is most agreeable, scenting the air for yards around with its honey fragrance.

So popular during Elizabethan times, lilies for gardens and greenhouses had by the beginning of the nineteenth century almost completely fallen from favour. Dahlias and the more exotic stove plants had taken their place, whilst flower beds filled with half-hardy plants had almost replaced the herbaceous border. It was the introduction to England in 1862 of *Lilium auratum* that began a new interest in the lily which has continued ever since with the Madonna Lily still retaining its popularity for it remains the only pure white species ever introduced and it seems to grow well anywhere.

Lilies may be divided into several groups each of which demand different cultural conditions. There are those which are lime-tolerant and those, mostly from China and Japan, which will not grow where lime is present. Several species, including *L. auratum* prefer an acid, peaty soil. Most Eastern lilies are stem rooting and require yearly top dressing, most European species form their roots from the base of the bulb. Some prefer partial shade whilst others enjoy an open, sunny situation. Again, not all lilies are pleasantly scented. Mrs. Constable Maxwell in her delightful *Lilies in their Homes* suggests that the European species of the *L. carniolicum* group, those lilies to be found growing in Elizabethan gardens, have the smell of decaying vegetable matter, something of the aroma of the compost heap. In addition, *L. bulbiferum* and *L. martagon* are almost scentless. Only the Madonna Lily of Elizabethan gardens possessed perfume in pleasant degree and from the ninety or more species grown today, no more than twenty to thirty bear flowers which may be described as being sweetly scented. Several lilies have become established cottage garden favourites.

SPECIES

Lilium candidum. It is unusual in that it forms its basal leaves as soon as the flower stem has died back in autumn and it is then that the bulbs should be moved. That the plant was always seen to advantage in cottage gardens was due to its liking for a rich soil and the company of other plants which provided the much desired shade to its roots during the heat of summer.

It bears its glistening white trumpets in June and July on 4-ft. stems and anything from twelve to twenty blooms to each stem which in the warmth of the summer sunshine, diffuse a sweet honey-like perfume. It is not stem rooting and should be planted with no more than 1 in. of soil covering the bulb. It prefers a chalk-laden soil, though one containing some moisture-retaining humus.

L. chalcedonicum. The Scarlet Turk's Cap Lily which Gerard has told us "groweth wild in the fields many days journey beyond Constantinople (Chalcedon)". It grew in almost every garden during Tudor times and by the turn of the century was so common that Parkinson said that "to all lovers of these delights, I shall seem to them to lose time to bestow many lines upon it". It is now rare.

It sends up its stem to a height of 3 ft. furnished with leaves which become smaller as they near the top. The flowers appear in July, six to eight and drooping, resembling a Turk's cap with the scarlet petals rolled back to expose the red stamens. It is stem rooting and so should be planted 6 ins. deep and about 10 ins. apart.

L. croceum. The Orange or Saffron Lily, native of the European Alps and grown by Gerard who described it as being "of a deep orange colour, spotted with black spots (at the base)" and borne in umbels on 4 to 5 ft. stems. It blooms early in July and came to be grown by Ulster Orangemen to celebrate the victory of William of Orange in 1691. It is now a familiar cottage garden plant throughout Northern Ireland from, it is said, original plantings made early in the eighteenth century, for once established, the plants are almost indestructible. From the base of the flat bulb, bulb-bearing stolons are produced, hence it was called *L. bulbiferum* by the French botanist De Candolle though it is a different plant from that so named by Linnaeus. It is now called *L. bulbiferum var. croceum.*

It flourishes in all soils and in sunshine or shade, the bulbs being planted 8 ins. deep and they should never be disturbed.

L. martagon. The Martagon Lily known as the Common Turk's

Cap and which Rev. Johns in *Flowers of the Field* said had become naturalized in woods near Mickleham in Surrey where it blooms during August and September. It grows 2 to 3 ft. tall with a downy stem and bears drooping flowers of pink or violet in chandelier-like racemes of twenty or more. The flowers have recurving petals.

The plant was described by Turner and also by Gerard as being native of Greece and Syria. Gerard mentions that "the small sort I have had many years but the greater I have not had till late", and he delightfully adds they were "given me by my loving friend Master James Garret, apothecary of London".

The bulbs should be planted as soon as flowering is over, in September, setting them 6 ins. deep and ordinary leafy loam will suit them well.

L. tigrinum. Though it did not reach Britain until the very beginning of the nineteenth century the Tiger Lily is so essentially a flower of the cottage garden from that time that it takes its place along with those of more ancient origin. In its native China however, it has been grown commercially for its food value for two thousand years and was highly valued for the purpose. It was originally known as the Chinese Lily and grows 3 to 4 ft. tall with dark green glossy leaves and from August until October bears large orange trumpets, heavily spotted with black. As many as twelve or more are borne on each truss.

The bulbs should be planted 6 to 8 ins. deep and any soil enriched with some humus will prove suitable.

LONICERA   Honeysuckle; Woodbine
Since earliest times no plant has been more representative of the cottage garden than the native honeysuckle, *L. periclymenum*, where it may be seen twining about old trees and from its flowers when "ripen'd by the sun" a delicious sweet aromatic scent reaches out to every part of the garden. The fragrance of the flowers is especially pronounced at nightfall for it relies upon the long-tongued moths for its pollination. Where growing near an open window the scent will reach in to the house during the warm evenings of summertime. About the hedgerows the plant grows profusely and in deciduous woodlands where the scent of its blossoms in summer may be enjoyed before one comes upon the twining stems.

Shakespeare describes a scene he must have known so well in *Much Ado About Nothing* when Hero requests "Good Margaret" to

> . . . run thee to the parlour;
> Where shalt thou find my cousin Beatrice
> Proposing with the prince and Claudio:
> Whisper her ear and tell her, I and Ursula
> Walk in the orchard, and our whole discourse
> Is all of her; say that thou overheards't us,
> And bid her steal into the pleached bower,
> Where honeysuckles, ripen'd by the sun,
> Forbid the sun to enter.

Ben Jonson, friend of Shakespeare, whose moving tribute, "he was not of an age, but for all time", appeared in the Folio of 1623, describes the charms of the honeysuckle bower in the "Vision of Delight" (see quotation on page 23). " I love the man and do honour his memory (on this side idolatry)," wrote Jonson in his *Discoveries* (1630). "He was (indeed) honest, and of an open and free nature: had an excellent Phantsie; brave notions and gentle expressions. . . ." From this we may conclude that the two men must have become close friends during Shakespeare's stay in London (Jonson was a Westminster man) for always does Jonson speak of him with great affection.

Honeysuckles are to be found growing in a corner of the orchard of Anne Hathaway's cottage. Where the turfy bank arises from the garden, there is a small bower, enclosed with the twining stems of the woodbine and beneath which one may sit on a summer's evening and inhale the spicy perfume. Could this be that same orchard that Hero mentions in *Much Ado About Nothing* and the grassy bank, that is so deliciously described by Oberon in *A Midsummer Night's Dream?*—

> I know a bank whereon the wild thyme blows,
> Where oxlips and the nodding violet grows;
> Quite over-canopied with luscious woodbine
> With sweet musk-roses, and with eglantine:
> There sleeps Titania, some time of the night
> Lull'd in these flowers, with dances and delight:

SPECIES AND VARIETIES

Lonicera caprifolium. It is found from Central Europe to Western Asia and has also become naturalized in parts of Britain. It is readily distinguished from the native honeysuckle *L. periclymenum* in that its leaves are united at the base. Its highly scented flowers which appear in June are yellow with a purple tube 2 ins. long and are borne in capitate whorls. They are followed by scarlet berries.

L. japonica. A slender Japanese climber with ovate, hairy leaves, pale beneath and it blooms from July until October. The red flowers, white inside and sweetly scented are small but borne in profusion at the tips of the shoots. The form *aureo-reticulata* has broader leaves which are attractively netted with gold.

L. periclymenum. The native honeysuckle or woodbine which loves to entwine about the trunks of forest trees, its roots in the shade and its head in the sun. It is deciduous, with ovate leaves, glaucous beneath and it is in bloom from the end of June until September. The flowers are borne in terminal heads and are yellow, dull red inside and covered with hairs.

The variety Serotina, known as the Late Dutch Honeysuckle is at its best in autumn when its flowers take on a deeper reddish hue.

LUNARIA BIENNIS   Honesty

It is suggested that the plant may have reached Britain during Tudor times but it is more likely to have arrived at a much earlier date for Gerard describes the White Satin flower as he names it, in detail and said that it was found growing wild "in the woods about Pinner and Harrow, on the hills about 12 miles from London and in Essex". It may therefore be a native plant and may be the "lunarie" of Chaucer. Honesty is its more common name for its seed is clearly (honestly) revealed through the transparent skin of the seed pod and appears as a piece of white satin.

"The stalks are charged or laden with many flowers like the common stock gillofloure, of a purple colour," wrote Gerard and these are followed by the flat seed cases which are produced in sprays like tiny moons, hence its name Lunaria. They are of the size of a ten pence piece. Parkinson called it the Pennyflower. If removed when the seeds have formed and dried, they provide pleasing indoor decoration for the winter.

The plant is biennial, the seed being sown where it is to bloom, in August, and thinning the seedlings to 6 ins. apart. The plant grows 2 ft. in height and its flowers, which appear in May, are of a most brilliant purple colouring. There is also a pure white form which is a striking contrast when in bloom with it.

During Tudor times and later, the roots were boiled and eaten with meat and were also grated into salads for they were thought to possess health-giving powers.

LUPINUS   Lupin

The Virginian Lupin, so called because it was introduced into England from Virginia in 1637 by John Tradescant, Jun., was the first perennial form to be grown in European gardens. The spikes of purple-blue with their peppery smell have long been seen in cottage gardens or were so until George Russell of York introduced his wonderful strain of Russell Lupins in 1937. He used *L. polyphyllus*, discovered in British Columbia in 1825 and *L. arboreus*, the Tree Lupin in his breeding programme and his introductions must be included amongst the finest garden plants of all time. The enormous spikes, some 3 ft. in length and stems 4 to 5 ft. above soil level, are packed with the familiar pea-like flowers of the family and are obtainable in the most exquisite shades and bi-colours. Amongst the best are Wheatsheaf, golden-yellow tinted with pink; Gladys Cooper, smoky-mauve, with a pink keel; Flaming June, orange; and Viscountess Cowdray, crimson. They bloom during June and early July and are amongst the first of the summer border plants to come into colour.

The lupins first introduced from S. Europe were annuals and may have come with the Romans for Pliny, who was living in Verona during Christ's lifetime, said that there was "nothing more wholesome and lighter of digestion than White Lupins (*L. albus*), eaten dry" and during ancient times, the plants were widely grown to provide food both for humans and for cattle. The earliest herbals in English describe the plant, also *L. luteus*, the yellow annual lupin, known as the Spanish Violet for its flowers carry the delicious sweet mossy fragrance of the violet. Rev. William Hanbury in 1770 wrote that of all annual plants, this was considered by him to be the best. It is raised by sowing seed in shallow drills in the border, in early April.

Equally fine is the perennial Tree Lupin, *L. arboreus*, introduced from California during the last year of the eighteenth century. It is a plant of shrubby habit, growing 5 ft. tall and in July bears multitudes of small spikes of laburnum-yellow. There is also a white and a mauve variety. The plants, which have become naturalized in parts of S. England, require a light sandy soil and resent moving. Seed should be sown where the plants are to bloom or in small pots so that the young plants may be set out without disturbing the roots. The flowers have the sweet mossy perfume of the sweet pea and laburnum of the same family.

All lupins appreciate a well-drained sandy soil, devoid of manure and other fertilizers nor do they like lime but one in which their tap roots can penetrate to a considerable depth. They like the sun for they are native of the warm temperate regions but are of extreme hardiness. For the plants to be long living, the flower spikes should be removed before they can set seed.

The plant takes its name from the Greek, *lupe*, sadness or grief, for it is said that the seeds if not boiled in several waters before being consumed, are so bitter as to cause contortions of the face and tears in the eyes. Virgil called it *Tristis lupinus*.

LYCHNIS CHALCEDONICA   Cross of Jerusalem
It is believed to have been introduced into Europe during the time of the Crusades for in all European countries it has the same name, Cross of Jerusalem from the cross formed by the petals of the tiny flowers, many of which go to make up a head of great brilliance.

The plant is native of southern Russia and Turkey from whence it reached the Middle East and it is possible it was brought back to W. Europe by those returning from the pilgrimages abroad, since when it has remained amongst the most beloved of all cottage garden plants.

With its dark green leaves and holding its flame-coloured flowers on stems 3 to 4 ft. long, it stands out in any company, an established plant having few rivals for the amount of colour it will produce compared with the amount of garden space it occupies. It is also of easy culture and has the endurance of the paeony.

Lyte in his *Herbal* (1578) said that the tiny flowers were "clustered together at the top of the stalks after the manner of Sweet Williams . . . of the colour of red-lead", an excellent description and of the double form which appeared just before the publication of the *Paradisus*, Parkinson wrote of "this glorious flower, as rare as it is beautiful . . ." Rev. Samuel Gilbert also described the "lusty strong great double-headed flower". At the same time appeared a double white-flowered variety, considered by the Dutch to be one of the most choice of all flowers.

It was first named *L. chalcedonica* by Gerard, denoting that it originated in Asia Minor. He also named it the Campion of Constantinople.

The plant is in bloom during July and August. It should be planted in November for it is not particular as to soil, neither is it troubled by excess moisture. Propagation is by division, removing the offsets and re-planting about 18 ins. apart and this should be done every 4 or 5 years. To prolong the life of the plant, the stems should be cut down to within 6 ins. of the ground as soon as possible after flowering. This is especially advisable with the double variety.

LYCHNIS VESPERTINA   White Campion

Its scent is so unmistakably like that of the pink carnation to which it is closely related, being sweet and clove-like, that the plants were grouped together by Michael Drayton in the *Polyolbion* as being suitable for a pot-pourri:

> Sweet William, sops-in-wine, the campion; and to these
> Some lavender they put, with rosemary and bays,
> Sweet marjoram, with her like sweet basil, rare for smell . . .

The Night-scented or White Campion (Syn.: *Lychnis alba*), blooms from May until September, its pure white flowers, 1 in. across, being spicily scented on a calm, damp evening, drawing the night-flying Lepidoptera from afar. It grows 2 ft. in height, and is a handsome plant, the icy whiteness of the flowers being enhanced by the purple stems and long tapering leaves which are sticky to the touch. Even more fragrant is the double form, *flore plena*, at one time a familiar plant of the cottage garden but now rarely seen. It is propagated either from cuttings or by division of the roots in autumn.

LYSIMACHIA   Loosestrife; Creeping Jenny

L. vulgaris is known as the Great Yellow Loosestrife to distinguish it from the Purple, of a different family. A native plant, to be found along the banks of rivers, its appearance was much welcomed by weary travellers who would sit down to rest beside it for it has the effect of keeping flies away. The dried herb possesses the same powers and for this reason was hung from the beams of almost every cottage room and no cottage garden was without at least one plant. It is a delightful plant of branching habit, growing 3 ft. tall and bearing spikes of golden-yellow during July and August. It is covered in short hairs and increases by underground runners.

L. nummularia, Creeping Jenny, is also a native plant and has for centuries been planted in gardens chiefly to suppress weeds. It is happy in shade and is an excellent ground-cover plant. It was also used as a valuable aid for whooping-cough in children, boiled in red wine with honey or mead added and for that reason alone no garden was without it.

It pulls itself over the ground, rooting as it does so and is increased by detaching the runners. The flowers are yellow and cup-shaped whilst its opposite leaves turn pink in autumn. Like *L. vulgaris*, it is a perennial plant, usually found in damp woods or the banks of rivers but as it grows well in partial shade it may be used as ground cover beneath mature trees.

MATTHIOLA   Stock

A genus of branching annual or biennial herbs amongst which is *M. bicornis*, the Night Scented Stock; the East Lothian stock; the spring-flowering Brompton stocks and the summer-flowering or Ten-week stocks. Each bears a flower with an exotic penetrating clove perfume which is more clove scented than in any other flower.

All the garden stocks are descended from a single species, *M. incana* and its variety *M. annua*, annual (or biennial) plants which are native of S. Europe. Both forms were common in Elizabethan gardens and were described by Lyte in his *New Herbal* (1578) as "Stock Gillofers". Another species, *M. sinuata*, figures in the parentage of the Intermediate stocks. Spenser wrote:

> Bring hither the Pinck and Purple Cullambine,
> With Gelliflowers.

And the poet Thomson in *The Seasons* mentions the

> ". . . lavish Stock, that scents the garden round."

Henry Phillips brings to our notice the enduring quality of the stock's perfume. "Though less graceful than the rose, and not so superb as the lily, its splendour is more durable, its fragrance of longer continuance." Indeed it is and no other plant, except perhaps the wallflower, is able to convey so readily its warm, aromatic perfume. There is no need to bend to inhale the perfume from a bed of stocks, the scent can be appreciated long before entering the garden, and is rich and satisfying.

Gerard said that the Gillyflowers were "greatly esteemed for the beautie of their flowers and pleasant sweet perfume". In Gerard's time, only the white stock was grown and the violet or purple from which the flower took its name of Dame's Violet or Purple Gillyflower to distinguish it from the Wall and Clove Gillyflowers. Dr. Turner in his *Herbal* called it the "Stock Gelouer" for the purpose of distinction. By the end of the century, stocks bearing double flowers were common and all the familiar stock colours, including rose, red and "carnation" (flesh).

Brompton Stocks

Stocks may be divided into four main groups, one for each season of the year. First come the spring-flowering or Brompton Stocks, developed at the Brompton Road Nurseries of Messrs. London and Wise (who laid out the gardens at Blenheim Palace) early in the eighteenth century. The plants are true biennials, obtainable in white, purple-crimson and rose and should be sown early in July removing the dark green seedlings (as with all stocks) as these will give only single flowers. The seedlings should be transplanted in August and they may either be set out in their flowering quarters in October or wintered under a frame and planted out in March. Or they may be grown on in pots to bloom under glass early in the year. Lavender Lady and the crimson Queen Astrid are outstanding varieties.

Summer Flowering or Ten-week Stocks

They are so called because they may be brought into bloom within ten weeks of sowing the seed in gentle heat early in March. Hansen's 100% Double is a recommended strain for bedding, making branched plants only 9 ins. tall and obtainable in all the stock shades including apple-blossom pink, light blue and yellow.

The Excelsior Mammoth Strain in a similar colour range, including blood red, grows 2 ft. tall, the large densely packed spikes having a most majestic appearance in the border whilst they are valuable for cutting so that their delicious clove scent may be enjoyed indoors.

Autumn Flowering Stocks

These are the Intermediate or East Lothian Stocks, discovered in a cottage garden in East Lothian. They should be sown in March for they take several weeks longer to come into bloom than the Ten-week type. They are at their best during the autumn and until the arrival of the November frosts. The Kelvedon strain in all the rich stock colours is outstanding.

Winter Flowering Stocks

They are the finest of all stocks, known as the Winter Beauty or Beauty of Nice strain. The seed should be sown in July for winter flowering under glass. Making plants of vigorous branching habit, they grow 18 to 20 ins. tall and produce their large dense spikes throughout winter under glass. Amongst the finest varieties are Mont Blanc (white); Queen Alexandra (rose-lilac); Crimson King and Salmon King. Under glass in a temperature of 50° F. the perfume of the flowers is almost overpowering.

MATTHIOLA BICORNIS   Night-scented Stock

Syn. : *Matthiola tristis*, it is a native of Greece and is a hardy annual which should be sown where it is to bloom as it resents transplanting. Sow the seed in March or April as an edging to a border or path, or in small circles to the front of a border. If the seed is sown thinly, it will not be necessary to thin the plants. A plant of slender habit, it grows 12 ins. tall and bears tiny flowers of dingy brown, lilac or purple colouring which emit a powerful fragrance at night. Where possible, sow seed near a window which may be kept open on a warm summer evening and the scent will penetrate and fill a large room. The plant was grown in Elizabethan England, often being flowered indoors to relieve the musty atmosphere of cottage and manor when it came to be called the "Night Violet".

MIMULUS MOSCHATUS   Musk

The plant takes its name of musk from *M. moschatus*, a plant discovered in British Columbia in 1824 and whose flowers smelled so strongly of musk that when removed from a room in which they had been for several hours, the musk-like scent remained for some time. The musk was planted in small pots and placed in cottage windows to counteract the often musty smell of the rooms for the damp course had not then been incorporated into houses. Then quite suddenly the flowers completely lost their perfume. This happened about the year 1913 when plants growing in all parts of the world behaved in the same way at almost exactly the same moment. The answer may lie in the glandular hairs which covered the old musk plant when it "sported", taking on the hairy characteristic and when at the same time it took on its musk-like perfume, the hairs being perfumed not the flowers themselves. It is said that when the sweet-scented mimulus was discovered there were some plants growing nearby which had not taken on the hairy covering and these were completely devoid of perfume. Plants of the musk lost their scent when they reverted to their original form and this happened in all gardens at the same time, in the same way that a rose which "sports" (takes on a different colour) may do so in many gardens at the same time. It is a phenomenon which has happened over and over again with plants through the centuries. Perhaps the best known example is the Moss Rose, *R. muscosa*, a hairy "sport" of *R. centifolia*, its glandular hairs leaving a strong smell of musk on the fingers after handling. In certain parts of the world the plant will lose its hairs and also its perfume.

M. moschatus has now disappeared from cottage gardens but *M. luteus*, the Monkey Flower which takes its name from the Greek *mimo*, a monkey and which was introduced from N. America early in the nineteenth century, has become naturalized in moist surroundings and is now looked upon as a native plant. It is a perennial enjoying the cool, moist conditions provided by most cottage gardens where it is usually to be seen, pulling itself over the ground by means of its creeping hollow stems. It bears large golden-yellow funnel-shaped flowers which remain in bloom from June until early October. Later introductions were *M. cupreus*, bearing flowers of coppery-red and *M. variegatus*, both natives of Chile and which when crossed with *M. luteus* produced a number of brilliantly coloured hybrids, the best known being the orange-flowered Whitecroft Scarlet and the crimson, Wisley Red.

It is best planted in March in time for it to become established before coming into bloom in May or early June. Growing only 6 ins. high it makes a striking edging to a border or path. A rich friable soil should be provided.

MIRABILIS JALAPA   Marvel of Peru
It reached England from Spain early in the sixteenth century and by the publication of his *Herbal*, Gerard said that it had long been

growing in his garden. The generic name was given to the plant on account of the diversity of colours in the flowers, being striped with yellow, white and red. They are so numerous that the whole plant is covered in them from early July until late October. On a warm day the flowers refuse to open until late afternoon for which reason it is also known as the Four O'clock plant. During autumn, the flowers are open throughout the day but in a warm climate, so exacting are the flowers in their opening at four o'clock that the plant is grown solely as a time keeper.

It is a half-hardy perennial with a tuberous root and in the British Isles it should be lifted after it has finished flowering, late in October and the roots stored during winter in moist sand. However, it grows so readily from seed that from a sowing made in gentle heat in March, the plants will come into bloom early in August. The seed is sown in boxes or pans and the seedlings transplanted to small pots from which they are set out early in June. The plants grow 4 ft. tall and grow bushy and so should be allowed 3 to 4 ft. in which to develop.

It was often to be seen in many a cottage garden, left to take care of itself for unless the winter was very severe, the roots received all the protection necessary from plants growing nearby and survived all but the most severe conditions.

MONARDA DIDYMA   Bergamot

No border will be complete without the monardas, natives of the deciduous woodlands of N. America and which will grow well in all soils and in partial shade or in full sun. Their leaves, stems and roots carry a delicious aromatic lemon perfume when crushed and are much used in perfumery and in pot-pourris, also to make Oswego Tea by an infusion of the leaves in hot water. Both the leaves and the flowers may also be eaten in salads. *M. didyma* bears its red, pink or purple flowers in whorls in candelabra fashion, on 3-ft. stems and is in bloom from early July until mid-September. It may easily be raised from seed sown in boxes of prepared compost under glass, a cold frame being most suitable whilst the named varieties are increased by root division. The genus is named in honour of Dr. Nicholas Monardes of Seville who published his *Herbal* in 1569, but the plant obtained the name Bergamot because of the likeness of its perfume to the Bergamot orange. The plant, which was first mentioned by Parkinson in his *Paradisus*, likes a cool, moist soil.

SPECIES AND VARIETIES

There are a number of excellent varieties of *Monarda didyma*, all of which grow 3 ft. tall, every part of the plant being aromatic.

ADAM. The blooms, borne in whorls, are of an attractive shade of cerise.

BLUE STOCKING. Of recent introduction, the large refined blooms are of deep violet colouring, the nearest to a "blue" bergamot.

CAMBRIDGE SCARLET. For long, one of the most striking of all border plants for the flowers are of richest crimson-red.

MELISSA. It has superseded Croftway Pink and bears flowers of a lovely shade of clear shell-pink.

PRAIRIE GLOW. A new colour amongst Bergamots, the blooms being of a lovely shade of salmon-pink.

SNOW MAIDEN. It should be planted as a contrast to Cambridge Scarlet for its flowers are of icy-white.

MUSCARI   Grape Hyacinth
It was *M. botryoides alba*, the pure white form of the more common Italian Grape Hyacinth that Parkinson called Pearls of Spain. It is a delightful spring-flowering plant, native of S. Spain with an unusual sweet perfume described by the author of the *Paradisus* as ". . . like unto starch when it is made new and hot". The flower is beautifully illustrated in the painting by J. Marellus (1614–81), in the Fitz-william Museum, Cambridge, presented by the 2nd Lord Fair-haven. Of the Italian Grape Hyacinth (*M. botryoides*), so called because the tiny blooms which made up the spike are the colour of black grapes, almost navy-blue, Gerard said smelled "strong . . . yet not unpleasant". Ruskin wrote of it in more romantic mood "as if a cluster of grapes and a hive of honey had been distilled and pressed together in one small boss of celled and beaded blue". It grows 6 ins. tall and is in bloom during April and May. There is also a white form, *album*.

The muscari takes its name from the musk-like perfume of *M. moschatum*, originally *Hyacinthus moschatus* which bears blooms of a dingy yellowish-purple but which will scent a large room with its incense-like perfume if several bulbs are grown in a small pot. Gerard said that they were "kept and maintained in gardens for the

Plate 9   Garden Pink, Solomon

Plate 10   Double red paeony

pleasant smell of their blooms but not for their beauty". If planted beneath a window, its perfume will be wafted indoors during the first warm days of April.

Another lovely form is *M. comosum monstrosum* which the American writer, Louise Wilder, described as "a quaint monstrosity". Gerard called it "the fair-haired hyacinth", a suitable description of its twisted filaments of purple and gold whilst it was also known as the Tassel Hyacinth.

Lovely too is *M. racemosum*, which is a native of the eastern Mediterranean and which became naturalized in East Anglia during Elizabethan times. On a 9-in. scape it bears cylindrical racemes of navy-blue and which have a thin rim of white. They are deliciously plum-scented.

M. plumosum, the Feather Hyacinth is another delightful reminder of the old cottage garden flowers. It grows 9 ins. tall and bears its violet-blue "feathers" in May. The blooms are sterile, the petals being drawn out into fine threads to give a plume-like appearance.

The muscari are amongst the most free flowering of all bulbs and flourish in a poor, dry soil, increasing rapidly each year and carpeting the ground.

MYOSOTIS   Forget-me-not

It was taken for his personal emblem by Henry of Lancaster, later to become Henry IV, believing that whosoever would wear it, would never be forgotten, yet the flower we know perhaps better than any other was first named by the poet Coleridge in "The Keepsake", written in 1817. It is a poem of sadness:

> . . . the corn sheaves in one field
> Show summer gone, ere come . . .
> Nor can I find, amid my lonely walk
> By rivulet or spring, or wet roadside,
> That blue and bright-eyed floweret of the brook,
> Hope's gentle gem, the sweet Forget-me-not.

The poet so well describes its natural habitat, by stream or in damp deciduous woodland, flowering in early summer, after the primrose and violet, enamelling the grass with its tiny flowers of brilliant blue and its central ring of gold.

A native plant it also grows in abundance in parts of N. France, Luxemburg and Germany, where it was prized by the florists and praised by the poets in the same way that the English love the violet and the primrose. Plants in bloom in pots meet a ready sale in the Paris markets and large quantities are grown for cutting.

In England, it was found only in the cottage garden, hiding its beauty beneath other plants and where it enjoyed the moist, cool soil. It was not used as a late spring bedding plant to accompany the tulips until towards the end of the nineteenth century when for this purpose new varieties began to appear.

It is called myosotis, mouse ear, from the small woolly leaves which are shaped like the ears of a mouse. It is a biennial, seed being sown in shallow drills in the open ground in May so that the plants will be of good size to move into beds prepared for the spring-flowering plants, late in October. Plant 6 ins. apart, with polyanthus or tulips between them. Yellow tulips or polyanthus provide a pleasing contrast to the blue of the forget-me-nots.

Amongst the best varieties are Blue Ball, growing only 6 ins. tall and bearing flowers of indigo-blue; Ultramarine, the deepest blue; Royal Blue; and Rose Pink.

MYRRHIS ODORATA   Sweet Cicely

A perennial plant of the mountain pastures of N. Europe, its leaves have a myrrh-like fragrance when handled whilst they taste as if they have been steeped in sugar, a quality which gives the plant its name. It was also called Sweet Fern with cottage gardeners for its highly scented bright green tripinnate leaves resemble those of the fern. They are delicious in a salad as John Evelyn recommended, whilst the roots, like those of the Horse-radish, are sweet and aromatic and were at one time used for braising or eaten with oil or vinegar. Bees are extremely partial to its aroma and it was the custom for bee-keepers to rub the leaves over the inside of the hives to induce newly cast swarms to enter.

The seeds, too, possess an attractive myrrh-like aroma and in N. Europe have, since earliest times, been used to polish oak floors and furniture to which they impart their pleasing scent and a glossy "finish".

It is a slow-growing plant which will eventually attain a height of 5 ft. or more. It dies back completely during winter to arise again in spring.

NARCISSUS Daffodil

Is there a more delightful expression of one's love for flowers than Perdita's speech in *A Winter's Tale* when, with masterly description, Shakespeare paints a picture of the countryside in springtime? This may have been the first of Shakespeare's works to be written following his return to dwell in his home town for it was completed in time for a performance to be given at the Globe on May 15th, 1611, when Simon Forman recorded his seeing it performed on that day. There is also recorded in the accounts of the King's Players for the 5th November of the same year, details of a "play called Ye Winter's Nightes tayle" and from it, one may imagine the joys experienced by the writer in being back by his beloved Avon with the willows showing palest green and the elms bursting from their winter's rest and the

> Daffodils
> That come before the swallow dares, and take
> The winds of March with beauty.

Again, in the same play when, on the way to the Shepherd's cottage, Autolycus bursts into the joyful song of springtime:

> When daffodils begin to peer,
> With heigh! the doxy o'er the dale,
> Why, then comes in the sweet o' the year;
> For the red blood reigns in the winter's pale.

Shakespeare here used the word "pale", meaning boundary, to tell us that in March, there is still the dividing line as the anger of winter gives way to the calm of spring.

Holding up their faces to the watery March sunshine, unmindful of the cold whistling winds, the daffodil has always been a favourite flower of the poets and none sings its praises more beautifully than Sir Aubrey de Vere in his *Ode to the Daffodil*:

> O love-star of the unbeloved March,
> When, cold and shrill,
> Forth flows beneath a low, dim-lighted arch,
> The wind that beats sharp crag and barren hill,
> And keeps unfilmed the lately torpid rill!
> Herald and harbinger! with thee
> Begins the year's great jubilee!

Wordsworth and his sister, Dorothy, loved the daffodil more than any flower and from their home in the Lake District would spend almost all the daylight hours of springtime walking in the woods near the water's edge. On one occasion Dorothy has written that the daffodils "grew among the mossy stones on which some rested their heads as on a pillow, the rest tossed and reeled and danced, and seemed as if they verily laughed with the wind, they looked so gay. . . ."

As early as 1548, Turner mentioned the wild daffodil *N. pseudonarcissus* and Gerard had much to say about it. "It is most common in our country gardens . . . The flower groweth at the top, of a yellowish-white colour with a yellow crown or circle in the middle and flowereth in the month of April or sometimes sooner." He continues, "we have them all and every one of them in our London gardens in great abundance" and he mentioned that the root "being stamped with the meal of Darnel and honey, draweth forth thorns". Of other writers of the time, only Shakespeare mentions darnel, a weed which is occasionally to be found growing amongst corn.

During Elizabethan times, wild daffodils or Lent Lilies grew so profusely around London that the women of Cheapside sold the flowers made up into large bunches, to those who were unable to grow their own. This daffodil has a long trumpet of deepest yellow and has the same woodland or moss-like fragrance as the primrose. It is early flowering, hence its name, Lent Lily.

The fairy-like miniature narcissus species are almost all plants of the Elizabethan garden being ideal for small knot beds. They are hardy and long lasting, the tiny blooms nodding in the spring breezes and they are well able to withstand wintry conditions. For the rockery, for planting around the roots of young trees, as an edging to a path, for a trough garden or window box, and for indoor culture in pots, the little daffodils could be more frequently planted. They are easily grown in any ordinary fibrous loam to which a little peat has been added. Small pockets should be prepared on the rockery to take four or five bulbs, planted early in September after the rockery has been thoroughly cleaned and the established plants stripped of any straggling growth. For a window box or tub it is not always convenient to plant before mid-October, which will not be too late, as the miniatures do not seem to require so long a season in which to make root growth. They may, however, take eighteen months to come into bloom, but then will bloom most prolifically and will rapidly increase, from bulblets, to form large clumps. They should be left untouched for as long as possible and only when they begin to show less bloom should they be lifted and divided. This is best done after flowering and before the foliage dies down, in the same way that snowdrops are divided. The foliage should not, of course, be removed until it has finally turned brown and died back.

SPECIES AND VARIETIES

Narcissus bulbocodium. The "Hoop Petticoat" Daffodil and a charming little plant which likes a sunny position and a light, sandy soil but one containing peat or leafmould to retain moisture. The tiny yellow trumpets, borne amidst rush-like foliage, are backed by star-like petals of pale yellow. The form, *citrinus*, has flowers of pale citron-yellow; *conspicuus* is bright golden-yellow. It will take fully a year to become established and will bloom in March on 6-in. stems. The form *romieuxii* is the earliest of all to bloom, for it will bear its sulphur-yellow flowers during February, if given a sunny, sheltered position.

N. canaliculatus. This little Polyanthus Narcissus bears three or four sweetly scented flowers to each stem, their tiny golden cups enhanced by a pure white perianth. The narrow, erect, greenish-blue foliage is also beautiful. It blooms during April and will appreciate the shelter of a sunny rockery. 6 ins.

N. capax plenus. This is "Queen Anne's Double Daffodil" with six rows of lemon-yellow petals so arranged as to give the bloom a star-like symmetry.

N. cyclamineus. The "Cyclamen-flowered" Daffodil, so called because of its reflexed perianth. It is one of the first daffodils to bloom and is at its best by the side of a stream, for it likes a peaty, moist soil and the protection of grass in summer. The most interesting variety is one of recent introduction called "Snipe", which grows to a height of nine inches and makes a delightful pot plant. The reflexed perianth is of pure white, the trumpet deep yellow. Another good new variety is "Peeping Tom", with long, elegant golden-yellow trumpet and a perianth of the same colour. Even more compact is "Beryl", which has a tiny globular orange cup and a reflexed perianth of primrose-yellow. 9 ins.

N. gracilis. It blooms early in June and is the latest of all the daffodils to flower, but well worth waiting for. Its blooms carry the strongest perfume of all the numerous bulbous plants. Four or five pale yellow blooms appear on each twelve-inch stem and their fragance is carried far from the plants.

N. juncifolius. The Rush-leaf Daffodil of the Pyrenees, in bloom in

April. It is quite happy in the shelter of rockery stones and is charming in pans in the alpine house, but does not like open ground planting. It is highly scented, with a unique large trumpet. After flowering its leaves die back almost out of sight. 4 ins.

N. lobularis. With *N. cyclamineus* and *N. minimus*, it is among the earliest to bloom. It is extremely dainty, with a primrose-yellow trumpet and sulphur perianth. 8 ins.

N. minimus. This is the smallest of all the trumpet daffodils, bearing its dainty fringed trumpets on stems of only 4 ins. Though useful along the edge of a path or border, this fairy-like daffodil is at its best in pans in the alpine house. Outdoors it enjoys a sunny situation and a peaty soil, well drained. It comes into bloom in March.

N. odorus. The Spanish Campernelle, highly scented. It should be planted at the edge of a border beneath a window to allow its fragrance to enter the house during May. The star-like blooms are borne in clusters of three or four on 8 in. stems. There is also an attractive double form known as "Queen Anne's Irish Jonquil".

N. tenuior. Known as the "Silver Jonquil", it comes late into bloom and is at its best at the end of May and early in June. Three or four blooms, richly perfumed, appear on each stem, with sulphur-yellow cups and a perianth of silvery cream. 8 ins.

N. triandrus albus. The Angel's Tears Daffodil produces a cluster of tiny creamy-white flowers of globular cup and reflexed perianth which droop gracefully like snowdrops, and give the impression of tear drops. It is in bloom during April.

NEPETA CATARIA   Catmint

It is so called because of its fascination to cats who eat the new leaves in spring and roll on the plants on warm days in summer. The catmints are hardy perennials, found in the British Isles and on chalk land from Portugal to Kashmir. The native *N. cataria* grows 2 ft. tall and the leaves are covered in soft hairs to give it a frosted appearance. The pale pink flowers are borne in whorls all summer.

N. mussinii is a lovely plant for the front of a border, growing 12 ins. tall and with small grey-green leaves whilst it bears neat spikes of misty purple all summer. Plant in spring and propagate by root division. The catmints like a sandy soil.

NICOTIANA AFFINIS   Tobacco Plant

A genus of about thirty species of usually hairy shrubs or plants with large undivided leaves and bearing tubular flowers in terminal panicles. The flowers are either white, green or crimson and are borne in continuous succession from July until September.

Nicotiana tabacum is the tobacco of commerce, so well known for the fragrance of its leaves when dried. It is named after Jean Nicot, Ambassador to Portugal in 1560 and who planted it in the garden of the Embassy in Lisbon for the valuable qualities of its dried leaves which were in demand for inhaling as snuff. It is believed that the word cigar is derived from the Spanish "cigarral", a word which means "little garden" for most small gardens of the Iberian Peninsula at one time grew a few plants of *N. tabacum* for its curative powers. The first cigars are believed to have been made about 1540 by one, Demetrio Pela, and by late Elizabethan times the tobacconist was as firmly established in the City of London as the herbalist. Gerard tells us that "the dry leaves are used to be taken in a pipe and set on fire and sucked into the stomach and thrust forth again at the nostrils. . . ."

Nicotiana affinis, the Tobacco Plant grows 3 to 4 ft. in height with glaucous ovate leaves some 6 ins. long and through late summer and autumn bears its starry white flowers, green on the outside, which open and emit a sweet perfume in the evening. The blooms remain closed by day but those of Dwarf White Bedder which are similar in all respects but which are borne on stems only 18 ins. tall, remain open and are fragrant by day as well as at night. The Tobacco plants are half-hardy annuals raised from seed sown in gentle heat early in the year and planted out when hardened, early in June.

NIGELLA   Love-in-a-Mist

It is one of the loveliest of annual flowers and its country name so well describes the flowers of misty blue which is half hidden in a frill of linear foliage, like that of fennel and of brilliant green. It takes its botanical name from *niger*, black, from the colour of its seeds, those of *N. sativa* having a nutmeg-like fragrance and from early Tudor times were imported from Egypt to use for flavouring cakes. The aromatic seeds were put in muslin bags to place amongst linen and clothes whilst Gerard advises warming the seed over hot ashes to scent a musty room or to be inhaled, to assist with the breathing from a cold in the head. Tournefort said that apothecaries distilled from the seed an oil used as a substitute for spikenard.

N. damascena, native of the Near East was first grown in English gardens during early Elizabethan times. It is illustrated in Gerard's *Herbal*, exactly as it is today and he writes, *"nigella* is both fair and pleasant". He also tells us that it had the old Anglo-Saxon name of Gith and was also called St. Catherine's flower. The seed crushed into powder and mixed with vinegar, Gerard says that "it taketh away freckles and is a most excellent remedie". The seeds of *N. damascena* are not aromatic.

By the end of the sixteenth century double-flowered forms were grown and every cottage garden grew the single form, seed being sown in the open early in April and thinning the seedlings to 3 to 4 ins. apart. Miller recommends making a sowing in August when the soil is well drained. The plants will come into bloom fully a month earlier than those from a spring sowing. They grow 18 ins. tall and are suitable for indoor decoration, looking most attractive in a pewter tankard.

The variety Miss Jekyll, bearing flowers of cornflower-blue; and Oxford-blue, are both lovely whilst equally fine is the new Persian Rose, bearing flowers of antique rose-pink.

OCYMUM BASILIUM   Sweet Basil
Ocymum basilium is known as the Sweet Basil and is an annual plant which is only half-hardy in the more exposed districts of the British Isles. The seed is sown in gentle heat or under cloches early in April, the young plants being set out late in May. The leaves possess a distinct sweet clove-like perfume and flavour and if used in salads with discretion, will impart a pleasant aromatic taste. In a good summer the plant, which grows 2 ft. tall, will form plenty of leaf which may be removed in September and dried and used for stuffings and in pot-pourris.

The plant figures in those lovely lines by Shelley:

> Madonna, wherefore hast thou sent to me
> Sweet basil and mignonette?
> Embleming love and health which never yet
> In the same wreath might be.

Michael Drayton, the Elizabethan poet describes two maidens both of whom make for themselves a chaplet. One, Glaia, gathers flowers only for their beauty whilst Lelipa picks hers for their fragrance:

> With Basil then I will begin,
> Whose scent is wondrous pleasing.

Shelley's reference to "sweet basil and mignonette" is interesting for in the Islands of the East Indies and in France, the essential oil of the Sweet Basil has such a distinct smell of mignonette that the two are often mixed together. The seeds are also scented and are used in muslin bags to place amongst clothes.

Of the Bush Basil, *Ocimum minimum*, which grows 6 ins. tall and is also an annual, Parkinson said, "it was used to make sweet washing waters and sometimes it is put into nosegays . . . to procure a cheerful and merry heart". Tusser includes both in his Herbs for Strewing and wrote in his *Five Hundred Points of Good Husbandry* (1573):

> Fine Basil desireth it may be her lot,
> To grow as the gilliflower trim in a pot . . .

It forms an erect plant with a round bushy head with leaves no larger than those of the thyme. Tusser's comparison to the clove-scented pink (gilliflower) may have been because of its similar clove-like fragrance.

OENOTHERA BIENNIS   Evening Primrose
It is a biennial plant and the most familiar of 100 or more species known to European gardeners, several of which bear flowers which are powerfully scented at night. The flowers sleep by day, the hooks of the tapering sepals clasping each other so that the bloom cannot open. Then as twilight descends, the bloom is seen to discard its protective hood and opens in all its fragrant loveliness.

> "You, Evening Primroses, when day has fled,
> Open your pallid flowers, by dews and moonlight fed."

John Keats had observed the phenomena:

> "But that 'tis ever startled by the leap
> Of buds into ripe flowers."

The plant comes into bloom at a height of 4 ft. but by the end of summer will have reached 6 ft. or more. It has downy, lance-shaped leaves and has one of the longest flowering seasons of all plants, coming into bloom early in June and continuing until October. The blooms, which measure 3 ins. across are of a lovely clear primrose-yellow colour and emit a delicious sweet perfume at night. They are pollinated by moths, nectar being secreted in the lower part of the calyx tube. The flowers soon die but others take their place in endless succession. The plants are readily raised from seed sown in July where they are to bloom and from then on they will seed themselves. It is believed that *O. biennis* first reached Europe in 1619, having been sent from Virginia to Padua and it must have been introduced into Britain a year or so later for Parkinson (1629) makes mention of it as the "tree primrose", since when it has been a favourite in every cottage garden for its evening perfume.

OMPHALODES VERNA　　　　　　　　　Venus' Navel-wort

A native of S. Europe, this delightful carpeting plant was introduced during the latter years of Charles I's reign when it quickly became a favourite of the cottage garden. Though quite happy in partial shade, in full sunlight it makes a superb display, during March and April being a sheet of brilliant blue, hence its name of Bright-eyed Mary, the flowers resembling forget-me-nots both in colour and in form. There is also a white variety, *alba*, which makes a fitting companion to the blue. The plants will form dense mats through which dwarf bulbs may push themselves up creating a delightful picture as soon as the snow has melted and the sun gathers strength.

The plant obtained its name Venus' Navel-wort from the peculiar dome shape of its seeds.

ORIGANUM MARJORANA　　　　　　　　Sweet Marjoram

The Sweet Marjoram is native of Spain but reached England early in her history and with its compact habit and staying green all year, it was planted in Tudor knot gardens (with hyssop), hence it became known as the Knotted Marjoram. It makes a spreading plant and has a camphor-like scent. The tiny leaves are dark green and there is a handsome golden variety, *aureum*, which forms a dense mat and in early summer is the most golden plant of the garden. Propagate by root division or by cuttings rooted in sandy compost and plant out in spring. They like a sandy soil and sunny situation.

The marjorams have many uses. They are an important part of a bouquet garni, with common and lemon thyme and a bay leaf, to flavour soups and stews (or dried and used in a similar way) and they make the best stuffings for pork and veal. Finely chopped, they are sprinkled into omelettes and over scrambled eggs and, like bay, a sprig placed in a glass of cold milk will impart a balsamic flavour.

ORNITHOGALUM Star of Bethlehem

Natives of the near East, the bulbs were brought back by returning Crusaders and soon were in every cottage garden. Parkinson knew ten species.

Possibly the best known is *O. umbellatum*, Star of Bethlehem, for its flowers have covered the hillsides about the little town since before Christ's time. The snow-white flowers may have been the "Dove's dung" mentioned in the Book of Kings for the bulbs were used as food in time of famine, whilst the flowers do resemble bits of bird's dung about the rocky hillsides.

Parkinson tells us that in Italy the bulbs were roasted and had a taste similar to that of the Sweet Chestnut, yet eaten raw they are poisonous.

O. pyrenaicum, now rarely seen, had also reached England early in her history and by Turner's time was grown as a commercial crop around Bath, the flower spikes being sold in bundles as "Bath asparagus".

SPECIES

Ornithogalum arabicum. The Arabian Star-flower which in June and July will bear heads of twelve or more starry white flowers on a stem nearly 2 ft. long. The jet black ovary at the centre of the flowers makes this a most striking flower for indoor decoration.

O. nutans. A most handsome species bearing on 15-in. stems, umbels of six to nine flowers of a most unusual shade of grey-green edged with white whilst the narrow petals are attractively reflexing. The flowers carry the sweet moss-like fragrance of the woodlands.

O. umbellatum. The Star of Bethlehem which grows 8 to 9 ins. tall and bears multitudes of snow-white flowers during early summer. It is a delightful plant for the alpine garden or for massing along a cottage path, planting the bulbs between clumps of red allwoodii to provide contrast in colour and protection during wintertime.

PAEONIA Paeony

It is the cottage gardener's plant without a rival and no plant is more steeped in history. It was named by the ancient Greeks after Paeon, who used the milk-like extract from the roots to cure the wounded Pluto. It was also described in detail by Theophrastus in his *Enquiry into Plants* written about 300 B.C. To the Greeks, and the peoples of those countries of the Eastern Mediterranean, the plant was held in something of awe for the seeds of certain species tend to give off a glow at night. This is due to a phosphorescent quality, and it was believed that both the seeds and the roots should be obtained only during the dead of night. At that time the roots were used for healing wounds, whilst the seeds were infused in rain water to make a special "tea". It was also believed that they would act as a charm against evil if carried in the pocket.

A paeony believed to be native to Britain, *P. mascula*, may well have been introduced from Europe by the early Christians, for the few places where the plants are now still to be found growing wild are situated close to the sites of ancient monasteries. One such place is at Steep Holme, a rocky islet in the estuary of the Severn where *P. mascula* produces flowers of red, pink and white, though chiefly they are of a purple-crimson colour. The beautiful single flowers are more than 4 ins. in diameter, the stamens being tipped with gold. The blooms are enhanced by the glossy, dark green foliage of the plant, whilst the seed vessels are most attractive during autumn when they open to reveal rose-red seeds which have the appearance of coral. For this reason the plant is also known as *P. corallina*. The same plant is occasionally to be found growing wild near Winchcombe in Gloucestershire, whilst Gerard recorded it at Southfleet in Kent. It is occasionally to be found in other out-of-the-way places, between the Bristol Channel and the mouth of the Thames but is one of the most rare of our native flowers and is mentioned in few books devoted to flowers of the British Isles.

During monastic times the paeony, and it would be *P. mascula*, for it is doubtful if others reached this country until the middle of the sixteenth century, about the time of the Dissolution of the Monasteries, was valued here as it was by the ancient Greeks, almost entirely for its medicinal purposes until the end of Stuart times. Parkinson, then botanist to Charles I, writing in his *Paradisus* says, ". . . we cherish them for their beauty and delight of their goodly flowers as well as for their physical virtues". Parkinson tells us that the root of *P. mascula* was "far above all else used as a remedy for all epileptical diseases". Culpeper in his *Herbal* also mentioned the use of the roots in much the same way.

It was Alexander Neckam, Abbot of Cirencester at the time of Richard I and of whom it is recorded that his mother reared both Richard and Alexander, born on the same night, the one at Windsor, the other at St. Albans, who gave us the first work devoted entirely to gardening in this country. In *De Naturis Rerum* he carefully lists those flowers and herbs which were grown in England at that time (1190), and it is of interest that he places the paeony along with the medicinal and culinary herbs rather than with those plants which were used to adorn the garden. In addition to the value of the root, the seeds were used for serving with meats for flavouring. Longland in *Piers Plowman* (1380), also mentions that the seeds were used for flavouring purposes.

Whereas *P. mascula* is known as the Male Paeony, *P. feminea* or *P. officinalis* was known as the Female Paeony. This was the plant so well known to the Greeks, but it was the double form of *P. officinalis* that was to become familiar in English gardens. It was from the Mediterranean regions that the first plants of the double paeony reached Britain some time before the beginning of the sixteenth century, but exactly when is not known, though it is believed that *P. officinalis* was cultivated here during Saxon times. In his delightful essay *Of Gardens*, first published in 1597, the same year in which Gerard published his *Herbal*, and Shakespeare was writing the two parts of *Henry IV*, Francis Bacon has written, ". . . there ought to be gardens for all the months of the year, in which severally, things of beauty may be then in season". For April, he suggests, "the tulip, the double paeony and the daffodil".

William Turner is the first to mention it. Writing in his *New Herbal* (1568), he said that he had seen the double crimson paeony in Newberry, "in the garden of a rich clothier", and Gerard in his *Herbal* (1597) has illustrated it. Parkinson has frequently mentioned the plant. "This double form is so frequent in every garden of note, that it is almost labour in vain to describe it," he writes in the *Paradisus* and he mentions that it blooms from the middle of May until the middle of June, or thereabouts, the paeony hybrids remaining later in bloom, until early July.

In Britain the reason why the crimson-flowered herbaceous paeony, *P. officinalis* (and its pink counterpart), is to be so often found in the gardens of ancient manor house and country cottage is the great durability of the plant. It has been described as being as hardy and as durable as the dock and this is true, for when once established, the plants will make dense bushes growing thicker than they grow tall and will bear as many as two dozen blooms per plant year after year.

Parkinson commented on the permanency of the paeony: "Double and single paeonies are fit flowers to furnish a garden and by reason of their durability give out fresh pleasure every year without any further trouble." Indeed, they may be considered amongst the most labour-saving of all plants, for they require only to be planted when they may be expected to last at least for a lifetime.

They resent disturbance and should be planted only where they will be fully permanent, in the same way as one plants a tree or a hedge. Even a single plant in a small border will produce a magnificent display each year and at a time when the border will generally be lacking in colour.

The herbaceous paeonies grow between 2 and $3\frac{1}{2}$ ft. in height but mostly flower at a height of around 3 ft. making them suitable for mid-border planting. The large globular multi-petalled blooms of the double varieties often measure 10 ins. in diameter, and no other flower can equal them for beauty. In Ireland they are called "Paeony-roses" for they greatly resemble the red cabbage rose of old, though they may be more likened to the Japanese chrysanthemum in their enormous size and fullness of bloom.

By comparison, the scented paeony is comparatively modern for it was not until the arrival of *P. lactiflora* towards the end of the eighteenth century that the herbaceous paeony took on its perfume. This is the white-flowered single paeony, known also as *P. albiflora* and The Bride and its flowers were heavily scented. It had been discovered in the Siberian wastes by a Russian traveller who found that its roots were cooked and eaten by the Mongols as a substitute for potatoes, whilst a pleasant drink was made by a diffusion of the seeds.

The plant appears to have been lost and re-introduced in 1805 by Sir Joseph Banks when he was Director of His Majesty's garden at Kew during the reign of George III and shortly before he took to a wheel chair to get about the gardens. But it was the French hybridizers who first took up the scented paeony, namely Calot, Dessert, Crousse and Lemoine, crossing it with *P. officinalis* and with a number of Chinese introductions. The result was a series of magnificent plants, all bearing scented flowers and which came to be planted in every cottage garden. They have survived until the present day. First came *P. edulis superba* from Lemoine in 1824 and Marie Crousse in 1832, bearing spice-scented flowers of shrimp-pink. Calot's Duchesse de Nemours followed in 1855 and has remained possibly the finest of all scented paeonies. Shortly after, James

Kelway began his life's work which brought his firm to the forefront of paeony growers, the lilac-tinted Lady Veronica Bruce which appeared in 1887, being one of his earliest introductions. But none is lovelier than the Single paeony The Bride and its pink companion, Mistral, with their rich perfume and conspicuous golden stamens.

With their appreciation of shade, the paeony may be used in a mixed border which is to be planted in a partially shaded position and devoted entirely to shade-loving plants. The ideal position for the paeony would be one where rays of the afternoon and evening sunshine may penetrate, the plants being protected from early morning sunshine and the heat of the mid-day sun. A position beneath mature trees, or where planted alongside an orchard, or beneath ornamental cherries and other flowering trees will prove most suitable for paeonies. For the same reason, and because the plants are so permanent, herbaceous paeonies should be more widely planted to the front of a shrubbery. With their attractive bottle-green foliage, which takes on rich bronze tints in early spring and autumn, the plants will provide valuable ground cover between the shrubs quite apart from the beauty of their blooms. But paeonies are gross feeders and they should not be planted where mature trees and shrubs will deprive the plants of moisture and food. In this respect they are like the primrose and polyanthus, enjoying a cool, partially shaded situation but one which is away from close proximity to tall trees which would deprive the soil of moisture and sustenance, and where dew and gentle rain could not penetrate. For this reason it is never satisfactory to plant against a hedge of privet used as a background, for like the paeony they, too, are gross feeders.

It is only during about ten weeks of the year that the paeony is quite dormant, from the middle of September until early December and if at all possible planting should be done at this time. By planting in October after the foliage has died back, the roots will become established before the severe weather and will get away to a good start as soon as the ground begins to warm in spring.

The actual planting of the roots is extremely important. Paeony roots are thick and fleshy, being woody and tuberous-like, and quite apart from the need to guard against breakage of the crown buds, is the need to handle the roots with care for they are easily broken. A two-year-old root containing two to three buds or eyes will be most suitable, for it will be vigorous and will grow away rapidly, whereas an old root will take considerably longer to establish.

When planting remove sufficient soil to accommodate the roots, without bunching them together. They should be spread out well, with the crown no more than 2 ins. below the surface of the ground. If the soil is on the heavy side then plant no more than 1 inch deep. This is of great importance, for too deep planting is the chief cause of failure.

SPECIES AND VARIETIES

P. lobata. The Lobed Paeony of Spain, a form of *P. peregrina* and bearing, on 2-ft. stems, throughout May and June, goblet-shaped flowers of an unusual shade of salmon-red. The variety, Sunshine, rather more dwarf, bears larger flowers of vermilion-red.

P. mascula. Also known as *P. corallina*, for its large seed pods have coral-coloured seeds. Native to Britain, it comes into bloom before the end of April and bears bright purple-red flowers on 2 ft. stems.

P. mlokosewitschi. From the Caucasus and now scarce. It makes a beautiful plant 2 ft. tall and bears, in April and May, its large, single, clear-yellow, bowl-shaped blooms which have coral-red stamens. The blooms are sweetly scented and are enhanced by the attractive sea-green foliage of the plant.

P. mollis. It makes a tiny plant only 15 ins. tall, and during May bears small flowers of purple-red.

P. officinalis. This is the old double paeony well known in its crimson-red form, "rubra", which reached Britain towards the middle of the sixteenth century. The blooms are large and cabbage-like, whilst the foliage of the plant is of rich bottle-green. The blooms are without perfume and appear early in May before those of the Chinese paeony. There is a pure white form, *alba plena*, and a double rose, *rosea plena*. The best named variety is "Charmer" and it bears a huge bloom of glowing crimson.

P. peregrina. It is a most outstanding paeony bearing large brilliant scarlet cup-shaped flowers which have a ring of vivid golden anthers. It blooms during May and was known to Parkinson and the Elizabethan gardeners, for it was the Red Paeony of Constantinople.

P. tenuifolia. The Adonis or Fennel-leaf paeony which has attractive fern-like foliage and grows only 18 ins. tall. It bears a single cup-shaped bloom of deep blood-red during May, but even more striking is the double form *P. tenuifolia plena*.

Of the many lovely varieties of herbaceous paeony, Alice Harding with its incurved blooms of creamy-white and Albatross, its huge white blooms being tipped with crimson, are outstanding. Claire Dubois bears large blooms of satin-pink edged with silver whilst Gayborder June bears flowers of carmine-red. Kelway's Queen bears flowers of shrimp-pink, likewise Marie Crousse. Magnificent is Phillipe Rivoire, its crimson blooms having a black sheen and the perfume of the "tea" rose.

In single varieties Admiral Harwood bears pale pink flowers with a central boss of golden petaloids whilst Mistral has flowers of cherry-red.

PAPAVER   Poppy
"Opium," wrote Gerard, "somewhat too plentifully taken doth also bring death." He described two forms of the poppy, the Red Poppy of the cornfields, *P. rhoeas* and the White-flowered Opium Poppy, *P. somniferum*, so that Shakespeare may. have seen this plant in Gerard's London garden with its shining leaves broad and oblong, in Gerard's own words, "like those of the lettuce". Like our native Red Poppy, it is an annual, the petals of the flower being almost transparent, in Ruskin's words "like painted glass".

Coulson Kernahan paints an impressive picture of the Red Poppy. "When I see a poppy, lifting the crimsoned cup of its chalice high above the heads of the growing corn, that one day will be made into bread, I think of the red of the wine cup and the bread in the hand of our Lord at the Last Supper, and bow my head in silent prayer."

On poor dry soils where most other annual plants would fail, the poppy flourishes and though the flowers do not last long, each day sees the appearance of new flowers of the most brilliant colours. It is remarkable that the poets made little or no reference to the fleeting appearance of the flowers of the poppy. Only Burns in "Tam o' Shanter" reminded us of this; that the petals will fall at the slightest touch but more buds are already opening:

> Pleasures are like poppies spread,
> You seize the flow'r, its bloom is shed.

Seed is sown in spring where the plants are to bloom, the best method being to scatter the seed about a circle made in the soil and thinning the plants to 3 to 4 ins. apart as soon as large enough to handle. They will not transplant with any degree of success.

Many excellent garden types have been developed from the Corn Poppy and also from the Opium Poppy. Hybrids of the former were first developed by the Dutch during the eighteenth century. Fairchild writing in 1722 described them as being "one of the most beautiful flowers that can be imagined. They are commonly as double as a Rose."

Crossing the so-called Dutch poppies with one that he found in his garden at Shirley in Warwickshire, the Rev. W. Wilks evolved a strain which came to be known as the Shirley Poppies. That which he first used was one found in a field near his home, bearing a red flower but with an unusual white edge and so popular did his strain become during the 1880's that the Red Poppy of the cornfields came to be known as the Shirley Poppy. From an April sowing where they are to bloom, the plants will begin to bloom early in July and continue until October.

SPECIES AND VARIETIES

PINK CHIFFON. A development of the Paeony-flowered strain and introduced in 1964 by Messrs. Samuel Dobie Limited of Chester, from seed supplied by Mr. W. Freeman of Derbyshire, the blooms are remarkably like enormous pink paeonies. The pale pink blooms are deep rose-pink at the centre and form a solid ball of curled petals held on sturdy stems 30 ins. tall.

P. pavonium. The Peacock Poppy, introduced from Turkestan. A hardy annual growing 18 ins. tall, the small flowers of brilliant scarlet having a contrasting black mark at the base of each petal.

P. rhoeas. The Shirley Poppy of which there are many forms.

REV. WILKS STRAIN. A re-selected form of the original bearing single flowers in many brilliant colours.

SHIRLEY DOUBLE QUEEN. The double form of the Rev. Wilks strain, the blooms having the appearance of paeonies, their petals being attractively frilled. The selection includes attractive pink and white bi-colours.

RANUNCULUS-FLOWERED. Also known as Pompadour, the blooms being smaller than the Double Shirley strain but more tightly packed with petals and in a wide range of attractive colours.

RYBURGH HYBRID. A double-flowered strain of outstanding beauty, colours including red, pink, salmon, scarlet.

PETASITES FRAGRANS   Winter Heliotrope
Syn.: *Tussilago fragrans*. It is known as the Scented Coltsfoot, Sweet
Scented Tussilage or the Scented Butterbur for it is a species of the
Common Butterbur. It is a native of S. Italy and though introduced
early in our history, became naturalized in the nineteenth century,
first in the south-east of England from whence it spread in a
northerly direction whilst it is also common in the East Coastal
regions of Ireland, especially near Dublin.

The plant was first discovered by a Monsieur Villan who was
attracted by its delicious fragrance when visiting Mount Pilat and
it is quite amazing how this little native of S. Europe has so readily
acclimatized itself to the British Isles where it delights us with its
perfume on the dullest days of the year. Many species of the Coltsfoot we have always had but this little intruder had been given a
special welcome to our shores long before it came to be so much
appreciated by the Victorians. It was planted in pots where its
fragrance during the coldest days of winter, freshened both cottage
and country house, where it remained in bloom for many weeks.
Phillips writing in the *Flora Historica* says, "and thus the plant which,
so short a time back, could not by all its fragrant charms, obtain a
corner in a cottage garden, now fills a situation in the proud saloon,
to the admiration of all the crowds that usually attend the decorated
apartments of gay routes."

It grows to a height of about 9 ins. with toothed leaves, lobed at
the base and it comes into flower early in January, its flowers of
lilac-grey having the delicious spicy scent of heliotrope. It is a
delightful plant to come across in the countryside but when introduced to the garden may become a nuisance with its invasiveness
unless confined to rough ground in some out-of-the-way corner.

PHILADELPHUS   Mock Orange; Orange Blossom
A genus closely related to the hydrangea, and taking the name
"mock orange" from the likeness of the blossom to the flowers of the
citrus, whilst the scent is similar. The Greeks named the plant after
Ptolomy Philadelphus, King of Egypt and with its hollow stems when
the pith is removed, it was with the lilac, given the name syringa, a
flute, thus giving rise to some confusion though botanically the true
syringa is the lilac.

Linnaeus has told us that *P. coronarius* is native of the country around Verona in Italy though the Near East is its more likely habitat where the pliable branches covered in blossom were used to make coronets.

The plant had reached England at an early date, possibly introduced by the Romans and by Tudor times it was to be found in most gardens. Gerard mentions that it grew in quantity in his garden and it is on record that at a much later date, the sailors of Captain Cook's expeditions used the dried blossoms and young shoots (also scented) to make an aromatic "tea".

P. coronarius is the earliest species to bloom, flowering before the end of May, bearing its creamy-white blossoms which measure about 1 inch across, in dense racemes. There is also a form *aureus* with golden leaves. The plant with its cane-like foliage was taken up by Lemoine, the French hybridizer during the last century and crossing it with *P. microphyllus* succeeded in raising a number of beautiful garden hybrids.

PHLOX PANICULATA Flame Flower

Pliny has told how the Greeks used a flower in their garlands known as phlox, a Greek word meaning "flame", but it is doubtful as to whether this was a reference to the plant we now call the phlox for *P. paniculata* is native only of N. America. It was introduced into Britain by Dr. Sherrard early in the eighteenth century and with its hardiness and ease of culture, quickly established itself in cottage gardens, enjoying the cool, moist and well-manured soil. But for some reason, the plant remained exactly as it was introduced for more than two centuries until Captain Symons Jeune took it up in the same way that George Russell improved the lupin and with the Simpsons of Otley, transformed it out of all recognition, introducing a range of striking new colours. Flowers of the type were of a delicate lilac shade and borne during July and August.

Planting should be done in late autumn, and every 3 to 4 years to maintain the quality of the flower trusses, the roots should be lifted and divided and replanted into (if possible) a fresh position. They appreciate a well-nourished soil.

VARIETIES

ENDURANCE. A lovely variety growing 3 ft. tall and bearing weather-resistant flowers of salmon-orange.

LOOK AGAIN. Well named for the huge trusses of purple blue compel one to "look again".

PARMA VIOLET. The trusses are large and refined and of a rich Parma-violet colour.

PHYSALIS   Winter Cherry; Chinese Lantern
As long ago as 1562, Turner wrote that this plant "had fruit in seed vessels lyke unto bladders", and indeed, the name "physalis" means "a bladder". It is a plant known to Dioscorides who was writing early in the sixth century when all parts of the plant were used in medicine, especially to treat gout. The plant was *P. alkekengi* which by Gerard's time was to be found in every cottage garden for its inflated scarlet seed pods were dried and used for winter decoration and had the appearance of Chinese lanterns. Phillips said that they were used "to ornament the chimney-pieces of cottage parlours".

A better form is *P. franchettii*, a native of Japan and introduced by the Chelsea nurseryman, Veitch, towards the end of the last century. Its "lanterns" are almost twice the size and of deep crimson-red.

The plant increases by means of underground runners, like mint, and requires a moist, well-manured soil in partial shade. It should be confined to one part of the border where it can spread unhindered by other plants.

PHYSOSTEGIA VIRGINIANA   Obedient Plant
The plant reached England from Virginia early in the 17th century and like most N. American plants, it is hardy, fully perennial and grows well in all soils. It also blooms during August and September when the border has lost its early colour. It grows about 2 ft. tall with lance-shaped leaves and it bears its tubular flowers in 4-sided tapering spikes. Their footstalks are so fixed to the stems that each individual flower can be moved into a new position and it will stay there, hence its country name of the obedient plant. The flowers are deep pink and there is a white variety, *alba*.

POLYGONATUM MULTIFLORUM   Solomon's Seal
Now so rarely seen, the Common Solomon's Seal has for centuries been one of the loveliest of cottage garden plants sending up its gracefully arching stems to a height of 2 ft. and bearing in May and

June, drooping bells of cool greenish-white. It is a perennial with dark green glossy leaves borne, like the flowers all along the stem like a ladder, hence its name Ladder-to-Heaven. A plant of deciduous woodlands, it loves the shade and beneath it primroses may be planted and will still be in bloom when the Solomon's Seal is opening its dainty bells in early summer. Miss Sinclair Rohde has described the flowers as having "a curious rich 'thick' smell, quite unlike the scent of any other English flower", but this is a reference to *P. odoratum*, a rare woodland plant whose scent resembles the perfume of the tuberose.

There is a belief that the name "seal" was given the plant because of the markings of the fleshy stem which when cut transversely, show the impression of the seal of Solomon. More credible is the theory of Dioscorides who said that the roots when dry and crushed and placed on flesh wounds caused them to be healed (sealed) in the quickest possible time, hence Solomon's Heal became Solomon's Seal. A medical authority of the reign of Elizabeth I has said that the roots "stamped whilst fresh and green and applied to the skin, taketh away in one night, any bruise gotten by woman's wilfulness in stumbling upon their hasty husband's fists". From the bells a toilet water was distilled.

The roots are best planted in November just below the surface of the soil which should contain some humus to help maintain moisture during the summer months.

POLYMONIUM COERULEUM Jacob's Ladder
Flourishing in both sunshine and shade and tolerant of all soil conditions, it is a wonderful plant for a newly-made garden, coming into bloom in May and covering itself with flowers of brilliant blue. The variety Blue Pearl grows about 12 ins. tall and Sapphire about 18 ins. Both are lovely and will bloom from May until the end of July. It is a native plant which may be traced back to the beginnings of time. It was loved by the first Elizabethan gardeners and has been grown in cottage gardens since earliest times under the name of the Blue or Greek Valerian.

PRIMULA AURICULA Bear's Ears
A race of plants descended from *P. auricula* and *P. pubescens* and differing from the Alpine auriculas in that their foliage and bloom

may be covered with farina. They were known as Mountain Cowslips or Bear's Ears from the shape of the leaves and its covering of farina (hairs). They are known as hardy border auriculas though with them must be included several which are entirely free from farina but which, with their vigorous coarse habit cannot be classed with the more refined Alpines. They are plants of great antiquity and with their hardy constitution, freedom of flowering, the rich "old master" colouring of the blooms and their exotic fragrance, they are amongst the loveliest of all flowers, in bloom from April until mid-June. So powerful is their scent that quite a small bed of plants will be almost overpowering when the early summer sun shines down upon them whilst they impregnate the sun-baked soil with their perfume. They are plants which, like the honeysuckle which their perfume so much resembles, give of their richest scent only when warmed by the sun.

Since their introduction into England about the year 1575, the border auriculas have come to be cherished in garden of cottage and manor alike. In the garden of Hardwick Hall in Derbyshire they grow where they may have been since the time of their introduction, the same year in which this gracious house was built by Bess, Countess of Shrewsbury and the rich colours of their flowers match those of the tapestries with which the magnificent Presence Chamber is hung. Here Mary, Queen of Scotland and France was held prisoner and she may well have seen auriculas in the walled gardens. Auriculas are also to be found in the tiny garden of Shakespeare's boyhood home in Stratford-on-Avon for they are flowers beloved by all and they have been with us for over four centuries. Parkinson wrote that "auriculas do seem every one of them to be a nosegay alone of itself . . . their pretty scent doth add an increase of pleasure in those that make them ornaments for their wearing".

They were the flowers of James Thomson's *The Seasons*, when

"fair-handed spring unbosoms every grace" with
. . . auriculas, enrich'd
With shining meal o'er all their velvet leaves.

And of Thomas Fuller's *Antheologia or The Speech of Flowers* (1660): "And now in the springtime earth did put on her new clothes. . . . For there was yellow marigolds, wallflowers, auriculusses, gold-knobs and abundance of other nameless flowers."

Not having been confined to pots under glass as have the show auriculas, the older border varieties have in no way lost their vigour and if they can be given a sunny situation and a soil which does not readily dry out during summer, they will prove adaptable to almost every garden, quickly growing into large vigorous clumps above which they bear on 9-in. stems, irregular heads of large velvety blooms. This irregularity adds to their old-world charm. There is nothing stiff about them and when cut and placed in small vases indoors, they will remain fresh for days and scent the house with their warm sweet honey fragrance. Plant in spring or in autumn and top dress each year.

VARIETIES

ADAM LORD. A variety of sturdy habit with serrated foliage which forms into numerous rosettes above which in large trusses appear the navy-blue flowers with their creamy-white centre.

AMETHYST. It forms a large truss of bright wine-purple flowers with a clearly defined white centre and is densely covered in farina.

BLUE MIST. Now rare but an outstanding variety and so well named for the medium-sized blooms are of pure sky blue with the farina providing a silvery, mist-like sheen.

BLUE VELVET. Of vigorous habit, it forms a symmetrical head of purple-blue flowers with a clearly defined creamy-white centre and emits a rich honey perfume.

BROADWELL GOLD. A superb variety found by Mr. Joe Elliott in a Cotswold cottage garden but it is now rare. It bears large blooms of brilliant golden-yellow with beautifully waved petals and they diffuse a musk-like fragrance. All parts of the plant are covered with farina.

CELTIC KING. A strong grower, its foliage is without farina whilst its flowers are of a lovely shade of lemon-yellow with attractively waved petals.

CRAIG NORDIE. The flowers are of burgundy-red with a golden centre and are almost free of farina whilst the foliage is grey-green.

GOLDEN QUEEN. It forms a large truss of pale sulphur-yellow flowers with a white centre and which carry a rich sweet perfume.

LINNET. An old favourite which now seems to have been lost. It is late into bloom and is well named for the blooms are of a combination of green, brown and mustard, the colours of the now almost equally rare bird of that name.

MCWATT'S BLUE. Raised by the late Dr. McWatt in Scotland, the rich mid-blue flowers with their white centre carry a delicious honey perfume. The foliage is heavily mealed.

MRS. NICHOLLS. A most attractive variety, the pale yellow blooms have a golden centre around which is a circle of white. The blooms have a pronounced musky scent.

OLD IRISH BLUE. A most beautiful auricula, with serrated foliage above which it bears large trusses of rich mid-blue. The flowers have a white centre and are heavily mealed whilst the perfume is outstanding.

OLD PURPLE DUSTY MILLER. Also known as Blue Dusty Miller but the flowers are really of purple colouring, with pronounced perfume and are held on 12-in. stems. All parts of the plant are heavily mealed.

OLD RED DUSTY MILLER. Of great antiquity, it is so heavily mealed as to appear as if covered in flour. The flowers are not large but the colour is unique, being of crimson-brown, wallflower colour and with a heavy scent.

OLD SUFFOLK BRONZE. A most interesting variety more Alpine than Border for it is quite free from farina. It makes a plant of robust habit and over a period of at least ten weeks bears large trusses of flowers of dollar size and of shades of gold, bronze and buff, almost impossible to describe. The scent is almost intoxicating and can be detected for a considerable distance. The plant was obtained by the author from a garden in Suffolk where it has been growing through the centuries.

OLD YELLOW DUSTY MILLER. The powerfully scented blooms are of deep golden yellow, whilst all parts are covered in farina.

PRIMULA VERIS Cowslip

It is one of the loveliest of all native flowers and with the exception of the rose and primrose, is given greater prominence by the poets than any other flower. Enjoying a more open situation than the primrose, the cowslip is usually to be found in water meadows where the plants enjoy the moisture and the sunshine.

In *Henry V*, written towards the latter part of 1599, King Henry and the King of France meet in a room in the King's Palace in Champagne. The Duke of Burgundy addresses the meeting, pleading for a return to more peaceful conditions:

My duty to you both, on equal love,
Great kings of France and England!
... all her husbandry doth lie in heaps, ...
The even mead, that erst brought sweetly forth
The freckled cowslip, burnet and green clover,
Wanting the scythe, all uncorrected, rank,
Conceives by idleness; and nothing teems
But hatefull docks, rough thistles, kecksies, burs,
Losing both beauty and utility.

Here Shakespeare compares the sweet perfume of the cowslip to that of burnet and clover; burnet which Sir Francis Bacon named as one of those plants which "perfume the air most delightfully" and which was planted with chamomile and thyme for walks, for these plants release their fragrance when trodden upon. It is a sweet refreshing fragrance from which the cowslip takes its name, cuslippe being the Saxon for "breath of a cow". In *Ælfric's Glossary*, it is cusloppe; countrymen call them Paigles. The calyx is the most delicate of all shades of green whilst the colour of the bloom is richly golden. The flowers, when in bud stand erect, in umbels but when fully open for fertilization they become pendulous. "Cowslips wan, that hang the pensive head," wrote John Milton. Then when fertilization has taken place, they take on the erect form again so that they do not readily lose their seeds when ripe. At the base of the cup of each flower is a tiny red or orange spot to which Shakespeare refers in *Cymbeline* when Iachimo describes Imogene as having

On her left breast
A mole cinque-spotted, like the crimson drops
I' the bottom of a Cowslip.

"Five spotted," wrote Shakespeare for the mark appears at the base of each of the five petals and it is these, states one authority and also Shakespeare himself, which give the bloom its sweet fragrance. In Elizabethan times, every part of the Cowslip had its uses. Cowslip wine, made from the petals, was taken to bring about sleep. Alexander Pope observed:

For want of rest,
Lettuce and cowslip wine: probatum est.

The ploughman poet, John Clare, alludes to the many uses of the Cowslip in his poem, "Cowslips", written in Northampton Asylum where he died in 1864:

The sheep and cows are crowding for a share
That basket-bearing children running there
Do think within their hearts they'll get them all
And hoot and drive them from their graceless waste.
For they want some for tea and some for wine
And some to maken up a cuckaball,
To throw across the garland's silken line
That reaches o'er the street from wall to wall.

The catching and throwing of cowslip "balls" was a favourite pastime with the young a century ago, whilst the "balls" were threaded on twine held by two people and allowed to run down the twine from one to the other, or, as Clare said, the "balls" were threaded on twine suspended across the road, sometimes from house to house.

Cowslip leaves were used with lettuce in salads, whilst the flowers were infused in boiling water to make a pleasant sweet "tea". Since earliest times, cowslip wine was and still is made and appreciated by countrymen as a refreshing drink. In his poem, "Cider", Phillips wrote of

. . . the Cowslip posies, faintly sweet,
From when thou artificial wines shalt drain
Of icy taste, that in mid fervors, best
Slack craving thirst and mitigate the day.

The Cowslip is so readily raised from seed sown in a cold frame, or in a seed pan early in April that it is rarely propagated by other methods. If kept moist, the seed will germinate within a month, the seedlings being transplanted to boxes of John Innes Compost where they may be grown on for planting into their flowering quarters during October. Or as soon as large enough, the seedlings may be transplanted to open ground beds, spacing them 6 ins. apart where they will bloom. The ground should be made clean of weeds and the soil brought into a friable condition, incorporating some peat and a little decayed manure. Old mushroom bed compost is excellent. The plants like a more open situation than primroses but will flourish in an orchard, planting them in beds to provide cut bloom for the home. They are valuable to have in the garden for they bloom several weeks later than primroses, bridging the gap between the spring and summer flowering plants.

The Polyanthus

The polyanthus has both *P. veris*, the cowslip and *P. vulgaris*, the primrose in its parentage for these species combined to pronounce the hybrid oxlip (as distinct from the true oxlip, *P. elatior*) from which the polyanthus has been evolved. The French botanist Clusius (De l'Ecluse) in his work *Rariorium Plantarum Historia* (1601) described it as *Primula veris pallida flore elatior*, the Larger Pale-flowered Cowslip and like the cowslip, it enjoys a more open situation than *P. elatior*. It was possibly from a crossing of the hybrid oxlip with John Tradescant's Red or Turkie-purple primrose obtained from the Caucasus, that the first red polyanthus or "big oxlip" was obtained and first described by Rea in his *Complete Florilege* (1665). He wrote: "The red cowslip or oxlip is of several sorts, all bearing many flowers on one stalk . . . some bigger, like oxlips" and which must have resembled a polyanthus of inferior quality. It was not until Miss Gertrude Jekyll in the year 1880, found in her garden a plant bearing yellow flowers, that a polyanthus of this colour appeared.

All carry the familiar mossy perfume of the family but in Hansen's F2 Hybrid strain, the perfume closely resembles that of the auricula and gold laced polyanthus, both of which may have a common ancestry in *Primula pubescens*. So powerful is the perfume of the Hansen strain that the author, on a first visit to the raiser's nursery, was able to fix the exact position from more than a mile away by the scent penetrating the open windows of a slowly moving car. The strain is without comparison in the thick stems and enormous flower heads which measure up to 18 ins. across, whilst the blooms are to be obtained in the richest of colours which includes tangerine, crimson, blue, pink, rose, apricot and gold.

The Gold Laced Polyanthus

It was about the year 1750 that the polyanthus took on the now familiar striking gold lacing or edging, at the same time that the auricula took its paste-like centre. The Gold Laced Polyanthus was possibly the result of a crossing of the red polyanthus (the yellow was not then known) with the natural hybrid *Primula pubescens*, to be found growing wild in the Austrian Tyrol. Several varieties of *P. pubescens* have the same golden centre as if the centre disc had been treated with gold leaf. The Gold Laced Polyanthus has a similar golden centre and an edging of gold which appears quite brilliant against the ground colour of crimson or black. It has also the same sweet perfume as *P. pubescens* and all the auriculas, so it would appear that they have a common ancestry in *P. pubescens*.

In 1759, James Justice who introduced the pineapple into Scotland, wrote that "the varieties that are obtained each year . . . are very great" and by 1780, Abercrombie said that the Gold Laced Polyanthus had become "one of the most noted prize (show) flowers amongst florists", being the special favourite of the small cutlers of Sheffield and of the weavers and spinners of Yorkshire and Lancashire. In "An Account of the Different Flower Shews" held in 1826, there is a record of over fifty shows held in the northern counties during April "open to All-England".

The polyanthus being the result of a cross between the primrose and cowslip may be said to have taken on the characteristics of both plants. It requires an abundance of moisture at its roots during the summer months and whilst it will flourish in shade it is happiest, in the words of Thomas Hogg, "in a situation exposed to the morning rays of the sun and excluded from them for the rest of the day". Here again in choice of situation the polyanthus may be said to come halfway between the primrose and cowslip, the former appreciating dappled shade, the latter a position of full sun. The primrose is a flower of the hedgerow, the cowslip of the open meadow especially where low lying, to enable it to receive sufficient moisture. Provided the plants are given an abundance of humus about the roots, the polyanthus will be quite happy in full sun for in such a situation are the plants set out by the cut-flower growers of Cornwall. Where a garden is exposed to the direct rays of the sun, the polyanthus may be grown to the same perfection as where grown in shade, though as Thomas Hogg has mentioned, shelter from the mid-day sun will prevent the blooms from fading and will ensure an extended flowering season.

A young orchard is the ideal place in which to grow on the plants during summer after they have finished flowering in the beds, when they must be divided and replanted into a humus-laden soil and kept well watered until the new roots have formed.

A light, sandy soil, which tends to dry out in summer, will never grow such sturdy plants as a heavier loam, unless well fortified with humus materials. With a heavy soil, humus is needed to disperse the clay particles so preventing the soil from "panning" and improving drainage; whilst with a sandy soil, humus is required for the retention of as much summer moisture as possible. Where in partial shade, a light soil well enriched with humus should be capable of supporting healthy plant growth even during periods of prolonged dryness. Liberal quantities of peat, used hops, shoddy, old mushroom bed compost and decayed farmyard manure should be used as liberally as possible, incorporating to a depth of at least 18 inches.

Growing from Seed

Polyanthuses are best raised from seed sown in boxes or pans in a cold frame. If seed is sown in April, the seedlings will be ready for transplanting to a frame or into the open ground during June. The John Innes Sowing compost is suitable. This is composed of:

2 parts sterilized loam
1 part coarse sand
1 part peat

to which is added per bushel:

1½ ozs. superphosphate of lime
½ oz. ground limestone (or chalk).

Careful watering at all times after sowing is essential for the seed will not germinate if the compost is dry, whilst the young plants will suffer irreparable harm if allowed to become too dry at the roots.

The seed will germinate in about three weeks and the seedlings will be ready to transplant in about a month, spacing them 2 to 3 ins. apart into fresh compost. The plants will come into bloom the following spring.

Dividing the Plants

Early July or springtime is the best time to divide old plants, when the ground is usually damp.

The plants should be lifted with care so that the fibrous roots, especially those near the surface, will be in no way damaged. Carefully shake away all surplus soil then, firmly holding the plant, pull apart the various crowns. In the very apt words of that great gardener, Miss Frances Perry, "tease them apart". In this way each crown will have its full quota of fibrous roots, whilst there will be no open wounds as may be the case where the plants are cut into sections. Every crown, however small, will grow into a flowering plant.

Where the plants have formed large clumps which they will do if given good cultivation, they should be divided like any other herbaceous plant, by placing two border forks back to back at the centre of the plant and gently prise apart. The two sections may then be divided as described into numerous offsets and these should be removed to a cool-shaded place without delay and where they remain until ready for replanting as soon as possible. Any unduly large leaves may be screwed off about 3 inches above the crown before replanting in the same way as when lifting and removing the tops of beetroot, for it is not necessary for the plants to have to re-establish these coarse outer leaves. Offsets with new and smaller leaves should be replanted without the removal of any foliage, for these young leaves will catch the dew and rains and direct the moisture to the roots thus enabling the plants to become more quickly established. The offsets should be set well into the ground and pressed firmly with the hand, or with the foot where the soil is friable. They should be kept well watered until established.

Polyanthus Strains

BLUE STRAINS. Quite excellent is Blackmore and Langdon's strain, the blooms being large, with a conspicuous yellow centre, the colours ranging from dark purple-blue to palest sky blue, the paler colours being more attractive. The American Marine Blue strain raised by the Barnhaven Gardens from G. F. Wilson's original blue stock has possibly not so sturdy a habit, neither is the bloom quite so large, but the colour is fixed somewhere between sky- and china-blue. The blooms possess that attractive smoky sheen which places the American polyanthus in a class to itself, whilst it is quite free from the red and purple colouring which spoils so many blue strains. The South Sea Island Blue strain is another combining the best of the several outstanding blue strains.

BRILLIANCY. This strain is excellent for cutting, the trusses being borne on long, wiry stems and whilst the individual pips are not large they are of the most vivid colourings imaginable; terracotta, tangerine, rust and orange being represented, whilst all other colours have been eliminated. One of the brightest flowers of the garden, and excellent for cloche culture.

CROWN PINK. This beautiful strain was introduced by Miss Linda Eickmann shortly before her death in 1956, and is the first real pink strain to give any degree of uniformity. The colour is clearest pink without any trace of rose or salmon. The blooms are large and well formed. Miss Eickmann introduced a number of named pinks from her strain such as Warm Laughter and Radiance.

MUNSTEAD STRAIN. The best strain of Miss Jekyll's original Munstead polyanthuses is that marketed by Messrs. Carter's Limited, who during recent years have improved it out of all recognition to that of sixty years ago. Though the colour range is comprised of only the original white and yellow tones, new oranges and pale yellows and much larger blooms now make this a most attractive strain, especially for planting in shaded positions where the more sombre colourings would not be shown to advantage.

PACIFIC STRAIN. Raised in California by Messrs. Vetterle and Reinelt, the colour range is wide, embracing blues, pinks, crimsons and pastel shades with a large golden centre. The plants are free flowering but as their place of introduction would suggest, they have not quite the extreme hardiness of British strains.

SUTTON'S FANCY. The blooms or pips are large with the truss flat and compact and the stems 9 to 10 ins. in length. The stems are extremely thick to withstand adverse weather, whilst the colour range includes chiefly the art or pastel shades of peach, pink, apricot, lilac and cream.

SUTTON'S SUPERB. Whilst the Fancy strain is composed chiefly of pastel shades, the Superb strain is made up of more brilliant colourings—bronzes, maroons and orange tints, the habit being similar to that of the Fancy strain and so making it very suitable for bedding.

TOOGOOD'S GIANT EXCELSIOR STRAIN. The large flower trusses are held on 10- to 12-in. stems and so are ideal for cutting or bedding though preferably for the latter purpose. The colour range includes most of the pastel shades of apricot, peach, pink and cream, the magentas having been eliminated.

Named Polyanthuses

There are a number of polyanthuses which may be the result of a primrose-polyanthus cross, but which because of their long stalk and the formation of a compact flower truss may be classed as of true polyanthus habit. The blooms of each are somewhat daintier than those of the modern polyanthus strains and the plants are of more compact habit. With their intensely rich colouring they are amongst the most attractive of all garden plants. All possess extreme hardiness, whilst they are very free flowering.

BARROWBY GEM. With Beltany Red this is one of the finest of all spring plants, ideal for window box or rockery with its sturdy habit.

Plate 11 *Above left* Green-edged Auricula, Buckley's Chloe,
above right Gold Laced Polyanthus, Burnard's Formosa, *below* Double
primrose

Plate 12   *Above Primula vulgaris*, Hose-in-Hose
Below Primula vulgaris (double), Barnhaven strain

It was raised in Scotland by Mrs. McColl and is now rarely seen, though in the author's garden are several hundred plants of the utmost vigour. It is the first polyanthus to come into bloom, the first pips opening on a mild February day, whilst its large umbrella-like heads remain colourful until June. The bloom may be described as primrose-yellow shaded green and it carries a pleasant almond perfume.

BARTIMEUS. This is believed to be a polyanthus of eighteenth-century days. It bears a bloom of velvety crimson-black and has no eye. In its place is a region of bronzy red. The blooms are not large nor does it form a large head in comparison with modern standards. This is the old Eyeless polyanthus, a connoisseur's plant.

BELTANY RED. Its origin is unknown, but it is one of the finest of all garden plants. It forms a stocky, compact plant and bears a large truss of tangerine-red blooms, which have an unusual green centre and an attractive wire-edge of gold. The leaves are vivid green. The plant remains ten weeks in bloom, and two or three planted together can be seen from afar.

FAIR MAID. The author obtained this magnificent variety from Perthshire, so it is well named. The small, but beautifully rounded blooms are freely produced on numerous 15-inch stems, their colour being burnt orange-scarlet with a most striking double centre of gold. The blooms remain fresh in water for fully two weeks.

HUNTER'S MOON. A modern polyanthus and a beauty, for like Barrowby Gem it comes into bloom before all others and carries a fragrance the equal of the Ena Harkness rose. Of sturdy habit, the bloom is of a lovely shade of apricot with a chrome yellow centre.

RALPH SPOONER. This is possibly the finest double polyanthus ever raised. It bears twenty or more fully double blooms on each stem, arranged in perfect exhibition form and they retain their perfection over a long period. The colour is Jersey-cream and they have a soft, sweet perfume.

PRIMULA VULGARIS   Primrose
Of all flowers native to the British Isles, none has continued to enjoy a greater popularity than the primrose, possibly because it is one of the first of spring's jewels. In the introductory song to *The Two Noble Kinsmen* it is written:

> Primrose, first-born child of Ver,
> Merry spring-time's harbinger,
> With her bells dim.

John Keats in his *Ode to Fancy* has also shown his excitement in finding the first primrose of the springtide:

> Thou shalt, at one glance, behold
> The daisy and the marigold,
> White-plumed lilies, and the first
> Hedge-grown primrose that hath burst.

The flower has since earliest times been a favourite of the poets for its simplicity, its freedom of flowering and its hardiness, being untroubled by the coldest winds as it finds shelter beneath the mossy bank. The serenity of this lovely flower is felt by Henry Kirke White in his lines *To an Early Primrose*:

> In this low vale, the promise of the year,
> Serene thou openest to the nipping gale,
> Unnoticed and alone
> Thy tender elegance.

Shakespeare conveys something of the same feeling in *Venus and Adonis*:

> Witness this primrose bank whereon I lie;
> These forceless flowers like sturdy trees support me;
> Two strengthless doves will draw me through the sky
> From morn till night, even where I list to sport me.

Again in *A Midsummer Night's Dream*, Hermia, in love with Lysander, exclaims:

> And in the wood, where often you and I
> Upon faint primrose beds were wont to lie,
> Emptying our bosoms of their councel sweet,
> There my Lysander and myself shall meet.

Perhaps Shakespeare's thoughts were of the grassy bank leading from the door of Anne Hathaway's cottage at Shottery to the orchard where to this day, primroses bloom in springtime.

> In dewy glades,
> The peering primrose, like sudden gladness,
> Gleams on the soul . . .

wrote Coleridge; and to Robert Herrick, writing shortly after Shakespeare's death, the primrose was "the Sweet Infanta of the year", a time when the willow spreads its golden arms about the river bank and "proud-pied April, dress'd in all his trim, hath put a spirit of youth in everything". John Clare captured the scene so well:

> Nor hath the sallow palms
> A peer for richness; ploughmen in their toils
> Will crop a branch, smit with its golden charms,
> Whilst at its root the primrose's burning eye
> Smiles in his face and blooms delicious by.

Though the primrose is associated with the joyful days of springtime, it has a paleness of colour which the poets so often associated with death. There is the touching scene in *Cymbeline* when Arviragus, bearing home the supposed dead body of Imogen says:

> With fairest flowers,
> Whilst summer lasts, and I live here, Fidele,
> I'll sweeten thy sad grave; thou shalt not lack
> The flower that's like thy face, pale primrose. Nor,
> The azur'd harebell, like thy veins.

Thoughts of his dead son Hamnet would most likely have been in Shakespeare's mind as he wrote these lines for he grieved throughout his life for his only son. In *The Winter's Tale*, Perdita shows us something of Shakespeare's keen botanical knowledge when describing the first primroses of the year:

> Pale primroses,
> That die unmarried ere they can behold
> Bright Phoebus in his strength.

Those blooms which appear early in the spring, before the fertilizing bees and insects are about, die without their being able to re-create. Here again, Shakespeare may have had his son in mind for the boy died before attaining manhood.

Milton makes a similar reference to the flower which was one of those chosen to line the hearse of Lycidas:

> Bring the rathe (early) primrose that forsaken dies,
> And every flower that sad embroidery wears.

The plant takes its name from primaverola, a diminute of *Prima vera*, meaning the first flower of springtime. From this word, the obvious development was primerole which soon became "primerose" which in Shakespeare's time was a plant held in so great esteem as to be the word most often used to denote excellence.

She is the pride and primrose of the rest,

wrote Spenser, and again in *The Shepherd's Calendar*:

Was not I (the Briar) planted of thine own hande
To bee the primrose of all thy lande . . .

In *Daphnidia*, the husband lamenting the loss of his young wife says:

Mine was the primrose in the lowly shade! . . .
Oh! that so fair a flower so soon should fade.

One of the earliest manuscripts to mention the flower was that of Walter de Biblesworth of the late thirteenth century:

Primerole et primeveyre
Sur tere aperunt entems de veyre

Chaucer, writing shortly after, also names it the primerole, using it to describe a lady of quality as in *The Miller's Tale*:

Her schoos were laced on hir-legges hyghe,
Sche was a primerole, a piggesneyghe
For any lord have lying in his bedde,
Or yet for any godde yoman to wedde.

It was not until Turner used the word "prymerose" did the name we know today, come to be used. Spenser and Shakespeare writing shortly afterwards, used the modern spelling. Sir Francis Bacon in *The Making of Gardens*, suggests planting "prime-roses" for February flowering which is early for all but the most sheltered gardens in Devon and Cornwall.

It was during the reigns of the Tudors that primroses first came to be widely grown for the beauty and interest of their flowers, for by then many variations of the yellow wild primrose had become known. Tabernaemontanus, writing in the year 1500, described the double yellow primrose which may still be found in its double form growing wild in various parts of Britain. Variations of the primrose *Primula acaulis* or *P. vulgaris*, are extremely numerous and quite apart from the lovely double forms, there are the dainty Hose-in-Hose forms and the Jack-in-the-Greens, which originally must have been found growing in the wild state in all parts of Britain. By Elizabethan times, these lovely primroses were widely grown in the dainty knot gardens of both manor house and cottage, for besides being of extremely perennial habit, the compact form of the plants made them ideal for this form of gardening.

Though the different forms of the white and yellow primrose must have been well known to cottage gardeners since earliest times, they had not been mentioned in any detail until the works of Gerard and Parkinson appeared during the last years of the sixteenth century and the beginning of the seventeenth century. John Gerard was a native of Nantwich but moved to London at an early age. Though he was not a gardener by profession he looked after Lord Burleigh's garden in the Strand and eventually had an equally famous garden of his own in Holborn. In his *Herbal*, he described and illustrated the double white primrose (*alba plena*) and also a number of the interesting forms, especially the Jack-in-the-Green primroses.

Jack-in-the-Greens

Here, the blooms are single and are backed by a ruff-like arrangement composed of tiny replicas of the primrose leaf, which provides a pleasing contrast to the clear colourings of the blooms. They were widely planted during the sixteenth century, the arrangement of the leaves behind the blooms greatly appealing to the Tudors, as could well be imagined. The plants later became known as Jack-in-the-Pulpits.

An interesting form of the Jack-in-the-Green is the Jack-a-napes-on-Horseback. This is the Franticke or Foolish primrose (or cowslip) described so well by Parkinson in his *Paradisus* of 1629. It is a plant of polyanthus form and in Parkinson's words, "it is called Foolish because it beareth at the top of the stalk a tuft of small, long, green leaves with some yellow leaves, as it were pieces of flowers broken and standing amongst the green leaves". It is well illustrated in Parkinson's *Paradisus*, the leaves being further apart and not held in close circular formation as for the Jack-in-the-Green. It should be said that the striping of the leaves is of the same colouring as the bloom. Gerard's Jack-a-napes has a larger flower which sits on a saucer of the same colour, striped with green. It possibly takes its name from a striped coat which was fashionable during the seventeenth century. In his diary dated July 5th, 1660, Samuel Pepys writes, "This morning my brother Jon brought me my Jackanapes coat . . ." Of the Franticke or Jack-a-napes-on-Horseback, the leaves are more jagged. A book of early Stuart times described the flower as being "all green and jagged", whilst Gerard says that it is so named by the women, "the flowers being wrinkled and curled after a most strange manner", though I have yet to understand where "the Horseback" part comes in. Most of the old Jacks during recent years have been rediscovered in Ireland, where its mild, moist climate is so suited to primrose culture and where many parts have been undisturbed for centuries.

Yet another form is the Gally Gaskin. This is a single bloom which has a swollen, distorted calyx and is now rarely to be found. It has also a frilled ruff beneath the bloom. A picture attributed to Henri Coiffier de Ruse in the National Gallery, aptly illustrates this form, a frilled ruff appearing beneath the knees of the gentlemen which appear large, like the swollen calyx of the Gally Gaskin.

Cup and Saucer Primroses

Perhaps the loveliest of all forms of the primrose is that of the Hose-in-Hose, where one bloom grows from another to give a plant in full bloom a most dainty, feathery appearance, the flowers seeming to dance in the spring breezes in a fairy-like manner. They are also known as Duplex, Double-decker or Cup and Saucer primroses, though Parkinson's Hose-in-Hose beautifully illustrates the form. "They remind one of breeches men do wear," he writes. Gerard called them Two-in-Hose and included an illustration in his *Histoire of Plants*. The hose worn by men at that time were knitted with a much stronger wool than used today and it was the custom for one stocking to be placed in another before being passed to the wearer. It was Mr. James Laver, keeper of Costumes at the Victoria and Albert Museum, London, who in a letter to the author kindly described the ancient forms of hose. He makes special mention of a delightful picture by Gabrielle Metsu, *A Gentleman and Lady at the Harpsichord*, which clearly shows the "Gentleman" wearing hose in this manner, one stocking being pulled up to the thighs with another turned down just below the knee to give the appearance of one growing out from another exactly like the flowers. The botanical explanation of this delightful effect is that the lower "bloom" is really a petaloid calyx. It is the primrose of Mrs. Ewing's Mary's Meadow. There is a variation to the Hose-in-Hose form where the calyx of the lower flower is striped with green, red or yellow. This has given rise to the name Pantaloon to describe the form which is perhaps more unusual rather than pretty.

HOSE-IN-HOSE VARIETIES

(p); Denotes Polyanthus form

ABERDEEN YELLOW. This is a very old variety bearing small clear yellow blooms, with the duplex clearly defined.

ASHFORT (p). It is tall growing and bears an umbel of brownish-red flowers above pale green foliage.

BRIMSTONE (p). May be said to be of semi-polyanthus form, for its large, clear sulphur-yellow bell-shaped blooms are borne from a main stem three inches long. An outstanding variety, remaining long in bloom.

CANARY BIRD. It is very early flowering, its bright, pure canary-yellow blooms being borne with great freedom.

CASTLE HOWARD. A lovely hose of true primrose habit, discovered in the grounds of the great Yorkshire house bearing that name. The blooms are of true primrose-yellow colour.

ERIN'S GEM. It bears a most interesting and dainty cream-coloured flower, the lower one having an attractive bright green stripe.

FLORA'S GARLAND. This is a lovely old hose-in-hose, bearing well-defined flowers of deep pink.

GOLDILOCKS (p). It bears its deep yellow blooms in umbels on long stems making it an excellent cut flower.

GOLD LACED HOSE (p). The Hose-in-Hose form of the florist's gold laced polyanthus and a most delightful plant of perfect cup and saucer form. The flowers resemble the gold laced in that the ground colour is of light or dark red (almost black) which accentuates the brilliant golden edge and centre. The flowers are deliciously scented.

IRISH MOLLY. A hose of great charm and of true primrose form, bearing a profusion of large flowers which are of a soft shade of mauve-pink. Also known as Lady Molly.

IRISH SPARKLER (p). This striking variety is frequently confused with "Old Vivid". Its blooms are similarly formed but are of a crimson-red colour without the conspicuous yellow centre. Like most of the Hose-in-Hose, it makes an excellent cut flower.

LADY DORA (p). I have seen this lovely variety in an Irish garden, but have not yet had the pleasure of having it in my own garden. The colour of the small, dainty blooms is brilliant golden-yellow, whilst they possess a powerful perfume.

LADY LETTICE. In his delightful book, *Old Fashioned Flowers*, Sir Sacheverell Sitwell so rightly says that this plant should be in every garden. Planted along a path, its fairy-like flowers provide a delightful effect. It comes early into bloom in March and continues until the end of May, bearing masses of apricot-yellow flowers which are tinged with salmon-pink. Sadly, it is now almost extinct.

OLD SPOTTED HOSE (p). Of polyanthus habit, the large crimson blooms are held on sturdy stems, the centre of each petal being quaintly spotted near the edge.

WANDA HOSE. This is the hose-in-hose form of the ever-popular Juliae primrose, Wanda. It has the same habit, the bright purple-red blooms being borne on short stems.

DOUBLE PRIMROSES

"Our garden Double Primrose, of all the rest is of the greatest beauty," wrote Gerard in 1597, and he makes special mention of the "Double White". Thirty years later, Parkinson gave a full description of double primroses in which he mentioned that the leaves were larger than those of the single primrose, "because it groweth in gardens". In other words, the double primroses were then popular garden plants. Parkinson describes the flowers as being "very thick and double and of the same sweet scent with them (as the common single primrose)". Indeed, the double primroses are among the most beautiful and interesting plants of the garden, and though they are considered by modern gardeners to be difficult to grow, the fact that Gerard's "Double White" and the "Double Sulphur" primrose of Tabernaemontanus are still with us and are still vigorous must surely do much to refute that charge.

The earliest writers repeatedly mention the ease with which the plants were grown. Phillip Miller, Curator of the Chelsea Physic Garden about the year 1720, wrote in his *Gardener's Dictionary* (1731), "they will grow in almost any earth provided they have a shady situation", and John Rea in his *Flora* published in 1665 said, "were it (the double primrose) not so common in every Countrywoman's garden, it would be more respected, for it is a sweet and dainty double flower . . ." Thus, through the years, the garden writers seem to have taken it for granted that those who grow the double primrose, and this would appear to be most gardeners, found it amongst the easiest of all plants to manage. Why, then, have these quite charming plants become little more than "collector's pieces" with present-day gardeners? The town garden with its acid and inert soil, due to continual deposits of soot and sulphur and complete lack of humus has now taken the place of the country cottage garden, where the soil was continually being revitalized with humus-forming manures. These took the form of night-soil, decayed farm-yard manure, sheep and poultry droppings, decayed leaves, supplying not only humus but food in the form of nitrogen, which the double primrose loves so well and without which the plants will not survive for long.

Though the double primrose will grow well in a town garden, given the right conditions, it has survived only in the cottage garden.

VARIETIES OF DOUBLE PRIMROSES

ARTHUR DE SMIT. Now rare but it is one of the loveliest of the doubles, and was raised in Germany. The blooms, borne on single footstalks, being of rich purple edged with yellow.

ARTHUR DU MOULIN. It goes by many names and is believed to have been introduced from Ireland towards the end of the nineteenth century, for de Moleyns is the family name of Lord Vertry. It is also known as "Dumoulin" and "des Moulens". It is the most important double, being the first to bloom and being the only variety to yield pollen in quantity, with the exception of the less double blooms of "Prince Silver-wings". The flowers are of beautiful formation and are of deepest violet, borne on short polyanthus stems.

BON ACCORDS. More than a dozen double primroses were raised at the Cocker Brothers' nurseries near Aberdeen during the first years of this century, and all, with but one or two exceptions. ("Bon Accord Salmon" and "Yellow") are still in cultivation and show no signs of losing their original vigour. Almost all the blooms are similar; having the somewhat flat appearance of "Red Paddy", being neat and symmetrical. They are of easy culture and flourish under average conditions, and for one wishing to start a collection of double primroses, the dozen Bon Accords still in cultivation would give the greatest satisfaction. Bon Accord is the motto of the City of Aberdeen. They are "bunch" primroses, a number of the flowers being borne on foot-stalks after the manner of the native primrose, whilst others on the same plant appear from a short polyanthus stem.

BON ACCORD BEAUTY. The blooms are large and of deep purple-blue, the petals being edged with white and spotted with white towards the edges.

BON ACCORD BLUE. The largest of all the Bon Accords, the blooms are of a lovely shade of rich blue borne on decidedly polyanthus stems. Though now scarce it is one of the easiest.

BON ACCORD BRIGHTNESS. Believed to be extinct, this must surely be the variety now called "Crathes Crimson", for it answers the description in every aspect.

BON ACCORD CERISE. The petals are flat and perfectly rounded, forming a near button-like rosette of a lovely shade of clear cerise-pink, the bloom being sweetly perfumed. Of strong constitution.

BON ACCORD ELEGANS. Outstanding amongst the Bon Accords but is the most difficult to grow well, requiring a rich diet. The attractive orchid-pink flowers are edged and flecked with white.

BON ACCORD GEM. The blooms are of bright rosy-red, shaded with mauve and are produced with freedom. The attractively waved petals accentuate the beauty of the blooms. The easiest and most vigorous in this section.

BON ACCORD JEWEL. A magnificent variety but is now rarely to be found. The large deep purple flowers are shaded with crimson on the reverse side.

BON ACCORD LAVENDER. The blooms are large with attractively waved petals and are of a lovely shade of purest lavender with a golden centre.

BON ACCORD LILAC. Of easy culture, the blooms are flat and are of a pleasing shade of lilac-mauve, the petals being marked with yellow at the base.

BON ACCORD PURITY. This must surely be one of the loveliest of all double primroses. The blooms, which are large and fully petalled, are of a lovely shade of creamy-white tinged with green, providing a most attractive appearance where growing in partial shade. The blooms, with their frilled petals, are held on sturdy footstalks so that they are held above the bright green foliage.

BON ACCORD PURPLE. The blooms are large and borne on poly-anthus stems and are of a glorious shade of burgundy-purple flushed with crimson on the reverse side.

BON ACCORD ROSE. This variety of robust constitution and of semi-polyanthus habit was sent to me as "Old Rose", yet I can find no trace of such a variety in any gardening literature, whilst Bon Accord Rose is said to be extinct. My belief, however, that it is Bon Accord Rose is because of the dainty, rounded bloom which is rather flat like most of the Bon Accords and has the same conspicuous orange markings at the base of each petal. The habit, too, is the same as the Bon Accords. The colour is deep old rose.

BURGUNDY. The plants in my garden bear a large well-shaped bloom of deep burgundy-red, flecked with white. This is an old variety which retains its original name but is tending to lose vigour unless well grown.

BUXTON'S BLUE. It bears bloom of pure turquoise-blue and is a plant of vigorous habit, though now rarely to be found. It is a "sport" from the single blue primrose, found in a garden at Bettws-y-Coed at the beginning of the century.

CASTLEDERG. A chance seedling raised by Mrs. Scott of Castlederg, Co. Tyrone, the large star-shaped blooms being of deep sulphur-yellow, splashed with pink and brown. The early blooms may open single, but it is quite lovely and a plant of vigorous habit.

CHEVITHORNE PINK. Found in the gardens of Chevithorne Barton in Devon, it makes a compact plant and is of easy culture. It remains long in bloom and bears small, beautifully formed flowers of a lovely shade of orchid-pink held on short polyanthus stems.

CHEVITHORNE PURPLE. This plant now seems much more rare than its pink counterpart but is of similar habit. The blooms are of deep purple-blue, the petals being edged with white.

CLOTH OF GOLD. A magnificent variety, of robust constitution and is extremely free flowering. It is thought to be a "sport" from the "Double Sulphur", for it possesses the same habit, having large pale green leaves. The bloom is bright yellow but is of not so deep a colour as Carter's "Cloth of Gold" which is now extinct.

CRATHES CRIMSON. This lovely variety was said to have been found in the grounds of Crathes Castle in Scotland, though from the familiar shape of the blooms it could be Bon Accord Brightness, thought to be extinct. The round, neat flowers are of bright purple-crimson and possess a sweet perfume.

CRIMSON EMPEROR. It possesses a rather stronger constitution than Crimson King, whilst the bloom has a slightly more purple tint. It is, however, said to be the same variety which may reveal variations of colour and vigour where growing in different gardens.

CRIMSON KING. This is the same variety as the Old Scottish Double Red. It makes a plant of reasonably sturdy constitution and bears large numbers of big, fully double blooms on a short polyanthus stem, the colour being deep ruby-red.

CURIOSITY. Also known as "Golden Pheasant", this variety was at one time grown in my garden in large numbers, but over-propagation to supply the demand has reduced its vigour. A pity, for the bloom is most interesting, the deep yellow ground colour being flecked with rose and bronzy markings. The blooms are borne on dwarf polyanthus stems.

DERNCLEUGHI. Like "Golden Ball" I have seen this variety growing only in a small garden in Ireland. The double blooms are of bronzy-crimson, the petals being margined with gold and born on poly-anthus stems.

DOUBLE CREAM. Now rare, it is a plant of robust habit and bears fully double blooms of a lovely shade of Jersey cream.

DOUBLE GREEN (a). This is not really a true double for it is caused by the sepals of the flower being developed as foliage leaves, a condition known as "phyllody". It is to be found occasionally among a batch of primroses in any part of the British Isles, but seems to be more prevalent in Ireland. For some unknown reason it is often called the "Exeter" primrose. In appearance it is unique and interesting rather than beautiful.

DOUBLE GREEN (b). There is also a true double green as mentioned by Parkinson, which was thought to be extinct; it has recently been found again in a Dorset garden, whilst plants may be obtained from Ireland.

DOUBLE SULPHUR. It is pleasing to know that this interesting primrose, mentioned by Tabernaemontanus in 1500, still exists and still retains its original name. Forming large sage-green leaves, it is similar in every respect to "Cloth of Gold", but the bloom is a shade paler.

DOUBLE WHITE. Gerard's "Double White" and a plant of the true primrose habit, the fully double blooms being of paper white and held on long, single footstalks making them ideal for posy bunches, for which purpose the plants should be grown under cloches, otherwise they may be washed into the soil by heavy rains. It is a plant of vigorous habit and of easy culture and is free flowering.

DOUBLE YELLOW. Obviously "sports" from the wild primrose must abound in various forms and especially with yellow flowering varieties. "Giant Yellow", "Giantess Yellow", "Early Yellow" and "Late Yellow" are all forms which at some time or other have been described in the garden Press. That in my garden, which is quite distinct from both the "Double-Sulphur" and "Cloth of Gold", bears a large, bright yellow bloom, the base of the petals being shaded with orange.

DOWNSHILL ENSIGN. It was raised with a number of others by Mr. Murray Thomson early this century. The then recently introduced *P. juliae* seems to have had some influence in their raising for each of the dozen or more varieties bear bloom of various shades of blue and purple. The variety "Bluebird", now lost but which received an Award of Merit in 1930, appears to have been the best for its blooms were 1½ inches across and were of a lovely shade of lavender-blue. "Ensign" is the last of the double primroses to bloom, its rather shaggy blooms being of bright violet-blue and held on very long footstalks from a short polyanthus stem. The foliage is smooth and of brilliant green.

FRENCH GREY. The earlier writers named this variety "Dingy", and the name fits the description well, the blooms being of a dirty white shade or French white or grey as it is called. The blooms are borne with freedom on long footstalks whilst the plant is of easy culture.

MADAME POMPADOUR. This lovely variety is often very difficult to grow and it bears a large double bloom of deep velvety crimson on single footstalks. The texture of its bloom is unique, hence it is always greatly in demand and expensive. It originated in France about 160 years ago and is also known as "Pompadour" and "Crimson Velvet".

MARIE CROUSSE. I could not disagree more with Sir Sacheverell Sitwell when he describes this variety as being "not of outstanding merit", for in my opinion it is everything a good garden plant should be. It is a strong, easy grower, increasing rapidly, and bears a large, densely double bloom on short, sturdy polyanthus stems. The blooms are of a lovely shade of Parma-violet, splashed and edged with white, and they carry a delicious perfume.

The description given in *The Garden* for April 1882, shortly after the plant had earned the Award of Merit from the Royal Horticultural Society, describes it well; "the blooms are one inch across and perfectly double, the petals forming a compact rosette . . ."

OUR PAT. It was found amongst a batch of *P. juliae* at the Daisy Hill Nurseries, Newry, and was named after the owner's daughter. It is unusual in that the olive-green foliage is veined with crimson-bronze. The small sapphire-blue flowers are borne in profusion on long footstalks. The plant is of vigorous habit and is of easy culture and is one of the last of the doubles to bloom, thus extending the season.

PRINCE SILVERWINGS. A beautiful variety of polyanthus habit, the crimson-lilac blooms being flaked with white and edged with silver. The petals are tinted with orange at the base to form a bloom of great beauty, but though in no way difficult to grow it is now rare. It sometimes bears semi-double blooms which yield pollen and so may be used for hybridizing.

QUAKER'S BONNET. A very old variety probably a "sport" from *P. rubra*. The bloom is the most beautifully formed of all the doubles, making a rosette of perfect symmetry and being of purest lilac-mauve. It blooms with as great a freedom as "Double White" and is a plant of sturdy constitution. Also, *Lilacina plena*.

RED PADDY. It is the *Sanguinea plena* and *Rubra plena* of old Irish gardens and a charming variety. It is a strong grower and bears large numbers of small, symmetrical rose-red blooms which have a salmon-pink flush and an attractive edge of silver. The blooms are flat and dainty and possess a sweet perfume.

REX THEODORE. Also known as "King Theodore" it was listed in the catalogues of all the hardy plant growers at the turn of the century, but is now rarely seen. The bloom is almost crimson-black borne on polyanthus stems, the petals being edged with silver. This may also have been the "double black polyanthus edged with white" called Queen Victoria and which was popular on the show bench during the Queen's reign.

ROSE DU BARRI. Without doubt this is one of the two or three loveliest of all double primroses. It is now extremely rare and seems to have been grown in one or two gardens for so long that it now resents moving to any other place. Sir Sacheverell Sitwell states that "it is probably of early Victorian origin" and I should not think him far wrong from what I have been told of those plants growing in a particular Wiltshire garden. The blooms are big and cabbage-like and are of a glorious shade of purest pink, flushed with orange.

TYRIAN PURPLE. One of the best of all primroses, indeed it is one of the best plants in the garden. The blooms are the size of a ten pence piece and held on sturdy primrose footstalks. The colour of the bloom is bright purple, flushed with crimson, whilst the foliage is brilliant green. It makes a large plant of robust constitution. Is said to have been found in Cornwall.

WILLIAM CHALMERS. Raised at Stonehaven in Scotland, it is a magnificent variety, the large well-formed blooms being of deep midnight blue, flushed with purple.

PULMONARIA OFFICINALE Lungwort
It is perhaps a native plant for it was mentioned in the earliest herbals under such names as Lungwort and Sage of Bethlehem. The leaves, with their peculiar markings, were thought to resemble a person's lungs and so were believed to be a cure for lung diseases whilst they were also used in potage, like those of the calendula. There is an old country superstition that the white markings on the leaves were made by drops of Our Lady's Milk for the plant grows wild in Palestine and around the shores of the Mediterranean, hence its connections with Bethlehem. It is also known as the Jerusalem cowslip.

The plant delights in shade and is in no way particular as to soil. It blooms during April and May, a time when few herbaceous plants will be in bloom and because its flowers which open pink, turn bright blue as they age, the plant was known to countrymen as "Soldiers and Sailors", the pink denoting the red tunics of the army of Waterloo days. The variety Bowles Red bears flowers of brightest reddish-pink whilst Pink Dawn bears flowers of soft strawberry-pink.

PULSATILLA VULGARIS Easter Flower
It used to be called *Anemone pulsatilla* and is a native plant, grown in English gardens since earliest times. It was until recently to be found in parts of Oxfordshire and Northamptonshire and as far east as the Gogmagog Hills near Cambridge for like the harebell, it is usually found about hilly pastures of limestone formation. It takes its name from an Italian word which is descriptive of the downy seeds being driven around by the wind and its name Pasque or Easter-flower because of its flowering at Eastertide. Miss Alice Coats, however, believes that it was so called for its pre-Christian association with the dawn goddess Easter. In medieval times, a bright green dye extracted from the plant was used to colour eggs at Eastertime and which is mentioned in the Royal accounts of Edward I.

P. vulgaris grows 4 to 6 ins. tall with thrice pinnatifid leaves which arise from the rootstock and develop after flowering has ended late in May. The flowers are of dull purple colouring, measuring about 2 ins. across and backed by six erect silky sepals.

Like the Hepatica, an established plant will resent disturbance but will appreciate an annual mulch of decayed manure alternating with a dressing of lime rubble. Also essential for its success are a deeply worked soil and an open situation.

Of several named varieties, the finest are the now rare Mrs. Van der Elst which bears flowers of strawberry-pink with golden anthers and Red Clock, with its large flowers of deep-velvety crimson. The pure white form, *alba*, provides a striking contrast.

When planting, make sure that the crown is not buried below the level of the soil.

RANUNCULUS ACONITIFOLIUS   Fair Maids of Kent
It is believed to have reached England with the Huguenots fleeing from the Massacre of St. Bartholomew in 1572 for the plants grow wild in parts of France. It is a delightful plant and came to be widely grown in cottage gardens but has almost disappeared, probably because it is difficult to establish. It grows 2 to 3 ft. tall and bears in June, on branching stems, multitudes of pure white buttons, double, like tiny pompon chrysanthemums, hence it was one of many flowers to be called Batchelor's Buttons. Gerard told us that it "grew in the gardens of lovers of strange and beautiful plants", denoting its rarity at the time the *Herbal* was published in 1596. The whiteness of the flowers is enhanced by the dark green leaves, attractively lobed like those of other flowering plants of the family. The plant came to be called Fair Maids of Kent but the origin of the name is unknown to the author.

Like most members of the Ranunculus family, it should be planted in April so that the tuberous roots do not decay through excessive winter moisture whilst still dormant.

Plant 12 ins. apart with the roots on a layer of sand or peat.

RANUNCULUS ACRIS PLENUS   Batchelor's Buttons
Though an obnoxious weed in the garden, several forms of the Buttercup are amongst the most delightful of plants and for centuries have occupied a place in the cottage garden. The Meadow Crow-

foot, so called because the leaves are shaped like a crow's foot, is a taller growing relation of the Common Buttercup, surprisingly not given its name Buttercup until the latter part of the eighteenth century. Before then, they were known as King Cups, as Gerard tells us: "the Crowfoot is called in English, King Kob (cup)" and he continues, "many do tie a little of the herb, stamped with salt unto any of the fingers against pain of the teeth; for it causes greater pain in the finger than in the tooth; by the means whereof the greater pain taketh away the lesser."

"I sought for the kingcup all cloth'd in the sun"

wrote John Clare in his poem, "The Sigh", written from Northampton Asylum during the latter days of his life.

It is the double form which came to be planted in gardens. Gerard tells that it was "brought forth out of Lancashire into our London gardens by . . . Master Thomas Hesketh who found it growing wild not far from Latham in Lancashire." In the *Herbal*, he calls it Batchelor's Buttons and the blooms do indeed resemble the highly polished brass buttons worn on soldiers' tunics. The flowers have more right to be called thus, than the double daisy which now appears to have taken the description.

The plant grows 2 ft. tall and early in summer the large buds begin to unfold to fully double blooms of brilliant gold.

RANUNCULUS ASIATICUS   Ranunculus; Crowfoot
A species of the Crowfoot it was grown in cottage gardens for three centuries and is now rarely to be found. It takes its name from *rana*, a frog, because it grew near marshy places. The Asiatic form was first found near Constantinople by the Vizier, Cara Mustapha, and brought to the attention of the Sultan. So beautiful were the flowers that the Sultan had his emissaries search the whole of the Middle East for further species and varieties. Several reached France during the reign of Louis IX (mid-thirteenth century) where they grew in the garden of his mother, Blanche of Castille but must have soon died after for there is no mention of the plant reaching England until Elizabethan times when Gerard tells us that "my Lord and Master, the Rt. Hon. the Lord Treasurer had plants sent to him" (from Constantinople) whilst others arrived from Syria ". . . for our gardens, where they flourish as in their own country". From that

time, under the influence of the Dutch breeders, the interest in the Turban Ranunculus increased with each year though today, like a number of the old florists' flowers, it is rarely to be found.

There were two chief forms, the Turban and the Persian, the latter being descended from a dark red form, named by Phillip Miller (1731), *R. sanguineus*. Miller has said that the blooms of the Ranunculus are so large and of such rich colours "as to vie with the carnation itself". By 1792 Maddock listed 800 varieties and *Mason's Catalogue of Ranunculus* (1820) listed over 400. Readily raised from seed, Maddock said that the seed never produced two flowers alike, hence the large number of varieties which were retained by regular division of the tubers.

The flower reached the height of its popularity by the beginning of the nineteenth century and fell from favour as quickly as it had increased in popularity. Even by 1851, it had become in Glenny's words, "a neglected flower" for they demanded care with their cultivation which an industrial age did not permit.

Perhaps the most sought-after variety was a Turban form bearing flowers of brilliant scarlet, spotted with gold which the French called Turban Doré whilst there were striped forms and blooms edged with gold, some of the finest originating at the nursery of Waterston and Lightbody of Selkirk.

Ordinary loam suits them well but some protection from cold winds should be given. The tubers are planted in April for they are only half-hardy, setting them claw downwards 2 ins. deep and 4 ins. apart. They are best planted on a layer of sand and should also be covered with sand. At all times, they should be kept moist and will greatly benefit from a top dressing (after planting) of decayed manure.

RESEDA ODORATA   Mignonette

This fragrant weed of Egypt, *Reseda odorata*, is a relatively new-comer to English gardens. Phillip Miller of the Botanic Gardens at Chelsea was the first to receive seed, sent to him by Dr. Van Royen of Leyden, shortly before publication of Miller's *Gardener's Dictionary* in 1752. The plant first found its way into southern France during the early part of the eighteenth century, possibly from the gardens of North Africa and the French named it mignonette, Little Darling, hence Cowper's reference to

". . . the fragrant weed,
The Frenchman's darling."

The poet made frequent mention of it for during his early manhood, the plant was at the height of its popularity and was to be found growing in pots on the balconies of London houses when, during the heat of summer, the perfume was so powerful as to obliterate the offensive odours of the streets, whilst it was thought to protect the inhabitants from numerous diseases of the time. As late as 1830, Phillips wrote that even those who considered the fragrance of the flower too powerful to have in the home "must be delighted with the scent it throws from the balconies into the streets, giving a breath of garden air to 'close-pent man' whose evocations will not permit a ramble beyond the squares of the fashionable part of the town".

It was also known as Sweet Reseda, taking its botanic name from *resedare*, "to assuage", for we learn from Pliny that the plant possessed the power of charming away many disorders. He tells us that it grew near Rimini, a Roman town on the Adriatic coast and seed may have been sent back from N. Africa during the Roman occupation for it was in Roman times widely used in Italy as a sedative.

During the early nineteenth century the plant became popular in France when grown in pots to release its perfume in the houses of the aristocracy. It is said that the fashion was begun by the Empress Josephine who had received seed of *R. odorata* from Napoleon, obtained during the Egyptian campaign. Both in France and in England, it was grown as a pot plant until the mid-nineteenth century. Only then did it become a garden flower, and came to be grown in France in large quantities to supply the Paris market with scented flowers for winter bouquets.

Though native of Egypt, the mignonette is a hardy annual and grows best when self-sown. It was absent from few cottage gardens during the nineteenth century, seed being sown either in autumn or early in spring where it was to bloom and an open, sunny situation should be provided.

To bloom in a sunny window early in summer, seed should be sown in autumn and the seedlings transplanted into small pots and wintered in a cold frame. They are taken indoors when coming into fresh growth in April.

ROSA ALBA   White Rose of York
It is a rose of erect bushy habit, growing 4 to 6 ft. tall and it is
steeped in the history of our islands. It is the national emblem of
England and of Yorkshire where it is most commonly found in the
wild. It is thought to be a hybrid of *R. canina*, the Dog Rose and its
milky-white flowers have a delicious scent. Shakespeare referred to it
in *Henry VI* when Somerset says:

> Then will I raise aloft the milk-white rose,
> With whose sweet smell the air shall be perfumed.

It has been since earliest times the symbol of the House of York
whose heir, Elizabeth, daughter of Edward IV and Elizabeth Wood-
ville and elder sister of the uncrowned Edward V had married the
Lancastrian, Henry Tudor, son of the Earl of Richmond and Lady
Margaret Beaufort to found the Tudor dynasty. The Red rose and
the White, imposed one upon another became the Tudor Rose,
which has remained the symbol of British royalty to this day.

Shakespeare made mention of the Red Rose and the White in
Henry VI where in the Temple Garden (London), Plantagenet and
Somerset commence the quarrel. "From off this brier pluck a white
rose, with me," says Plantagenet to which Somerset replies:

> Let him that is no coward nor no flatterer,
> But dare maintain the party of the truth,
> Pluck a Red Rose from off this thorn with me.

The tragedy of the Wars of the Roses is summed up by the Earl of
Warwick when he says:

> This brave today
> Grown to this faction in the Temple Garden,
> Shall send, between the Red Rose and the White,
> A thousand souls to death and deadly night.

Of the White Rose, the Roman historian Pliny said, "The Isle of
Albion is so called from the white roses with which it abounds," and
he was the first to give an account of the culture of roses, saying that
"they should be transplanted in February . . . and replanted with
a foot distance one from another". This would be too close for the
White Rose which makes a plant almost as bushy as it grows tall
and so requires planting about 3 to 4 ft. apart, any time when the
ground is in suitable condition, between November and March.
The White roses require little attention as to their pruning, merely

cutting out dead and straggling wood in spring. The flowers are followed by handsome hips.

VARIETIES

R. ALBA MAXIMA. The Great Double White or Jacobite Rose, used as their symbol by the supporters of Bonnie Prince Charlie, the Young Pretender. It makes a large bush 6 ft. tall and the same across and blooms early in June, being one of the earliest of all roses. The large flat flowers are folded at the centre.

R. ALBA SEMI-PLENA. It is the semi-double White Rose of York. The blooms with their attractive golden stamens are borne on graceful arching stems.

BELLE D'AMOUR. Thought to have originated in a convent garden in Germany, it grows 4 to 5 ft. tall and bears attractively shaped blooms of a lovely shade of palest pink with a clove-like perfume.

FELICITÉ PARMENTIER. A delightful rose, growing only 4 ft. tall and 3 ft. across. Its cream-coloured buds open to flowers of rosette-shape, like those of the ranunculus and which are of palest pink with the scent of honeysuckle.

GREAT MAIDEN'S BLUSH. It was grown during medieval times and the late Lady Nicolson (Miss Sackville West) of Sissinghurst Castle has said that it retains its petals longer than any other rose. It has blue-green foliage and bears double flowers of blush-white with a pink centre.

POMPONE BLANCHE PARFAIT. It makes a compact bush 3 ft. tall and the same across and on short laterals, bears pompom-like blossoms of blush-white during July. It is almost thornless.

ROSE DE RESHT. It reached Britain from the Persian city of Resht and is usually classed with the White roses and is the most compact of them. It is an arresting sight when in bloom, it's camellia-shaped flowers being of ruby-red, veined with purple.

ROSA BOURBONIANA   Bourbon Rose

It came about by a natural crossing of the China rose (*R. chinensis*) and the autumn-flowering Damask, *R. damascena bifera* which took place on the French Isle of Bourbon in 1817. The result is the wonderful Bourbon roses which, unlike most of the old shrub roses, are of recurrent-flowering habit. There are those who consider them the most exquisite of all roses, being quartered at the centre and filled with overlapping petals. They are also deliciously scented. Requiring little or no pruning they were during the last century planted in many cottage gardens, often as a hedge or against a wall where their "old-fashioned" flowers enhance the white-washed walls of the cottage.

VARIETIES

BOULE DE NEIGE. Introduced a century ago, it does best against a wall which it will cover to a height of 7 ft. It has dark green foliage and bears its symmetrical camellia-shaped flowers of snow-white from June until October.

LA REINE VICTORIA. A delightful Victorian plant and with its compact habit is suitable for the smallest of cottage gardens. The circular cup-shaped blooms of rosy-pink are tightly packed with small petals and filled with exquisite perfume.

LOUISE ODIER. It is one of the loveliest of garden roses growing 4 to 5 ft. tall with dark leathery foliage and bears circular quartered blooms of rose-pink, flushed with lilac and with a soft sweet perfume.

MME I. PERIÈRE. Against a wall it will reach a height of 12 ft or more and bears handsome flowers of rosy pink flushed with crimson and which appear in profusion in autumn.

MME PIERRE OGER. It is a "sport" from *La Reine Victoria* and like Zéphyrine Drouhin is always in bloom whatever the weather. The cup-shaped blooms have almost transparent petals of creamy-pink with outstanding perfume.

ZÉPHYRINE DROUHIN. It is possibly the most valuable of all garden roses and may be Queen Elizabeth I's "Rose-without-a-thorn". It is thornless and bears, from June until November, double Hybrid Tea-type flowers of brilliant cerise-pink with a silvery sheen and pronounced fragrance. It may be used against a wall or as a hedge or wind-break for only during 3 to 4 months of the year is it without foliage. It may be trained to cover a wall of cottage or outhouse within two years of its planting.

ROSA CENTIFOLIA   Provence Rose; Cabbage Rose
The old Cabbage Rose, so called because the petals fold over like the leaves which form the "heart" of a cabbage. It is also the rose of Provence, the most southerly of French states, situated close to the

Italian border where the rose grew in abundance having reached there from the mountainous regions of Greece and Bulgaria where the plant grows naturally. It takes its botanical name from the flowers having a hundred petals. It was known to Pliny who said that the blooms were the largest of all roses. *R. centifolia* grows 3 to 5 ft. tall and bears blooms of China-pink which were depicted by the Dutch flower painters of old. The blooms are borne on short lateral shoots during June and July. The plants with their thorny stems require the minimum of pruning; occasionally shortening the shoots and cutting out dead wood.

VARIETIES

BULLATA. With its large pale green leaves deeply grooved and with their serrated edges it is known as the Lettuce-leaf rose and figured in Redouté's great work. It was known in the seventeenth century, the large globular blooms being of a lovely shade of cherry-blossom-pink and are powerfully scented.

FANTIN-LATOUR. Its arching stems and cup-like blooms of shell-pink, made it a great favourite of the French painter after whom it was named.

GROS CHOUX D'HOLLANDE. It is the Dutch Hundred-leaved rose, known to the flower painters of the seventeenth century and grown in gardens in earlier times. It makes a compact bush 4 ft. tall with small pale green leaves and bears tightly petalled flowers of a unique shade of mushroom-pink.

ROSA DAMASCENA
Damask Rose

Herodotus tells us that the Damask rose flourished in Macedonia where existed the Gardens of Midas "with a scent surpassing all others" but its origin is lost in antiquity. It may be descended from *R. gallica* and as it is closely allied to *R. centifolia*, both may have a common ancestor in the Rose of Gaul. No rose excels it for perfume and it is almost the only one grown for its attar in Turkey, Persia, Syria and Bulgaria. *R. damascena*, named after the city of Damascus is depicted on the walls of the Palace of Knossos in Crete (2000 B.C.) whilst the Autumn Damask mentioned by Virgil in the *Georgics*, ancestor of the Bourbon roses was grown by the Romans at Pompeii. It was a seedling of this rose, obtained from a crossing with *R. gallica* (possibly a back cross) which when crossed with the China rose gave rise to the Portland rose, ancestor of the hybrid perpetuals and later the hybrid teas in which is perpetuated the repeat flowering qualities of the Autumn Damask and China rose.

It was loved by Shakespeare more than any of the old roses for he makes frequent references to it. It was most probably the Blush Damask with its flesh-coloured blooms and which grew in Henry VIII's gardens that was best known to the poet for he speaks of "cherry lips and cheeks of Damask roses" and in *Two Noble Kinsmen*, probably written jointly with John Fletcher:

> Of all flowers
> Methinks a rose is best.
>   Why gentle maiden?
> It is the very emblem of a maid
> For when the west wind courts her gently,
> How modestly she blooms, and paints the sun
> With her chaste blushes!

The Damask rose may have been introduced into England with the returning Crusaders for it is mentioned in a "bill of medicynes" furnished for the use of Edward I in 1306.

The Damask and Provence roses; the Apothecary's rose, *R. gallica*; and the White rose, *R. alba*, all grew in the gardens of the Bishops of Ely in Holborn and in the nearby gardens of the Earl of Lincoln, granted by Edward I in 1286. The Earl took in law students whilst his successor Thomas of Lincoln leased a part of the garden to the Honourable Society of Lincoln's Inn and over the years the Lincoln's Inn as we know it, took shape. The York and Lancaster Rose was described by Shakespeare in *The Sonnets*:

> "I have seen roses damask'd Red and White."

That it was a Damask, the poet well knew, with its petals a mixture of rose-red and white and delicious scent.

The Damask rose is known as the Holy Rose for it is usually shown surrounding the Virgin as when she appeared to St. Bernadette at Lourdes. Whilst in the Wilton Diptych, which shows the oldest known portrait of an English king, Richard II is being presented to the Virgin and Child with Saint Edward the Confessor, St. Edmund of Bury and St. John the Baptist in attendance and with the Virgin crowned with pink Damask roses whilst the blooms litter the ground about her feet.

The Damasks should be pruned early in March, merely tipping back unduly long shoots and removing any dead wood.

VARIETIES

BLUSH DAMASK. Attaining a height of 6 ft. it makes an excellent hedge. It begins to flower in June, the flowers being of a lovely shade of clearest pale pink with a deeper flush at the centre.

CHÂTEAU GAILLARD. It was discovered growing on the walls of Richard the Lion Heart's Castle in Normandy and may have been brought back by him from the early Crusades. It has emerald foliage and bears flowers of fuchsia-pink which turn lavender with age.

LEDA. Known as the Painted Damask, it is right for a small cottage garden for it grows only a yard tall and bears, in profusion, blooms of purest white tipped with crimson to give a picotee appearance.

MME HARDY. It was raised by M. Hardy in the Luxembourg Gardens and Mr. G. S. Thomas in *The Old Shrub Roses* says that "it is unsurpassed by any rose". It bears circular cup-shaped blooms of ivory-white with a tight button eye of jade-green. The petals are attractively folded.

YORK AND LANCASTER. Syn. *R. damascena versicolor*. It has a history surpassing that of almost any other rose and grows 6 ft. tall, its blooms being a mixture of rose-pink and white, splashed and in stripes and with delicious perfume.

ROSA GALLICA   Red Rose of Lancaster
It has a history which goes back to the beginning of time and it was used by Persian warriors some 1000 B.C. to adorn their shields. It is believed to have been introduced into Britain by the Romans. Shakespeare knew it well and it would be familiar to him as the Apothecary's rose for it was widely grown for its medicinal qualities, especially around the old walled town of Provins, near Paris, hence the poets reference in *Hamlet* to "two Provincial roses in my razed shoes". The petals of the rose retain their perfume when dry longer than any other and were in great demand for making pot-pourris to place in the often musty-smelling rooms of cottage and manor house and for strewing over the floors. Shakespeare referred to their ability to retain their perfume in *The Sonnets*:

The rose looks fair, but fairer we it deem
For that sweet odor that doth in it live

The poet speaks of the "perfumed tincture of the roses" and "of their sweet deaths are sweetest odours made". Shakespeare makes reference to the Red Rose, taken for their symbol by the House of Lancaster in the Wars of the Roses. It may be recalled that Edmund, brother of Edward I and first Earl of Lancaster, second son of Henry III was also Count of Champagne in which territory was situated the town of Provins. The rose was the emblem of Blanche, his second wife and widow of Henry of Navarre and upon his return to England in 1277, Edmund took *R. gallica*, the Rose of Gaul, as his emblem too. Having no issue by his first wife, it is likely that the descendants of his wife Blanche and himself, also adopted the Red Rose as their emblem.

The Gallicas flourish in all soils and are completely hardy and easy to manage. They grow especially well in a sandy soil. They should be pruned in March, shortening the previous season's wood to half their length. The plants have no real thorns but are covered in strong hairs. They make neat upright bushes about 3 to 4 ft. tall and are mid-summer-flowering only.

VARIETIES

BELLE DE CRÉCY. One of the most beautiful of the old roses, it has bottle-green foliage and bears flat honey-scented blooms of violet-pink flushed with grey.

CAMAIEUX. It grows only 2 ft. tall and bears pretty cup-shaped flowers of crimson-maroon, striped with white; the stripes later turn to a lavender colour.

CHAMOISIE PICOTÉE. It makes a small upright plant with dainty leaves and bears rosette-like flowers of light red, edged with crimson and spotted with brown.

DUCHESSE D'ANGOULEME. Growing less than 3 ft. tall, it is thornless and bears dainty rosettes of soft Malmaison-pink.

ROSA MUNDI. Redouté rightly names it Fair Rosamond's rose and it is one of the oldest of all named roses, named after Rosamond Clifford, mistress of Henry II who was buried in the old Nunnery at Godstow in Oxfordshire. The best and most free flowering of all the striped roses, the white blooms are striped and blotched with purple, pink and red.

ROSA MUSCOSA   Moss Rose
With its distinctive musky perfume, the Moss rose has occupied a
special place in the cottage garden since early in the nineteenth
century. It is really a mutation of the Provence rose, the moss-like
hairs appearing on the calyx and on the stems and leaves. Its origin
is undecided. Mr. Edward Bunyard in his *Old Garden Roses*, suggested
that it was discovered in Holland about the year 1700 but Mme de
Genlis said that the mutation appeared first in Provence from which
plants reached England early in the eighteenth century. Most, however, date from the time of the Napoleonic Wars and by 1860 there
were, as William Paul the famous rose grower of Cheshunt told us,
more than fifty named varieties, the rich purple, pink and burgundy
colouring of their blooms providing a striking effect against the
crimson moss on the stems.

The plants should be harder pruned than most of the old roses,
cutting back the old wood to about half way and the side shoots to
the third bud.

VARIETIES

BLANCHE MOREAU. One of the loveliest of the moss roses, bearing
pure white cup-shaped blooms and being covered with striking
crimson moss.

CAPT. INGRAM. More than a century old, it remains one of the
loveliest roses of all with purple-tinted foliage and bearing rosette-
shaped blooms of deep velvety purple.

COMMON MOSS. It grows 4 ft. tall and the same wide, the chalice-
shaped buds opening to large cup-shaped flowers of clearest pink.

MARECHAL DAVOUST. One of the loveliest roses in cultivation, it
grows less than 4 ft. tall and is covered in crimson moss whilst its
cup-shaped blooms are of carmine-pink with a lilac edge.

WHITE BATH. It was introduced in 1817 by William Shailer, a
nurseryman and was known originally as the White Moss rose,
being a "sport" from the Common Pink Moss. It makes a compact
bush 3 ft. tall, its heavily mossed pink buds opening to large cups of
ivory-white.

WILLIAM LOBB. Known as the Old Velvet Moss, its tall vigorous
habit confined it to planting against a wall. The dense mossed
crimson buds open to flowers of purple, grey and lilac with outstanding fragrance.

ROSA RUBIGINOSA Sweet Briar; Eglantine
A native rose and like *R. canina*, the Dog rose, it bears flowers of
clearest pink which are delicately fragrant. It sends out its long
arching stems to 10 ft. or more in length and which may be trained to
form a canopy or bower beneath which the refreshing fruity fragrance
of its leaves may be enjoyed during the warmth of summertime for
which purpose it was planted in cottage gardens of old.

"The vulgar Sweet Briar," wrote John Worlidge in his *Systema
Horticulturae* (1677), "for its excellent odour in the spring, deserves
a place near your house or places of repose, yet not so much as that
which bears a double blossom for which it is preferred to it, and is
one of the best of odoriferous plants."

It is a rose frequently to be found about the hedgerows of Shakespeare's countryside, mingling with the woodbine and the musk-
rose. No scent can compare with that of eglantine leaves, especially
after a gentle shower or when the air is moist and heavy before a
storm for then the aroma takes on a refreshing spicy scent like that of
well-ripened apples and is capable of bringing comfort to the most
tired mind. From the fragrance of its leaves, the plant was named the
Sweet Brier. The leaf scent is released through minute glandular
hairs on the leaves, which actually leave their fruity perfume on the
hands when pressed.

Shakespeare, when writing those lovely words spoken by Arviragus
in *Cymbeline*, is believed to have had in mind his son, Hamnet:

> With fairest flowers,
> Whilst summer lasts, and I live here, Fidele,
> I'll sweeten thy sad grave: . . .
> The leaf of eglantine, whom not to slander,
> Outsweeten'd not thy breath.

Here, the comparison of the sweet, refreshing fragrance of the eglantine to a child's breath is delightful for to hold a child in one's arms
and to smell his sweet warm breath is one of life's pleasures. "Not
amongst the roses shall we find a more delicious perfume," wrote
Dean Hole.

The eglantine was, with its sweetly fragrant leaves and large,
angry thorns, used as a symbol of pleasure and of pain as Spenser
wrote in *Sonnet XXVI*:

> Sweet is the Eglantine but pricketh nere.

And Robert Herrick of the same period wrote:

> From this bleeding hand of mine
> Take this sprig of Eglantine,
> Which, though sweet into your smell,
> Yet the fretful briar will tell,
> He who plucks the sweets shall prove
> Many thorns to be in love.

The eglantine makes a delightful scented hedge as Thomas Hyll mentioned in *The Gardener's Labyrinth*, a book on the art of gardening, published in 1577. Here, he suggests planting "either privet alone or sweet bryar and whitethorn interlaced together, and roses one, two or three sorts placed here and there amongst them". But long before the appearance of Hyll's book, Chaucer, in *The Flower and the Leaf* had written:

> And closed in all the greene herbere
> With sicamour was set and eglanteres.

"Sicamour" was, in Chaucer's day, the honeysuckle or woodbine. The rose must have been a particular favourite of Chaucer for he mentions it often:

> Where she sate in a fresh greene laurey-tree,
> On that further side right by me,
> That gave so passing a delicious smell,
> According to the Eglantere full well.

Not least of its attractive qualities is its scarlet hips which follow the blooms in autumn and persist right through winter, providing colour when the plant has shed its leaves. Gerard wrote that "the fruit when ripe maketh most pleasant, meats and banqueting dishes (using it as an alternative to red current jelly), as tarts and suchlike; the making whereof I commit to the cunning cooke. . . ."

To form an impenetrable hedge, the plants should be set 4 ft. apart when they will quickly close up the gaps and will eventually grow to a height of about 6 ft. and the same distance in width. With their large hooked thorns, such a hedge will deter the most savage beast as well as providing colour almost the whole year round.

VARIETIES

JANET'S PRIDE. It was illustrated in Miss Ellen Willmott's book, *The Genus Rosa* (1910) in which she quotes the Rev. Wolley-Dod that this variety of the Eglantine was found growing in a

Cheshire lane. Of similar habit to the parent, the flowers are of a lovely shade of bright pink with a white centre but the foliage is less aromatic than that of the parent.

LA BELLE DISTINGUÉE. It is the Double Scarlet Sweet Briar, less vigorous than the parent and not nearly so thorny. The deep red flowers are followed by hips of similar colouring. The foliage however is not very fragrant.

MORNING'S BLUSH. Of compact habit, rarely exceeding 5 ft. in height, the fully double blooms are quite small and of a lovely shade of blush-pink, enhanced by the neat bottle-green leaves.

In 1890, Lord Penzance began a long programme of breeding, using *R. rubiginosa* as a parent and a number of Hybrid Perpetual and Bourbon roses as the pollinating parents. The result was a number of fine hybrid varieties bearing scented flowers and with the same strongly aromatic foliage of the sweet-briar. Amongst the best are:

AMY ROBSART. The blooms are large and semi-double and of a rich shade of reddish-pink.

FLORA MCIVOR. The large single flowers are white, attractively flushed with pale pink.

JEANNIE DEANS. One of the best, the semi-double blooms being of a startling shade of crimson-scarlet.

LUCY ASHTON. One of the loveliest of all roses for a hedge, the blooms being of purest white with a distinctive rose-pink edge to the petals.

ROSA WICHURAIANA   Rambler Rose
Though the familiar pictures of Cotswold cottages clothed with rambling roses present an appearance of antiquity, it is only since the beginning of the century that the climbing rose has been grown in British gardens when *R. wichuraiana* was introduced from Japan by way of America. Previously, only one or two varieties of *R. sempervirens* were grown, noteworthy being Felicité et Perpetué, raised by Louis-Philippe's gardener at Château Neuilly in 1827 and which bears its creamy-white pompoms only during July. Another was the Crimson Rambler, a variety of *R. multiflora* introduced by Turner of Slough, introducer also of Cox's Orange Pippin. Of vigorous habit, the brilliant red flowers are borne in heavy clusters. The Garland was also known to cottage gardeners. Raised in 1835 by crossing

R. multiflora with *R. moschata*, Shakespeare's musk rose, it bears pure white flowers in large clusters and which have the fragrance of the musk rose of the hedgerow. Zéphyrine Drouhin was used to cover a wall and with its large hybrid tea type blooms of deepest pink and its outstanding perfume where is none lovelier to this day. Another was *Gloire de Dijon*, the hardiest of the Noisette hybrids, introduced in 1853. In his *Book about Roses*, the Rev. Reynolds Hole, Dean of Rochester and founder of the Royal National Rose Society said, "I lose no time in stating that the best climbing rose with which I am acquainted is . . . *Gloire de Dijon* . . . of robust habit and hardy constitution. It is what cricketers call an all-rounder, good in every point for wall, arcade, pillar, standard. . . ." With its quartered blooms of buff-yellow, it remains one of the most delightful roses in cultivation.

The introduction of *R. wichuraiana* into America towards the end of the nineteenth century began a new interest in climbing roses. The American breeders began by crossing it with the Tea Roses in an attempt to prolong the flowering period and the first hybrid variety to appear was May Queen in 1899 when its warm pink flowers and delicate perfume quickly earned it high praise. Then came Jersey Beauty from a crossing with the tea rose *Perle des Jardins* and from the French came that fine rose, Alberic Barbier, its creamy-white blooms having the refreshing perfume of ripe apples. The following year came Dorothy Perkins, a rose known to all cottage gardeners for its dark foliage and bright pink flowers borne in huge clusters. Shortly after came Excelsa, known as the Ulster Rose. It was raised by M. H. Walsh of Massachusetts but soon came to be planted in every cottage garden in Northern Ireland and in the South too for it readily grew from shoots inserted in the open ground. It was raised by crossing *R. wichuraiana* with Turner's Crimson Rambler and bears clusters of bright crimson flowers. It still remains the best of all standards in the weeping form. Next year (1910) saw the introduction of Dr. van Fleet, bearing fragrant flowers of clearest pink. It was important in that from it appeared a rose in 1930, of repeat-flowering habit and bearing hybrid tea type blooms of a unique shade of silvery pink. It was called The New Dawn and it was from this rose that so many of the modern climbers have been evolved. It was well named for it was the dawn of a new era in roses to cover a wall, for they now sent up their new shoots of healthy foliage from the base and were also known as pillar roses.

The new climbers are perpetual flowering and bear large flowers, equal in form to the best of the modern hybrid tea roses. They bear their flowers on the lateral growths formed during the previous season, hence they should be pruned only moderately, cutting back small lateral shoots to four buds.

VARIETIES OF CLIMBING ROSE

ALOHA (1949). A New Dawn seedling which bears its lovely coral pink blooms on long stems and which are the equal in form to the hybrid teas.

CHAPLIN'S PINK CLIMBER (1928). Raised from Paul's Scarlet × American Pillar; it will attain a height of 20 ft. in all soil types and bears shell-pink flowers with attractive golden stamens.

CHAPLIN'S PINK COMPANION (1961). Bred from Chaplin's Pink Climber × Opera, it is one of the best roses to cover a wall quickly. It has plenty of glossy foliage and bears its silvery-pink flowers in large clusters.

CASINO (1963). Raised from Coral Dawn and Buccaneer, it is a climbing hybrid tea of perpetual-flowering habit, growing 10 ft. tall, its flowers of soft yellow having forty-two petals.

CÉCILE BRUNNER (1880). Known as the Sweetheart Rose for its dainty quilled-petalled blooms of soft pink were so often used in Victorian posies, it will attain a height of 12 ft. in the climbing form and bears its flowers in graceful arching sprays.

COPENHAGEN (1963). Raised by Niels Poulsen in Denmark, it will cover a pillar or wall to a height of 10 ft., its scarlet flowers having fifty petals and a distinct old rose perfume.

CORAL SATIN (1956). Raised from New Dawn × Fashion, it is hardy and vigorous, bearing clusters of large coral pink amidst dark green glossy foliage.

DANSE DU FEU (1954). Raised in France by Chas. Mallerin, it is one of the finest of all modern climbers, reaching a height of 10 ft. with bronzy-green foliage. It has Paul's Scarlet in its parentage and bears hybrid tea-type blooms of orange-scarlet which are quite untroubled by wet weather.

HANDEL (1966). Raised by McGredy's by crossing the vigorous floribunda Columbine with Heidelberg, it grows 10 ft. tall and bears flowers of deep cream, shaded and edged cerise.

MEG (1954). Raised from Paul's Lemon Pillar and Mme Butterfly, it is a vigorous climbing rose that would grace any cottage wall. The

Plate 13   *Rosa gallica officinalis* and *Rosa gallica*, Rosa mundi

Plate 14   *Lonicera periclymenum* – Honeysuckle

blooms are single (or semi-double) of shell-pink, shaded with coral and peach and enhanced by crimson stamens.

PARADE (1955). A New Dawn seedling growing to a height of 12 ft. and one of the most free flowering of all climbers, its rose-red blooms borne singly and in clusters.

ROYAL GOLD (1957). It is a Climbing Goldilocks seedling and will cover a wall 8 to 9 ft. tall. It is unique in that it will bloom well the first summer after planting and is the best of all yellow climbers for its old gold flowers do not fade.

SCHOOLGIRL (1964). A McGredy introduction and raised from Coral Dawn and the wonderful hybrid tea, Belle Blonde, it is a most distinctive rose bearing pointed flowers of a unique shade of apricot-orange and is perpetually in bloom.

ROSMARINUS OFFICINALIS   Rosemary
Has any plant a lovelier name—or is there one more steeped in history? It is said to have taken its name from the Virgin Mary who rested against the evergreen shrub, covering it with her cloak, during the flight into Egypt. A Spanish legend goes further, believing that from that time onwards its white flowers changed to those of the rich purple-blue colour we know so well. An old English legend tells us that rosemary never grows taller than the height of Christ; afterwards it continues to grow only in width. More probably because of its liking for the salt-laden atmosphere of the sea coast, did it takes its name *Rose marinus*.

The plant is believed to have been introduced into England by Queen Philippa, who married Edward III in York Minster on January 30th, 1328, and who, it may be recalled, implored her husband to spare the lives of the six burghers of Calais. Queen's College, Oxford, founded by Robert of Eglesfield in 1340 was named after her and rosemary still figures in the bringing in of the Boar's Head each Christmastide in College Hall to commemorate the lovely queen. A manuscript in the library at Trinity College, Cambridge, sent by the Countess of Hainault to her daughter, Philippa, describes the value of rosemary in numerous ways. It was said to "gladden the spirits" of all who crushed its fragrant leaves, and its refreshingly pungent smell, quite unlike that of any other plant does seem to act in the same way as smelling salts, especially during a period of hot dry weather which brings out its fragrance as strongly as when growing in its native haunts, around the shores of the Mediterranean. In fact, rosemary is always at its best in the dry, sandy soil and salt-laden atmosphere of the seashore, from which it has been called the "dew of the sea". But it loves a wall more than any plant and where it will receive the maximum amount of sunshine to bring out its fragrance to the full. It must have some lime or lime rubble about its roots. As the young plants, until firmly established, may become "burnt" by cold winds, late April or early May is the best planting time. If the soil is heavy, add some coarse sand. Space the plants 2 ft. apart.

Rosemary may also be easily grown from seed sown in shallow drills in April; and cuttings will strike readily in a trench of sand and peat if taken between May and August and kept moist.

The stems should be gathered early in September when the fragrance is more pronounced. Distilled oil of rosemary is one of the ingredients of eau-de-Cologne and the water from simmered leaves acts an an excellent hair tonic and as a freshener and purifier of the face. The ancients recommended simmering in white wine. But it is the freshly gathered foliage that is most valuable, for if placed under the pillow-case it will bring about peaceful sleep. Bancke's *Herbal* of 1525, the first in the English language, mentions that "the leaves laid under the pillow deliver one from evil dreams". Bancke also advised one to "smell of it oft and it shall keep thee youngly".

William Langham writing in *The Garden of Health* (1579) said, "carry powder of the flower about thee to make thee merry, glad, gracious and well-beloved of all men. Lay the flowers on thy bed to keepe thee from all eveil dreames . . . To comfort the heart, seethe Rosemary and the flowers with Rose water, and drinke it. The conserve of the flowers comforteth the heart marvellously. To preserve youth, make a box of the wood and smell to it."

The potent seeds dried and placed in muslin bags and hung about the bedroom will encourage sleep. Thomas Newton in *A Butler's Recipe Book* wrote, "Flowers of rosemary being distilled, the water drunke morning and evening first and last make the breath very sweet."

No plant was more beloved by the Tudors. Barnaby Googe tells us in his *Husbandry* (1578) that it was widely used in topiary, "sette by women for their pleasure, to grow in sundry proportions as in the fashion of a cart, a peacock, or such things as they fancy."

Rosemary was trained against almost every available wall, for in some way it was in constant use. No more so than used as garlands at weddings, for rosemary has always represented "friendship". Sir Thomas More wrote, "as for Rosemarine, I let it run over my garden walls not only because the bees love it, but because it is the herb sacred to remembrance, to love and friendship." This same Thomas More, beheaded by command of Henry VIII on Tower Hill for refusing to recognize his divorce and re-marriage and whose head was conveyed through the night by his daughter, Margaret Roper, to her home at Canterbury. Here it remained until her death and it now rests in a leaden casket in St. Dunstan's church in the city.

Sir Thomas More has said that during Tudor times rosemary was the herb consecrated to remembrance, and Shakespeare also makes mention of this in *Hamlet*:

> "There's Rosemary, that's for remembrance; pray,
> love, remember."

Paul Hentzner in his *Travels* (1598) wrote that at Hampton Court "it was so planted and nailed to the walls as to cover them entirely". It is said that Anne of Cleves wore a head-dress of rosemary leaves at her marriage to Henry VIII, but in her case it cannot be said that "where rosemary flourished the woman rules".

Each year on April 23rd, St. George's Day, and which is also Shakespeare's birthday, the people of Stratford wear a sprig of rosemary and carry wreaths of scented flowers and herbs in procession through the town, preceded by a band and the Town Beadle dressed in crimson livery.

In a delightful sonnet written in 1584 by Thomas Robinson and entitled, "A Nosegay for Lovers", it is written:

> Rosemary is for remembrance
> Between us day and night,
> Wishing that I might always have
> You present in my sight.

Rosemary was the favourite evergreen for all solemn occasions. "Be't for my bridall or my buriall," wrote Herrick and indeed the herb was in great demand at weddings and at funerals, for its ability to retain its fragrance throughout the year. This is due to the microscopic pores through which water evaporates from the plant, being in the Rosemary sunk deep into the leaves and which are also covered by hairs. Thus the leaves remain fresh for a considerable time when removed from the plant and retain their perfume.

> "With sweet Rosemary in your hand—
> A perfect token of your Virgin's life."

it is written in the Roxburgh Ballads.

Brand in *Popular Antiquities* gives an account of a wedding where the bride was led to church "between two sweet boys with bride-laces and rose-mary tied to their silken sleeves", in this case used as a symbol of the bride's virginity. At weddings, the sprigs were placed in glasses of wine as a token of respect and happiness whilst they were often made more colourful by gilding. In *The Shepherd's Calender* for November, Spenser wrote of "The knotted rush-rings and gilt rosemarie".

Ben Jonson said that it was the custom for bridesmaids to present the bridegroom with "rosemary bound with ribands" on his wedding morn. In Jonson's *Christmas Masque*, New Year's Gift enters "in a blue coat . . . with an orange and a sprig of rosemary, gilt, on his head".

At funerals, sprigs were distributed to the mourners to be carried to the church as a token of remembrance and were then thrown onto the coffin. Shakespeare refers to this custom in *Romeo and Juliet* when Friar Laurence tells the mourners to take the rosemary which was to be used at Juliet's wedding and to place it on her dead body:

> Dry up your tears and stick your Rosemary
> On this fair corpse.

In France, at the time, and maybe in England, too, it was the custom to decorate bodies of the dead with Rosemary for the reason that it would remain fresh and fragrant longer than any other herb and because it was an emblem of perpetual remembrance, hence the saying "keeping the memory green".

A genus of only one species *Rosemarinus officinalis* makes a large spreading evergreen bush 5 to 6 ft. tall and bears flowers like tiny white orchids. Jessop's variety is of more upright habit and bears lavender-coloured flowers. The form, *R. prostratus*, almost hugs the ground, though it is not so hardy and should be given a place in full sun and where it is sheltered by other herbs of shrubby habit. It grows only 9 ins. tall and in early summer bears bright lavender-coloured flowers. There is also a most attractive pink-flowered form, *roseus*.

RUDBECKIA PURPUREA   Cone-flower

The first species to reach Britain was *R. laciniata* which Parkinson said first came to the gardener of the King of France from French settlers in Quebec. It was he who gave several roots to John Trades-cant, who passed them on to Parkinson. Parkinson knew it as *Doronicum americanum* and it did not receive its now well-known name until given it by Linnaeus in 1740. He named it after the Swedish physicians who founded the botanic garden at Uppsala University shortly before Linnaeus' time, Rudbeck, father and son.

Also introduced during the seventeenth century was *R. purpurea* (Syn.: *Echinacea purpurea*) which was brought from Virginia by Rev. J. Banister. Like *R. laciniata*, it came to be planted in every cottage garden for it possessed extreme hardiness, took kindly to all soil types and flowered in autumn when colour in the garden was much needed. They are best planted after flowering, in November, allowing 2 ft. between the plants for like all the American composites, they make dense growth.

Of *R. purpurea*, Phillips tells us that it was the second flower to be illustrated in *Curtis's Botanical Magazine* and he makes mention of the singular shape of the petals which are pendulous and curve inwards, "having the appearance of so many pieces of narrow ribbon notched at the end". The flower and stems are crimson-purple.

VARIETIES

AUTUMN SUN. A stately plant in all respects, growing 6 ft. tall and bearing during autumn flowers of deep golden-yellow.

GOLDEN GLOW. Tall growing, it bears fully double flowers of a lovely shade of lemon-yellow.

GOLDQUELLE. It makes a compact plant 3 ft. tall and from July until October bears double flowers of richest gold.

RUTA GRAVEOLENS   Rue

Because of its extreme bitterness, Rue was the herb of repentance or Herb of Grace.

> "For you there's Rosemary and Rue: . . .
> Grace and remembrance be to you both."

said Perdita in *A Winter's Tale*, and again in *Hamlet*, Ophelia says:

"There's Rue for you; and here's some for
me: we may call it Herb—Grace o' Sundays:
O, you must wear your Rue with a difference."

In *Richard II*, one of Shakespeare's early plays, the theme was the
curse put on the House of Lancaster by Henry Bolingbroke, Duke of
Lancaster, for having imprisoned Richard in Pontefract Castle and
proclaimed himself King. And after the Queen has departed; the
gardener says:

Poor queen! so that thy state might be no worse,
I would my skill were subject to thy curse.
Here did she drop a tear; here, in this place
I'll set a bank of Rue, sour herb of grace:
Rue, even for truth, here shortly shall be seen,
In the remembrance of a weeping queen.

In this context, Shakespeare uses the word to denote pity, the
meaning of the Anglo-Saxon word "Ruth" from which the plant
takes its name.

Like Rosemary, the herb had many uses. Turner said that rue
"made hott in the fyle (nipple) of a pomegranate (a fruit widely
grown in Britain before the introduction of the orange) was good for
ake of the ears". Milton mentions its use as an eye ointment as in
Paradise Lost:

"To nobler sights,
Michael from Adam's eye the filme removed
Which that false fruit which promised clearer sight
Had bred; then purged with Euphrasie and Rue
The visual nerve, for he had much to see."

Rue was also believed to guard one against witches and it was used
by inn-keepers to give to travellers before continuing their way, to
keep them safe on their journey. The herb appears on the Arms of
the Duke of Saxony, granted by the Emperor Barbarossa in 1181 and
in 1202 it was announced that the King of Saxony had conferred the
Order of the Crown of Rue on the Prince of Wales. The herb appears
in the *Collar of the Order of the Thistle*. Parkinson wrote of it, "without
doubt it is a most wholesome herb, although bitter and strong". And
Spenser wrote of "Rank-smelling rue".

The attractive leaves have a pleasing, powerful, aromatic perfume, like the smell of freshly cut hay in the stack which made the
stackyard so popular in boyhood days.

Culpeper tells us that the leaves were used to strew the floor of workhouse and prison, for as Walfred Strabo wrote in the ninth century, "great is its power over evil odours".

Rue is a perennial plant which grows to a height of about 2 ft. It has attractively serrated leaves, blue-green in colour and bears pale yellow flowers. It likes best a dry, sandy soil and does well in chalk. Plants are readily raised from seed sown in summer or from cuttings taken in spring.

SALVIA OFFICINALIS   Sage

The ancients gave pride of place amongst all aromantic plants to *Salvia officinalis*. In his poem, Walfred Strabo wrote, "Amongst my herbs, sage holds place of honour, of good scent it is and full of virtue for many ills." As it has since earliest times been considered so "full of virtue", "sage" has become firmly established in the English language, meaning "wise", "mellow", "learned" and it is in this context that it was frequently used by Shakespeare for curiously, he made no direct reference to the plant in any of his plays. In *Richard III*, in the Court of Baynard's Castle, the Earl of Gloucester addresses the Lord Mayor, Alderman and Citizens of London:

"Cousin of Buckingham and sage grown men."

And again in *Henry IV* (part II) Shakespeare uses the words "sage counsellors" but there is no direct mention of the plant.

Sage is reputed to give long life to those who use it, hence its name of Salvia (Salvation). It has certainly been used through the years for curing all manner of complaints. Sage cordial, made from Red Leaf sage, is most valuable for a sore throat, whilst an infusion of sage (an ounce of dried leaves to a pint of boiling water) taken when cold, is an excellent help to the digestion and for those who suffer from anaemia. It may also be used as a hair tonic, and will prevent the falling out of hair better than any other preparation, whilst it will darken greying hair. A little of an infusion of sage water should be massaged into the scalp every day upon rising, using a little conditioner once a week to prevent the hair from becoming too dry. It is surprising how quickly the hair will respond to this treatment. Since earliest times, sage has been used in stuffing for the richer meats.

Sage enjoys a sandy soil but being shallow rooting it will appreciate a mulch of well-decayed manure given in autumn. To keep the plants tidy and to prevent them forming an excess of old wood, cut in June and again at the end of summer, and for market make up liberal sized bunches. For this purpose and for supplying sage for packeting dry, only the broad leaf form will be wanted and a stock may generally be obtained only from cuttings. These will root quickly in frames or in the open in a sandy soil. When planting, space the plants 2 ft. apart for they form large bushes and require the maximum amount of sunlight and air.

With their handsome grey foliage and bearing racemes of sky-blue flowers, several of the sages are valuable garden plants.

SPECIES AND VARIETIES

Salvia argentea. A native of S. Europe, it grows to a height of 3 ft. Its oval, wedge-shaped leaves and the stems are covered in down and grey hairs and it bears its whorls of pinkish-white flowers throughout summer.

S. azurea. A native of N. America, it will eventually reach a height of 5 ft. with smooth grey-green leaves whilst it bears its slender spikes of deepest blue during July and August.

S. officinalis. The culinary sage which grows 3 ft. tall and bears its purple flowers throughout summer. The form *aurea*, is more compact than the grey-leaved type. It has golden leaves and bears yellow flowers whilst tricolor is an interesting variegated leaf form.

S. superba. Also *S. virgata*, it is a European species with rough oblong leaves and bearing long elegant spikes of violet-blue. The form East Friesland is similar but grows less than 18 ins. tall.

SANTOLINA INCANA   Cotton Lavender

The Cotton or French Lavender, *Santolina incana*, which is in no way related to the true lavender is a most interesting plant. It has beautifully serrated silvery-grey leaves which it retains through winter and so it is a valuable plant for a low hedge. It grows almost 2 ft. tall (though there are more dwarf forms) but it may be clipped in spring and maintained at a height of no more than 12 to 15 ins. Its leaves are pleasantly pungent and may be used to keep away moths from clothes, for which purpose it is best dried and mixed with lavender and Southernwood. The French name it Guarde Robe. It reached England during Tudor times for it was still rare at the beginning of the seventeenth century. Parkinson wrote: "The rarity and novelty of this herb being for the most part in the gardens of great persons doth cause it to be of greater regard."

To make a hedge, the plants should be set out 18 ins. apart in autumn and it will be quite happy in ordinary soil provided it is well drained. The cuttings removed with a heel, strike readily in a sandy soil in the open and if inserted during mid-summer will have become well rooted in time for transplanting before winter. The plant bears masses of bright yellow daisy-like flowers which will be lost if the plants are clipped later than early April. In the less exposed areas the plants are clipped in autumn.

SPECIES AND VARIETIES

Santolina incana. It grows to a height of 2 ft. with small fleshy leaves covered with silvery hairs and in July it bears rounded heads of yellow flowers.

The form *S. incana nana* is more compact, attaining a height of no more than 15 ins. whilst its foliage is more pungent than the type.

Finer still is the variety Weston, which grows less than 12 ins. tall but 15 to 18 ins. across. The stems are made up of numerous tiny "lambs' tails" or "catkins" which are brightly silvered and which possess a strong pungent scent.

S. neapolitana. It grows to a height of 3 to 4 ft. with finely cut silvered foliage which is most aromatic and in July bears lime-green flowers which have an unpleasant smell.

S. serratifolia. A hybrid between *S. incana* and *S. neapolitana*, it more closely resembles the latter, having finely cut feathery foliage, as if dusted with silver though its rich golden flowers have not the same unpleasant smell.

SAPONARIA OFFICINALIS Soapwort

Of about thirty species, that which is native to the British Isles and grown in cottage gardens is *S. officinalis*. It is a plant of the hedgerows and ditches which was highly prized by the countryman for its leaves when crushed and rubbed on the hands, form a lather like soap and remove dirt and stains, hence its name "soapwort". Gerard said that the leaves "yielded a juice which when bruised, scoureth almost as well as soap". The leaves were also placed on cut fingers when they would disinfect the wound whilst an infusion was considered a certain cure for jaundice.

The plant was also known as Bouncing Bet for as Parkinson said, once planted, it spread about the garden and was difficult to eradicate.

In its double form, it is a charming old garden plant, coming into bloom by mid-July and continuing until October, its flesh-pink flowers being in the words of Thomas Hanmer, "fulsomely sweet" which is an apt description. There is a handsome double white form, *alba plena* which has an undertone of clove in its perfume. Both forms grow 2 ft. tall and have handsome glaucous foliage.

SATUREIA MONTANA   Winter Savory
In *A Winter's Tale*, Perdita says:

> "Here's flowers for you;
> Hot Lavender; Mints; Savory; Marjoram."

This was the perennial form of *Satureia montana*, or Winter Savory, propagated from cuttings or from pieces of the root. The leaves, which are small, are dried and mixed with other herbs and possess the refreshing pungency of thyme. Thomas Hyll in *The Art of Gardening* (1563) wrote that mazes or knots are sometimes "sette with Isope and Thyme or with Winter Savory and Thyme, for these endure all the winter through green". The fresh leaves, boiled with broad beans, greatly improve the flavour.

Winter Savory was included by Tusser in the twenty-one plants for strewing for the pungency of its leaves rivalled lavender and fennel whilst it is said that if rubbed on wasp stings they provide immediate relief. Winter Savory is a most delightful little plant which will retain its leaves (which turn bronze) and its aromatic fragrance, likened to that of sweet marjoram, under a covering of snow and ice. The flowers, though insignificant, are a valuable source of nectar.

SAXIFRAGA UMBROSA   London Pride
It is a plant which has been grown since earliest times for its properties of "breaking up stone" in the bladder which is the meaning of its name. It is a native plant, to be found about the mountains of Donegal and Mayo and of the craggy hills of North Yorkshire and was in almost every cottage garden in that part of the county where its name was None-so-Pretty. Indeed, few flowers have been more

attractively served by nature for the tiny petals are pointed with a delicacy seen in few other flowers and which may be fully appreciated only through a miscroscope. The flowers are borne in sprays which arise on 12-in. stems from a rosette of dark green glossy leaves and because of its neat habit, it was widely used for an edging to small garden beds and borders. It is a plant of extreme hardiness and also flourishes under town garden conditions so that by Parkinson's time it had become widely planted in London gardens, hence its name London Pride. Miss Alice Coats however, in *Flowers and their Histories*, believes the plant received its name from Mr. George London, Royal Gardener to William III in 1688 and who made liberal use of it in the Royal gardens of Hampton Court and Kensington Palace. Parkinson named it Prince's Feathers. It grows well in shade and will rapidly propagate itself by offsets. Native of the rocky limestone formations, it enjoys a soil containing limestone chippings and also grows well in a rockery constructed of limestone.

SCABIOSA   Pincushion-flower
Of several species native to or naturalized in the British Isles, that grown as a garden flower is *S. atropurpurea*, the Sweet Scabious which is a hardy annual and is usually sown where it is to bloom, in early April. From its deep purple flowers, like pincushions, it takes its country name and is also known as widow-in-mourning. It grows 3 ft. tall and is in bloom during August and September.

The plant may be a native of southern Europe and became naturalized in parts of Britain at an early date but there is no mention of it in garden literature until the beginning of the seventeenth century when it was said to be growing in the garden of William Coys in Essex and from then on it came to be grown in most cottage gardens. In those countries of S. Europe bordering the Mediterranean, the flowers were much used at funerals for the colour of the slightly clove-scented flowers is of "in memoriam" purple.

Of a number of lovely modern varieties, Azure Fairy bears flowers of azure-blue whilst King of the Blacks bears deep blackish-maroon flowers.

The perennial scabious, *S. caucasica*, reached this country from Mt. Caucasus at the beginning of the nineteenth century, since when it has been a popular cottage garden flower and of recent years the most profitable of all summer cut flowers for those who make a living from the land. Not only are the flowers extremely long lasting when in water and do not drop their petals, but it blooms profusely from July until October. It should always be planted in March for the roots have few fibres and will perish if planted in autumn.

Of several lovely varieties, Clive Greaves, bearing flowers of powder-blue; Miss Willmot, white; and Pride of Exmouth, navy-blue are outstanding.

SEDUM   Stonecrop

For a starved soil and a sun-baked situation, the sedums are without rival in diversity of form and colouring. They take their name from the Latin, "to sit", for they are at their best when "sitting" upon a stone wall with their roots in the mortar and baked by the sun and wind. At one time they were widely planted on the walls of cottage and manor house and were known as stonecrops or wall-peppers. The best known is *Sedum acre*, the native stonecrop or wallpepper, so named from its acrid leaves. It bears sprays of tiny brilliant golden flowers on stems less than 3 ins. long. Like all the cushion stonecrops, it is a splendid plant to use for a colourful "lawn", planting it with the creeping thymes when they will quickly cover the soil and present a picture of brilliance throughout summer.

Like the sempervivums, the stonecrops are succulents, members of the Crassulaceae family and where baked by the sun, the fleshy foliage will take on the richest shades of bronze and crimson towards the end of a dry summer. They may be planted on a sun-baked bank where little else would grow and are delightful growing between the crevices of paving stone. Many are ideal for growing in troughs and are always happy where allowed to grow around the sides. A gritty, well-drained soil is all they require but they must have sun. Only *S. pulchellum* enjoys a moist soil and partial shade where it will produce its pink flower heads above emerald-green foliage from June until September.

SPECIES AND VARIETIES

Sedum rhodiola or *S. roseum* is a plant which has been grown in cottage gardens since earliest times. It was known as Rose-root for the dried roots have the unmistakable smell of a pot-pourri made of Ena Harkness rose petals. From the roots, a rose-scented toilet water was made. It frequents mountainous slopes and sea cliffs in N. England

and Ireland and is a perennial plant with glaucous leaves above which it bears on 9-in. stems, greenish-yellow flowers in terminal cymes. It is in bloom from May until August and like most of the stonecrops may be planted between the cracks of an old wall.

Of those most suitable for a trough garden, outstanding is *S. rubrotinctum* which grows only 3 ins. tall and has the most unusual salmon-pink foliage which turns brilliant scarlet during a dry, sunny summer. The tiny star-like flowers are yellow. Another beauty is *S. oreganum* which bears heads of golden flowers above orange rosettes. *S. lydium*, also grows less than 3 ins. tall and forms an erect tuft of narrow bright green leaves which turn red in autumn.

S. spathulifolium, another native of Oregon, in its various forms is a beauty. *Aureum* has bright yellow foliage whilst *purpureum* forms rosettes of crimson-purple covered with grey "bloom" like a black grape. The two provide a pleasing contrast. Lovely too, is *S. dasyphyllum album*, found by the late Mr. Clarence Elliott at St. Martin Vesubie. It bears snow-white flowers amidst beautiful grey leaves and carpets the ground. Striking in that its glistening white flowers have black anthers is *S. nevii* which makes a tiny hummock 2 ins. high.

Of the more upright sedums, *S. rupestre* is a handsome European species and is to be found growing between limestone rocks. Its pale green leaves take on purple tinting during sunny weather whilst it sends up its yellow flowers on 6-in. stems. Outstanding too, is *S. aizoon* which is said to have reached Britain in 1753. It has handsome grey foliage, the stems reaching a height of 18 ins., at the end of which it bears large heads of golden-orange. It is a useful plant to edge a dry shrub border and will die back in winter coming up fresh in spring.

S. tatarinowii is a handsome Chinese species, bearing on 6-in. stems, heads of pinky-white whilst *S. cauticolum* is from Japan and has grey-green glaucous foliage. It bears its heads of rich rose-red on 6-in. stems during autumn when the rock garden will have lost the full beauty of spring and summer and so is especially valuable.

SEMPERVIVUM   Houseleek

Natives of the alpine regions of Central Europe but naturalized in England since earliest times, *S. tectorum* the Common Houseleek is the best known, to be found growing from ancient walls and on the roofs of houses, for it was thought to protect the home from fire and from witches.

Of the same Crassulaceae family as the Sedum and Cotyledon, both native plants, it lends charm to its surroundings wherever it grows, forming dense clusters of spiny rosettes of darkest green tinted with crimson and it remains colourful all the year through. It takes its name from two Latin words *semper* (always) and *vivo* (I live), for it is almost indestructible. It is usually seen on walls but is charming where used for summer bedding, planting 6 ins. apart, with blue lobelia between. Other species may also be used and never fail to create interest. After the lobelia has finished flowering it may be replaced with dwarf early flowering tulips in red or yellow and for which the sempervivums provide a pleasing ground cover. The plants like a soil containing lime rubble and one which is well drained in winter. Or they may be planted in the cracks of old walls and on tiles becoming anchored with the minimum of soil about their roots. To increase them, offsets may be removed without disturbing the main plant. They are charming where growing in the company of *Sedum acre* which bears tiny sprays of golden-yellow flowers. The leaves of sempervivum quickly stay bleeding and are also effective in the treatment of skin diseases.

SPECIES AND VARIETIES

Sempervivum arachnoideum Stansfieldii. This distinct species has wedge-shaped leaves formed in dense rosettes of crimson-bronze and veiled with white cobweb-like hairs. In June it bears bright red flowers on 4-in. stems.

S. atlanticum. Native of the Atlas Mountains, it has been growing in English gardens for at least a century. It forms pale green rosettes of 2 ins. diameter, the leaves being tipped with bronze and fringed. In June it bears pinky-red flowers on 12-in. stems.

S. fimbriatum. An old favourite of the European Alps forming a neat dark green rosette, tipped with purple and fringed with hairs. In July it bears brilliant red flowers on hair stems 9 ins. long.

S. glaucum. Native of the Alpine regions of Central Europe, it forms a large rosette of glaucous mauve tipped with brown above which it bears in July, bright red flowers on 6-in. stems.

S. schlehanii rubrifolium. One of the most striking of all, forming huge rosettes of plum-red and bearing crimson flowers on 12-in. stems.

S. tectorum. The Common Houseleek, forming pale green rosettes of 3 ins. diameter, the leaves being tipped with reddish-brown. In June it bears pale red flowers on hairy stems 12 ins. tall, the flowers being enhanced by their bright purple filaments.

SOLIDAGO Golden Rod

The Common Golden Rod, *S. virgaurea* is a plant native to the British Isles where it is the sole representative of the genus. It is a perennial, found in woodlands and on mountainous heath-lands, mostly in Wales and Northern England. It grows 3 ft. tall and bears terminal clusters of small yellow flowers. Its leaves are hoary and sharply pointed. It was to be found in every cottage garden since earliest times for a decoction taken internally was able to stop the flow of blood from open wounds, hence its country name, Wound-wort. At one time, the dried plant was imported in considerable quantity from Germany and Gerard tells us that it was sold in Bucklersbury, London, for half a crown an ounce. "Yet since it was found in Hampstead wood," says Gerard, "no man will give half a crown for a hundredweight of it . . . This verifies our English proverb, 'Far fetch and dear bought is best for ladies'." Gerard goes on to admonish the physicians of the time who search the world for medicines when those just as effective are obtainable near at hand.

The Golden Rod of gardens has been developed from *S. canadensis* which was introduced from N. America by John Tradescant the younger about the mid-seventeenth century. Like all the North American composites, it takes kindly to any soil, shows extreme hardiness and blooms towards the end of summer and early autumn. The most modern varieties have a compact habit, making them ideal for the smallest garden.

Planting should be done in November when they are cut back after flowering and allowing about 18 ins. between the plants.

VARIETIES

GOLDEN SHOWER. It grows 2 ft. tall and is well named for it bears its deep yellow flowers in graceful arching sprays.

LAURIN. A 1966 introduction, it grows only 12 ins. tall and from early August until October bears dainty sprays of clearest yellow.

LEMORE. A most attractive form, coming into bloom earlier than the others and bearing branched sprays of soft primrose-yellow.

SYRINGA VULGARIS Lilac

In bloom May and June, it heralds the summer and its perfume can be inhaled from a distance. Lilac is the Persian word for flower and it remained with the plant after its introduction into Europe from that country and to this day. When it first reached England is not recorded, though in a survey of the Royal gardens at Nonsuch in Surrey, planted by Henry VIII, mention is made of fountains, one being "set round with six lilac trees which bear no fruit but only a pleasant smell".

Though native of the near east, the lilac is hardy almost everywhere and flourishes in ordinary well-drained soil but they do appreciate a mulch of garden compost each year. They grow 15 ft. tall and make rather sparse, twiggy growth. They also bear their bloom at the ends of the new seasons shoots, so that they should be pruned little or not at all. The flowers appear in large panicles or pyramidal clusters. Clark's Giant bears deep blue flowers; Sensation, reddish-purple edged with white; Primrose is pale yellow. These bear single flowers. Of the doubles, Charles Joly bears crimson-purple flowers and Mme Buchner, carmine rose.

Propagate from suckers or by layering; also from cuttings rooted in sandy compost.

TAGETES French and African Marigold

The Tagetes family comprise about twenty species amongst which are included *T. erectus*, the co-called African Marigold; *T. patula*, the French Marigold; and *T. signata*, the true tagetes, named after Tages, a God famed for his beauty. They are all native of Mexico, hence the need to provide them with half-hardy treatment in the British Isles. With their refreshingly pungent foliage, neat, compact habit and brilliance of colour, they are amongst the finest of all summer-flowering plants.

Most closely allied to *T. signata*, a modern plant for it reached us only in 1825, being introduced by Dr. Sutton when Archbishop of Canterbury, is *T. patula* which reached England with the Huguenot refugees in 1573. A native of Mexico, it was thought that the golden flowers became stained with red when the people of that country were slain by the Spaniards.

It is believed that the plants reached Spain together with *T. erecta*, early in the sixteenth century and it was known as the Rose of the

48 *Left: Thunbergia alata*, Black-eyed Susan. 49 *Below left:* Old English Tulip, Attraction.
50 *Below right:* Old English Tulip, Queen of May

51   *Narcissus triandrus—*
Angel's Tears Daffodil

52   *Narcissus poetaz,*
Geranium

53   *Fritillaria meleagris*

54   *Puschkinia libanotica—*
Lebanon Squill

56 *Erythronium dens-canis*—Dog's Tooth Violet

55 *Colchicum autumnale*—Meadow Saffron

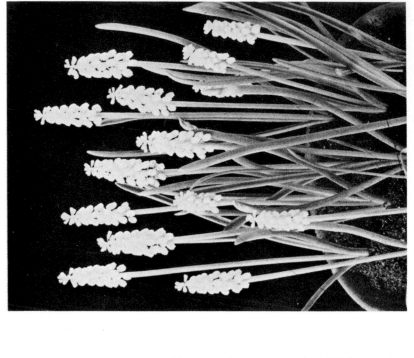

58 *Muscari botryoides*, Pearls of Spain

57 *Galanthus nivalis*, Arnott's Seedling

Indies. It is thought that *T. erecta* became naturalized along the coast of North Africa during the early years of the century and was introduced into France in 1535, when the Emperor Charles V sought to free Tunis from the Moors, hence it took on the name of African Marigold.

M. Pirolle tells us that the plants were held in such esteem in France during the eighteenth century that they were really called Tagetes from *tagé* meaning "principality", which shows the rank they commanded on the parterre.

Both the French and African forms were known to Gerard and to Parkinson who wrote of *T. erecta* as "this goodly double flower which is the grace and glory of a garden in the time of his beauty . . ." A century later, Thomas Fairchild called *T. patula*, "one of the most agreeable annuals we have" and it had by then attained the distinction of being a florist's flower for the perfect symmetry of the double blooms made it a favourite with exhibitors.

All the Tagetes are half-hardy annuals and seed should be sown in gentle heat in March and the seedlings transplanted when large enough to handle. They should be planted out after hardening, towards the end of May or early June, spacing the African varieties 12 ins. apart and the others 6 ins. apart.

VARIETIES

MONARCH LEMON GEM. It grows only 4 ins. tall, with fern-like leaves, and bears single flowers of brilliant lemon-yellow (variety *T. signata*).

DOUBLOON. Growing 2 ft. tall, it bears enormous numbers of large golden-yellow flowers (variety *T. erecta*).

GOLDEN FRILLS. Growing only 5 to 6 ins. tall, it has flowers of mahogany-red, margined with gold (variety *T. patula*).

TEUCRIUM CHAMAEDRYS   Germander

Tusser included it amongst his "strewing herbs" whilst, with its dainty upright habit, it was widely grown during Tudor times for "knot" gardens. It is perennial, growing 6 to 8 ins. tall, with shining green, deeply toothed leaves and it bears its rosy-pink flowers from July until September. It is a pleasing rockery plant and does well planted about old walls where its evergreen leaves and short pink spikes are most pleasing against the stone. The leaves have a pungent, aromatic smell, most pronounced when trodden upon, hence its value for strewing and which Michael Drayton mentions in the *Muses' Elysium*:

> Germander, marjoram and thyme,
> Which used are for strewing,
> With hisope an herb most prime,
> Herein my wreath bestowing.

Culpeper writes of its virtues in restoring the spirits, like so many other fragrant plants. "It is good against a continual headache," he writes, "melancholy, drowsiness and dullness of the spirits."

The Cat Thyme, *Teucrium marum* of the same family as Cat Mint, *Nepeta mussini*, is so called because its pungent leaves, in shape like those of the thyme, are enjoyed by cats which love to roll on it and eat the leaves.

A native of Europe, it is a shrub growing 12 to 15 ins. tall with short lance-shaped leaves, downy above and woolly beneath which gives a silvery appearance. Like the nepeta, the flowers of reddish-purple are borne in pairs in the axils of the leaves.

THALICTRUM   Meadow Rue
A native plant, *Thalictrum flavum* the yellow Meadow Rue, the Fenland Rue, has been growing in English gardens since earliest times and was known also as the Yellow Maidenhair. Like all members of the Buttercup family, it enjoys a moist soil and is to be found about hedgerows and ditches, usually with its roots in moisture. It grows 3 to 4 ft. tall and is a much-branched plant with attractive bi-pinnate leaves and bears its pale yellow flowers in crowded racemes. It was grown in most country gardens where the spinning of wool was carried on as was usual during earlier times for the root was used for dyeing wool a pale yellow colour.

Another form which was widely planted was *T. aquilegifolium* which bears fluffy purple flowers on 3 ft. stems whilst *album* bears clouds of purest white. It is a plant native of southern and eastern Europe and of Asia. It first came to be planted in English gardens early in the eighteenth century when it was known as the Purple Tufted Columbine for its thrice-pinnate leaves and deeply toothed leaflets resemble those of the closely related Aquilegia. Again, like most of the Buttercup family, it blooms early in summer on 2-ft.

stems, the flower being represented by purple stamens. Parkinson tells us that the roots were eaten in the belief that this would ward off the plague.

T. minus, the Maidenhair Meadow Rue prefers drier conditions. Its glaucous leaves are divided into rounded leaflets, toothed at the apex whilst the greenish-yellow flowers are borne in drooping panicles. The thalictrums are perennial and their foliage is valuable for use with cut flowers.

THUNBERGIA ALATA   Black-eyed Susan
A half-hardy climbing plant that once came to be grown in almost every cottage garden, it is a native of central Africa, named after Dr. Karl Thunberg, Professor of Botany at Uppsala University during the first years of the nineteenth century when the plant reached Britain. It is a perennial but where it cannot be grown under glass, it is usually treated as a half-hardy annual and is planted out in June. It requires a warm, sunny position and may be allowed to pull itself up a trellis or about other plants when in a single season it will reach a height of 6 ft. Or it may be allowed to trail over the ground and is particularly suited to cover a sunny bank.

The plant has heart-shaped leaves and bears masses of creamy, buff flowers with a purple-black centre, hence its cottage name. It will be in bloom from mid-July until mid-October. There is also an attractive lemon-yellow form, *sulphurea*.

THYMUS   Thyme
Tennyson wrote of "the thymy plots of Paradise" and indeed the creeping thymes are amongst the loveliest of all plants with their tiny flower spikes and small leaves, forming a carpet of colour when in full bloom. The thymes may be divided into two main groups, (*a*) the prostrate or creeping thymes and (*b*) those of upright bushy habit like miniature shrubs. The former are members of the *T. serpyllus* (serpent-like in habit) group, whilst the latter are representatives of the *T. citriodorus* and *T. nitidus* groups and are valued for their culinary qualities. It was Francis Bacon who wrote of "those flowers which perfume the air most delightfully . . . being trodden upon and crushed, Burnet, Wild Thyme and Water Mint". But not only are they planted to make a fragrant "lawn"; they may be used about a rockery or trough garden and planted between crazy paving

stones where they are to be seen at their best creeping over the stones.

All the thymes have aromatic foliage, each one possessing a different aroma, like the mints but more pungent.

"I like also little heaps, in the nature of mole hills," wrote Bacon, "to be set, some with wild Thyme, some with Pinks, some with Germander."

"The bees on the bells of thyme," wrote the poet Shelley for thyme is a plant especially loved by bees; thyme honey collected by the bees of Mt. Hymettus in Greece and upon Mt. Hybla in Sicily being world famous. Spenser speaks of "the bees alluring Tyme" and possibly due to the great activity of the bees about the flowers, the plant became an emblem of activity and valour in the days of chivalry. Ingram in his *Flora Symbolica* wrote that ladies "embroidered their knightly lover's scarves with the figure of a bee hovering about a sprig of thyme" whilst "to smell of thyme" was an expression of praise. Virgil made it the highest compliment the shepherd could pay to his mistress:

> "*Nerine Galatea, Thymo mihi dulcior Hyblae.*"

Relying upon honey for sweetening, bees were highly looked upon in medieval times, hence those plants visited by bees were considered of great importance and first amongst these were the sweet-smelling flowers. In *The Parliament of Bees*, a charming little play written by John Daye in 1641, all but one of the characters are bees. The Master Bee proclaims the freedom of gardens and of meadows:

> "Of wanton Cowslips, Daisies in their prime
> Sun-loving Marigolds, the blossom'd Thyme,
> The blew vein'd violets, and the Damask Rose,
> The statelie lily, mistree of alle those . . ."

"The owners of hives have a perfite forsight and knowledge what the increase or yields of honey will be every year by the plentiful or small numbers of flowers growing and appearing on the thyme about the Summer solstice," wrote Thomas Hyll in *The Gardener's Labyrinth*.

In an Anglo-Saxon work of the tenth century, Serpulum is mentioned and in the *Promptorium parvulorum* of 1440, the plant is referred to as *Sepillum piretrum*. The herb first appears in the Latin form *timum* in the *Catholic Anglicum* since when the name has been used.

Of a number of lovely species and varieties, *T. serpyllus* is a plant of almost prostrate habit. It is lovely for covering the sides of a trough. Almost as prostrate is the variety Annie Hall, which forms mats of fleshy-pink flowers, whilst Pink Chintz is of similar habit and bears flowers of a beautiful shade of salmon pink. The new Bressingham Pink is valuable in that it comes early into bloom, whilst Russettings has rosy-red flowers and very dark foliage. With them plant Snow-drift, a pure white counterpart, or *T. serpyllus sandersi* of prostrate habit and which also bears white flowers. Another lovely white form, *T. serpyllus albus*, has leaves of a paler green colouring than the others. Gerard described its flowers as being "as white as snow".

Another creeping thyme is *T. serpyllus lanuginosus*, which has silvery leaves and which are as if covered with wool. Also having woolly leaves is *T. doeffleri*, its carmine-pink flowers, which are sweetly fragrant, being accentuated by the woolly white foliage. *T. micans* is interesting in that it forms large grey-green mats, studded with attractive mauve blooms and carries a distinct aromatic pine fragrance. It is not quite as prostrate as *T. serpyllus* but may be planted with the creeping thyme, as may T. Lemon Curd, a hybrid which carries the real scent of lemons.

To plant between crazy paving, soil should be removed to accommodate the plant with its ball of soil as it is shaken from the pot. Where the plants have not been pot grown, the soil between the stones should be removed to be replaced by prepared compost made up of a mixture of loam, sand and a little decayed manure into which the young plants are set out. This will provide the plants with a friable soil where the original soil may be heavy or not too well drained. Early spring is the best time to plant between crazy paving stones.

A thyme alley, as mentioned by Bacon, may be made alongside a pathway, possibly between a path and a lawn where the alley may be approached from both sides. The plants may be set out in groups of three or four to provide a carpet of rich colour, using those of contrasting colours near together. Set out the plants 10 to 12 ins. apart, preferably from pots and during the first summer hand weed the bed which, if made 5 ft. wide, may be reached from both sides without treading. By the end of summer, the plants will have completely covered the ground with their mat-like foliage and if the bed was cleared of all perennial weeds before planting, no further weeding should be necessary.

Those thymes of upright, shrubby habit possess individual

aromatic qualities and are most valuable for stuffings and for flavouring meats. Natives of the Mediterranean shores, the thymes prefer a sandy soil and like so many of the shrubby herbs, the plants grow well over limestone formations and are always happy in a soil which has a high lime content. Whilst the grey-leaved thyme may be raised true from seed, sown in shallow drills under cloches or in frames during summer, the individual species and varieties are best propagated from cuttings. These should be removed with a heel and inserted into sandy soil either in the open or in a frame during summer. Alternatively, plants may be increased by root division, the outer portions of the clumps being the most vigorous. Select a sunny position and a well-drained soil and allow 15 to 18 ins. between the plants. To prevent the plants becoming untidy, cut the shoots almost to ground level in early June and again at the end of August, and where growing commercially make up into bunches of a thickness that will fit between finger and thumb joined together.

TIGRIDIA Tiger Flower

This native of Mexico has been known to cottage gardeners only since the eighteenth century but its existence was known to Gerard long before, information possibly having reached him by our ambassador to Spain for Philip II's physician had first seen it in Mexico in 1570. It was named Tigridia on account of its leopard-like spots which cluster around the centre of the propeller-shaped flowers of red, white or yellow.

The bulbs should be planted in March, 3 to 4 ins. deep in a sunny position, and covering them with sand before replacing the soil. The best method is to remove a circle of soil of about 15 ins. diameter, spacing the bulbs 4 ins. apart. A dozen bulbs will cost no more than a crown piece and from June until September will provide a succession of brilliantly coloured flowers.

After flowering, the bulbs should be lifted and stored in damp sand over winter, except where the garden is situated in a warm part of the British Isles.

TRADESCANTIA Spiderwort

Since its introduction from Virginia very early in the seventeenth century, this most interesting plant has been cherished in most cottage gardens. It was introduced by John Tradescant the Elder who received plants whilst travelling in Europe and which had reached Holland from Virginia several years previously. Tradescant was then gardener to Charles I and Queen Henrietta Maria, when Parkinson was the Royal botanist. In the *Paradisus*, Parkinson has told us that "the Christian world is indebted to that painful and industrious lover of all natures varieties . . ." for the introduction of the plant.

By the mid-seventeenth century it was to be found in every cottager's garden, Sir Thomas Hanmer when describing it in 1659, saying that it had "deep blew-coloured flowers" but by then the original plant had been joined by others bearing red, pale blue and white flowers.

It received its country name of Spiderwort from the belief that the plant was of the same family as the Phalangium, the juice of which was used as a cure for the bite of poisonous spiders. It is a member of the Commelina family and is an excellent plant for a town garden whilst it also grows well in partial shade. It has dark green purple-veined leaves which grow from the stem and throughout the early weeks of summer, bears its attractive three-petalled flowers backed by three long green outer sepals, on 2 ft. stems. Of extreme hardiness, it is a most interesting plant, bridging the gap between the spring and summer flowering plants and it needs the minimum of attention, dividing every fourth year or so to maintain its vigour and re-planting into a well-drained loamy soil for like most blue flowering plants it is not tolerant of excess moisture during the dormant season.

Amongst the best varieties is Osprey, bearing large flowers of purest white, enhanced by the green sepals; *coerulea plena*, sky-blue and double; Purple Dome; and Valour, crimson-purple.

TROLLIUS   Globe Flower

T. europeus is native to the British Isles and is most common in the meadows of Lancashire, Yorkshire and Derbyshire where it blooms during May and June. It was introduced to country gardens at an early date. Clusius has said that he saw it in London gardens about 1580 and it has remained, like the Christmas Rose, virtually unchanged since its cultivation as a garden plant. *T. asiaticus*, the Orange Globe-flower of N. China is similar in every way except that its flowers are more orange in colour. It was introduced early in the eighteenth century and has since given rise to a number of varieties such as Salamander, fiery orange; Goldquelle, golden-yellow; and Canary Bird; canary-yellow. They grow 2 to 3 ft. in height and enjoy a damp soil and partial shade when the flowers will be long lasting.

Propagation is by division of the roots in autumn, re-planting them 18 ins. apart.

In his *Flowers of the Field*, Rev. C. A. Johns says that the plant takes its name from the Scandinavian *troll*, a witch, for it was supposed to have supernatural powers, hence its country name of Witch's Gowan, from the Celtic *gulan*, a flower.

TROPAEOLUM   Indian Cress
This popular flower was named Indian Cress for it was first found growing in the islands of the West Indies. It is also native of Peru, seed being sent to Europe by Spanish settlers in the fifteenth century. Some seed reached Jean Robin, gardener to the King of France, about 1580 and in his *Herbal*, Gerard tells that he in turn had received some from "my loving friend, Jean Robin". This was *T. minus* (not the better-known climbing form which is *T. majus*), and which bears small yellow flowers splashed with orange, each petal terminating in a point with the upper one forming a spur. Hence, it was known to Parkinson as the Yellow Larkspur and he described its perfume as "most pleasing", whilst also telling us that by the beginning of the seventeenth century it was "familiar in most gardens of any curiosity". It is of vaguely trailing habit and was planted along the side of paths but because of its weakly habit, constantly disappeared from our gardens and had to be re-introduced.

T. majus, a vigorous climber, was not introduced until a century after the appearance of Gerard's *Herbal*. Samuel Gilbert advised training up a "craggy pole" when it would make "a glorious show" and this was how it was grown in many a cottage garden—against old apple trees or allowing it to festoon rustic arches. A delightful way of growing the plant and shown to the author by an old cottage gardener was to plant a few seeds between the stones at the top of an old wall which by July would be completely covered in brilliant colours. Or loving a sun-baked impoverished soil, seeds may be planted at the top of an unsightly bank which it will cover in a matter of weeks. This is the Great Indian Cress, bearing large flowers of orange-scarlet, marked with crimson-brown. Early in the nineteenth century dwarf forms were introduced and making dwarf bushy plants, are suitable for window boxes.

The plant was named by Linnaeus from the Roman *tropaeum*, a pole upon which was hung armour captured in battle, for the botanist thought the round leaf resembled a warrior's shield and the red flowers the spears which were covered in blood.

Evelyn had recommended that the seeds and the flower buds be pickled in vinegar to be served with meat and this was a favourite condiment of Lincolnshire cottagers until recent times and may still be so. They have a "hot" appetizing taste. The leaves too, like those of the watercress of the same family, are most nourishing and are tasty served in a salad.

The annual climber *T. canariensis* was discovered at Lima, capital of Peru and reached Britain about 1750. It was thought to have been named after the Canary Islands, wrongly believed to be its native land, but it was most likely named after the canary bird which its flowers resemble in colour. It is an annual of rapid growth and will cover a trellis or archway during a single season.

T. speciosum, the Flame Flower of Chile, reached the British Isles in 1850. With its pale green clover-like leaves, six-lobed and flowers of brilliant scarlet it is the brightest flowering plant of the garden. It is tuberous rooted and is perennial and though native of Chile is quite hardy. It prefers to have its roots in shade and enjoys best a cool climate so that it is seen at its best in N. England and in Scotland.

TULIPA   Tulip

Native of Persia, the tulip takes its name from the Eastern head-dress known as a tolipan or turban which the flower so much resembles in form and colour. It was from Turkey that both seeds and bulbs were sent to the Emperor Ferdinand I of Germany by Auger Busbec. This was in 1554 and in 1559, the German botanist Conrad Gesner wrote of first seeing the flower in the garden of John Harwart at Augsburg but it was not until about twenty years later that the tulip reached England. In his *History of Plants* which Turner dedicated to Queen Elizabeth I, no mention is made of the tulip but in 1582 Richard Hakluyt wrote: "Within these four years there have been brought into England from Vienna in Austria, divers kinds of flowers called Tulipas." Gerard also confirms the date of introduction as 1577-8. This was the Common Tulip, *T. gesneriana* (named after Conrad Gesner) and now widely distributed in the wild state throughout S. Europe. From the sweetly scented scarlet flowers, the most fragrant of the cottage tulips are descended. Writing of the plant in 1559, Gesner said ". . . it was like a red lily with a pleasant smell, soothing and delicate". The fact of the flower being fragrant was given great prominence. In the sixteenth century this was the most important quality of any flower. For this reason, tulips were in demand for evening wear by the ladies of the French aristocracy during the seventeenth century. But so magnificent is the colouring of the modern bedding tulip that there is a tendency to select a particular variety entirely for its colour when its most endearing quality may be absent. Scent in tulips is present in all colours, this being one of the few flowers where perfume in the scarlet flowering varieties is as pronounced as in those bearing white or pale yellow blooms, though it is most pronounced in those bearing double flowers.

The earliest forms to capture the imagination of florists were striped and streaked in the most amazing fashion and were divided into groups known as Bizarres, Bybloemens and Edgers. This was due to a virus disease which caused the self-coloured forms to "break" into stripes and feathering. These forms could be propagated only vegetatively and so the bulbs always commanded a high price yet so great was the demand that in 1796, the catalogue of Maddock, a London nurseryman, contained nearly 700 varieties and Hogg writing in 1823 said that "a moderate collection of choice tulips could not be purchased for a sum less than £1000".

One of the earliest named tulips still obtainable is Keizerskroon, a single which has no scent. The double tulip appeared first in 1581, in Vienna and was recorded, in Hakluyt's words, "by an excellent man called Carolus Clusius". In the double Murillo tulips, scent is most pronounced, also in the Breeder tulips, the lily-of-the-valley perfume being most noticeable in the purple and bronze Cherbourg. Indeed, its perfume is so delicious as to make this variety worthy of planting solely for this quality. Several flowers near an open window will, on a calm day, scent a large room.

Almost every known species of the tulip is to be found in its natural state in those countries bordering the Black Sea and the shores of the Mediterranean and in Persia. In Rumania and Bulgaria and in that part of the U.S.S.R. around the Sea of Azov, also in the Caucasus and Turkey appear most of the scented species including *T. suaveolens* from which was evolved the scarlet single tulips which are also scented.

Completely perennial, the taller growing species may be naturalized in grass whilst the more dwarf forms may be used in the alpine-garden. The taller growing Cottage and Darwin tulips, usually planted in beds, may also be naturalized and will prove quite long lasting if the flower heads are removed as soon as they fade. Delightful together, planted against a background of cupressus trees are the almond-scented Mrs. Moon of palest yellow colouring and the violet-blue Demeter which has the perfume of dried cloves. Or plant a bed of the white honey-scented Schoonoord with Marie Crousse primrose for an edging for its double purple flowers have a similar perfume.

SPECIES (SCENTED)

Tulipa gesneriana. It is distributed throughout south-eastern Europe and Asia Minor and has broad, ovate, lance-shaped, glaucous leaves. In May and June it bears on 9-in. stems, brilliant scarlet flowers with a striking black centre and they are sweetly scented.

T. macrospeila. Probably a hybrid form of *T. gesneriana* for it is in all respects similar, producing in early summer large fragrant crimson flowers.

P. persica. The handsome Persian tulip, its deep green leaves being edged with crimson whilst it bears, on 4- to 6-in. branched stems, several scented star-like flowers of brilliant yellow, shaded with bronze on the exterior and which are deliciously scented. It blooms in June being one of the latest species.

T. primulina. Native of the mountains of eastern Algeria, it is closely related to *T. sylvestris* which inhabits the lower regions of the same area and extends north into the British Isles. It has smooth pale green leaves and bears bell-shaped flowers of primrose-yellow, tinted red on the outside and they emit the lily-of-the-valley perfume.

T. suaveolens. A native of south-eastern Europe it is believed to be the parent of the scented red (crimson) Duc Van Thoe tulips which bear their flowers on 3- to 4-in. stems and which at one time were forced in large numbers for bowls at Christmastime. *T. suaveolens* is of similar habit, its sweetly scented bright scarlet blooms, edged with gold appear on a 6-in. stem and outdoors in the alpine garden, appear early in April.

T. saxatilis. In the wild state, it is to be found close to the seashore around the Island of Crete, with broad leaves of bright shining green, unlike those of any other tulip. It blooms in April, bearing several flowers of clearest lilac to each 9-in. stem and they have a delicate sweet primrose perfume.

T. sylvestris. It is present in low-lying ground from N. Africa through Europe and in the British Isles and Scandinavia. It is probably the French Tulip of Gerard's *Herbal.* It is usually to be found in chalk pits and in low-lying waste land and once established, is difficult to eradicate, increasing by underground stolons. It bears two or three flowers to a stem some 18 ins. tall and has a more graceful appearance than any other tulip. The flowers appear in mid-April and are of richest yellow, shaded with green on the outside and with a most pronounced perfume, even more noticeable in the Algerian form *T. fragrans* but which is however not so hardy.

SINGLE EARLY TULIPS

They are ideal for pot culture and outdoors will bloom in April. Several of the scarlet varieties descended from *T. suaveolens* bear scented flowers.

BELLONA. A most beautiful tulip, bearing huge globes of buttery-yellow shaded with orange and with the scent of orange blossom.

DOCTOR PLESMAN. A most showy tulip, the globular blooms being of ox-blood red throughout and with the lily-of-the-valley perfume.

FRED MOORE. One of the finest tulips ever raised, the large globular blooms are of terracotta colouring, flushed with orange-scarlet and have a honey perfume.

GENERAL DE WET. It is a "sport" of Prince of Austria which had *T. suaveolens* in its parentage, hence the delicious perfume of the fiery orange blooms which defy all the laws of nature. It grows 12 ins. tall and may be brought into bloom indoors by Christmas.

PRINCE CARNIVAL. Also a "sport" of Prince of Austria, its flowers of scarlet and gold possess outstanding perfume.

PRINCE OF AUSTRIA. Unsurpassed for forcing, its orange-scarlet blooms scented like orange blossom have enormous substance.

VERMILION BRILLIANT. A "sport" from Prince of Austria, the dazzling scarlet blooms are long lasting and sweetly scented.

DOUBLE EARLY TULIPS

Like the single early tulips, they may be grown in pots of five or six bulbs indoors or are long lasting and early flowering in outdoor beds. Deliciously honey scented is the old Murillo and its several "sports".

MARQUETTE. Another Murillo "sport", the huge globular blooms being of richest crimson-red and provide a striking contrast to the White Schoonoord.

MME TESTOUT. One of the most attractive of the Murillo "sports", the blooms of satin-pink had a striking golden base.

MURILLO. The multi-petalled blooms are large and are white flushed and shaded with rose-pink.

SCHOONOORD. A beautiful white Murillo "sport".

TEA ROSE. It bears a bloom of exquisite charm, being of primrose-yellow flushed with salmon in which the honey scent is most pronounced.

BREEDER TULIPS

These are early summer flowering and of enormous size whilst the colours include shades of copper, orange and bronze to provide a display of great richness. They grow about 30 ins. tall and in addition to their beauty, one or two have pronounced perfume.

CHERBOURG. The large globular blooms are of orange-yellow, shaded with bronze and flushed with purple and have the refreshing sweet scent of lily-of-the-valley.

MOROCCAN BEAUTY. One of the finest of all May-flowering tulips, the huge blooms are of Moroccan-red over a gold base and shaded bronze inside. The blooms have an almost lily-like perfume.

PRINCE OF ORANGE. An old variety bearing large orange blooms of outstanding fragrance.

DARWIN TULIPS

A race of tulips imported into Holland from northern France in 1889 but their origin is unknown. They are the latest of all to bloom, continuing until almost the end of June.

DEMETER. It is the first of the Darwins to bloom, its deep violet-blue flowers, held on 30-in. stems having a distinct clove perfume.

PHILIPE DE COMMINES. An older variety but its purple-maroon flowers stand out in any company and are sweetly scented.

WHITE VICTORY. The large refined flowers are purest white with the scent of white jasmine.

COTTAGE TULIPS

They were discovered in an old English cottage garden and are early May flowering. They grow rather less than 2 ft. in height and are ideal for bedding or for naturalizing. Several bear scented blooms.

GRANDIER. The large orange-scarlet blooms have a striking golden base and a delicious perfume to make it one of the finest of all tulips.

MRS. MOON. An old favourite of distinct form, the long flowers of clear canary-yellow having pointed reflexed petals and an unmistakable almond perfume.

LILY-FLOWERED TULIPS

Unsurpassed for elegance and charm with their pointed reflexed petals. They grow 2 ft. tall and are early May flowering. Several have pronounced scent.

ELLEN WILLMOTT. It honey perfume is most noticeable whilst the long slender flowers with their reflexing petals are most elegant.

LA MERVEILLE. One of the most exquisite and most sweetly scented of all tulips, the flowers with their pointed petals being of scarlet-orange, flushed with rose at the margins.

PARROT TULIPS

They are "sports" of all the various sections and have heavily laciniated petals and an unusual brilliance of colouring. They are May flowering and are scented.

BLACK PARROT. A "sport" of Philippe de Commines bearing large glossy maroon-black flowers of delicious perfume.

ORANGE FAVOURITE. Probably the most striking tulip in existence, the orange-scarlet blooms being tinged with old-rose and with featherings of apple-green on the outside. It is sweetly scented.

VERBASCUM   Mullein

Of the same family as the foxglove and mimulus (musk), the verbascums are biennials, to be found about hedgerows and waste ground where they grow up to 6 ft. tall. The plant takes its name from the Latin, *barbascum*, bearded, on account of the hairy stems and flannel-like leaves which were grown by cottagers to dip into tallow when they would burn for hours with an iridescent light. Hence, the countryman's name of Candlewick. The plant had other uses. One was to put the fresh leaves into children's worn shoes to give comfort against the shingly roads. Another was to use an infusion of the leaves to relieve chest troubles whilst it was in great demand to stop an attack of diarrhoea. It was also used to cure coughing in cows hence its name of Cow's Lungwort.

Like the foxglove, the mulleins sow themselves from seed with the greatest of ease and once planted will persist as long as required. They are handsome back of the border plants, in bloom during July and August when they send up their club-shaped spikes of yellow or biscuit-coloured flowers and all parts of the plant are covered in hairs. They like a light sandy soil and are readily raised from seed sown in July where they are to bloom.

SPECIES AND VARIETIES

Verbascum nigrum. A native plant, it remains in bloom from June until October and bears branched spikes, densely packed with bright yellow flowers. Known as the Black or Dark Mullein, on account of its dark green hue, it was to be found in most cottage gardens of Tudor times.

V. phoenicium. Known as the Purple Mullein, it reached England from southern Europe during early times. It grows 3 ft. tall with ovate leaves, smooth above, downy beneath and it bears its flowers of lilac or purple from the end of May until September.

Of the numerous lovely hybrid varieties, *hartleyi* bears massive spikes of fawn-yellow suffused with plum-red; Cotswold Gem bears flowers of terracotta; and Pink Domino, spikes of deepest rose.

V. thapsus. Present from the British Isles across central and southern Europe to the islands of Greece, it was the species most grown in cottage gardens where it has been found since earliest times. Even the Romans appreciated its valuable qualities, and Pliny has said that figs keep almost indefinitely if wrapped in its leaves. Gerard has said that the plants "grow in plenty near a lime kiln upon the end of Blackheath, next to London; also about the Queen's (Elizabeth) house at Eltham Palace, near Dartford". It is known as the Great Mullein and has leaves so densely covered in hairs as to give it a frosted appearance whilst the spikes of yellow flowers have white hairs on their filaments.

VINCA MINOR Lesser Periwinkle
It is one of the few plants which takes its botanic name from its country name for it was called Pervinca by Pliny, a name which the writers of *The Romance of the Rose* have spelt Pervinke a spelling used by Chaucer, who is believed to be the translator into English:

There sprange the violet all newe,
And fresh Pervinke, rich of hewe.

Its name Pervinca is from the Latin *vincere*, to conquer, for by its low, creeping habit, it is said to subdue other plants.

It is a pretty plant and at one time was widely used to cover banks or waste ground; it was often to be found in those dark corners where little else would flourish. *Vinca minor* with its more compact habit and dark green leaves, evergreen and always fresh, is a most suitable plant to grow with the common yellow primrose. It also blooms at the same time, the brilliant grey-blue proving a delightful contrast to the pale moonlight-yellow of the primrose. Both plants enjoy a situation sheltered from the mid-day sun and a moist, friable soil. The form *azurea flore plena* is even lovelier, the double flowers having an intensity of colour equalled only by the Gentian. There is also a form *multiplex*, bearing fully double plum-coloured flowers.

The white form *alba*, was discovered at Chiltington in Sussex by a Mr. Woolgar early in the nineteenth century and is a pleasing counterpart.

The plant was delightfully described by Miss Mary Russell Mitford in Our Village. It is, she wrote ". . . the very Robin-redbreast of flowers, a winter friend. . . . It blossoms from September until June . . . peeping out from beneath the snow, smiling through the tempests of life and yet welcoming and enjoying the sunbeams."

The trailing stems root easily and propagation is a simple matter, achieved by cutting away pieces from the parent plant and lifting with the roots attached. It rarely produces seed.

VISCUM ALBUM Mistletoe
It is a parasitic shrub which bears tiny green flowers during April and May which are followed by semi-transparent berries which become ripe by the year end. It fixes itself to the branches of certain host trees, usually as undigested seed left by birds but it may be planted artificially by pressing the seeds into cracks in the bark,

Plate 15   *Rosa bourboniana*, Zéphyrine Drouhin

Plate 16   Fancy pansies

preferably of apple trees when the sticky juice surrounding the seed will enable the seed to remain in position and to germinate. To prevent birds taking the seed, a mixture of soil and cow manure made moist, should be smeared over the seed when "set".

In spring, the seedlings will send out yellowish branches shaped like the antlers of a stag. It is mostly found in apple orchards of Somerset, Herefordshire and Worcestershire, situated in England's western side which are the chief suppliers of cut mistletoe for Christmas festivities. The plant is mostly to be found on neglected apple trees so often associated with cottage gardens. In *Titus Andronicus*, it is Tamora, Queen of the Goths who says:

> These two have 'ticed me hither to this place,
> A barren, detested vale you see it is;
> The trees, though summer, yet forlorn and lean,
> O'ercome with moss and baleful mistletoe.

The Druids considered it to be semi-sacred, able to drive out evil spirits and for this reason, mistletoe has always been refused entry to our churches. Culpeper sings its praises as being a cure for palsy and fits and in parts of Scandinavia, those who suffer in this way wear rings made of mistletoe, in the belief that a cure will be effected.

VIOLA CORNUTA   Horned Violet
Viola cornuta, known as the Alpine or Horned Violet of the Pyrenees, was introduced into England in 1776 and was used in the breeding of the garden viola and the violettas. A fibrous rooted plant of short tufted habit with hart-shaped toothed leaves, it blooms from May until August, the pale blue flowers having an awl-shaped spur. There is also a white form, *alba*, both of which bear sweetly scented flowers.

Using the tufted *V. cornuta* as the seed-bearing parent and by crossing this with a pansy called Blue King, Dr. Stuart of Chairnside obtained a strain of rayless violas which he called violettas. The plants have the same tufty habit as *V. cornuta*, yet the blooms are larger, being longer in shape, quite rayless and possessing a delicious fragrance, like that of vanilla.

In *Pansies and Violas* published in 1892 by Messrs. Dobbie and Co., appeared in Dr. Stuart's own words, a short account of his hybridizing, which is worthy of reproduction. He writes, "In 1874, I took pollen from pansy, Blue King, a bedding variety then in fashion, and applied it to *V. cornuta*. There was a podful of seed which produced twelve plants and which were all blue in colour, but with a good tufted habit. I then took pollen from a pink pansy and fertilized the flowers of the first cross. The seed from this cross gave more variety of colour and the same tufted habit (of *V. cornuta*). The best were sent to the R.H.S. for trials at Chiswick. After being in the ground for some time, I received a letter from a member of the Floral Committee inquiring how they had been raised as they were all different in habit from all other violas sent for trial. I heard no more until the autumn of 1875 and was surprised when informed that I had received six First Class Certificates.

"It was, however, ten years before I succeeded in finding a really rayless viola. In Queen Victoria's Jubillee Year whilst walking round a seed bed, I found what I had for long been seeking—a pure white rayless self. It was a warm night and the perfume from the blooms attracted my attention. The plant was pulled to pieces and every bit propagated."

A box of bloom was sent to Mr. William Robinson, editor of *The Garden*, who at once recognized a new strain. It was given the name of Violetta and quickly became a favourite in the cottage garden. It was Robinson who wrote in *The English Flower Garden*, "No family has given our gardens anything more precious." Almost a century later, the same may be said of it and yet it is known to few gardeners.

D. B. Crane continued with violettas where Dr. Stuart had left off towards the end of the century, and amongst his finest introductions were Diana, with its lovely clear primrose-yellow blooms; Eileen, pale blue with a gold eye; and the blue and white Winifred Phillips. Though more long flowering than any of the pansies and violas, and being of more perennial habit it is surprising that these charming plants have never become as popular as the ordinary bedding violas. They come into bloom in April, with the primroses and continue until the frosts, the dainty flowers hovering like butterflies about the neat dark green foliage. On a year-old plant, as many as fifty-six blooms have been counted at one time. Also, with their fibrous roots and tufted habit the plants present no difficulty in their propagation, being lifted and divided in March like any other herbaceous plant whilst they are extremely long lasting. Above all is their delicious vanilla perfume.

VARIETIES OF VIOLETTA

ADMIRATION. The larger than usual flowers are of a rich shade of purple-violet.

BABY GRANDE. The oval-shaped blooms are pale crimson-pink.

BUTTERCUP. One of the loveliest of all the violettas, the oval blooms being of a rich orange-yellow colour.

COMPACTUM. The pale lavender blooms have a bright yellow eye.

DAWN. Lovely for planting with Iden Gem or Jersey Gem, for the blooms are of a pale shade of primrose-yellow.

DUCHESS. A lovely variety, the cream-coloured blooms being margined with lavender-blue.

GERTRUDE JEKYLL. A lovely bi-colour with the upper petals pale primrose; the lower petals golden-yellow.

HEATHER BELL. The blooms are of rich mauve-pink.

IDEN GEM. The dark blue flowers are held on long stems.

JERSEY GEM. Also known as Blue Gem. The dainty flowers are of deep aniline-blue.

LE GRANDEUR. The blooms, which are rather larger than usual, are of a lovely shade of mid-blue.

LITTLE DAVID. The cream-coloured blooms held well above the foliage possess the rich fragrance of freesias.

LORNA. The blooms are of a lovely shade of deep lavender-blue.

LYRIC. An original variety, the pale lilac blooms being attractively marbled with lavender-mauve.

MAUVE QUEEN. The flowers are reddish-violet borne in profusion.

MRS. GRIMSHAW. A recent introduction, bearing blooms of a lovely shade of rose-pink.

VIOLETTA. The original hybrid and still obtainable. The blooms are white-suffused-yellow on the lower petals, and are produced over a long period.

VIOLA ODORATA   Sweet Violet

Included in this genus of annual or perennial plants are many of which must be numbered amongst the most delightful of all plants to be found growing in the wild and in the garden. Mostly of the temp. regions they are to be found across N. America and in N.

Europe extending from the British Isles to the Urals, inhabitating those countries with a cool climate, for with but one or two exceptions they are intolerant of hot, dry conditions. Even where growing under cold conditions the plants will seek the coolness and moisture of the hedgerows and woodlands and crevices between rocks, for they must have moisture at their roots. Many of the species of viola are of tufted or creeping habit, the dainty flowers being held above the foliage on thin wiry stems. In their native haunts, the plants remain inconspicuous, like the violet itself, requiring careful search and for this reason are all the more appreciated. They also possess the charming habit of blooming at the most unexpected times, generally when there is little other bloom in the countryside and garden. The flowers are cleistogamic, i.e., the first to appear do not set seed. Seed is set by the smaller blooms which appear later. They are not scented and are self-pollinating whilst the plants bury their own seed-capsules. The earlier flowers are insect pollinated, drawn by the sweet perfume in their search for nectar, which is stored in the spur formed by the front or lower petal.

Most important of all the species is *V. odorata*, the Sweet Violet which long before the birth of Christ was in cultivation, even in commercial cultivation, for the blooms were used by the ancient Greeks for sweetening purposes, and it was so highly regarded that it became the symbol of ancient Athens. In France a vast quantity of bloom is grown each year, as it has been from earliest times, not only for sale as posy bunches, but for the perfume industry. There, the violet has always been held in reverence and shortly before his exile, Napoleon picked blooms from the grave of his beloved Josephine and which were found in a locket he was wearing on his death bed. But it was for its culinary and medicinal properties that the violet was chiefly cultivated during medieval times. In England, the blooms were cooked with food for sweetening as an alternative to honey for sugar was not imported into England until a much later date. Surprisingly, both meat and game were sweetened in olden times, the violet being much in demand for this purpose. In the treatise on gardening written in rhyme by "Mayster Jon, Gardener", the violet is quoted as being amongst several flowers then in cultivation:

"Peruynke, violet, cowslyppe and lyly . . .
Holyhocks, coryawnder, pyony."

All were used either for flavouring or for medicinal purposes. Violet blooms were also in great demand to strew about the floor of church, manor house and cottage to relieve that damp, musty smell all too familiar to those who have occupied such places, and which have been built without a satisfactory damp course.

Thomas Tusser, mentions the violet in a list of twenty-one herbs and flowers all of which possess fragrance either in their flowers or foliage, and which were suitable for strewing floors. In his *Five Hundred Points of Good Husbandry*, Tusser mentions the violet, together with pansies, sweet williams, wallflowers, stocks and cowslips, as being suitable also for "windows and pots", under the heading, "For those who have no garden". Indeed these richly perfumed flowers were widely grown in earthenware pots to be placed on the inside window ledge of houses where their fragrance was much appreciated.

In a similar way, the violet was widely used during ancient times as a cure for headaches, to relieve melancholia and to bring about sleep, the blooms being placed upon the head, especially at night. An interesting cure for sleeplessness is given by Anthony Ascham in *The Little Herbal* of 1525. He writes, "for they that may not sleep, seep this herb in water and at even let him soak well his feet in the water to the ankles, and when he goeth to bed, bind of this herb both temples and he shall sleep well by the Grace of God."

The blooms, dried and crystallized have been used for cake decoration and as a sweetmeat since medieval times. Today they are used to decorate chocolates usually containing a violet-flavoured cream. Candied violets are made by dipping the flower heads in a solution of gum arabic and rose water, then sprinkling with fine sugar. They are placed in a slightly warm oven to dry.

V. odorata is propagated by runners, the first of which will have formed and become rooted by the end of April. Only those which have formed a "rosette" or cluster of leaves should be used. The removal of the runners continues throughout summer.

The plants may also be increased by division of the crowns, a method usually adopted by the gardeners of old. The double flowering varieties especially lend themselves to this method for they form tight clumps of numerous crowns.

Usually to be found in their natural state growing in the filtered shade of deciduous woodlands, or on grassy banks canopied by hedgerow plants, similar conditions should be provided for those plants to be grown in the garden and an old orchard is ideal. Here the plants will receive the fullness of the early spring sunshine yet will be protected from the heat of the sun during midsummer.

April is the most suitable time to make a planting, small raised beds being most suitable, setting out the runners 12 to 15 ins. apart in each direction.

The plants enjoy best a soil containing ample supplies of humus and one giving a slightly acid reaction (like the strawberry). Peat is therefore a valuable source of humus whilst hop manure and clearings from ditches is also of value. In addition, some decayed farm yard manure should be incorporated but where this is unobtainable, give a dressing of 2 ozs. per sq. yd. of bone meal, together with 1 oz. of superphosphate of lime and 1 oz. of sulphate of potash which should be raked into the ground just prior to planting.

Plant when the soil is in a moist but friable condition, placing the crowns level with the surface of the soil. Keeping the soil stirred with the hoe and in a moist condition during summer, together with an occasional application of dilute manure water will ensure a plant capable of blooming profusely the following year.

VARIETIES

Of many lovely garden varieties, Admiral Avellan with its blooms of reddish-purple is one of the most sweetly scented; likewise John Raddenbury with its blooms of brilliant china-blue. Rawson's White is equally strongly scented, also Sulphurea, the only yellow violet, the pale yellow blooms being flushed with apricot. These are single varieties. In double flowering, outstanding is Countess of Shaftesbury, the lavender flowers having a rose-pink centre, whilst Marie Louise also bears lavender-blue flowers but with a white centre. Exquisite too, is Mrs. J. J. Astor, the very double blooms being of an unusual shade of rose-pink.

VIOLA TRICOLOR   Pansy

Widely distributed throughout the N. Hemisphere, the wild pansy has been loved by countrymen since earliest times. The poets too, have been captivated by its charms. Milton was particularly fond of the flower for he includes it in the wreath of Sabrina:

Pansies, pinks and gaudy daffodils

and places it on Eve's couch:

Pansies and violets, and asphodel,
And hyacinth, earth's freshest, softest lap.

The Anglo-Saxon name for the flower was bonewort and it is not difficult to understand why it took the more pleasing name "pansy" from the French *pensées*, "thoughts", derived it would seem from *pensare*, to ponder or contemplate, hence "pensive mood".

"And there is pansies—that's for thoughts," utters Ophelia in *Hamlet*, in what must surely be one of the most touching of all of Shakespeare's passages.

Viola tricolor seems to have taken the name pansy during Elizabethan times, possibly because of its appeal to the illustrious poets of the age who were ever ready to capture some sweet and pretty superstition in association with a name, especially if belonging to a native flower. The same "pancyes" appears in William Webbe's *Discourse of English Poetric* (1586). Michael Drayton wrote of "The pansie heart's-ease Maidens call", and Lyte in his *Herbal* mentions "pances or hartes-ease". He also calls it "love-in-idleness", a name used in Warwickshire and in other Midland counties to this day and to which Shakespeare made reference in *A Midsummer Night's Dream*, when Oberon bids Puck to obtain "a little western flower . . ." In Elizabeth Barber's *Glossary of Northamptonshire* (1854) appears the entry, "Love-in-idleness—the very small old-fashioned purple pansy called Pinkeney John", yet another name by which it was known, the great affection for the plant being shown by its many delightful names, though usually they were in some way connected with the French derivation and with lovers in happy pensive mood.

I pray, what flowers are these?
The pansie this;
O, that's for lovers' thoughts.

wrote Ben Jonson. The plant was also called Flamy because the colours of the flowers are those of the flames of burning wood. For the same reason, it was known to the Greeks as the "flame flower" whilst the people of Italy knew it as Herb Trinity for the three colours of its flowers, hence its botanical name *Viola tricolor*. In his *Names of Herbes* (1548) Turner also used the name *Trinitatio herba*. To the Americans, pansies are known as johnny-jump-ups or johnnies.

Gerard called the pansy, the heart-ease and gave a full description of *V. tricolor* in his *Herbal*. He also mentioned the other native pansy, *V. lutea* of which he said, "there is found in sundry places of England, a wilde kind thereof, having floweres of a feint yellow colour without mixture of any other colour, yet having a deeper yellow spot on the lowest leafe (petal) with four or five blackish-purple lines. This has been taken by some young herbalists to be the yellow violet." Parkinson (1626) also describes *V. lutea* as the Great Yellow Pansy "which better abideth our winters" which was his way of showing this species to be of more perennial habit. This was later proved correct by the first pansy hybridizers when raising the Tufted Pansies, now known as violas but in Parkinson's time, *V. lutea* was grown for its purging qualities, "being taken either fresh, or dried and made into powder, especially the flowers".

The pansy may be divided into two main classes:

(*a*) The Show or Scottish Pansy, and

(*b*) The Fancy or Continental Pansy.

The Show pansy was firmly established by 1841 with the formation of the first Pansy Society whose definition of an exhibition variety was that the bloom should have "a white or cream ground to the lower petals, with the upper petals of the same colour". Since that time, however, the pansy has been greatly developed so that the Show pansy may be sub-divided into:

(*a*) Belted or Margined bi-colour pansies, and

(*b*) Self colours.

The blooms should be thick, smooth and circular, with no waviness in the petals, whilst they should possess a glossy, velvety appearance. The face of the bloom should be slightly arched or convex, with a small eye. The two centre petals should meet above the eye and reach well up the top petals. The lower petal should be sufficiently deep and broad to balance the others and each should lie evenly upon each other. To elaborate further, the top of the lower petal should be straight and horizontal, with the two centre petals arranged evenly on either side of an imaginary perpendicular line drawn through the eye. The tops of these petals should reach to the same height on the upper petals so that the whole of the bloom is evenly balanced. As to the correct marking of the Margined or Two-colour varieties, the ground colour should be the same throughout, with the margin well defined and of uniform width, and the same colour as that of the two upper petals. The blotches should be dense, solid and as near circular as possible. The eye should be well defined and circular and be of a bright golden yellow colour. It is important that there is no suffusion of colour of the margin into the ground colour.

The Self colours may again be sub-divided into light and dark self-coloured varieties, where the upper and lower petals are of the same dark colour, free of any blotch. The same remarks as to smoothness of petal, form, and texture of bloom apply equally with the selfs as with the belted bicolours.

Here is a selection of the true Show pansies which should be grown where open competition is desired. The plants, however, have not the habit which makes them suitable for bedding and where this is required, the modern hybrid strains raised from seed will prove more satisfactory in this respect.

VARIETIES

ALICE RUTHERFORD. A deep golden yellow self of great beauty.

BLUE BELL. A dark blue self colour of great beauty.

CHARLES MC'CRERIE. A belted variety, the ground colour is pale sulphur, with a margin of violet.

GOLDEN GIFT. The ground is rich yellow, the belting and upper petals being of violet.

JAMES FERGUSON. The ground is of rich Jersey cream colouring, the belting and upper petals being of violet.

JAMES GRAME. The ground is deep creamy-yellow, the belting and upper petals being deep purple.

JAMES RUTHERFORD. This is a pure yellow self.

JAMES THOM. An old favourite having a bright yellow ground, the belting and upper petals being of a chocolate-violet colour.

MAGGIE MYERS. A pure yellow self of fine form.

MRS. PETER THOMSON. The ground is primrose-yellow with the margin and upper petals being rosy-purple.

As with the Show pansies, the Fancy or Belgian pansies should bear a circular bloom with smooth, velvet-like petals, lying evenly over each other. It is in this respect that the Exhibition pansies made most headway during the nineteenth century. The earliest introductions had a ragged appearance, the petals being spaced apart whilst the blooms were oval or long in shape rather than circular, which is the hall-mark of the Exhibition pansy. The two centre petals should reach well up on the two upper petals, whilst the lower petal should be broad and deep to give a balanced or circular effect to the bloom. There is no definition as to colourings. The blotch, of violet or chocolate colour should almost cover the whole of the three lower petals with the exception of a wide margin which may be of any colour or of more than one colour. The top petals need not be the same colour as that of the margin of the lower petals and may be rose, cream, gold, purple or intermediate shades. The eye should be bright yellow and clearly defined.

VARIETIES

ADAM WHITE the large blotches are of chocolate, the edges and top petals being of golden-yellow, suffused with violet.

ALDERLEY. A Jackson introduction, the refined blooms having large circular blotches of deep plum, the lower petals being margined rosy-pink, The upper petals are white, flushed with purple and edged white.

ALEX LISTER. The dense blotches are of chocolate, the edges rose and cream with the top petals rosy-purple.

ANNIE LISTER. The bloom has a large almost black blotch and a margin of cream. The upper petals are of violet-mauve also with a broad margin of cream.

CATHERINE. The blotches are violet, the edges ruby with the upper petals a rich shade of purple.

DR. MCKINNON. The blotches are violet, the petals being edged with cream, with the upper petals cream and rosy-violet.

ENA WHITELAW. The blotches are chocolate, the petals being edged with gold with the upper petals soft purple.

ERNEST CHEETHAM. A magnificent variety of great size with deep plum blotches and a narrow edging of white round the lower petals; the upper petals being plum-coloured.

MRS. A. B. COCHRANE. A huge bloom with purple blotches and cream margins; the upper petals being purple and cream.

MRS. CAMPBELL. A grand yellow self with huge circular claret-coloured blotches.

NEILL MC'COLL. The blotches are plum, the lower petals being margined with rose and white. The top petals are cream and purple.

T. B. COCHRANE. The blotches are dark blue, the lower petals being margined white with the top petals purple and white.

W. B. CHILD. A variety of refined form having a huge purple

blotch with a margin of gold. The upper petals are deep golden, yellow with purple blotches.

VIOLAS

In 1867, James Grieve of the Scottish firm of Dicksons of Edinburgh, after whom the famous apple was named, began to improve the habit of the pansy to make it more suitable for bedding. For his work he was to become "the father of the bedding viola" as we know it today. James Grieve was to make use of as many species as possible in his effort to produce a pansy of more compact habit. He collected plants of *Viola lutea* on the Pentland Hills; *V. amoena* at Moffat; and *V. cornuta*, which had been introduced in 1776 from Spain, especially the variety Perfection which had just been raised by Mr. B. S. Williams, gardener at Rotherfield Park.

To each of the numerous species James Grieve crossed the most modern of the Show and Fancy pansies, taking pollen from the pansies and applying it to the species in turn. Pollen of a dark Show pansy applied to *V. cornuta* Perfection produced violas Tory and Vanguard, whilst applied to *V. striata* it gave that still popular yellow bedding viola Bullion, which was rightly hailed at that time as an introduction of enormous value, though the bloom by modern standards is not of the best. From *V. lutea* he obtained Golden Gem and *V. grievii*, two fine yellows. With their compact habit and forming a mass of fibrous roots, Grieve's introductions were first known as tufted pansies, later violas.

EXHIBITION VARIETIES

ADA JACKSON. A new colour break. The large white blooms have an edge of rosy-mauve on the three lower petals, the upper petals being suffused rosy-mauve.

ANDREW JACKSON. The refined bloom is of a rich shade of purple, striped with amethyst and pale mauve.

A. S. FRATER. The large blooms are creamy-white margined with mauve.

BARBARA BENNETT. A crimson purple self of refined form.

C. S. ROBERTSON. A pure cream self of excellent form.

DOUGLAS UPTON. The rose-pink blooms are striped with crimson.

ELIZABETH WILLIAMS. The blooms are deep mauve with a cream centre.

HELEN COCHRANE. Possibly the finest pure white yet raised.

H. H. HODGE. A fine variety having a lemon ground with a wire edge of lavender.

JOHN ADAMSON. A grand pure golden-yellow.

LADY TENNYSON. An outstanding pure white.

LOIS MILNER. A lovely yellow, edged bright blue, the two upper petals also being suffused with blue.

MARY ANDERSON. An outstanding viola, the pale sulphur-yellow blooms are edged with mauve.

MAY CHEETHAM. A variety of superb form and likely to be the most popular viola of its colour on the show bench for many years. The huge bloom is pure primrose-yellow, rayless and of great substance.

MAY JACKSON. The primrose-yellow lower petals are edged with mauve, the upper petals suffused-mauve.

MILNER'S FANCY. The bloom is most striking, being large and of deep purple-red, striped with rose.

MOSELEY PERFECTION. The beautifully formed golden-yellow blooms are entirely rayless.

MRS. A. BLEARS. The pale cream blooms have a wire edge of purple.

MRS. A. COCHRANE. The large blooms have a cream centre and are edged and suffused pale lavender.

MRS. J. H. LITTLE. The primrose-yellow blooms are heavily banded with an unusual slate-blue colour.

MRS. J. ROBERTSON. The sulphur-yellow blooms have an attractive picotee edge of lavender. The top petals are also pencilled lavender.

MRS. M. WALLACE. Unusual in that the bloom is lavender, speckled or marbled with purple.

MRS. T. BATES. A fine pure yellow self of lovely form.

PICKERING BLUE. One or the most popular of all violas for exhibition and bedding. The large, sweetly scented blooms are of deep sky-blue.

R. N. DENBY. An outstanding variety, the pale lemon yellow bloom being edged with pale blue.

SUE STEVENSON. The large blooms are of a rich shade of violet with a large clear yellow centre.

SUSAN. A seedling from the popular Ada Jackson. The white bloom has a margin of mid-blue on the lower petals, the top petals being suffused blue.

WILLIAM JACKSON. The refined blooms are brilliant golden-yellow with a picotee edge of white.

BEDDING VARIETIES

ADMIRAL OF THE BLUES. A fine old exhibition variety, now used chiefly for bedding. The mid-blue flowers suffused with crimson and a striking yellow eye make this one of the best violas ever introduced.

AMY BARR. A fine bedding variety. The blooms are deep pink with a white centre.

ARABELLA. A most beautiful viola the bloom being pale mauve deepening to violet at the edges.

BARBARA. A most colourful variety, the top petals being mauve-blue, the side petals mauve-pink, the lower petals yellow, edged with mauve.

BLUESTONE. An old variety of compact habit. The clear mid-blue colour of the medium-sized blooms with their striking golden eye surrounded by a small purple blotch make it unbeatable for bedding. Very long in bloom.

BRENDA RUSHWORTH. An unusual variety, the large lemon-yellow blooms being flushed with lilac at the edges.

BULLION. Almost a hundred years old and for its freedom of flowering still widely planted. Brilliant golden-yellow and rayed. Very compact and early to bloom.

CRIMSON BEDDER. The blooms are of a rich crimson-purple shade, produced with great freedom.

DOBBIE'S BRONZE. Probably the best bronze for bedding. The blooms are bright, with a terracotta flush, and with a bronze blotch at the centre.

IRISH MOLLY. The colourings are so diverse as to make it difficult to describe. It may be described as bronzy-yellow, with a copper centre. The bloom has quite a green appearance. Of excellent habit.

JACKANAPES. An old variety, the upper petals being crimson-brown, the lower petals bright yellow.

JAMES PILLING. A fine belted pansy, the white bloom being margined with lavender-blue.

J. B. RIDING. An old favourite, a "sport" from Wm. Neil, the bright slightly rayed purple blooms being produced with freedom.

KATHLEEN. The white blooms have a thick edge of reddish-mauve and have a mauve-pink blotch on the upper petals.

MAGGIE MOTT. Long and free flowering, it bears silvery-mauve blooms of great beauty. One of the best ever introduced.

MISS BROOKS. A uniquely coloured viola, the large blooms being of a deep cerise-pink self colour.

MOSELEY CREAM. The large refined blooms are of a lovely Jersey cream colour.

PALMER'S WHITE. A fine white for massing, the blooms are medium-sized, the habit of the plant being most compact. Should accompany Blue-stone or Maggie Mott.

Index